D0934454

# Down Where My Love Lives

### THE DEAD DON'T DANCE
### MAGGIE

# CHARLES
# MARTIN

### THOMAS NELSON
*Since 1798*

NASHVILLE  DALLAS  MEXICO CITY  RIO DE JANEIRO  BEIJING

Published in Nashville, Tennessee, by Thomas Nelson. Thomas Nelson is a registered trademark of Thomas Nelson, Inc.

Thomas Nelson, Inc., titles may be purchased in bulk for educational, business, fund-raising, or sales promotional use. For information, please e-mail SpecialMarkets@ThomasNelson.com.

ISBN: 978-1-59554-609-8

*Printed in the United States of America*

08 09 10 11 12 QW 6 5 4 3 2 1

the
Dead
don't
Dance

🦋 *For Christy* 🦋

*Thank you for throwing your blanket over me.*
*Without it, I would have grown cold.*

# *chapter one*

LAST OCTOBER, AFTER THE SOYBEANS HAD PEAKED at four feet, the corn had spiraled to almost twice that, and the wisteria had shed its purple, a November breeze picked up, pushed out the summer heat, and woke Maggie. She rolled over, tapped me on the shoulder, and whispered, "Let's go swimming." It was two in the morning under a full moon, and I said, "Okay." The tap on the shoulder usually meant she knew something I didn't, and from the moment I'd met her, Maggie had known a lot that I didn't.

We rolled out, grabbed a couple of towels, and held hands down to the river, where Maggie took a swan dive into the South Carolina moonlight. I dropped the towels on the bank and waded in, letting the sandy bottom sift through my toes and the bream shoot between my knees. Leaning backward, I dunked my head, closed my eyes, then let the water roll down my neck as I stood in the waist-deep black river. Summer had run too long, as summers in Digger often do, and the breeze was a welcome comfort. We swam around in the dark water long enough to cool off, and Maggie spread a towel over the bleached white sand. Then she lay down and rested her head on my shoulder, and the moon fell behind the cypress canopy.

A while later, as we walked back to the house, her shoulder tucked under mine, Maggie knew that we had just made our son. I didn't know until four weeks later, when she came bouncing off the front porch and tackled me in the corn-field. Grinning, she shoved a little white stick in my face and pointed at the pink line.

Soon after, I started noticing the changes. They began in our second bedroom. Previously an office, it quickly became "the nursery." Maggie returned from the hardware store with two gallons of blue paint for the walls and one gallon of white for the trim and molding.

"What if she's a girl?" I asked.

"He's not," she said and handed me a paintbrush. So we spread some old sheets across the hardwood floors and started goofing off like Tom and Huck. By the end of the night, we were covered in blue paint and the walls were not, but at least we'd made a start.

The smell of paint drove us out of the house, so Maggie

and I shopped the Saturday morning garage sales. We found a used crib for sixty dollars, the top railing dented with teeth marks. Maggie ran her fingers along the dents like Helen Keller reading Braille. "It's perfect," she said.

We set up the crib in the corner of the nursery and made a Sunday afternoon drive to Charleston to the so-called "wholesale" baby outlet. I have never seen more baby stuff in one place in my entire life. And to be honest, before going there, I didn't know half of it existed. When we walked through the sliding glass doors, a recorded voice said, "Welcome to Baby World! If we don't have it, your baby doesn't need it!" The tone of voice gave me my first hint that I was in trouble.

Maggie grabbed two pushcarts, shoved one into my stomach, put on her game face, and said, "Come on!" Midway down the first aisle I was in way over my head. We bought diapers, wipes, pacifiers, a tether for the pacifiers, bottles, nipples for the bottles, liners for the bottles, bottles to hold the bottles and keep the bottles warm, cream for diaper rash, ointment for diaper rash, powder for diaper rash, a car seat, blankets, rattles, a changing table, little buckets to organize all the stuff we had just bought, a baby bag, extra ointment, cream, and powder just for the baby bag, booties, a little hat to keep his head warm, and little books. About halfway through the store I quit counting and just said, "Yes, ma'am."

To Maggie, every detail, no matter how small, had meaning. She must have said, "Oh, look at this," or "Isn't this cute?" a hundred times. When we reached the checkout counter, we were leaning on two ridiculously overflowing carts.

Some marketing genius had stacked the most expensive teddy bears right up in front. Only a blind man was without excuse. Maggie, wearing a baggy pair of denim overalls, batted her big brown eyes and tilted her head. In a deep, whispery, and all-too-seductive voice, she said, "Dylan, this bear's name is Huckleberry."

I just laughed. What else could I do?

I loaded up the truck and started to breathe easy, thinking the damage was over, but we didn't even make it out of the parking lot. Just next door to Baby World stood a maternity clothing store. Maggie, the possessed power shopper, stalked the racks and piled me high for over an hour. When I could no longer see above the heap of clothes in my arms, she led me to the changing room, where, for the first time in my life, a woman actually told me to come inside with her. Maggie shut the door, slid the latch, and pulled her hair up into a bouncy ponytail.

Over the next hour, my wife modeled each item of clothing while I marveled. The only light was a recessed forty-watt bulb above her head, but when she turned, lifted the ponytail off her neck, and whispered, "Unzip me," the light showered her five-eight frame like Tinkerbell's pixie dust. It fluttered off the blond, fuzzy hair on the back of her neck and the sweat on her top lip, over her square tan shoulders and down into the small of her back, along her thin hips and long runner's legs, and then finally swirled around the muscular shape of her calves.

*God, I love my wife.*

From shorts to shirts, pants, dresses, skirts, maternity bras, nursing bras, six-month underwear, nine-month underwear, jackets, and sweatshirts, the fashion show continued. As she tried on each item, Maggie stuffed the "eight-pound" pillow inside her waistband, put her hand on her hip, leaned forward on her toes, and looked at herself in the mirror. "Do you think this makes me look fat?"

"Maggs, no man in his right mind would ever answer that question."

"Dylan," she said, pointing her finger, "answer my question."

"You're beautiful."

"If you're lying to me," she said, raising her eyebrows and cocking her head, "you're on the couch."

"Yes, ma'am."

Leaving the dressing room, Maggie shone in full, glorious, pregnant-woman glow. Three hundred and twenty-seven dollars later, she was ready for any occasion.

Life had never been more vivid, more colorful, as if God had poured the other end of the rainbow all around us. Rows of cotton, corn, soybean, peanuts, and watermelon rose from the dirt and formed a quilted patchwork, sewing itself with kudzu along the sides of the old South Carolina highway. Ancient gnarled and sprawling oaks covered in moss and crawling with red bugs and history swayed in the breeze and stood like silent sentinels over the plowed rows. Naïve and unaware, we rumbled along the seams while Maggie placed my hand on her tummy and smiled.

At twelve weeks we went for the first ultrasound. Maggie was starting to get what she called a "pooch" and could not have been prouder. When the doctor walked in, Maggie was lying on the table with a fetal monitor Velcroed across her stomach, holding my hand. The doc switched on the ultrasound machine, squeezed some gel on her stomach, and started waving the wand over her tummy. When she heard the heartbeat for the first time, Maggie started crying. "Dylan," she whispered, "that's our son."

At sixteen weeks, the nurse confirmed Maggie's intuition. Maggie lay on the same table as the nurse searched her tummy with the ultrasound wand and then stopped when my son gave us a peek at his equipment. "Yep," the nurse said, "it's a boy. Right proud of himself too."

I hit my knees. At twenty-nine years old, I had looked inside my wife's tummy and seen our son. As big as life, with his heart beating, and wiggling around for all the world to see.

"Hey, Sport."

That started my conversations with Maggie's stomach. Every night from that day forward, I'd talk to my small and growing son. The three of us would lie in bed; I'd lift Maggie's shirt just over her tummy, press my lips next to the peach-fuzzy skin near her belly button, and we'd talk. Football, girls, school, farming, tractors, dogs, cornfields, friends, colors, anything I could think of. I just wanted my son to know the sound of my voice. After a few days, he started kicking my lips. Before I told him good night, I'd sing "Johnny Appleseed," "Daddy Loves His Sweet Little Boy," "The Itsy-Bitsy Spider," or "Jesus Loves Me."

Sometimes in the middle of the night, when the baby kicked or pushed his foot into the side of her stomach, Maggie would grab my hand and place it on her tummy. She never said a word, but I woke up feeling the warmth of my wife's stomach and the outline of my son's foot.

Toward the end of the first trimester, while rummaging through a yard sale, I found a rickety old rocking horse that needed a lot of glue, some elbow grease, and a few coats of white paint. I brought it home, set up my woodworking shop in the barn, and told Maggie to stay out. A week later, I brought it inside and set it next to the crib. Maggie looked at it, and the tears came forth in a flood. I think that was my first realization that new hormones had taken over my wife's body and mind.

Pretty soon the cravings hit. "Sweetheart." It was that whispery, seductive voice again. "I want some fresh, natural peanut butter and Häagen Dazs raspberry sorbet."

I never knew it would be so difficult to find freshly churned natural peanut butter at ten o'clock at night. When I got back to the house, Maggie was standing on the front porch, tapping her foot and wielding a spoon. As soon as I got the lids off, we plopped down in the middle of the den and started double dipping. When she'd polished off the sorbet, she said, "Now, how about a cheeseburger?"

At the end of her second trimester, she became pretty self-conscious. The least little thing really set her off. One morning, while studying her face in the mirror, she screamed, *"What is that? Dylan Styles, get in here!"*

Usually when Maggs calls me by both names, it means I've done something wrong. Left the toilet seat up or the toothpaste cap off, not taken the trash out, not killed every single roach and spider within two square miles of the house, or tried something sneaky and gotten caught. The tone in her voice told me I had just gotten caught.

I walked into the bathroom and found Maggs up on her toes, leaning over the sink and looking down at her chin, which was just a few inches from the mirror. Holding a magnifying glass, she said again, *"What is that?"*

I took the magnifying glass and smiled. Studying her chin, I saw a single black hair about a centimeter long protruding from it. "Well, Maggs, I'd say you're growing a beard." I know, I know, but I couldn't resist.

She shrieked and slapped me on the shoulder. "Get it off! Right now! Hurry!"

I reached into the drawer and pulled out a Swiss Army knife and slipped the little tweezers out of the side with my fingernail. "You know, Maggs, if this thing really takes off, we might be able to get you a job with the carnival."

"Dylan Styles," she said, pointing that crooked finger again, "if you want any loving for the rest of your life, you better quit right now." Maybe I was pushing it a little, but Maggs needed a perspective change. So I handed her the shaving cream and said, "Here, it's for sensitive skin."

Thirty seconds later, she had me balled up in the fetal position on the den floor, trying to pull out what few chest hairs I have. When she had adequately plucked me, she raised her fists like a boxer ready to start round two. "Dylan Styles, you better shut up and pull this evil thing off my chin."

Underneath the bathroom light, I pulled out the single rogue hair, placed it on her outstretched palm, and returned to the kitchen, laughing. Maggs spent the next hour poring over her face in the mirror.

Soon after, she lost sight of her toes. The baby was getting bigger and growing straight out like a basketball attached to a pole. Maggs stood helplessly in front of the mirror with an open nail polish bottle and wailed, "I'm fat! How can you love me when I look like this?" Then the tears came, so I did the only thing I could. I took her hand, sat her down on the couch, poured her a glass of ice water with a slice of orange, stretched out her legs, and painted her toenails.

When she was seven months along, I came in after dark one evening and heard her sloshing in the bathtub, talking to herself. I poked my head in and saw her holding a pink razor, trying to shave her legs. She had already cut her ankle. So I sat on the ledge, took the razor, held her heel, and shaved my wife's legs.

Somewhere around seven and a half months, I sat down to dinner—a dinner Maggie insisted on cooking—and found a package wrapped in brown paper. Untying the ribbon, I peeled open the paper to find a green T-shirt with *World's Greatest Dad* sewn on the front. I wore it every day for a week.

Getting heavier and feeling less mobile every day, Maggie nevertheless sewed the bumper for the crib and tied it in. The pattern featured stripes, baseballs, footballs, bats, and little freckle-faced boys. I bought a Pop Warner football and a Little League baseball glove and placed them inside the crib. On the floor beneath I clustered Matchbox cars, a miniature train set, and building blocks. When we were finished decorating, there was little room left for our son.

In the late afternoons of her last trimester, Maggie tired more easily, and I tried to convince her to take naps. Occasionally she'd give in. Two weeks before her due date, which was August 1, her legs, hands, and feet swelled, and her breasts became sore and tender. A week away, Braxton Hicks contractions set in, and the doctor told her to keep her feet up and get more rest.

"Try not to get too excited," he said. "This could take a while."

For some reason, and I'm not sure why, I had thought that as Maggie's tummy grew larger and she got more uncomfortable, she'd have less affection for me. I mean, physically. It only made sense. I had tried to prepare myself by blocking it out—*Don't even think about it*—but that time never came. Just three days before delivery, she tapped me on the shoulder. . . .

A week past her due date, the first real contraction hit. Maggie could tell the difference immediately. She was walking across the kitchen when she grabbed the countertop, bit her bottom lip, and closed her eyes. I grabbed The Bag and Huckleberry and met her at the truck. I was driving ninety miles an hour and honking at every car that got in my way when Maggs gently put her hand on my thigh and whispered, "Dylan, we have time."

I pulled into the maternity drop-off, and a nurse met us at

the car. When I found Maggie on the second floor, the doctor was checking her.

"Two centimeters," he said, taking off his latex gloves. "Go home; get some sleep. I'll see you tomorrow."

"See you tomorrow?" I said. "You can't send us home. My wife's having a baby."

The doctor smiled. "Yes, she is. But not today. Go get a nice dinner, then take her home. And"—he handed two pills to Maggie—"this will help take the edge off."

Helping Maggie into the truck, I said, "Your choice. Anywhere you want."

Maggie smiled, licked her lips, and pointed. A few minutes later we were sitting in the Burger King, where Maggie downed a Whopper with cheese, large fries, a cheeseburger, and a chocolate shake. I ate half a cheeseburger and two French fries.

That night Maggie slept in fits, and I slept not at all. I just lay there in the dark, watching her face and brushing her Audrey Hepburn hair out of her Bette Davis eyes.

At six o'clock Maggie bit her lip again, and I carried her to the truck.

"Four centimeters," the doctor said as he pulled the gown over Maggie's legs. "It's time to walk."

So we did. Every floor. Every hallway. Every sidewalk.

Walking through the orthopedic ward six hours later, Maggie grunted and grabbed the railing, and one of her knees buckled. I grabbed a wheelchair, punched the elevator button, and tapped my foot down to the second floor.

The doctor was on the phone at the nurses' station, but he hung up quickly when he saw her face. We stretched her out on the bed, strapped the fetal monitor over her stomach, and I cradled her head in my hands while the doctor listened.

"Okay, Maggie, get comfortable." Then he pulled out this long plastic thing and asked the nurse to cover it with gel. "I'm going to break your water and start you on Pitocin."

While I was thinking, *You're not sticking that thing in my wife,* Maggie sighed and gripped my hand so hard her knuckles turned white.

"That means two things: it will bring on your labor more quickly, and"—he paused as the fluid gushed out—"your contractions will hurt a bit more."

"That's okay," Maggie said, while the nurse swabbed her right arm with alcohol and inserted the IV needle.

Fifteen minutes later, the pain really started. I sat next to the bed, holding a wet towel on her forehead, and fought the growing knot in my stomach. By midnight Maggie was drenched in sweat and growing pale. I called the nurse and asked, "Can we do anything? Please!"

Within a few minutes the anesthesiologist came in and asked Maggie, "You about ready for some drugs?"

Without batting an eye, I said, "Yes, sir."

Maggie sat up and leaned as far forward as her stomach would let her. The doctor walked around behind her and inserted the epidural in the middle of her spine just as another contraction hit. Maggie moaned but didn't move an inch.

*God, please take care of my wife.*

Breathing heavily, Maggie lay back down and propped her knees up. After one more contraction, the epidural kicked in. Her shoulders relaxed, and she lost the feeling in her legs. At that moment, if I had had a million dollars, I would have given every penny to that man. I almost kissed him on the mouth.

The next two hours were better than the last two days together. We watched the monitor, the rise and fall of every contraction—"Oh, that was a good one," listened to the heartbeat, laughed, talked about names, and tried not to think about what was next. It was surreal to think our son would be there, in our arms, in a matter of moments. We held hands, I sang to her tummy, and we sat there in quiet most of the time.

About one-thirty, the lady next door had trouble with her delivery, and they had to wheel her off for an emergency C-section. I've never heard anybody scream like that in all my life. I didn't know what to think. I do know that it got to Maggie. She tried not to show it, but it did.

At two o'clock, the doctor checked her for the last time. "Ten centimeters, and 100 percent effaced. Okay, Maggie, you can start pushing. We'll have a birthday today."

Maggie was a champ. I was real proud of her. She pushed and I coached, "One-two-three . . . " I'd count and she'd crunch her chin to her stomach, eyes closed and with a death grip on my hand, and push.

That was two days and ten lifetimes ago.

*chapter two*

THE SMALL, PRIVATE ROOM THEY PUT US IN WAS dark, overlooked the parking lot, and sat at one end of a long, quiet hallway. The only lights in the room shone from the machines connected to Maggie, and the only noise was her heart-rate monitor and occasionally the janitor shuffling down the hall, rolling a bucket that smelled of Pine Sol over urine. Somebody had shoved Maggie's bed against the far wall, so I rolled her over next to the window, where she could feel the moonlight. By rolling the bed, I unplugged all the monitors, setting off several alarms at the nurses' station.

A pale-faced nurse slid through the doorway and into the room. She stopped short when she saw me sitting next to the bed, quietly holding Maggs's hand. She almost said something but changed her mind and went to work instead, repairing what I'd torn apart. Before she left, she grabbed a blanket from the closet, put it over my shoulders, and asked, "You want some coffee, honey?" I shook my head and she patted me on the shoulder.

Maggie has lain there "sleeping," unconscious, ever since the delivery. I wiped her arms and cheeks with a warm, damp rag and then felt her toes. They were cold, so I looked through our bag, found a pair of socks that I gently slid over her heels, and put another blanket over her feet. After pulling the sheets up around her shoulders, I sat down next to the bed and tucked her hair behind her ears, where I still felt some dried blood. For the third time, I ran a towel under some warm water and wiped her face, arms, and neck.

I don't remember my arms being sore afterwards, but I do remember it took the nurse three tries before she found my vein. Maggie needed a lot of blood pretty quick, so I gave one more pint than they normally would allow. The nurse knew Maggie needed it, so when I grabbed the needle and told her to keep going, she looked at me over the top of her glasses, opened another Coca-Cola for me, and kept drawing. I walked back to the delivery room with both pits of my elbows taped up, sat next to the bed, and watched my blood drip into my wife.

While I was sitting in the quiet beneath the moon, a wrinkle appeared on Maggie's forehead between her eyebrows—her trademark expression. A sure sign that she was determined to figure something out. I placed my palm on her forehead and held it there for a few seconds while the wrinkle melted away and her breathing slowed.

"Maggs?"

I slid my hand under hers and thought how her callused fingers seemed so out of place on someone so beautiful. Under the rhythm and short blips of the heart-rate monitor, I watched her heart beat, listened to her short, quick breaths, and waited for her big brown eyes to open and look at me.

They did not.

I stared out the window over the parking lot, but there wasn't much to look at. South Carolina is one of the more beautiful places on God's earth—especially where the wisteria crawls out of the weeds that can't choke it—but the parking lot of Digger Community Hospital is not. I turned back to Maggie and remembered the river, the way the light followed Maggie's eyes, her smile, her back, and how the water had dripped off her skin and puddled on her stomach. "Maggs," I said, "let's go swimming."

# *chapter three*

THE DAYS TURNED INTO NIGHTS AND BACK INTO days, and I became afraid to blink, thinking I'd miss the opening of her eyes. During that time, I'm pretty sure other people came in and out of the room, but I never saw them. I think I remember Amos putting his hand on my shoulder and telling me, "Don't worry, I'll take care of the farm." And somewhere during one of the nights, I think I remember smelling the lingering aroma of Bryce's beer breath, but for seven days my entire world consisted of Maggie and me. Anything outside that picture never came into focus. The periphery of my life had blurred.

On the afternoon of the seventh day, the doctor took me

out into the hall and gave me his prognosis. Consternation was painted across his face, and it was clear this wasn't easy for him, no matter how much practice he must have had at delivering bad news. "Dylan, I'll give it to you straight," he said.

The seconds melted into days.

"Maggie's out of what we call the hopeful window. The longer she stays in this vegetative state, the more involuntary muscle responses she'll begin to have. Unfortunately, these muscle responses are from spinal activity, not brain activity. Within the next few weeks, she's got a 50 percent chance of waking up. The following month, it drops in half. Following that . . . " He shook his head. "Of course, this is all just statistics; miracles can happen. But they don't happen often."

Later that afternoon, the hospital executive responsible for accounts receivable stopped in for a visit. "Mr. Styles, I'm Mr. Thentwhistle. Jason Thentwhistle." He stepped into the room and extended his hand.

I immediately didn't like him.

"Yes, well, I think we should talk about your financial arrangements."

I turned my head slightly and narrowed my eyes.

"Coma patients often require long-term hospital care. . . ."

That was all I needed to hear. I hit him as hard as I could—maybe as hard as I've ever hit anybody. When I looked down, he was crumpled on the floor, his glasses were broken in three pieces, his nose was twisted sideways and smashed into his face, and blood was pouring out of his nostrils. I picked up his heels and dragged him out into the hallway because I didn't want him bleeding on Maggie's floor.

"D.S., YOU BEEN HERE SINCE YOU LEFT THE HOSPITAL?"

I opened my eyes, remembered Thentwhistle, and looked around. The head hovering over me was familiar.

"Dylan?" A big, meaty black hand gently slapped me twice in the face.

That was definitely familiar. "Amos?"

Slapping my cheek again, he said, "Hey, pal? You in there?"

I must have moaned, because Amos grabbed me by the shoulders and shook me.

"Yeah, yeah," I said, swatting at his hands, "I'm in here." My head was killing me, and the world was spinning way too fast. Amos's hands stopped the spinning but not the pain.

"D.S.?" Amos brought his face closer to mine. "Have you been here since you left the hospital?" He was still out of focus.

"I don't know. When did I leave the hospital?"

"Tuesday," he said, shading my face with his hat.

I swatted at it because it looked like a buzzard. "What day is today?" I asked, still swatting.

"Thursday." Amos crinkled his nose and waved his hand. "And it's a good thing it rained too." Waving the air with his hat, Amos said, "D.S., you stink bad. Whatchoo been doing out here?"

I reached for the tractor, pulled at the tire rod, which my

grandfather had bent twenty-one years ago pulling stumps, and tried to pull myself up. I could not. I thought for a minute, but I couldn't remember. "Thursday?"

I pulled my knees up and scratched my neck and the four itchy bumps on my ankles under my jeans.

Amos looked doubtful.

I guessed again, "Tuesday?" The rush of blood to my head caused my head to bob, rock, and crash into the cornstalk that was growing up out of an anthill.

Amos caught my head. "Here, you better sit still. I think you been sitting in the sun a little too long. How long you been out here?"

Ordinarily Amos's English is pretty good. He only drops into the South Carolina farm-boy dialect when talking with me. After twenty-five years of friendship, we had developed our own language. People say marriage works the same way.

"I need to get to the hospital," I muttered.

"Hold on a minute, Mr. Cornfield. She's not going anywhere." Amos tapped the plastic cover on the tractor's fuel gauge. "And neither is this old tractor. We got to get you cleaned up. If it weren't for Blue, I'd still be driving around looking for you."

Blue is a blue heeler and the most intelligent dog I've ever known. He's seven years old and is better known as the "outdoor dog" that sleeps at the foot of our bed.

I rubbed my eyes and tried to focus. No improvement. Amos was about to brush my shirt off with his hand, but he took a second look and thought better of it.

"My truck's low on gas. Where's your car?" I said. "Can you take me there?"

Seeing me return to life, Blue hopped off the tractor, licked my face, and then sat between my legs and rested his head on my thigh.

"Yes, I can," Amos said, articulating every letter. "But no, I will not. I'm taking you to work."

Amos wasn't making a lot of sense.

"Work?" I looked around. "Amos, I was working until . . . well, until you showed up." I shoved Blue out of the way. When he gets excited, he drools a good bit. "Go on, Blue. Quit it."

Blue ignored me. Instead he rolled over like a dead bug, turned his head to one side, hung out his tongue, and propped his paws in the air.

"D.S." Amos ran his fingers around inside his deputy's belt. "Don't start with me. I ain't in the mood." He put his hat back on, hefted his holster a bit. Then he raised his voice. "I've been looking for you all morning in every corner of every pasture. All thirty-five hundred acres." Amos waved his hands as if he were on stage or telling a fish story. He could get animated when he wanted to. "Then a few minutes ago, I'm driving past this field, and I see this rusty old thing your grandfather called a tractor sitting driverless and parked out here at the intersection of Nowhere and No Place Else. Except one thing sticks out and grabs my attention."

Amos reached over and began scratching Blue between the ears. "Ol' Blue here is sitting at attention on top of your tractor like he's trying to be seen. So I turn the car around and think to myself, *That'd be just like that old fool to go through one week of hell and then walk out of the hospital, only to end up out here and act like he's farming.*

He reached over, picked up a handful of sand, and slung it into the corn. "Dylan Styles"—he looked down a long row of corn that was planted in more of an arc than a straight line—"you're an idiot. Even with all your education. You can just about strap an alphabet behind your name, but I'm your friend and I'll tell it to you straight: You're a sorry farmer and a danged idiot."

Amos is smart. Don't let the deputy's badge fool you. He took this job because he wanted it, not because he couldn't find anything else. Amos takes nothing from nobody—except me. He's big, articulate, black as black comes, and my oldest friend. He's a year older than I am and was a year ahead in school. In my junior year of high school, we were the two starting running backs. They called us Ebony and Ivory, for obvious reasons.

Amos was always faster, always stronger, and he never once let anybody pile on me. I've seen him take two linebackers and shove them back into the free safety on more than one occasion. The only reason I scored my first touchdown was because he carried me. I got the ball, grabbed his jersey, shut my eyes, and he dragged me eight yards to glory, where I saw the goal line pass under my feet. When I looked up and saw the crowd screaming, Amos was standing off to the side alone, letting me take the credit and soak it all in.

Later that year, the Gamecocks gave him a scholarship. He lettered four years and was an all-American three. From day one he studied criminal justice and learned everything about it that he could. Right after graduation, Amos applied with Colleton County and came home. He's worn that badge ever since. Last year they sewed sergeant's stripes to his shirtsleeves.

I rubbed my eyes and steadied my head between my hands. The world was spinning again, and the ants at my feet weren't helping my perspective any.

"Is there somebody else around here I can talk to?" My voice was pretty much gone, and all I could muster was a smoker's whisper. "Amos, have you had your coffee this morning? Because I'm tired and I don't quite remember how I got here, but I think you're riding me. And if you're riding me, that's a pretty good sign that you have not had your coffee."

Amos was really animated now. "I've been traipsing around this piece of dirt you two call home all morning. Thanks to you and your disappearing stunt, I ain't had the pleasure of my morning cup of coffee. What is it with you Styleses and this piece of dirt? If you're gonna choose someplace to catch up on a week with no sleep, you could have picked a better place than the middle of a cornfield. In the last hour I have ruined my pants, scuffed my boots, torn my shirt, and there is no telling how much pig crap I've got smeared on me right now. Why do you keep that old pig?"

"Who? Pinky?"

"Well, of course, Pinky. Who else makes all this stuff?" Amos pointed at his boots. "In all my life, I have never seen a pig crap the way she can. You ought to enter her in a contest. It's everywhere. What do you feed that thing?"

"Amos . . . A-Amos." I stuttered and shivered. "It's got to be close to ninety, and I feel like crap. I'm itching everywhere, and I've got a headache. All I want to do is see my wife. Please, just help get me back to my house."

Amos knew when to quit.

"Come on, D.S. Inside." He picked me up and hooked his shoulder under mine. "Ivory, did I already tell you that you need a shower?"

"Yeah, I heard you the first time."

We crashed through the corn and limped toward the house.

Pulling me along, Amos asked, "What's the last thing you remember?"

"Well," I said, aiming my toes toward the porch, "I was sitting with Maggs when this suit from the hospital poked his pointy head through the door and asked me how I intend to pay my bills. He started to say something about how expensive it was to keep Maggie there. So I did what any husband would have done. I turned around and clocked the pointy-headed son of a—"

Amos held up his hands. "I get the picture."

"I dragged him out in the hall, and Maggie's nurses started looking him over. But to be honest, they didn't seem real eager to start tending to him." I glanced at the cut on the knuckle of my right hand. It was still puffy and stiff, so I guessed I had hit him pretty hard. "I don't remember too much after that."

Amos carried me a few more steps to the house. Without looking at me, he said, "An executive from the hospital named Jason Thentwhistle, with two loose teeth, a broken nose, new pair of glasses, and one very black and swollen eye, came to the station to file a complaint against one Dylan Styles. Said he wanted to press charges."

Amos kept his eyes aimed on the back door, but a smile cracked his face. "I told him that I was really sorry to hear about his altercation, but without a witness we really couldn't do anything." He turned and held me up by my shoulders. "D.S., you can't go around hitting the very people who are taking care of your wife."

"But Amos, he wasn't taking care of my wife. He was being an—"

Amos held up his hand again. "You gonna let me finish?"

"I should have hit him harder. I was trying to break his jaw."

"I didn't hear that." Amos wrapped his arm tight about my waist, and we took a few more steps.

I stopped Amos and tried to look him in the eyes. "Amos, is Maggs okay?"

Amos shook his head side to side. "No real change. Physically, she seems to be healing. No more bleeding."

"I'd drive myself, but I might have to push my truck to the station, so can you please just take me there without a bunch of conversation?" I asked again.

Amos dug his shoulder further under mine, dragged me closer to the back porch, and said, "After your interview." He grunted and hoisted me up onto the steps.

"Interview?" I sat down on the back steps and scratched my head. "What interview?"

Catching his breath, Amos wiped his brow, straightened

his shirt, gave his gun belt another two-handed law enforcement lift, and said, "Mr. Winter. Digger Junior College. If you can survive the interview, you'll be teaching English 202: Research and Writing."

It took a minute, but the word *teaching* finally registered. "Amos, what are you talking about? Speak English."

"I am speaking English, Dr. Styles. And in about two hours, you'll be speaking it with Mr. Winter about the class you're going to teach." He smiled and took off his sunglasses.

Amos only calls me doctor on rare occasions. I finished my doctorate a few years back, but because I quit teaching after graduate school, few knew it, and fewer still called me by the title. Although I was proud of my accomplishment, I had little reason to make sure everybody knew about it. My corn didn't care what kind of education I'd had. It sure didn't help me drive that tractor any straighter.

"One thing at a time," I said, shaking my head. "Will you or will you not take me to see my wife?"

"D.S., have you been listening to me?" Amos raised his eyebrows and looked at me. "Dr. Dylan Styles Jr. is soon to be an adjunct professor at Digger Junior College, teaching English 202: Research and Writing. And"—Amos looked at his watch—"Mr. Winter is expecting you in his office in an hour and fifty-seven minutes."

He unfolded a slip of paper from his shirt pocket and handed it to me. "Don't fight me on this. They need a teacher, and for a lot of reasons, you need this."

"Name one," I said.

Amos wiped the sweat off his brow with a white handker-chief. "Taxes, to begin with. Followed by your loan payment. Both of which are coming due at the end of the month, and the chances of you actually producing anything but a loss on this piece of dirt are slim to none. Teaching is your insurance policy, and right now you need one."

"Amos, I've got a job." I waved my arms out in front of me. "Right here. Right out there. All of this is my job." I pointed to the fields surrounding the house. "And how do you know when my taxes and loan payments are due?"

Amos dropped his head and pointed to the soil. "D.S., you and I grew up right here, playing ball on this field. You busted my lip right over there, and"—he pointed to his house—"two hundred yards across that field and over that dirt road is my house and my dirt. So I know about dirt. I don't want to see you and Maggie lose it." He spat. "Heck, I don't want to lose it. So don't fight me. Put your education to work, listen to what I'm saying, and get in the shower while you can still afford to pay for hot water."

"How's Maggie?" I asked again.

"She'll live. She's stable. At least physically. Mentally . . . I don't know. That's His call." Amos's eyes shot skyward.

"Amos," I said, as the world came slowly into focus, "tell me about this whole teaching thing."

During graduate school in Virginia, I had taught seven classes as an adjunct at two different universities to help us pay the bills, and, I hoped, secure myself a job when I got out. But after I defended my dissertation and graduated, nobody would hire me. I got a feeling it wasn't my credentials as much as it was my background. A farm-boy-turned-teacher, at least this one anyway, was not something they wanted on their faculties.

Unable to get a job in the field that I had chosen, I hunkered down in the field that I owned. I was not my grandfather, Papa Styles, and nobody was knocking on my door, asking for advice, but for three years Maggie and I had been making ends meet out here in this dirt. Amos knew this. He also knew that having been snubbed once, I wasn't too eager to go crawling back in there—especially at a community college as an adjunct. I had moved on.

"Digs, room one, English 202. You've taught it before."

"But Amos, why? Between what's in the ground, what will be, the pine straw lease, and the two leased pastures, we'll make it. My place is with Maggie, not nurse-maiding a bunch of dropouts who couldn't get into a real school."

"D.S., don't make me look foolish. Not after I went to bat for you. And don't thumb your nose at those kids. They're not the only ones who couldn't get into a 'real school.'" Amos had a brutal way of being honest. He also had a real gentle way of making me eat my pride. "And this isn't my doing. It's Maggie's."

"Maggie's?"

"She saw an ad in the paper that Digs was hiring adjuncts. So she called Mr. Winter a month or so ago and inquired about it. She was going to talk with you after the baby was born."

"Yeah, well . . . " I felt numb. "She didn't get a chance."

"And as for your tax records and loan payment, Shireen at the station pulled your file and ran a credit check for me.

Which, by the way, is real good. I'm just trying to help you keep it that way."

I shook my head and suppressed a wave of nausea. "Amos, if I could throw you in general quarters with all your law-abiding buddies . . . "

"D.S, how long are you going to fight me on this? You know good and well that every one of my jailbird buddies deserves to be there. They know it too."

Amos was right. He pegged it pretty square on the head. Everybody knew he was fair, even the folks he arrested. Amos was who you wanted to catch you if you ever broke the law. You'd get what you deserved, but he'd be fair about it. Amos enforced the law. He didn't rub it in your face.

"Besides," he whispered, "it's Maggie's wish."

Somewhere in the last three days I had rolled in pig excrement. Now it was smeared on Amos's hands and shirt. He brushed himself off, making it worse, paused, and then looked right at me.

"D.S., here I am. My uniform is now covered in pig crap, and I've got a radio, loaded gun, big stick, and this badge. If I could trade places with you, I would. But since I can't, I'm here to ask you, please go inside, shower twice, shave, and get dressed. Because deep down, you know it's best for you." He scanned the cornfield. "It's best for your wife, and it's best for this place."

Sometimes I wished Amos weren't so honest.

"Who's staying with her?" I asked.

"I was until a little bit ago. The nurse is now. She's a sweet girl. Pastor's daughter. She'll take good care of her. D.S., there's nothing you can do for Maggie. That's God's deal. I don't understand it and I don't like it, but there is nothing you or I can do for her. Right now what we need to worry about is you and making sure that the mailbox out front goes right on saying 'Styles.'

"And for that to happen, you got to teach. This is what it comes down to. And don't give me any of that stuff about not teaching again." Amos pointed his finger at me and poked me in the chest. "You are a teacher. Why do you think God gave you Nanny to begin with? You think that was just some big cosmic mistake?" He spat again. "You think she just shared all that with you so you could keep it bottled up and to your lonesome?"

Amos put one foot up on the steps and rested his elbow on his knee. "Not likely. You may like farming, but you're no Papa, at least not yet. You can hide out here if you want to, but it'd be a sorry shame. Now are you gonna get cleaned up, or do I have to hose you down myself?"

I opened the screen door and stumbled into the house, mumbling, "Dang you, Amos . . . "

"Hey, I'm just honoring my promise to your wife. You married her. Not me. If you want to complain"—Amos pointed toward the hospital—"complain to her."

"I would if I could get there."

"After your little chat with Mr. Winter." Amos smiled, grumbled something else to himself, and then walked to the kitchen and began washing out the percolator.

# chapter four

I SUPPOSE YOU COULD CALL ME A LATE-LIFE MIRACLE.
At least I'm told my parents thought so, because my dad was
forty-two and my mom forty when she gave birth to me. I have
sweet memories, but not many because Dad died in a car accident pretty close to my fifth birthday and Mom suffered a
stroke strolling down the cereal aisle of the grocery store six
months later.

My grandparents took me in after their daughter's funeral
and raised me until I turned eighteen and headed off to college. Despite the absence of my parents, love lived in our
house. Papa and Nanny saw to that. They poured their love
into three things: each other, me, and this house.

When my grandfather built our two-bedroom brick farm-house more than sixty years ago, he pieced the floors out of twelve-inch-wide magnolia planks and dovetailed them together without using nails. They were strong, creaky, marred with an occasional deep groove, and in the den where my grandparents danced in their socks to the big band music of Lawrence Welk, polished to a mirror shine.

Papa covered the walls in eight-inch cypress plank, the ceilings in four-inch tongue-and-groove oak, and the roof in corrugated tin. I have no memory of the house ever being any other color but white with green trim and shutters. Why? Because that's the way Nanny liked it, and Papa never objected.

One summer, standing on a ladder and painting the underside of a soffit for the umpteenth time, he looked down and said with a smile, "Never argue with a woman about her house. Remember that. It's hers, not yours." He waved his paintbrush toward the kitchen and whispered, "I may have built it, but in truth, we're just lucky she lets us sleep here."

Whenever I think of Nanny's home, I remember it glistening white and green under a fresh coat of springtime paint, landscaped with whatever was blooming, and cool from the whispering breeze ushering through the front and back doors, which she propped open with two retired irons.

Papa had several eccentricities. The top three were overalls, pocketknives, and Rice Krispies. The first two fit most farmers, but the third did not. He'd pull a saucepan from the cupboard, fill it to the brim with cereal, cover it in peaches, douse it with half a pint of cream, and polish off an entire box in one sitting. Not surprisingly, the first few words I learned to read were *snap, crackle,* and *pop.*

Born poor country folk, Nanny and Papa didn't make it too far in school. Born before the Depression and raised when a dollar was worth one, they were too busy working to pursue higher education. But please don't think they were uneducated. Both were studious, just in a nonacademic way. Papa studied farming, and he was good at it. For the sixty years that he turned this earth, it stayed green more often than not. His reputation spread, and people drove for miles just to rub shoulders at the hardware store and ask his opinion in between the feed and seed.

While Papa plowed, Nanny cooked and sewed. And late at night, after she had untied her apron and hung it over the back screen door, she read. We owned a TV, but if given my choice, I preferred Nanny's voice. After Walter Cronkite told us everything was all right with the world, Papa clicked the television off and Nanny opened her book.

After school, I'd spot Papa on the tractor, run across the back pasture, climb into his lap, and listen to him talk about the need for terraced drainage, the sight of early-morning sunshine, the smell of an afternoon rain, the taste of sweet corn, and Nanny. When our necks were caked in dust and burnt red from a low-hanging sun, Papa and I would lift our noses and follow the smell of Nanny's cooking back to the house like two hounds on a scent.

One morning when I was about twelve, I was standing in the bathroom, getting ready for school, listening to a loud rock 'n' roll station hosted by an obnoxious DJ that all my friends listened to.

Papa walked in with a raised brow, turned down the volume, and said, "Son, I rarely tell you what to do, but today I am. You can listen to this"—he pointed to the radio, which, thanks to his tuning, was now spewing country music—"or this." He turned the dial, and hymns from the local gospel station filled the air.

It was one of the best things my grandfather ever did for me. Listen to Willie singing "My Heroes Have Always Been Cowboys," and you'll understand what I mean. About the same time I was flipping through the three channels we received on our dusty Zenith and came across a show called *The Dukes of Hazzard*. I heard the same voices from the radio singing their theme song and put two and two together.

Before long, I planned my week by what I was doing at eight o'clock on Friday nights. Nanny and Papa watched with me because *Dallas* followed, and they had to know who had shot J.R. But from eight to nine, the TV was mine. I fell in love with Bo and Luke Duke and amused myself by mimicking everything they did. With Papa's help I bought a guitar, learned to play "Mommas, Don't Let Your Babies Grow Up to Be Cowboys," and began wearing boots. All the time.

Papa worked hard six days a week, but like most Bible-Belters, never on Sundays. Sundays were reserved solely for the Lord, Nanny, and me. We'd spend the morning in church, then gorge ourselves on Nanny's fried chicken or pork chops. After a lazy afternoon nap we would walk down to the river, where we would feed hooked earthworms to the bream or listen to the wood ducks sing through the air just after dark.

Papa was never real vocal about his faith, but for some reason, he loved putting up church steeples. In the fifteen years I lived with Nanny and Papa, I saw him organize twelve steeple-raising parties for nearby churches. Pastors from all around would call and ask his help, and as far as I know he never told one no. The denomination of the church mattered little, but the height of the steeple did. The taller, the better. The closest stands a mile from our house, atop Pastor John Lovett's church—a rowdy AME where the sign out front reads, "Pentecost was not a onetime event."

After attending my fourth or fifth raising, I asked him, "Papa, why steeples?"

He smiled, pulled out his pocketknife, began scraping it under each fingernail, and looked out over the pasture. "Some people need pointing in the right direction," he said. "Myself included."

Nanny grew sick my junior year of college. When we knew it was serious, I broke every posted speed limit on the drive home. I bounded up the back steps just in time to hear Papa hit his knees and say, "Lord, I'm begging You. Please give me one more day with this woman."

After sixty-two years, the music stopped, the lights dimmed, and their dance atop the magnolia planks ended. The loneliness broke Papa, and he followed three weeks later. The doctor said his heart simply quit working, but there's no medical terminology for a broken heart. Papa just died. That's all.

Growing up, I had always wanted to travel out west. When Nanny and Papa died, I found my excuse, so I dropped out of school and drove toward the setting sun. I had grown up watching Westerns with Papa, so all that wide-open space held some attraction. Besides, that's where the Rockies were. I spent weeks driving through mountain after mountain. Saw the Grand Canyon; even sank my toes in the Pacific Ocean. I'm pretty low maintenance, so I ate a lot of peanut butter and slept in the back of the truck with Blue. We kept each other warm.

When I got to New Mexico, I came pretty close to running out of money, so we loaded up and came home. When I finally made it back to Digger, almost a year after Papa's death, the vines and weeds had almost covered the house, a few shutters had blown off, the paint had flaked, and a fence post or two had fallen, pulling the barbed wire with it. But the well water still tasted sweet, the house was dry, and Nanny's breeze blew cool even on stagnant August afternoons. Papa knew what he was doing when he built the place.

I spent six weeks cleaning, painting, sanding floors, repairing the plumbing, oiling doorknobs and hinges, and fixing fence posts and barbed wire. I also spent a lot of time on the tractor, just trying to get it working again. The sound reminded me of Papa, but it had sat up too long and a few of the hoses had rotted. I drained the fluids and changed the plugs, distributor, and hoses. After some careful cussing and a few phone calls to Amos, she cranked right up.

On a trip to the hardware store, I bumped into Maggie. We had known each other in high school but never dated. In hindsight, that was really dumb. But I was too busy hunting, fishing, or playing football. At any rate, I wasn't dating, or studying, for that matter. That came later.

Papa once told me that before he met Nanny, his heart always felt funny. Like a jigsaw puzzle with about two-thirds of the pieces missing. When I met Maggie, I realized what he was talking about. Most guys talk about their wives' figures, and yes, mine has one, but it was her Audrey Hepburn hair and Bette Davis eyes that stopped me.

After two or three more "accidental" hardware meetings, I got my nerve up and asked her out, and it didn't take long. If I had had any guts, I would have proposed after two weeks, but I needed six months to work up the courage. I bought a golden band, we married, and somewhere on the beach at Jekyll Island beneath the stars, she persuaded me to finish my degree.

I enrolled and started night school at the South Carolina satellite campus in Walterboro. If Nanny and Papa's deaths had taken the wind out of my sails, then Maggie helped me hoist anchor, raise the sails, and steady the rudder.

For most of my life, and thanks in large part to Nanny's prodding, the only thing I was any good at was writing. When I enrolled as a freshman at the University of South Carolina, I registered in the English program and started down the track toward a creative writing degree. It's what I was good at, or so I thought.

During my first three years of college, I wrote some stories and sent them off to all the magazines you're supposed to send stuff to if you're a writer. *The Saturday Evening Post. The New Yorker.* I've still got a folder of all my rejections. Once my folder got pretty full, I quit sending my stories.

But Maggie continued to believe in me. One day while I was finishing my senior year at the satellite, she printed a few of my pieces and sent them to Virginia along with an application for graduate school. For some reason, they accepted me into their master's program and even said they'd pay for my classes and books. I don't know if that's because I wrote well or because I couldn't afford it, but either way, they paid for it.

So Maggie and I charted a new course, and I returned to school. It was not long after, though, that my grand illusions of plumbing the deeper meanings in storytelling, fired by Nanny's love of reading, were shattered. Graduate school was no lighthouse. If it weren't for Victor Graves, a gnarly old professor who laughed like a rum-drunk sailor, I'd have never made it. Vic took me under his wing and helped me navigate.

After I wrote my thesis, Vic encouraged me to apply to the doctoral program. With little hope but no other direction, I did. Three weeks later I received my acceptance letter, which Maggie framed and hung above my desk. I couldn't believe it. *Me? A doctoral student? You've got to be kidding. I'm the guy who didn't study in high school.* But the letter said they wanted me, and once again they said they'd pay for it—which was nice, because without the financial backing, I wasn't going. They gave me a fellowship, and I got to work.

Thanks to Vic, lightbulbs began clicking on like a Fourth

of July celebration, and it was there that I really discovered just how smart Nanny really was.

It wasn't easy, but we made it. We lived in an upstairs, one-room apartment, and while Maggie waited tables, I worked the morning preload at UPS. I woke early and she worked late, so for about two years, we didn't see each other much.

Despite Vic's best encouragement, I quickly found that my grandmother had forgotten more stories than most experts would read in a lifetime. And not only did she understand them better, but she had a knack at helping others do the same. Just because you know something, or think you do, doesn't mean you can teach it.

Beneath the sly, academic façade, and hidden behind their glossy degrees, most of my teachers were just frustrated hacks who couldn't write a great story if their lives depended on it. Out of the void of their own missing talent, they found a sick joy in tearing others' apart. Maybe I could do better, I hoped. Maybe I could teach Nanny's wonder through Papa's pocket-knife practicality and shield the students from the poisonous cynicism around me.

I accepted an adjunct position at my university, teaching freshman and sophomore English. I enjoyed the classroom and the interaction with the students and even helped click on a few lightbulbs myself. All I wanted to do was introduce other people to the power and wonder of language. But all the covert backstabbing and infighting along the tortuous path to tenure drove me to the brink of drinking. If the pen is mightier than the sword, it's also a good bit bloodier.

Instead of finding Nanny's fireside wonder shared amid my colleagues, I found ivory-tower experts ripe with stoic discontent and bent on tearing down castles they could never rebuild, simply for the sake of saying something.

While I struggled to help kids look for universal truths and themes that great stories revealed in unforgettable ways—themes like love, humor, hope, and forgiveness—and maybe encourage them to transpose those through their fingers and onto paper, my colleagues stood on soapboxes with raised brows and asked, "Maybe, but what is *hidden?*" They reminded me of pharmacists who crushed their pills into powder and studied the contents under a microscope while never bothering to swallow the medicine.

Caught in a postmodern pinball machine, I became pretty well disillusioned. I never voiced it to Maggie, but she could read me. She knew. After graduation, she gave me a good talking to. So I swallowed my disgust and filled out twenty applications for schools scattered about the South. I licked the stamps, dropped them in the box, and hoped the grass grew greener in some other pasture. When the last "we're-sorry-to-inform-you-letter" arrived from my own hometown junior college, we quit our jobs, packed up my books, and came back here.

Virginia is pretty, but it can't hold a candle to South Carolina. We hadn't even walked in the front door when I realized that my love for farming had much deeper roots than the shallow shoots I'd put down in academia. As I looked out over those fields where I had passed many a happy day, I knew I'd miss the students, the lively exchange of ideas, and the sight of lightbulbs turning on, but little else. I was glad to be home.

The well water smelled like eggs, the faucets dripped like Chinese water torture, and both toilets ran constantly, but Maggie never complained. She loved the narrow, coal-burning fireplace, the front and back porches, and the two swinging screen doors that slammed too loudly and squeaked in spite of oil. But her two favorite pleasures were the tin roof beneath a gentle rain and Nanny's breeze.

I had never measured it, but including the porches, the house probably covered twelve hundred square feet. But it was ours, and for sixty-two years, love had lived here.

Like riding a bicycle after the training wheels had been removed, I hopped on the tractor, sniffed the air for any hint of rain, and cried like a baby all the way to the river. Papa had taught me well, and once away from the classroom cobwebs and textbook chains, I remembered how to farm. In our first year, I sold the pine straw from beneath our fifteen hundred acres of planted pines, leased two five-hundred-acre blocks to part-time farmers who lived in Walterboro, and drilled soybean seed into the remaining five hundred acres of our thirty-five-hundred-acre tract. By the end of that year, we had made money.

Maggie looked at Papa's picture on the mantel, stroked the skin around my eyes, and said, "You two have the same wrinkles." And that was okay with me. I liked watching things grow.

It was shortly thereafter that Maggie tapped me on the shoulder and said, "Let's go swimming." I remember lying on the riverbank, with my wife's head resting on my chest, looking at the water droplets fall down her pale skin and thinking that God must be pleased. At least I thought He was.

Then came the delivery.

THE FUNERAL PARLOR HAD PREPARED MY SON'S BODY. Amos and I drove by in my truck and picked up the cold metal coffin. I walked through the double swinging doors, bent down, picked it up, and walked back to the truck, where Amos lowered the tailgate. I gently slid it into the back. While Amos thanked the mortician for preparing things and giving us a few extra days, I climbed into the back and braced the coffin between my knees so it wouldn't slide around.

Shutting the tailgate, Amos climbed into the cab and drove us the twenty minutes back to the farm. Underneath a sprawling oak tree on the sloping riverside, next to my grandparents, I had dug a hole with the backhoe for the larger cement casket. Amos parked. I picked up the box that held my son, and we walked over to the hole.

After we stood there for some time, Amos cleared his throat, and I set my son down next to the hole. Then Amos handed me his Bible. It had been a while. Maybe last Christmas. Maggie always liked to read about the Nativity scene.

"What should I read?"

"Psalm 139."

I split the big book down the middle with my index finger. The thin pages crinkled and blew in the breeze, and I had a hard time finding the right page. When I found the psalm, I read what I could.

> *O LORD, You have searched me and known me.*
> *You know my sitting down and my rising up;*
> *You understand my thought afar off.*
> *. . . Where can I go from Your Spirit?*
> *Or where can I flee from Your presence? . . .*
> *If I make my bed in hell, behold, You are there.*

About midway through, I fell silent and Amos took over from memory.

> *. . . For you formed my inward parts,*
> *You covered me in my mother's womb.*
> *. . . My frame was not hidden from You,*
> *When I was made in secret . . .*
> *And in Your book they were all written,*
> *The days fashioned for me.*

When he finished, he stood with his head bowed and hands folded in front of him. The breeze picked up and blew against our backs. Then in a deep, low voice he began singing "Amazing Grace."

I did not.

While Amos sang, I knelt down next to my son and put my head on his casket. I thought about the things that were not going to happen. Baseball. The tractor. Finger painting.

"Dad, can I have the keys?" Buying his first pair of boots. Girls. The first step. Fishing. A runny nose. Tag. Swimming. Building a sandbox. Vacation. Big brother. All the stuff we had talked about. I faded out somewhere into a blank and empty space.

Amos's singing brought me back. With each of the six verses, he sang louder. When the song was over, Amos wasn't finished. "D.S., you mind if I sing one more?"

I shook my head, and Amos, looking out over the river, started up again.

> *When peace, like a river, attendeth my way,*
> *when sorrows like sea billows roll . . .*

Since college, Amos had spent two days a week singing in the church choir. He was a church history buff and especially liked the stories surrounding the writing of hymns. Years ago, floating on our raft down the river, he'd told me the story behind "It Is Well with My Soul," and I'd never forgotten it. I sat there, resting my head on the cold metal coffin of my baby son, a child I never knew, a child I never held, and thought about Horatio G. Spafford.

Spafford was a Chicago lawyer, traveling to Europe with his family for the summer. There he is, boarding a steamer with his family for an Atlantic cruise, but he gets called away for business. He sends his family ahead and plans to meet them in England. A storm comes up, sinks the ship, and all four of Spafford's children drown while holding hands on the bow.

A strong swimmer, his wife reaches land and sends him a telegram, saying simply, "Survived alone."

Broken, Spafford catches the next steamer. When the ship gets to the place where his children drowned, the captain brings him up to the bow.

"Here. This is where." He leaves Spafford to stand alone on the bow.

I want to know if he broke down. Fell to his knees. How strong was the urge to Peter Pan off the bow? Had it not been for his wife waiting on the other shore, would he have jumped? I think I would have. That dark water would have reached up and swallowed me whole—frozen man. But not Spafford. He stands up, wipes the tears, scans the water, and returns to his cabin, where he writes a poem.

What kind of a guy writes a poem at the place where his four kids went down? What kind of a guy writes anything when his children die? Well, the poem got off the boat in Spafford's pocket in Europe, somebody tied some notes to it, and there it was, coming out Amos's mouth.

The doctors say Maggie "probably" won't be alive long. Tell me yes or no, but don't tell me probably. Yet had it not been for probably, and the picture in my mind of Maggs lying there, limp and bleeding, I'd have lowered my son down on top of me and let Amos sing for both of us.

He finished his song, his face a mixture of sweat and tears, and I laid my son in the hole. Amos grabbed a shovel.

"Hold it," I said.

I walked back to the truck, picked Huckleberry off the

front seat, and tucked him under my arm. I brushed him off, straightened the red bow tie around his neck, and then knelt next to the hole and laid the bear on top of the casket.

The cement made a grinding sound as we slid the casket into place. I let the first shovelful spill slowly. Gently. Quietly.

The riverbank sloped to the water. The river was quiet and dark. Minutes passed. Amos wiped his face, put on his glasses, and walked to the truck. Sweat and cold trickled down my back in the ninety-eight-degree heat.

I looked at my hands. My eyes followed the intersections of wrinkle and callus and the veins that traveled out of my palm, over my wrist and up my forearm where, for the first time, I saw flecks of blood caked around the hair follicles. It was dark, had dried hard, and had blended with the sun freckles. Maggie's blood. I picked up a handful of dirt and gripped it tight, squeezing the edges out of my palm like an hourglass. It was damp, coarse, and smelled of earth.

I needed to tell Maggie about the funeral.

The tops of the cornstalks gently brushed my arms and legs, almost like mourners, as I walked back to the house. On the way, I rubbed the dirt from my son's grave into my arm, grinding it like a cleanser, until my forearm was raw and clean. The old blood gone and new blood come.

# *chapter five*

THE DIGGER AMPHITHEATRE, BUILT ABOUT SIX YEARS
ago, is one of South Carolina's best-kept secrets. It's ten miles
from my house and a long way from nowhere. It rises up like
a bugle out of pine trees and hardwoods, covering about
three acres, most of which is parking lot. Whoever built it
was far more interested in quality acoustics than quantity
seating. During the construction, throughout the public
hoopla surrounding the opening, and ever since, the donor
has remained anonymous.

The amphitheatre is used about three times a year; the rest
of the time it just sits there. It's hosted Garth Brooks, George
Strait, Randy Travis. Vince Gill, James Taylor. Mostly country

and bluegrass folks. The unplugged types. But we've had other names. Even George Winston. Bruce Springsteen came through once. Brought only his guitar. Maggie and I got to that one.

There are all kinds of myths about who built it. Some bigwig in Charleston with more money than sense. A divorcee from New York who was angry at her husband. An eccentric from California whose family homesteaded this area. Who built it depends on whom you talk to. One night a few years back, I learned the truth.

I was driving home at about two in the morning, and I swore I heard bagpipes. I stopped my truck and crept through the woods to the top of the hill. Sure enough. A broad-shouldered man stood center stage in the amphitheatre, wearing a kilt and playing the pipes. I sat and listened for about half an hour. Curiosity eventually got the best of me, and I found myself standing on the stage with a half-naked man. Once his eyes focused on me, he adjusted his skirt and shook my hand. We struck up a conversation, and somewhere in there the guy decided that he liked me. His full name, I learned, was Bryce Kai MacGregor, and when he plays the bagpipes, he wears a kilt. But after six or eight beers, the plaid skirt is optional. He has fiery red hair and freckles, and looks like a cross between a coal miner and a troll—just one big flexed muscle. Bryce is not ugly, although he could take better care of himself, and he has penetrating green eyes.

North of town, where things are more hilly, sits his home— a drive-in movie theater. Though the drive-in has been closed for more than fifteen years, Bryce is a Friday night regular who watches whatever strikes his fancy. The Silver Screen is actually more white than silver, and the largest of the three screens has a big hole in the left corner where a buzzard flew into it. Unfortunately for the buzzard, it got itself stuck and just hung there, flapping its wings in a panic. Bryce climbed up the back of the screen and shot the bird out with a twelve-gauge. A Greener, no less. He just stuck its head in the left barrel and pulled the trigger. "Buzzard removal," he called it, and opened another beer.

His usual sundown activity is to sit in the bed of his truck, drink beer, and watch the same old movies by himself. He owns hundreds of reel movies, of which his favorites are John Wayne Westerns. Normally at a drive-in, a moviegoer sits in the front seat of the car and hangs the speaker on the window. But Bryce's truck window is broken, and he can't fit his cooler in the front seat, so he backs his truck up front and center and spreads out on a lawn chair in the bed.

Most of the speakers in the parking lot are broken and dangling from frayed wires, so he starts the movie and then drives around until he finds one that works. When he finds a live one, he duct-tapes it onto the tailgate or the handle of the cooler. That often takes a while, because Bryce is usually so drunk that he can't remember where he last found one that worked. In his speaker search he has run into or over most of the speaker poles, which presents a bit of a problem to the exterior of his truck.

But that's not a concern to him, because he hardly ever goes into town, not even to buy groceries. He does most of that on-line now, which is odd if you think about it. As drunk as he stays, he can still find the computer when he needs it, and he can usually make it work. In about two days, a white delivery truck drops a half dozen boxes at his gate. An exception to the no-town rule is if he runs out of beer before the truck arrives.

Some folks think he's a rebel or some sort of burnt-out Vietnam kook. Bryce is no rebel. Different, yes, and in a world of his own, but he quit rebelling a long time ago. He has no one. No family. No wife. No kids. Look up "alone" in the dictionary and you see a picture of Bryce. As best I can gather, he dropped out of high school, lied about his age, and got shipped off to Vietnam for his senior trip.

They put him in a Special Forces unit, and from what I eventually gathered, they kept him busy. In the bottom of his closet is a fifty-caliber ammunition can where he keeps all his medals. All seventeen. He brought them out and showed them to me one night while we were watching *The Green Berets*. He was quick to tell me that five of them weren't his. They belonged to a buddy who didn't come back. That meant Bryce had been awarded twelve. Twelve medals. They were all colors, purple, bronze, silver. Mostly purple.

Like most boys, Bryce came home different, and he's been the same ever since—living alone with his beer and his bagpipes and his movies—and his trust fund.

So occasionally, ever since that first night in the amphitheatre, I check up on him. I'll sneak up the path to the parking area of the drive-in, and there stands Bryce. Front and center. Butt naked, except for his boots. Blowing 'til his face looks like a glow plug. Drunk as a skunk. Rattling off "Amazing Grace," "A Hundred Bottles of Beer on the Wall," or "Taps."

We usually end up watching movies together. We'll drink beer and sit in the silence, or if we can find a speaker that works, listen to the static spewing from the box between us. The poor audio doesn't seem to bother Bryce. He knows most every word of every film by heart.

SHORTLY AFTER THE DAY MAGGIE TACKLED ME OFF THE front porch and shoved the pink line under my nose, we climbed the hill and knocked on Bryce's trailer door, because we figured he'd want to know. Ever since I first introduced him to her, he'd shown a special affection for Maggie. I guess after so much killing, Bryce is attracted to things that are tender and full of life.

Hand in hand, we knocked and listened while Bryce cussed and tripped over the empty beer cans on his way to answer the door. He greeted us wearing nothing but his boots and a straw hat. When he saw Maggie, he slowly reached behind the door and grabbed a framed poster of John Wayne to cover himself from belly button to kneecap.

I nudged Maggs, and she leaned in on her tiptoes and whispered in Bryce's ear, "Dylan's gonna be a daddy."

It took a second to register, but when it did, Bryce's already dilated pupils grew as large as the end of a beer bottle. His eyes darted from side to side, he held up a finger and slowly shut the door. To call Bryce a friend, you have to be willing to live with a few eccentricities.

The noises behind the door told us that Bryce was tearing apart the inside of his trailer, looking for a pair of pants. A few minutes later he opened the door, wearing a yellowed and stretched-out T-shirt—as a pair of shorts. He had shoved his boots through the armholes, hiked it up around his waist, and buckled a belt over it to hold it around his hips. The neck hole hung down around his knees and flapped when he walked.

Bryce crept up to Maggie, knelt, and slowly placed his ear to her stomach like a safecracker. Then he wrapped his arms around her waist and pressed his ear farther into her stomach. Maggie is more ticklish than any human being alive, so the pressure of his forearms on her ribs and his ear pressed against her tummy started her to giggling. With Maggie laughing, Bryce could no longer hear whatever he was listening for, so he squeezed tighter. The crescendo grew, and thirty seconds later, Maggie was laughing so hard and wiggling around so much that Bryce just picked her up off the ground, tossing her over his shoulder like a duffel bag, and continued listening while Maggie flung her feet and laughed hysterically.

"Bryce Kai MacGregor!" she said, pounding him on the back.

Bryce set Maggs on her feet, nodded as if satisfied that there actually was a baby in her tummy, and held up his index finger again. He disappeared into the trailer, only to return half a minute later holding a beer and two dirty Styrofoam cups. After popping the tab, he poured half a sip in Maggs's cup, a full sip in mine, and kept the remainder for himself.

Beneath the shadow of the silver screen, Bryce raised his can, we clinked Styrofoam to aluminum, and the three of us drank to our son. We set down our cups and started walking toward the fence when Bryce shouted after us. "Maggie, what's your favorite movie?"

All true Southern girls have only one favorite movie, and they've all seen it ten thousand times. It's stitched into their persons like sinew and veins, and if you listen close enough, they'll whisper dialogue from entire scenes in their sleep. When it comes to their education, Scarlett O'Hara may have as much practical authority as the Bible. Maybe more.

Maggs curtsied beneath an imaginary dress and batted her eyelids. Dragging out her sweetest Southern drawl, she said, "Why, Rhett Butler!"

Bryce looked at me for interpretation, but I just shrugged. "You're on your own, pal."

Bryce scratched his head, and pretty soon the *Ohhh* look spread across his face as the lightbulb clicked on.

A couple weeks later, the UPS man delivered two oversized boxes to our front porch, saying they had been drop-shipped direct from the manufacturer—one that specialized in Southern plantation period furniture.

I looked at the box and wondered if Maggs had taken her nursery shopping on-line, but she read my face and said, "Don't look at me. I had nothing to do with it."

We cut away the cardboard and there, mummified by eight layers of bubble-wrap, sat a handmade and hand-oiled rocking chair with matching foot cradle. Finding no card, and wanting to make sure it was ours, we called the manufacturer and spoke with the owner. He told us that a man who was definitely not from south Georgia called and asked if his company could build nursery furniture for a Southern lady who already owned a crib but little else.

The owner responded, "Sir, we can build most anything if you can give us an idea of what you want." The next day they received an express package containing a videocassette.

Want to guess which one? Handwritten instructions scribbled on a yellow sticky note told them to "take notes and furnish the nursery, minus the crib." The buyer paid them double to speed manufacturing and delivery, so the guys in the shop spent their lunch breaks watching the movie clip and then arguing over the drawings for Maggs's chair and cradle.

Maggie wanted to thank Bryce without embarrassing him, so she cooked him a roast, smothered it in gravy, carrots, and potatoes, and bought him a key lime pie to satisfy his sweet tooth. She wrote a note, left the dinner at his front door, and spent the next two days swaying in that chair and nudging the cradle with her big toe.

On the third night I waited until she fell asleep, then picked her up and laid her down beside me. When I woke the next morning, she was still there, but somewhere during the night she had carried that chair and cradle in from the nursery and slid them over next to the bed.

# chapter six

DESPITE THE HEAT, I ROLLED DOWN MY SLEEVES, walked into my second-story classroom, opened the windows, straightened the desks into rows, and cleaned the chalkboard. Soon kids shuffled in, eyed the available seats, and chose ones that suited them. The room was hot, and proximity to airflow was prime real estate.

The second bell rang, and I cleared my throat. "Good morning."

Faces looked back at me blankly. The silence was heavy, but the nonverbals were raucous. The silence said, "Look, man, we ain't no happier about being here than you are, so let's get this over with."

I let a few more minutes pass, thinking eager stragglers might rush in, but they didn't. Clearing my voice again, I picked up my roll book and eyed the first name. "Alan Scruggs?"

"Here."

In my first year of teaching, I established the habit of identifying students by their places in the classroom until I got to know their work and personalities. When Alan said "Here," my mental note sounded something like, *Second row from the window. Center of room. Reading a book.*

"Wait, you skipped me."

I looked up. "Who are you?"

"Marvin Johnson!" The speaker leaned back in his chair. "See, *J* come befo' *S*."

It doesn't take the class clown long to identify himself.

"I don't usually start with the *A*'s."

"Oh, tha's cool." He looked around at the other students. "I's jus' lettin' you know. Thought you mighta forgot." My new friend smiled, showing a mouthful of white teeth.

I returned to the roll. "Russell Dixon Jr.?"

"Yeah."

A deep voice came from my left. *Against the window, front row. Big, broad shoulders. Sitting sideways. Looking out the window. Never looked at me.*

"Eugene Banks?"

"Uh-huh."

*Left side next to the window. Two back from Deep Voice. Looking out the window. Also never looked at me.*

"That was enthusiastic. Marvin Johnson?"

"Yo." It was my alphabetically conscientious friend. *Front-and-center and liking it. Smiling. Big ears. Sweatpants. Tall and athletic. Shoes in a tangle.*

The contrast between my non-air-conditioned room and his sweatpants room struck me. "You look like you just rolled out of bed. Aren't you hot?"

"Who, me? Naw." He waved his hand. "See, dis' what I wear." The kid was a walking attitude, an uncrackable nut—or so he hoped.

"Amanda Lovett?"

"Yes, sir. Both of us." A sweet, gentle voice rose from next to the window. *Front left, against the window, in between Uh-Huh and Deep Voice, and . . .*

"Both?"

She patted her stomach gently. "Joshua David."

I admit it, I'm not proud of my second reaction—the one that questioned her morals. I thought it before I had time to wish I hadn't thought it, but it didn't last very long.

"Joshua David?"

"Yes, sir," she said again, holding her hand on top of her stomach.

"Well," I said, recovering, "you make sure that young man makes it to class on time."

She broke into an even larger smile that poked two dimples into the sides of her cheeks. "Yes, sir."

Laughter rippled through the room. Somebody against the window said, "Yes, sir" in that mocking tone that kids are so good at. I looked up and waited for him to finish.

"Kaitlin Jones?"

"Koy," a voice from the right rear of the class said quietly.

I looked up at a young woman whose face was nearly covered by a combination of sunglasses and long hair.

"Koy?"

"K-o-y."

"I could see you better without those sunglasses."

She half smiled. "Probably." She didn't move a finger.

Uh-Huh, Deep Voice, and Front-and-Center laughed, but I didn't push it. The first day was not the time to draw lines. I finished the roll, noted the changes and preferred nicknames, and leaned back against the desk. There I was again, in the front of a classroom. Roped in by Maggs and Amos.

"My name is Dylan Styles."

Marvin interrupted. "Professuh, is you a doctuh?"

"I am."

"So, we should call you Doctuh?"

I checked my seating chart, although I already knew his name. "Marvin, my students have called me Mr. Styles, Professor Styles, Professor, or Dr. Styles. Do you have a preference?"

My question surprised him. When he saw that I was serious, he said matter-of-factly, "Professuh."

"Fair enough." I paused. "My wife . . ." Bad way to start. ". . . calls . . . me Dylan, but school administrators don't usually like students and teachers operating on a first-name basis. So the rest of you can pick from the list. This is English 202: Research and Writing. If you're not supposed to be here, you may leave now, or if you don't want to embarrass yourself, just don't come back after class is over. I suppose if you don't want to be here, you can leave too."

A voice from the back, next to the window, interrupted me. Its owner wore dreadlocks down to his shoulders, and when he had passed my desk on the way in, I was hit by a strong smell of cigarettes and something else. Maybe cloves. Whatever it was, he had been in a lot of it. His eyes were glassy and looked like roadmaps. "Professuh, ain't none us want to be here. Why don't we all leave?"

A wave of laughter spread across the room. Yo high-fived Uh-Huh and then slapped Deep Voice on the knee. I checked my seating chart and started again.

"B.B., I understand. But the fact is that 'not wanting to be here' is what landed each of you in this particular class a second time. Do you really want to make that mistake again?" Scanning the room, I said, "Anyone?"

Quiet replaced the laughter. Watching their faces straighten, I thought, *Maybe that was too much, too soon.* From the far right middle I heard somebody say, "Uh-umm. That's right too." I checked my seating chart. Charlene Grey.

From the middle of the room someone asked, "Professuh, was yo' granddaddy that farmer that everybody used to talk to in the hardware store? The one that raised all the steeples? I think they called him Papa Styles."

"Well, a lot of farmers fit that description, but yes, I called my grandfather Papa, he made a lot of friends in the feed and seed section, and he had a thing for steeples."

Marvin sat back in his chair, tossed his head up, and pointed in the air. "Yo, Dylan, answer me something. Why they send the grandson of a steeple-raising farmer to teach us how to write? I mean"—he looked over each shoulder, garnering support, and then pointed at me—"you don't look like much of a professor. What makes you think you can teach us anything?"

The class got real quiet, as though someone had pressed an invisible pause button. Three minutes in, and we had reached a silent impasse.

What struck me was not that he asked the question. Except for the gold-rim glasses I wear when I'm reading, I look more as though I should be riding or selling a tractor than teaching an English class—cropped blond hair, oxford shirt, Wranglers, and cowboy boots. No, it was a fair question. He could have phrased it differently, but it was fair. Actually, I had already asked it of myself. What surprised me was that Marvin had the guts to express it.

"I don't know. Availability, I suppose. Mr. Winter's probably got an answer." I was losing ground. "Okay, English 20—"

Marvin interrupted again. "But I don't want Mr. Winter's answer. I asked you, Professuh."

Sneers and quiet laughter spread through the room. Marvin sat low in his chair, in control, on stage and loving it.

I walked to the front of his desk and put my toes next to his. To be honest, I was too scattered to have said it the way I should. My body may have been in that classroom, but my heart was lying next to Maggie.

I took a deep breath. "Marvin, if you want the title of Class Clown, I really don't care." I waved my hand across the class.

"I don't think you'll get much of a challenge. What I do care about is whether or not you can pass my class. Your ability to make everybody laugh is secondary to your ability to think well and learn to write even better. Do we understand each other?" I leaned over, laid my hands on his desk, and put my eyes about two feet from his.

Marvin half nodded and looked away. I had called his bluff, and everybody knew it. I had also embarrassed him, which I wouldn't recommend. For the first time that hour, no papers were ruffling, nobody was trying to outtalk me, and nobody was looking out the window.

I let it go.

I backed up, walked to my desk, and leaned against it because I needed to. I then made a few procedural announcements and mentioned the syllabus. Everyone followed along. Point made. *That's probably enough for one day.*

My introduction had taken, at most, four minutes. Once finished, I said, "It's too hot to think in here." I gathered my papers and began packing up. "See you Tuesday. Check your syllabus, and read whatever is printed there. I have no idea because I didn't write it."

My class beelined for the door, shooting glances at one another and whispering as they left.

*Funny. What had taken ten minutes before class now took less than thirty seconds. Maybe it was something I said.*

The only student to stop at my desk was Amanda Lovett. She rested her hand on the top of her tummy. "Professor, are you the one who's been at the hospital the last week, sitting next to the coma patient on the third floor? The pretty woman, um . . . Miss Maggie?"

When I first learned to drive, I always wondered what it would be like to throw the gear shift into reverse while driving down the highway at seventy miles an hour.

"Yes, I am."

Amanda chose her words carefully. Her eyes never left mine. "I work the night shift at Community as a CNA. I . . . I was working the day you two—I mean three—came in." She fumbled with the zipper on her backpack. "I'm real sorry, Professor. I help to look after your wife. Change her bed linens, bathe her, stuff like that." Amanda paused. "I hope you don't mind, but when you're not there, I talk to her. I figure, I would want someone to talk to me, if . . . if I was lying there."

I now knew how the emperor felt with no clothes.

"Professor?" Amanda asked, looking up through her glasses, her face just two feet from mine. I noticed the skin right below her eyes. It was soft, not wrinkled, and covered with small droplets of sweat. It startled me. I saw beauty there. "I'm real sorry about your son . . . and your wife." She swung her backpack over her shoulder and left.

I stood there. Naked. The only comfort I found was that she didn't even realize she had done it. Her eyes had told me that.

Going out the door, she stopped, turned around, and said, "Professor, if you want, I won't talk to her any more. I should've asked. I just thought . . . "

"No," I interrupted, rummaging through my papers. "You talk to her . . . anytime. Please."

Amanda nodded. As she walked away, I noticed that the shirt she was wearing was one Maggie had tried on in the maternity store. I sat down at my desk, stared out the window, and felt absolutely nothing.

## chapter seven

FEW FOLKS KNOW THIS, BUT BRYCE MACGREGOR IS probably the richest man in Digger. His dad invented a gadget, something to do with how railroad cars hook together, that made his whole family a bunch of money. I know that doesn't sound like a gold mine, but Bryce said that every train that's been produced in the last fifty years uses this contraption. I guess that would add up. Bryce gets a royalty check about once a week. Sometimes more than one.

Three years ago I was in his trailer and saw a bunch of envelopes scattered about. One of them had been opened, and its contents lay on the floor. It was a check for twenty-seven thousand dollars. Bryce saw me looking at it and said,

"Take it. You can have it. Most of 'em are like that. Some are more. Some less." A few minutes later, Bryce passed out. One beer too many.

I couldn't find a pillow, so I wadded up a couple sweatshirts and propped up Bryce's head. He was snoring pretty good and could have really used a bath, so I opened a few windows and didn't bother to shut the door behind me. Nobody ever went up there anyway. The breeze would do him more good than harm.

I don't think Bryce ever remembered that night, but I did. There was more than a quarter of a million dollars on the floor in checks made out to him. I left that check, and all the other checks, right there on the floor. I didn't want Bryce's money, and the secret of his trust fund was safe with me. But I didn't want him taken advantage of, either. And there are enough money-grubbers in Digger, small town or not, to rob Bryce blind.

So a few weeks after that, I got to thinking about Bryce while harrowing a section of pasture. What was a half-naked drunk, probably the richest man in South Carolina, doing, living in a trailer next to a drive-in movie theater that had been closed since the early seventies? I said to myself, "This is just not right. This could turn out real bad if someone doesn't start taking care of Bryce." So I went up to the Silver Screen and gathered up all those envelopes. Bryce showered once a week, and I made sure that once a week was that day. Once Bryce was smelling sociable, we loaded up my truck and the three of us—Bryce, Blue, and I—drove to Charleston to talk to the man who Bryce said handled his trust fund.

The man's name was John Caglestock. A skinny little man with rosy cheeks and round glasses that hung on the end of his bulbous nose. Legally, the man had no actual control over the fund, but he was careful to make it his daily priority. His firm made some good commissions from handling Bryce's affairs. But Bryce could be intimidating when he wanted to. Whatever Bryce said, Mr. Caglestock did.

After our meeting, due in large part to the way Bryce talked about me, Mr. Caglestock did whatever I said. Bryce called me his brother, and the man brought out some paperwork and had me sign it. I told him I wasn't anybody's brother and I wouldn't sign anything, but Bryce told me to do it. That way I wouldn't have to "drag his butt" down here again.

So I read it, got the gist of it, and signed it. From then on, the firm had to run every transaction by me before it did anything. Bryce's orders. In essence, I couldn't spend any of Bryce's money on personal matters, but I could look over the firm's shoulder and see where it wanted to invest it. And Bryce thought that was good.

About once a month Mr. Caglestock would call me, and we'd have a real polite conversation in which I approved or denied every transaction he wanted to make. The more time I spent with Bryce, the more I realized that behind the drunk façade, Bryce had moments of lucidity in which he really knew what he was doing. I guess he knew the day I took him to Charleston.

In the three years since I've been talking with Mr. Caglestock, Bryce has made a pile of money. He's more than doubled his fund. Looking back, I realize that has more to do with the market and Mr. Caglestock's research and advice than my input. Caglestock knows his stuff, and he taught me a lot.

One day Maggie asked me if Bryce had a will, and I said I didn't know. I started doing some digging and found out that he did not. And he had no one to leave anything to. That worried us, so I went up to his trailer one afternoon and asked him, "Bryce, if you were to die tomorrow, who would you want at your funeral?" Without batting an eye, he said, "The bugler."

That didn't give Maggie and me much to go on. Just whom do you leave forty or fifty million dollars to when the guy who owns it isn't saying? We decided that while we had no right to play God, we could do a better job than the state. So we had Mr. Caglestock draw up a will that left the whole kit and caboodle to the children of the men who had served with Bryce in his unit in Vietnam. Most of them never knew their fathers, but Bryce did. He kept their dog tags in his ammunition box. About fifteen in all.

So why did I do all this if I didn't want the money? I guess because Bryce couldn't, or at least didn't, and I didn't want him getting taken advantage of by a bunch of Charleston lawyers who found him incompetent to handle his own affairs. And since Bryce's fund has doubled, they can't accuse me of that. Besides, between Caglestock and me, they've made good money. I'm not sure even Bryce knows how directly I handle his fund. It's an odd thing. Caglestock will call me, we'll move two to three million dollars from one stock or fund to another, and yet personally, I'm scratching to pay the taxes on our property. Bryce makes more money off the interest in his investments in one week, or sometimes even a day, than I'll make all year.

A TORNADO BOUNCED OVER DIGGER LAST NIGHT. IT PICKED up a couple of houses, disassembled them piece by piece, and scattered the remains for miles. I didn't hear it, but those who did said it sounded like a really mad freight train. After a phone call reassured me that the hospital hadn't been in its path, I wanted to see the damage, so I loaded up and drove across town. It was an odd thing. On one side of the road, everything was exactly as it had been the night before. On the other side, it looked as though God had taken a two-mile razor to the earth's face. One man woke up to a neighbor phoning to say his tractor was sitting upside down in his tomato patch more than a mile from where the owner had parked it the night before. Others didn't wake up. There were three of those.

I finished my chores around the house, cleaned the yard and then myself, and drove out to Bryce's. By the time I crested the top of the hill by the Silver Screen, it was late in the afternoon. Bryce was standing in a kilt and wearing combat boots, holding bagpipes in one hand and a beer in the other. "Morning, Dylan," he said with a smile. His white barrel chest glistened in the afternoon sun. Bryce had quit wearing a watch long ago, and sometimes, if his nights ran long, so did his mornings.

"Morning." Blue ran up to smell and greet Bryce. "Thought I'd come see how the storm left you. Everything still here?"

"No problem," Bryce barked in his best Scottish brogue.

Looking around, I noticed that one of the screens he no longer used had been torn from top to bottom. The canvas that was once tacked to plywood now flapped in the wind, exposing the splintered plywood that was separated and ripped right down the middle.

"Looks like that one didn't fare too well," I said, pointing.

"Yup," Bryce said between gulps. "No big deal. Only need one." Bryce threw his now-empty can on the ground and walked toward his trailer. He came back carrying a blowtorch. To my amazement, he walked across the parking lot into the second lot and up to the wooden housing at the base of the torn screen. He sparked the blowtorch, adjusted the flame, and held it against the wooden housing. After a few seconds, flames appeared. After a few minutes, the wind caught it, fueling the fire, and it rose up to the screen. The screen and structure behind it caught fire and burned like film in a projector.

Bryce walked back to his trailer and returned to me without the blowtorch but with a beer in each hand. He handed me one, and we watched the screen burn to the ground. Bryce lifted his beer above his head and said, "To the Silver Screen."

IT WAS WELL PAST DARK WHEN I CRANKED MY TRUCK. I passed the amphitheatre, and all was quiet. I pulled off the shoulder, and Blue let out a big breath and lay down in the back. I cut the engine and sat in the quiet.

One night after a show, Maggie and I had lain in bed, ears ringing and too wired to sleep. Bathed in darkness and the sweat of a South Carolina summer night, she asked me why I was so quiet. And taking a chance, I told her what was on my mind.

"When I see those people on stage, sometimes I think about the little drummer boy. Standing there, offering his gift. All he had. Right there at the foot of the King. I wonder what that moment was like. Was it quiet all except for the sound of a drum? Were the animals shuffling about? Chewing hay? Where was Joseph? Was Jesus sleeping, up 'til He smiled? And the smile. What did He feel? I . . . I wish I could wring out my soul, like the drummer boy, and then stop midwring, and know, in that minute, that that—whatever *that* was—was the perfect expression of a gift."

I pointed out the window toward the amphitheatre. "Those people, when they stand before the world, just before the sound fades, they know that they're doing the very thing they were created to do. Their faces show it. Gift affirmed. They know life. That's it. That moment, when the fans come alive and the King smiles, is living. Sometimes, I just wonder what it'd be like to play my drum for the King. Did the drummer boy stand like Pavarotti, hang the notes off the balcony, stop midbeat, and listen to himself? Did he notice the moment, or did it pass by unmarked?"

I thought she'd laugh, maybe lecture me. Not Maggie. When I had finished, she ran her fingers through my hair, wrapped her arm and leg around me, and pressed her chest to mine. "Have you ever had that feeling? Ever?"

"I think so."

"Where?"

I looked up at the ceiling fan, hypnotized by the backward-spinning mirage caused by the forward spin of the blades. "Maybe a time or two in class. It's hard to say."

A few nights later, Maggie packed a brown-bag dinner, blindfolded me, put me in the truck, and started driving.

"Where're we going?" I asked.

She just kept driving, and after fifteen minutes of U-turns and "shortcuts," we got where we were going. She pulled over, grabbed my hands, and led me to a gate, where she fumbled with some keys and unlocked what sounded like a padlock. Loosing the chain, she pushed open a creaky fence and then led me a hundred or so yards to a series of steps. At the top of them, my feet told me that the surface had changed from concrete to something hollow, maybe wood. She led me a few feet farther, then placed her finger across my lips. It was quiet. Pin-drop quiet.

I heard her shuffle away from me and down the steps. Then, while I stood there wondering what in the world was going on, she started screaming at the top of her lungs.

"Whooooo! More! More! More! Whooooo!"

It scared me so bad I ripped off the bandanna, only to find myself on the stage of the amphitheatre and Maggie running up and down the rows of seats, holding a candle, waving her arms in the air and screaming like a wild woman. Throughout the rows she had placed cardboard people, maybe fifteen in all, and each held a burning candle. She whooped and hollered for ten minutes, dancing around as if she'd struck gold or come to hear the man at the mike. It took me ten minutes to get her to stop.

When I finally got her calmed down, we sat in the second row, propped our feet up on the first, ate turkey sandwiches, and watched a show that existed only in our minds. When I finished my sandwich and leaned over to kiss her, she had mustard dabbed in the corner of her mouth. I can still taste it.

Maggie could have made me feel foolish, even stupid for wondering outside myself. But she didn't. She took me down there, set me on the stage, and then acted like my own private audience no matter how foolish it made her feel.

Now I sat there in the moonlight and looked down at the amphitheatre through blurred vision. I opened the truck door, slid down the hill, and hopped the fence. I walked down the center aisle and climbed up on the stage. The moon reflected off the tops of the chairs like ten thousand candles, but I never opened my mouth. I knew no sound would come. Only tears. I lay down on the stage and hid from the demons that fed my doubts.

*chapter eight*

THE DIGS ENGLISH DEPARTMENT HAD TITLED MY class "Research and Writing," hoping that the students would do just that. This meant that from day one, they would need to be thinking about and working toward a term paper. It also meant that anyone waiting until the last minute would land him- or herself right back in the class a third time. I suppose most of my students knew this. The syllabus allowed for weekly, sometimes daily, quizzes, but the bulk of each student's grade would be determined by one single term paper.

With this in mind, I set aside the third day of class as optional. On the second day I told them, "The most important aspect of your paper is not your topic—there are thousands of interesting topics. The most important aspect is your question. You ask a vague question, you get a vague answer. Ask a specific question, and you tend to get a specific answer. I want specific questions and specific answers. If you have any doubt as to the effectiveness of your question, such as, 'Is it tight?' you'd better come see me on Thursday."

I was willing to answer questions, no kidding, but more than that, I just wanted to see who would show up if I gave them the option.

No one came.

That meant one of two things. Either they all had good questions, or they could not care less. The proof would be in the paper, and we'd find out toward Christmas.

BLUE AND I ARRIVED AT THE HOSPITAL AROUND FOUR IN the afternoon. We walked into Maggie's room, where her brushed hair told me that Amanda had been working. Around Maggie, the sun hung a peaceful light. The lack of tension in her facial muscles told me that she liked it. Aware but unaware, peaceful but not at peace, rested but tired, sleeping but not asleep.

I wanted to wake her up. To nudge her shoulder, watch her stretch and yawn, reach for a hug, sip coffee, and then head for the barn or slip along the river and watch the bass and bream break water or the wood ducks whistle overhead. I sat down next to Maggie, kissed her cheek, and she moved not at all.

The doctors say her brain registers "normal activity for a

person in this condition," whatever that means. They say, "All we can do is wait. Sometimes shock does the unexplainable to a person."

I'm having a hard time with this. If we can put a man on the moon, split an atom, move a heart from one man to another, cure polio, or build a hundred-story building, we ought to be able to wake up my wife. One minute she was awake and crying, reaching for our son. The next minute she was vomiting and then not awake. I can't explain that.

I sat with Maggie while the sun went down. Blue settled in on the blanket someone had folded in the corner. The same someone had filled a bowl of water next to it.

Just a couple days after the delivery, my friend Mr. Thentwhistle had sent a nurse to tell me that he was calling animal control to remove my "filthy canine."

"Ma'am," I said politely and pointing at Blue, "I've tried to tell him, but he won't listen to me. The dog goes with the girl."

She had left, reported to Mr. Administrator, and he called animal control. Animal control is a voluntary position in this county, and it happens to be held by Amos's dad, Mr. Carter. When Mr. Carter found out what kind of dog it was, he put two and two together and said, "No sir, that girl might need that dog. You best leave it alone."

I sipped coffee and held Maggie's hand in silence.

Maggie wasn't a real touchy-feely person, but she loved for me to rub her feet. In her bedside table she kept some moisturizing cream that she got at one of those sensory-overload stores in the mall. You know, the kind full of creams, candles, and all the fluffy crap that sits unused in your medicine cabinet. I didn't really like the smell, but she did. She said it smelled like honeysuckle. The label said "Body Butter."

For some reason, I don't smell too well. I mean, I can smell gardenias or bacon cooking or that perfume of Maggie's called Eternity, but on the whole, I don't walk around smelling life the way she does. Maggie can smell anything. We'll be walking in the mall, stop at the perfume counter, and she can close her eyes and differentiate between eight perfumes. To me, they all smell the same.

But a week ago, I brought that cream from the house and put it in her bedside table. I opened the drawer, pulled out the cream, slid my chair to the end of the bed, gently slipped off her socks, and rubbed. Starting with her heel, up through the length of her arch, between her toes, and finally up her calf.

Maggie has beautiful feet. Her toes are small, callused, trimmed. I used to kid her about having interchangeable toes, because they're all the same size. She has strong feet, a high arch, a slender heel, and a strong calf—working feet, I call them. She's a natural runner, with a much better gait than I have, and occasionally we jog along the river. But that's her second hobby. Her first love is her garden. She'd much rather dig in the dirt than run.

AT FIRST, MAGGIE AND I COULDN'T SEEM TO DEVELOP A routine at the hospital. At some times we were like two kids on a continual first date, and at others we were like Papa and

Nanny after fifty years. Sometimes I'd sit there and talk to her. Sometimes not. Sometimes the rubbing did all the talking. And sometimes, I just didn't know what else to say.

Sometimes when I walked into the room, Maggie's forehead was real tense. Today she had a wrinkle between her eyes, so I started rubbing her feet and the wrinkle disappeared. Who knows what coma patients are doing or thinking on the other side of their eyelids? Maggie's forehead made me think that they don't sleep all the time. I'm no expert, but sometimes when I walked into the room, I could tell Maggie was awake even though her eyes were closed and she looked asleep. Her face showed it. Sometimes it was her hands, but mostly it was her face. Then there were other times when she looked asleep, and I knew she was asleep. Her whole body looked relaxed. Sitting at the end of the bed, I rubbed a few more minutes, and Maggie slipped off to sleep. And no, I never told her about the funeral.

A wristwatch alarm on the arm of a nurse walking down the hall sounded at nine o'clock, and I woke up with my head slumped over next to Maggie's. I wiped off my drool and sat there a few minutes in the dark, letting her breath wash my face. The moon hung full, and a couple of clouds blocked the stars, but for the most part, it was clear and breezy. A sweet, South Carolina starlight serenade. If we were home right then, we'd be wrapped up in a blanket on the front porch. I tucked the covers up around Maggie's shoulders, checked her socks to make sure they covered her heels, set the cream next to the bed with the cap off, and pulled the door shut behind me.

Walking out Maggie's door, I noticed that Amanda had taped a note to the doorjamb. *Professor, come to church tonight. Daddy's preaching. 7:30. I'll save you a seat. Amanda.*

I pulled the note down, read it a second time, and thought to myself, *The life of a preacher's kid. Probably front and center every time the door is open.*

Blue and I slipped down the hallway, and a fat old nurse nodded at me as I left. She glanced over her reading glasses, looked me up and down, and continued reading. The silver chains hanging down both sides of her glasses outlined her square jaw and double chin like a cowbell. Blue and I walked down the stairs and out the ER, and I started my truck. We drove out the main entrance of the hospital, and I pitched Amanda's crumpled note out the window.

At 9:30 I rounded the last corner before home, and Pastor John's church came into view. The AME church was built in 1952. Since then, Sunday mornings had become a local spectacle. Almost a parade of sorts. Just prior to the ringing of the 10:30 AM bells, women in all shapes, sizes, and colors, escorted by their families, walked smack down the middle of the highway en route to their pew.

And hats? Hats galore. You've never seen so many hats. They say sometimes Pastor John stops midsermon to point out a new or good-looking hat. The women love it. They also love his preaching, which, according to his reputation, is pretty heavy on the fire and brimstone. People say he tells it like it is, and they like him for it.

The church is a good mixture of all races and sizes, and if

you drive by during the singing, it'll resonate through your windows. Even in winter when the front doors are shut. It's a good thing that steeple is tall and well built; otherwise they'd bring it down. Clapping, singing, even some dancing. You want good hymn singing? Go to Pastor John's church. You'll get it there.

Tonight, like every Wednesday night, was no exception. The place was packed. I slowed to an idle and found myself parked on the shoulder opposite Amos's Crown Vic. His radio was squawking voices and radio checks.

"Seven-twelve to HQ."

"HQ to 712. Go ahead, 712."

"Ah, I've got a . . . " An eighteen-wheeler carrying a load of pine trees whizzed by my window, causing me to miss the rest of the mumbo jumbo. After Amos had been appointed deputy, he told me, "D.S., if I don't learn my ABCs, they'll park my B-U-T-T in HQ and I'll be sorta-outta-luck." He spent weeks reading flashcards that he kept in his shirt pocket.

Law enforcement definitely has its own language. I guess it's a good thing. If I'm sitting there with a telephone pole lying over the top of my car and my feet resting on the engine block, I don't want a deputy with flowery language. I want somebody who can cut through the c-r-a-p and get my b-u-t-t to the h-o-s-p-i-t-a-l. Right n-o-w. Amos says that pretty much eliminates me from law enforcement. He's probably right. I'd be explaining to HQ what the situation looked like rather than what was needed. I see colors, not structure.

Based on the squawking, it was a dull night in Digger.

Apparently most of the population was in church, because every parking space was taken. Even the dirt spillover lot was full. I left my truck on the shoulder and slipped in the side door, where I was immediately met by an usher in a three-piece suit. An older, gray-haired gentleman, probably seventy-five. He smiled from earlobe to earlobe and held the door while I walked through it. You have never seen so many teeth. And straight? You could have drawn a line with them.

I stood there in jeans, scuffed boots, and a flannel shirt that I was rapidly trying to tuck in. I keep my hair pretty short, so that's never really a problem. Even when it's messed up, it can't look too messed up. The entrance to the church was warm and empty, except for Mr. Smiles and me. He asked me if I was a visitor, and I thought briefly about lying to him but figured the narthex of the church, beneath the apex of my grandfather's steeple, was not the place. I nodded without meeting his eyes.

Through the window of the door leading into the sanctuary, I could see Pastor John pacing slowly back and forth, wearing a purple robe and holding a well-worn book in his right hand. He'd aged, and his hair had grown white since I last saw him. The usher gently opened the door and stepped in. A sea of three hundred to four hundred people, pressed elbow to elbow, filled the upright pews, and lines of latecomers filled folding chairs all the way down the aisle and around the back of the pews. *This would never pass the fire marshal's inspection.*

The rounded sanctuary fanned out before me like a half circle. At the flat end stood the pulpit and Pastor John. Behind him stood an organ and forty or fifty folks in matching robes shouting "Amen" and "Umm-hmmm." The pews must have been fashioned by the Oompa Loompas because they were little; but judging from appearance, the size of the pew didn't seem to bother anybody. The pews did have padded seats, but I'd have given up the padding for a little shoulder room.

Before I realized what he was doing, the usher had walked smack-dab down the middle of the center aisle, intending to lead me to the front of the church where, wonder of wonders, Amanda sat next to an empty spot. I tried to stop him. I coughed and even thought about whistling, but Amanda turned, saw me, and started scooting over to make more room. I followed while the whispers grew out from me like aftershocks resonating from an epicenter.

When the usher got to the front row, he turned, opened his arm so the palm of his hand showed, and nodded his head. Still smiling. *Dang, that's a lot of teeth.* With my shirt starting to stick to my back, I slithered into the seat.

Amanda smiled, whispered, "Hi, Professor, I thought you might come," and folded her hands in front of her tummy.

I looked down and said nothing. Studying the carpet, I noticed that Amanda had slipped off her shoes, and it wasn't hard to see why. Her feet were pretty swollen. I looked up, and Pastor John stopped midsentence, waved his hands, and placed his right index finger against his lips.

After the congregation quieted and people stopped talking about me behind my back, he said, "For those of you who don't know him, Dr. Dylan Styles has just joined us. As you all know, we've been praying for his wife, Maggie, for several weeks now, and we will continue to do so."

Someone behind me said, "That's right." Across the room, someone muttered, "Ummm-hummm" and farther over to the left came, "Amen."

Walking to the other side of the stage, he said, "Please, make sure that all of you greet Professor Styles when I finish." Pastor John smiled and looked at me, then back at the congregation. "But not until I finish."

Looking back at me, sweat pouring off his face like a spigot, he said, "Welcome, son." It looked as though he wanted to say something else, but he didn't. Without skipping a beat, he picked up where he had left off and continued thumping that Bible across the pulpit. Based on his speaking and the audience's reaction, I had interrupted his sermon at the crescendo. After another ten minutes, once he had worked everybody into a pretty good frenzy, he finished and sat down in a big, wide, ornate wooden chair next to the choir.

An organ started, and my armpits were soaked. The place was like my classroom: real hot. Several women were methodically waving pieces of paper in tempo with the ceiling fans, which only served to circulate the warmth. My forehead was dripping, and I kept rubbing it with my shirtsleeve. Shortly, the music stopped, the sanctuary fell silent save the rustling of the choir's robes, and next thing I knew, the ushers were leading the choir to the railing. That only meant one thing.

Communion.

The choir made their way to the rail and knelt in unison.

Following Pastor John's prayer, the assistant pastor walked down the row of purple robes and placed white wafers in black hands. "The body of Christ. The bread of heaven."

After they had time to swallow, Pastor John followed with a great big silver cup. He moved methodically down the aisle. "Brother Michael, the blood of Christ. Sister Annie, the cup of salvation." When he had finished, the choir stood in unison and returned to their seats where, swaying in rhythm like the women's fans, they began to hum quietly. Like my cornfield, this place was constant movement.

Then out of nowhere, Mr. Smiles appeared next to me. He turned, extended his arm, showed his palm, and beckoned. I looked straight ahead and pretended not to notice him.

Amanda whispered, "It's okay, Professor. We ain't Catholic. You can go with us."

The row opposite me was filing out and up to the railing on the left. Mr. Smiles beckoned a second time, and my forehead wrinkled.

Pastor John broke in, waved at the organ, which went silent, and pointed his face toward the balcony. Looking at no one in particular but everyone in general, he said, "You all know how I feel about this." His hand swept across the railing. "Before you strut up here, remember what waits." His articulation was crisp and powerful, his wording careful and precise. He paused, moved the cup from one hand to another, pulled out his handkerchief, and wiped his forehead and cheeks.

"You all face a choice. You can rise from your seat, follow the person in front of you, stroll down this aisle, critique somebody else's Sunday best which they happened to wear on a Wednesday night, think about how hungry you are or where, when, and what you are going to eat when you leave here, and then kneel, nod, nip and sip, and return to your seat, having thought the bread stale and wine cheap." Pastor John wiped his brow again after unfolding and refolding the handkerchief.

"Or"—he moved the cup to the other hand—"you can slide from your seat, limp to this rail . . ." The humming grew louder. "Reach down, grab these splintery timbers, fall, rest your baggage against it"—Pastor John's voice rose above the humming—"extend your hands, take tenderly, place the body on your tongue, taste the grit, swallow, and feel the hunger build in your stomach. Then you can grasp this cup." Pastor John held the cup above his head with two hands, his powerful arms rippling through his robe. "Tremble, sip violently, feel the burn, taste the acrid smell, feel the splinters pierce your elbows, lean more heavily, and then look upon this cross." Pastor John pointed behind him without looking.

"You can reach up and place your trembling hands on callused, blood-soaked feet, let the red, slippery liquid run down your fingers, underneath your watchband, and come to rest in the crack of your elbow. You can lean your forehead against His shin, notice the crude and rusted nail, the shake and strain in His arms and legs, stick your hand in the hole in His side, notice the dried blood on His face, the thorns poking through the skin, smell the vinegar, feel the raw skin on His back, and hear the gurgle drowning out His breathing." Pastor John took a long, deep breath.

"Lastly, you can raise your head and feel the breath of God. And in that instant, if you so choose, you can see your own reflection. With all your zits, warts, blemishes, and scars. And there, amongst the scar tissue, are your demons. But having chewed, sipped, and swallowed, you can chase." The choir was humming louder. Pastor John's voice was calm, controlled, soothing, and resonating.

"People." He paused, knelt, leaned his arms on the railing, held the cup between both hands, and faced the congregation. "This is where you chase the demons that feed your doubts, your anger, your bitterness, and your lack of faith." Then in almost a whisper, he said, "Every last one." He stood and wiped his forehead. Except for the choir, you could hear a pin drop.

"Brothers and sisters, a demon's job is to kill you. To beat you to death. To rob you of anything that is not painful. This railing is where you give more than you take. Where you steal back. Where you kill what's killing you. Then, having chased and slain, you return"—Pastor John pointed to the pews and folding chairs—"bloody but unharmed, different but the same, changed but unchanged, moved but unmoved. A living battleground.

"People, we got hurting brothers and sisters here. Every one of us has a closet, and in that closet, we keep and feed our demons. Some's more full than others, but they're all busting at the seams. You all know most of mine. I've told you. What I haven't told you is in my criminal record. That's public. You're welcome to read it."

85

I shot a glance at Amanda. Peace bounced off the glisten on her face as she watched her father.

"People," Pastor John continued, "that space between your pew and this altar, between the red velvet cushion and these splintery timbers. Whether it's twenty feet or a million miles, it's not a question of distance. It's one of position." He calmly turned, walked to the end of the railing, and waited.

The humming continued. Mr. Smiles put his hand on my shoulder. The people next to Amanda were standing, waiting.

I rose.

I took three steps and knelt. Or rather, fell. If the railing had been much farther, I'm not sure I'd have made it. Amanda knelt next to me. I looked straight forward and followed Amanda's lead, holding out my hands, one clasped beneath the other. The assistant pastor gently placed a small white wafer in my white hand. I took it. If he said anything, I didn't hear it. Amanda did likewise and immediately placed it on her tongue and closed her mouth. I held mine out and looked at it, then placed it on my tongue. It was gritty, but I swallowed. I think my stomach growled, because out of the corner of my eye, I saw Amanda smile.

Silently Pastor John appeared with the cup that he held to my lips. "Dylan, this is Christ's blood, which was shed for you. Take it in remembrance of Him who died on the cross." He placed the cold silver cup to my lips.

I sipped.

My tongue and throat burned as I forced the liquid into my belly.

Then he moved to Amanda. "Baby, this is Jesus." He placed his hand on her forehead and prayed quietly.

When I opened my eyes, the railing was empty but for me. I don't know how long I had been there, but when I turned, everyone else was seated and about eight hundred eyes were turned directly at me. I quickly rose and plopped into my seat with an embarrassing thud.

Amanda sat with her eyes closed. Quiet. I hadn't seen Amos until now. Out of the corner of my left eye, I noticed that he was sitting at the end of the row opposite me with his attention focused on Pastor John. His uniform stood out, and his badge glistened in the lights. His belt, and Kimber, were noticeably absent.

At 10:47 PM Pastor John said a closing prayer, and as the choir sang, people filed out of their seats. A few headed for the door, but most headed for me. I was the center of several hundred people's attention and hands. After eight or ten minutes, Amos rescued me. He put his arm around me and led me toward the side door.

"Professuh," he said in his cornfield tone, "how 'bout a burger?"

"No." I paused. "I'm not hungry."

"Doc, that's horsepucky."

"What?" I said, looking at Amos.

"A few minutes ago, back over there, your stomach told me you were starving and needed a fat, juicy, greasy cheeseburger with bacon, extra pickles, and a little of Amos's secret sauce on the side."

"No . . . " I fumbled for my keys. "Thanks." I left Amos standing with three hundred people who had just heard him describe the cheeseburger. I started my truck, noticed a new exhaust leak, bumped the stick into drive, and drove home.

Pulling into the drive, I circled around back, parked on the grass, walked up the back porch, and pulled on the screen door, where the smell of Maggie's house tugged at my loneliness. Unable to face an empty house, I grabbed the blanket off the front porch, walked out into the cornfield, lay down with Blue, and named my demons.

*chapter nine*

WHEN I WOKE UP, THE SUN WAS JUST BREAKING
the tree line. It was cold, I was shivering, and Pinky was rooting
at my feet. Pinky appeared on our doorstep about two years
ago. I looked at her and saw three months' worth of breakfast,
but Maggs gave me the pointed finger and said, "Dylan Styles,
if you shoot that pig, you're on the couch for a month."

So Pinky ended up in the barn with her own stall and two
permanent slots in our daily calendar. Maggs even painted
*Pinky* in bright-red letters above the gate. I feed her bulk dog
food or kernel corn, sometimes a combination, but she'll eat
anything that's not nailed down—and even some stuff that is.
When she first appeared, she weighed maybe eighty pounds

and needed a bath and a vet. Now she weighs a little over three hundred and expects to be hosed down weekly.

I'll never understand how someone so beautiful and so tender could love something so ugly. But make no mistake, that pig loves her back. Dang thing hates me, craps on my foot every chance she gets, but she just adores my wife. You've never heard such grunting and squealing as when Maggie rubs Pinky's ears and stomach. Pinky rolls and wallows and then rubs up against Maggie's overalls. Maggie doesn't care.

Maggie would squat down in the middle of the stall, and Pinky, holding her curlicue tail high in the air, would nose all the piglets out of the corner and up to Maggie, where she'd rub each one until it squealed with delight. Every now and then, Pinky would stick her nose under Maggs's hand, get a scratch between the ears, and then shove a piglet under Maggie's leg. Thirty minutes later, Maggie would walk out of the barn and smell like a pig all day. One morning last summer it was so bad, I had to hose *her* down. Maggie didn't care. She just laughed. Squealed just like Pinky.

Maggie loved the farm. Everything about it, from the creaking floors to the noisy screen door. The chipped paint, the front porch, Papa's swing, the smell of hay in the barn, the way the cotton bloomed in summer, the short walk through the oaks down to the river, the oak tree spreading across the barn that was bigger around than the hood of my truck, the artesian well and its sulfur water, the corn that waved in rows to the wind that sifted through it.

Maggie probably loved the corn best. Every night when the

breeze picked up off the river, she'd disappear to the front porch with hot herbal tea and stand there, watching the waves rise and fall atop the stalks. And on moonlit summer nights when she couldn't sleep or Blue woke her up barking at a deer, she'd grab a blanket, tiptoe to the porch, and sit on the steps as the moonlight streamed through the rows like a prism and lit the sandy soil beneath.

Daybreak would come, and I'd find her asleep against the column at the top step. I'd crack the screen door, Blue would pick his head up off her lap, and without saying a word, Maggie would lift her eyelids, smile, throw off the blanket, and then tear off the front steps with a giggle like a kid let out of church. We'd race through the cornrows all the way to the river, where she'd leap off the bluff and into the deep, black water below. Blue and I followed as if we were trapped in a Mountain Dew commercial.

One of Maggie's favorite foods was creamed corn. After our swim, she'd cut ten or fifteen ears, haul them into the kitchen, rub them over the creamer, and come out looking as though somebody had just shot her with corn puree.

When I was finishing my dissertation, she'd walk in late at night, silently offering a bowl of chocolate ice cream or coffee or whatever I needed to help me continue writing. If she sensed frustration and knew I was about ready to set a match to the whole blasted thing, she'd grab me by the hand, pull me to the porch, set me on the swing, and tell me to breathe deeply and watch the corn roll in waves. Thirty minutes later, she'd put her foot in my back and tell me to get back there and keep writing.

I miss that.

When I raised my head, Pinky stopped rooting, perked her ears, and snorted, showering me in pig snot. With her tail sticking straight up into the air, she ran back to the barn with her Charlie Chaplin gait. I have no idea how she got out in the first place, but I bet the answer will require new lumber.

I lifted myself off the sand and brushed off my face and clothes. They were cold and damp.

In the barn, Pinky huddled her little ones around her, although they weren't all that little anymore, and she made sure to keep me at a good distance. I threw some corn and tried to step closer, but she got her body in between me and them and then crapped on my foot. So I dumped the corn in a pile, hung up my bucket, locked the barn door, and headed for the porch. "Pigs!"

Back in the house, I made myself a pot of coffee and spent thirty minutes studying my classroom seating chart, trying to memorize appearance and characteristics with name. It would only work if the kids sat in the same place each class, but most kids do because people are creatures of habit. Take church, for example. Ever visited a new church and sat in somebody else's pew? Try it sometime. Whoever owns that pew will let you know.

I HAD BEEN IN MY CLASSROOM ONLY A FEW MINUTES WHEN Amanda walked in and smiled. Then she took one look at my forearm and raised an eyebrow. "Professor, what happened to your arm?"

I quickly pulled my pushed-up sleeve back down over the scabs and pus on my left forearm, cursing myself for letting it show. "Little run-in with a big pig," I lied.

She could tell I was covering up more than my arm. "You make sure you let me clean that for you at the hospital. You don't want it infected. I've seen that. And you don't want it."

Amanda sat down, and I stuffed my hand into my pocket. The midmorning sun was streaming through the magnolia and heating the classroom up pretty good. I had the fans set on "breeze," but the sun convinced me to crank them over to "hurricane" and really get the air flowing.

Marvin walked in, and I greeted him.

"Morning," he replied. Apparently not a good one. Under his breath, I heard him mutter, "It's hotter than a snake's butt in a wagon rut in here."

Russell followed, said "Mornin', Professuh," sat down, rubbed his eyes, wiped his forehead with a towel, and looked out the window.

Koy slipped in and sat silently in her chair near the back. So far, everyone was true to form.

I walked down the far-right aisle and stood next to an empty desk, just smiling. "Good morning, Sunglasses."

Koy half smiled, looked over the rim of her glasses, showed me the whites of her eyes, and said with a whisper, "Morning." Then she ducked her eyes, placed her hand on her forehead, and continued reading.

I counted heads, checked my chart, faced the class, and sat on the top of my desk with my legs dangling off the end.

Noticing this as an address posture, everyone quieted and looked at me with suspicion. "Would you please take out a piece of paper and—"

The class groaned.

"What are you moaning for? I told you there would be a quiz."

Russell turned to Amanda, who already had paper and pencil on her desk, and said, "Could I have a piece of papuh?" Marvin did likewise. Eugene and Alan had their own.

All my quizzes were ten questions. All of them together, which after a semester could total more than twenty, only counted for 10 percent of the grade, so fretting over one or two scores wasn't worth it. In addition, if a student was present for every quiz, I'd tack on 10 percent to the final grade anyway. None of my students ever knew this, but it worked. The process of knowing they were going to get a quiz, and not wanting to fail another one, had a way of causing people like Marvin to read and at least familiarize themselves with something they might not otherwise bother with.

"Question number one," I said, as my students leaned over their desks and placed pen to the paper. "What is your name?"

Everybody laughed, and Marvin said, "I always knew I liked you, Professuh."

"Question number two. Where are you from?"

Marvin smiled and licked his lips. Amanda quickly wrote her answer and looked back at me. Koy wrote without looking up or expression. Russell propped his feet up on the desk next to him.

CHARLES MARTIN

"Question number three. What is your favorite color?"

Marvin, starting to take me seriously because he was looking at the possibility of acing my quiz, said, "You go, Professuh."

"Question number four. Why?"

"What?" Marvin's face was suddenly real tense. "Wha' you mean 'why?'"

Half the class wrote without comment. Marvin waited for my explanation, so I repeated the question. "Why is your favorite color, your favorite color?"

Marvin shook his head. "But there ain't no right answer. How you gonna grade it?"

Russell, Eugene, Alan, B.B., M & M, and Jimbo all waited for my answer. Everybody else wrote furiously.

"Take as long as you need," I said.

Marvin dropped his head and said beneath his breath, "How do I know why my color is my favorite color? It just is."

"Question number five."

Marvin's hand shot up. "Wait, I ain't finished."

"You can come back to it." Looking back at the class, I said. "What is your major?"

"Question number six. Why?"

Marvin dropped his pencil and looked at me with disgust. "Come on, Professuh."

"Question number seven. How many brothers and/or sisters do you have?" The room was really starting to heat up. The morning sun was turning into midday sun, and the fans were now blowing hot air. "Eight. How old are you?"

Marvin said, "You ain't allowed to ask that."

95

"Marvin," I said, smiling, "this is not a job interview. Just answer the question."

A few kids laughed. Marvin huffed.

"Nine and ten. Tell me your story. You have the rest of the period to do so."

Marvin raised his hand.

"Yes, Marvin?"

"What you mean, 'Tell you my story'? That could take a long time."

"Write what you can. Tell me what you would like me to know about you."

He raised his hand again.

"Marvin, get to writing."

"But Professuh," Marvin objected.

I looked at him. Tall. Trim. Fit looking. Probably pretty fast. I had heard he was a cornerback on the football team. "Marvin, how fast are you?"

"Wha' you mean?"

"I mean how fast do you run the forty?"

He tilted his head and rolled his eyes around as if he were trying to figure out whether or not this was a trick question. Then he said, "Fo-fo."

"Good," I said. "Then how about getting your mind and hand to work as fast as your feet?"

Marvin relaxed, smiled, and began to write.

# chapter ten

I WAS STANDING IN THE SHOWER, BREATHING THE steam, when Amos climbed the porch steps. I had just finished cleaning in the barn and stank something fierce. I heard the creak of the springs, the slam of the screen door, and then, "D.S., you ready?"

"Ready?" I asked, poking my head around the corner.

"Ivory. Man, put a filter on that thing." Amos saw me walk past the door wearing my towel and put his sunglasses back on. "The UV is killing me. You need to get out more. A little tan here and there wouldn't hurt you."

My ancestors were Scottish. They came in through South Carolina, then through Tennessee, and ended up in Texas.

You'd think that hot Texas sun would have brought out some tan, but it didn't. Too many years in the highlands, I suppose. I've never had a tan, but I've been burnt a thousand times.

Amos covered his eyes, then made himself at home with my refrigerator, which was empty. "Don't you ever buy anything to eat? You're gonna wither away."

"There's PB & J and tuna in the pantry," I said from behind the door.

Amos poked around in the kitchen, rattled some plates and silverware, then yelled, "Boy, I'm tired of waiting on you. Would you get it in gear?"

I pulled a T-shirt over my head and said, "Amos, I don't know why you're here, but I've got a notion I'm not going to like it. And the last time you had that look, I ended up standing in front of a class of college kids, which I'm still trying to figure my way out of. Shouldn't you be working or something?"

"Ivory, Ivory, Ivory," Amos said, not looking up from the four pieces of bread on which he was spreading peanut butter. To Amos, a PB & J was not a snack, it was an experience. Too much peanut butter, and it was hard to swallow. Too much jelly, and it was too sweet. Too much of both, and it drowned out the bread. And Amos did not like wheat bread. White only. The kind you ordinarily feed to ducks or put on a hook.

Judging from his flair with the knife and the way he was putting the peanut butter on the bread, I could tell that he was in a good mood. I just wasn't sure why. Amos was a real prankster when we were younger, but when he got hired by the sheriff's department, he shelved a lot of that. Occupational hazard, I suppose. Show criminals you're a real human being with emotions and feelings, and they'll take you for a loop or leave you in a ditch somewhere, putting pressure on a real bad gunshot wound.

Nope, this was unusual. But it was the Amos I knew. It was also the Amos I needed to see. In the past, when he let his hair down this far, we usually got in trouble, but that was before the badge.

"Amos," I started, "when was the last time we got into trouble?"

"Tonight," he said, kind of dancing around the kitchen with a sandwich in one hand and another in his mouth. He was dressed in cut-off shorts, a worn and ragged John Deere cap, his beeper, a torn-up T-shirt that said "Protected by Kimber," and no shoes. This could only mean one thing.

The river.

WHEN AMOS AND I WERE TWELVE AND ELEVEN RESPECTIVELY, we built a raft. We had spent the previous month reading *Robinson Crusoe* and were in the middle of *Huckleberry Finn,* so we had a hankering. The raft took us most of a month, but we were a lot smarter about it than Crusoe. We cut cedars growing out of the water, so that when they fell, they fell into the water. We couldn't understand why old Rob didn't think about that before he cut that big tree so far from the ocean. We saw it coming the moment he cut it. I said, "He'll never get that thing in the water," and Amos said, "Yeah, how's he gonna drag it? It's not like he can move it." We were right. Rob never got it to the water.

We trimmed the top branches and bound together twelve cedar trees, about a foot in diameter each, and then floated the whole thing downstream to the main river, where we floated it into shallow water and tied it up. We did most of the work in the water, covering the base with about thirty smaller trees. We cut them in half and sanded the tops so that we actually had a flat floor that fit rather tightly into the subfloor beneath it. Made for a pretty good raft. At least Papa thought so.

On top of the flooring, which was twelve by twelve, we built a lean-to that could sleep both of us. We even put a wood-burning stove in it. We had planned to float to the Gulf, but then found out that our river didn't dump into the Gulf. Whoops.

The whole thing weighed a ton, and once it got good and waterlogged, probably more. Cedar trees are pretty heavy. It needed about eight inches of water to float. We'd travel down-river, however far we could get in a night, and then hook the raft to a barge going north to pick up soy, corn, or whatever the farmers were trying to get to the railroad in Brunswick.

In the span of a summer, we got to know most of the usual captains. We'd float a day or two, fish, eat whatever we caught, smoke a pipe like Rob and Huck, get dizzy, sleep, and then about Sunday afternoon, we'd throw a rope, hook a barge, and it'd pull us north. We could reverse in five hours what had taken us nearly two or three days.

That's not entirely fair. On our float down, we'd tie up and fish for a few hours, sometimes a day. It depended on if and where the fish were biting. Then we'd float until we felt like fishing again. On several occasions we thought about ditching the raft, but after all that work, we just couldn't do it. Too much invested. Besides, the barge captains were lonely and liked having somebody to talk to, and we liked not having to row that thing back up that river.

We tried that just once. Floated downriver about twelve miles, spent the night, then thought we'd paddle back up it. Not a chance. You'd think, as critical as we'd been of Crusoe, we'd have thought of that. Funny how you can think of some things and not others.

Then about fifteen years ago, I found an old forty-horse Evinrude that belonged to Papa. All the times I worked and played in that barn, and I never knew it was there. We took it to Bobby's small engine-repair shop in town, and Bobby spent a week tinkering with it, replacing this hose and that seal. Pretty soon he had it puttering like a champ.

Bobby helped us rig up a platform out of steel. We sank the bolts all the way through the timber and hooked the Evinrude to the back of the raft. That was the day that heaven came to Digger. A couple of five-gallon gas cans, and we could putter all the way back from a three-day float. It really changed the way we traveled. Sometimes we puttered upriver ten or so miles and then just floated back. The motor was a nice addition, but the floating was why we built the raft.

Floating the river is a delicate dance. Tenuous at best. If you've ever floated, you know what I mean. It's slow and silent progress, but you're not in control. Nobody controls the river.

To float the river you've got to trust something bigger than yourself, and you better not mind living halfway between Nowhere and No Place Else, because the river's not interested in the destination, only the process. Otherwise all rivers would be straight.

The river's got its own rhythm, and you either dance to it or you don't. Whether you're man or woman matters not because the river leads, and if you're stepping out of time, then it's your fault because the river changes its beat for no one. You want to go swimming? Go swimming. You want to sleep? Sleep. You want to fish? Fish. You want to go faster? Too bad. You want to slow down? Good luck. The river's got one speed, and it's not going to stop and wait on you. And unless it rains, it's not going to hurry you along either.

Amos and I made our pact with the river long ago. We built a raft, shoved off, and never complained. Rain, no rain, sun, no sun, wind, no wind, hot, cold, fast, slow, wet, dry. It really didn't matter to us. We were just boys, happy to go wherever the river carried us. And all the river cared about was that we were going in the same direction it was and that we could swim, because it didn't like us dying.

Rivers don't do death, that's why they flow. You may drown, sink to the bottom, and lie there a few days, swelling, getting all puffy. You might even get caught on a downed tree with bream and bass nibbling on your nose, but eventually the river's going to lift you up and beach you. Spit you out like Jonah. You're not going to make the trip. You can't go where the river goes. Rivers do life, and the dead don't dance.

On our maiden voyage, a three-day float, we read *Huckleberry Finn,* switching turns every chapter. Our favorite scene was Huck sitting on the raft, deciding whether or not to rescue Jim. "All right then, I'll go to hell" became our motto.

For us, the raft was a safe and easy place. While I read, Amos would lie flat, listen, and try to smoke a pipe. He coughed and sputtered a good bit, about like the Evinrude, but eventually he got it and seemed to enjoy it. I, on the other hand, tried Red Man. A mistake. Every time I put that stuff in my mouth, I'd end up chumming. Why in the world I continued to try still amazes me. Glutton for punishment, I suppose. I figured if Josey Wales and John Wayne could chew, then so could I. The only difference was that my life was not a movie. Mine was real life and showed all the unedited stuff, like me hanging my head overboard.

My dancing with the river was never poetic, but Amos got pretty close.

I JUMPED INTO SOME SHORTS AND GRABBED MY POCKET-knife, Papa's yellow-handled, two-bladed Case Trapper.

Amos started in again. "Come on, boy. I'm always waiting on you."

Amos and I lit out the front door and headed for the barn, where Pinky met us at the gate and tried to flip me with a stiff shoulder. She's got about 130 pounds on me.

Amos laughed, and I shooed her away. "Get out of here, you ol' biddy."

"That is one mean pig," Amos said as Pinky grunted and ran in circles around her offspring.

"You ain't seen nothing. That pig is the Antichrist," I said.

The Evinrude hung on a little rack I'd made years back. Even though we hadn't used it in a few years, I started it up every now and again just to hear the sound. We loaded it into the wheelbarrow—actually it was more of a manure cart, but we called it a wheelbarrow—and grabbed a couple of gas cans. Two cans were plenty for a one-night float.

It was getting dark, but the trail alongside the cornfield was light enough. The moon shimmered off the sand, and shadows followed us through the long, tall grass and even taller corn. Blue bounced along beside us.

"What happened to your arm?" Amos asked while pushing the wheelbarrow and nodding at my forearm. "That's a pretty good one."

"Oh, that's just, uh . . . I was moving some stuff in the barn, and Pinky tripped me up. Just came down on it wrong."

"You ought to send that thing to Smithfield. I'd tell you to make sausage out of her, but she's probably too dang tough."

"You got a point there," I agreed. A half mile later we rolled up to the riverbank and into the hollow where we hid the raft. The river was high, due to the moon, so floating it out would be easy. We pulled off all the branches that had either fallen on it or we had put on it, but there didn't seem to be as many as the last time we had done this.

"I think somebody's been on our boat," I said, pointing. "Less cover."

Amos nodded and looked at the raft. "Sometimes a man likes to be alone."

"When?" I asked.

"'Bout four weeks ago. I got tired of sitting there feeling useless and watching you hold Maggs's hand."

"Oh."

Amos mounted the motor and loaded the gas inside the lean-to. We had sealed it when we built it, so it was pretty good and dry. Matches even lit. Which would be nice once we got going. A fire helped keep the mosquitoes at bay, and this end of the Salkehatchie Swamp produced some big mosquitoes.

I grabbed the push pole, jumped on top of the poling platform, and backed out the raft.

We bumped into some old cedars, and Amos said, "D.S., you're getting rusty."

I gave a hard push and Amos, who was standing, lost his balance and almost went in the water.

"D.S., you get my Kimber wet and I'm gonna beat you like a drum right here on this raft in the middle of the river."

I laughed. "I ain't that rusty. And you might could whup me, but you're gonna have to catch me first, Mr. Donut."

Amos was actually pretty fit. He had gained a few pounds since high school—I'd say about ten—but it was mostly muscle. After high school his hair started thinning up top, so he just shaved it off. He said it was cooler and less hassle. Although I'd never tell him, Amos is a pretty handsome man, and he takes good care of himself. Spends about four days a week in the weight room. So between his head, his muscles, and the moon, he looked like a shorter, thicker, blacker version of Mr. Clean. I was glad we were on the same side.

"Listen here, half-pint, I'm within ten pounds of my playing weight. What are you? 'Bout a buck-seventy?" He eyed me up and down.

"One sixty-eight," I said.

"That's what I thought. You're almost thirty pounds *under* your playing weight."

"Yeah, but I can still outrun you," I said, laughing and looking downriver.

"But when I catch you," Amos said, flexing his right arm, "I'm gonna put you in the Carolina cruncher."

"Ebony," I said, smirking, "I think you're losing a bit. Your arms ain't what they used to be."

He took two steps, grabbed my legs, and tossed. The whole thing didn't take a second and a half. I went about fifteen feet in the air, then dived deep into the water. I swam back over to the raft and climbed up, something I'd done a hundred times. I wrung out my shirt and watched Amos stand atop the polling platform, smiling. It was good to be back on the raft.

We floated a few hours, not saying much. About three o'clock in the morning, Amos looked up from his pipe and broke the silence. "Have you been thinking what I think you're thinking?"

I knew what he was asking. This was why he had brought me to the river. Amos was checking my pulse, but it hurt too much just to come outright and say it. We needed the river and a few hours beneath the shadow of the moon to get him to the place where he could ask and me to the place where I could answer.

I looked up from my seat on the front of the raft. "If Maggs is already sitting in heaven, rocking our son, laughing with Nanny and Papa and our folks, and looking down on me, then she's never coming back, and I might live another sixty years." I shook my head. "I just don't know that I can make it through those years without her."

We floated along in the quiet, listening to the ripple and flap of water against the cedar timbers. An owl hooted, and on the air I smelled a charcoal fire thick with lighter fluid. Amos stood atop the poling platform on the back of the raft, his sweat glistening in the moonlight. Minutes passed, during which neither of us said a word.

My pulse must have been pretty weak, because Amos pressed me one more time. "What keeps you?"

I splashed water on my face and rubbed my eyes. "The thought of Maggie waking up. Her hand without mine. Her without me, staring at the same future that's bearing down on me."

Blue slept next to me, his ears pricking up every once in a while. We probably floated four or five miles while Amos wordlessly and methodically worked the pole. It was a warm night, so I dunked my head in the water and let it drip down and soak my neck and chest. Amos lit his pipe, and in the flash of the match I saw tears streaking his cheeks. At daybreak, we napped and fished. We caught a few bream, one or two bass, and ate lunch around noon. About dusk, we cranked the Evinrude and puttered back home, arriving around midnight.

I stepped onto the porch and pointed to the stringer. "Keep the fish. I'm not too hungry."

Amos nodded, looked as if he wanted to say something, and then stuck his right index finger in the air. He opened the trunk of his squad car, pulled out a cardboard box about two feet square, and set it on the porch. "Maggie found this at an antique shop in Walterboro. She was real excited. Stored it at my house so you wouldn't find it. I think she meant to give it to you on your first day of class. After the, uh . . . well, I didn't know what to do with it. So here it is." Amos looked out over the field toward the river. "I don't think she ever got around to writing a card."

Amos turned while tears slid off his square chin. He nodded and spoke quietly, as if his voice would amplify across the cornfield. "When you boil it down," he said, holding out his hand and counting with his fingers, "all we got left, all anybody's got, is faith . . . and hope . . . and love." He looked at his three fingers. "And we all gonna make it. All three of us."

I watched him cross the dirt road and head into his own driveway. I turned on all the lights, showered, wrapped myself in a towel, and stood in the den, staring at that box. An hour later, I sat on the floor and slit the brown wrapping tape. Inside, wrapped in dirty burlap, were a leather-strung drum and two hand-cut drumsticks.

I cried like a baby all the way to the hospital.

# chapter eleven

I CONSIDER MYSELF A FAIR TEACHER. I DON'T ASK anything of my students that I wouldn't ask of myself. And one thing I would not ask of myself is to jump into a cold pool without sticking my toes in it first. Now, Amos, he's a different breed. It can be thirty degrees outside with a film of ice covering the surface of the water, and it's "Aw, just jump in. Get it over with. You'll warm up." Not me. Especially not when it comes to being cold.

I like to get comfortable with an idea before I take it on. Give me time to ruminate, and I can face most anything, but don't allow me an experience, and then with the sweat still rolling off my face, ask me to interpret it for you. I don't know what I think until I've had time to look in my rearview mirror.

The English department had structured my class around three papers, but it only cared about the third, the research paper. A passing paper was my student's ticket out of here. While the third paper had to meet certain length and style requirements, the first two were left up to the teacher's discretion, meaning I could tailor the assignment to need. Theirs and mine.

They needed to get their feet wet, get their engines running, get comfortable, and I needed to get to know them. I needed to place a face with a writing voice and so have a starting line against which I could compare their other two works. I needed to know who could and who could not. Who did and who did not. The first paper was the plumb line against which I compared the other two. It would also keep them honest.

The first assignment was an autobiographical essay. Easy enough. Everyone is an instant expert on the subject. No research needed. The only requirement is honesty, and sometimes a good sense of humor.

I spent most of Saturday reading essays to Maggie at the hospital. From prom night to car crashes to summer nights with bronzed, big-breasted women, they gave me real and honest stuff.

Marvin wrote about his last football game as a senior in high school. State champions. All-state player of the year. Marvin was no master of the English language, but he was able to get across his humor. He wrote the way he spoke, which to me is the sign of a good beginning. Good beginnings breed hope. And I had hope for Marvin.

Amanda wrote about growing up in Digger, about her dad and his past. She wrote about her desire to be a nurse for the critically ill. She wrote about being pregnant. She had an informative voice, similar to her speech. Her paper told the reader everything you'd want to know about Amanda in three pages. Except for one detail.

Alan wrote about his first car, a '69 Chevy Camaro. He bought it off a junk lot and set it on blocks for two years. He literally took it apart one piece at a time and put it back together again with new parts. Paint, interior, bodywork, engine, gears, transmission. It was all new, and he had built, rebuilt, or custom-ordered all of it. It sounded like a showpiece, and he provided me with proof. A certificate, "Best of Show," from the Walterboro Classic Car Roundup was stapled to the last page of his paper. Alan's voice was rough and his writing skills poor, yet he, too, got his point across. And judging by the erasure marks, he had put some real time and work into this. In some ways, it was clear Alan knew his writing skills needed taking apart and rebuilding, just like his first car. I had hope for Alan too.

Eugene wrote about his experiences in last year's Freak-Nik in Atlanta. He described four days of bars, the backseat of a big Oldsmobile, and bad indigestion. His paper was essentially his personal chronicle of four days of booze, women, and a dirty hotel, and he didn't spare any details. Even down to the little machine next to the bed that required four quarters for five minutes' worth of bad decisions. Eugene's paper confirmed what I had suspected: here was a ladies' man who was interested in one thing. His paper also confirmed something else I had suspected: here was an intelligent guy who had yet to put his mind to something other than the next girl or the next good time. Eugene was an entrepreneur, and without his knowing it, his paper illustrated that. He had a unique ability to handle details, to turn a bad situation into a better one, and to say the right word at the right time. I didn't need to hope for Eugene. He'd get out of there, which was all he wanted.

Koy, the silent one, hidden behind sunglasses and long hair in the back of the room, turned in a one-paragraph paper. I had specifically requested three pages. I don't understand why students do that. If the instructions say three pages, then at least make a go at it. If you want to run the race, then at least do it from the starting line. In Koy's one paragraph she attempted to hide herself the same way her sunglasses hid her eyes. Problem was, her ability to write was as effective a concealment as her glasses. Ironically, by her effectiveness in keeping the reader at bay, she revealed her remarkable writing ability. Her language skills surprised me. I wanted to hope for Koy, but I couldn't figure out what or why she was hiding.

The rest of the papers fell in line along the same ideas. Most were informational and dry; the students gave me what they thought I wanted, hoping, no doubt, that I in turn would give them what they wanted: an A.

The last paper in the pile was Russell's. I had little expectation for Russell because I have known and even played with a few Russells before. He was a gifted athlete, a walking Adonis, and he had no need for school because school was not his ticket. The NFL would be his ticket. Though he was only a sophomore, word was that scouts had been looking at him this year. For Russell's academic future that meant one thing only: he would transfer out of DJC, but he wasn't planning to graduate with a four-year degree. In his version of his prospects, Russell didn't need my class. At least not yet. If he blew out a knee, then he'd need it.

I refilled my coffee cup and propped my feet up on the end of Maggs's bed, slowly swaying in rhythm with the hum of her monitor. A cool breeze blew in through the window and swept the parking lot clean. The almanac predicted the coldest winter in twenty years. Maggs liked cold winters. One of the things she missed about Virginia was the snow. I liked to watch it fall but not stick, drift, or melt. Not Maggs. She loved being snowed in.

I picked up Russell's paper and began to read. To my surprise, it bled honesty. It seeped through the pores and bubbled over. And Russell didn't need to be honest. Why should he? Being honest showed that he could be vulnerable. And to show that he could be vulnerable showed that he could be touched, even beaten. Football players on their way up cannot afford to show what Russell's first paragraph showed me. Or so I thought. Two pages in, and I felt myself wanting to offer Russell an apology. I had misjudged him. He hid nothing.

Russell wrote about his folks and last year's homecoming game. His mom and dad drove from Roanoke, checked into their hotel, went to the game, and stood in the rain while their son played football. That night, Russell's dad caught a cold. The next day they all drove home to Roanoke for Thanksgiving. Russell wrote about his dad's lifelong work with the railroad. Several times, he flashed back from the action of the football game to times spent with his dad playing catch, fishing, saying "Yes sir," and just hanging out together.

I'm not sure Russell was aware of the extent to which it came across, but his paper made it evident that he and his dad had something most fathers and sons do not: a friendship. Without sounding clichéd, these two guys loved each other. Following Thanksgiving in Roanoke, Russell's dad developed pneumonia and died in the hospital two days later.

Two things struck me. One was that I couldn't possibly put a grade on it. It was one of those rare papers that existed outside of a grade. Two, it was apparent that Russell and his dad shared tenderness, intimacy, and trust. They probably hugged each other good night. Russell's description of his father's death was vivid and convincing: the sound of his cough, the color of the mucous, his dad's wrinkled face, the fear in his mom's eyes, the last time he kissed him.

I put down the essay, picked up my coffee cup, and watched the clouds roll past the window. Russell had put his heart on that page. All 280-plus pounds of it. Russell, whom I had wrongly put in the proverbial football player's box, with his big shoulders and deep voice and eyes always looking disinterestedly out the window, had done something no other student in my pile of papers had done. He had touched me.

# chapter twelve

I WOKE UP IN A CHAIR NEXT TO MAGGIE, WHERE THE air smelled like magnolias. The Sunday morning sun was bouncing off her face, which had regained its color.

Amanda poked her head into the room and said, "Good morning, Professor. How about some orange juice?"

I nodded and wiped the sleep from my eyes. "Thanks."

She returned, placed it on the table, checked Maggie's IV and her blood pressure cuff, and then rubbed Blue between the ears on her way out. Around ten o'clock she returned, carrying some antiseptic and gauze pads. She motioned to my arm. "Professor, I'm cleaning that before it gets infected."

I looked at my arm and rolled my sleeve back down. "No thanks. It'll be fine."

"Professor, if I had a problem with my paper, I'd expect you to help me out. Same goes here, only it's reversed." She pointed to my arm. "Whatever was here is long since gone. You can quit now."

She pulled a chair up beside me and rolled up my shirtsleeve. Amanda worked quietly and quickly. She doused me with hydrogen peroxide, cleaned out all the dirt, and then poured some brown stuff all over it that stung so bad I almost cussed.

"Professor." Amanda studied my arm, dabbing it periodically with a Betadine-soaked cotton ball. "My daddy's having a baptism down at the river this afternoon. You're invited. Your deputy friend will be there. Daddy asked him to help the older folks down to the river."

"You think I need help getting into that river?"

"No, sir. I just thought you might want to come. It's a good time. Always lots of food." She smiled.

"How's the baby?" I said, nodding at her stomach.

"Healthy and growing," she said with a smile. "I'm eating everything that's not nailed down and some that is." She continued working on my arm.

"Do you talk to God at your daddy's church?" I asked bluntly.

Amanda didn't bat an eye. "I talk to God most everywhere and most all the time." She thought for a minute. "And yes, one of those places is my daddy's church." She fiddled with her hair, a little self-consciously. "Professor, do you ever talk to God?"

"No. Not since He quit listening."

She gathered her dirty pads and antiseptic and headed for the door. "At the river, down below my daddy's church, at two. You'll see the cars." She disappeared around the corner.

"Amanda?"

She poked her face back around the door. "Yes, sir?"

"You think I need to get in that water?"

"No, sir. I just thought you might like to come. Lots of people. And if you haven't had Mrs. Baxter's chicken, you haven't had fried chicken."

"You think I need to get cleaned up?"

She walked over to the head of the bed. "Professor, it's not just you. Everybody needs to get cleaned up sometime."

"What if there's not enough water?"

She tucked Maggie's hair behind her left ear. "It's not the water, Professor. And you don't have to get cleaned up to take a bath."

Amanda walked out of the room, and I placed my head next to Maggie's hand and slept.

# chapter thirteen

I DRIVE AN OLD PICKUP BECAUSE I UNDERSTAND IT. It's simple. I don't understand a car that does not require a tune-up for a hundred thousand miles. What kind of car is that? Self-timing and loaded with computer chips. I understand a distributor cap, a carburetor, eight cylinders, a timing belt, and how to change the oil. When I first met Maggie, she owned a foreign car that we nursed through graduate school. Not long after graduation, it died, and we sold it to a parts supplier at a junkyard for three hundred dollars. But the first time I changed the oil, it took me the better part of a day just to find the filter. And even when I did, I had to be a contortionist to get to it. The human hand is not designed to do that. My truck is made so that regular people like me can change the oil every few thousand miles. Maggie's car was made so I had to pay a professional twenty-eight dollars to locate and unscrew the filter with a tool that cost him ninety-eight dollars.

My truck is a 1972 Chevy C-10, possibly the best truck Chevy ever made. It's got a long bed, which is partly rusted, a bench seat torn in several places, and it burns oil. It looks used because it is.

If it's knocking, I pull over, adjust the timing to fit the grade of gas, and keep going. Sometimes in the mornings, it needs a few minutes. I do too. What's wrong with that? I hit the starter, give it some gas; it coughs, spits, churns, and hacks itself to life, for one more morning, anyway.

When I get more than two hundred thousand miles on me, I'm quitting. There won't be any coughing, spitting, and churning. I'm just going to bump myself into neutral and coast.

I've thought about restoring it. Maybe new interior, new paint, an engine overhaul. Then I think, *No, I'm not going to do that. It's got more character the way it is.*

If Maggie had a choice, she would prefer not to ride in my truck. And that's putting it nicely. She laughs at me everytime I climb in. "I can't believe you actually own that thing, Dylan Styles. It's pitiful. You look like *Sanford and Son.* All you need is some furniture sticking out of the back, and you could have your own sitcom."

I tried to tell her that Red Foxx drove a Ford, but she wouldn't hear it. She just shook her head and said, "I married a man in love with a truck that's the same age as me. I guess I should be happy. At least it's not another woman."

A pickup truck just fits the way my brain works. I can throw stuff in the back and forget about it until I need it. I like the way the starter sounds when you crank it. I like the way the door sounds when you close it. I like the way the tailgate sounds when you lower it. I like the way the muffler sounds at idle. I like the play in the steering wheel. I like manual door locks. I like the horn because it's loud. I like the rattles my truck makes when I drive it. I like the way it trusts me to read the gauges and the way the gas cap screws completely off—no strings attached. And I like the way it drives.

Some folks like that "new car smell." I like that old truck smell. Sweat. Dirt. Oil. Preemissions-controlled exhaust. Hay. Pig feed. And whatever's blooming. Leave your windows down. Let it breathe. Wipe the dew off the seats in the morning. Automobiles take on the smell of their environment.

In May, when Maggie's gardenias bloom, I park it so close that the branches hang in the window and the blooms spill over the seats and dash. The next morning I get in, and it smells like Maggie. Who would want new car smell when you can have Maggie's gardenias?

AROUND TWO ON SUNDAY, I CLIMBED INTO THE TRUCK, feeling dangerously hungry. Blue and I cranked her up and idled out of the hospital parking lot. I rolled down the window, stuck my arm out into the hot breeze, and surfed my hand through the waves of air coming off the front fender. The new bandage was thick, bulky, and my arm throbbed inside it.

The cars stretched down the road about a mile before the church came into view. I rounded the corner before the final straightaway that intersected the dirt road that runs in front of my house and saw the river. I slowly passed the church and saw a line of people headed for the water. White robes for the women and shorts for the men. Probably two hundred people. I didn't see Amos, but I figured he was already down in the water. I could see Pastor John holding Amanda's hand as they stepped over the roots of an oak tree. Her other hand was cupped under the swelling her baby had made in her belly.

Pulling up under the oaks, I cut the engine and listened to the late-summer crickets; it's a lazy, psychedelic, summer sound that can send any man to the crazy house or into a deep summer nap. Blue whined and stuck his head from around the back of the cab and looked at me. I hesitated and sat sweating inside, still buckled in.

"All right, but just to look."

We slipped through the oaks and sat down on some moss on the south side of the folks in the river. Up on the bank, just downriver of the church, there were ten or fifteen picnic tables covered with checkered tablecloths and plates of fried chicken, potatoes, coleslaw, and what smelled like peach pie. I was hungry.

Up the river a bit, a father squatted next to his son, who stood with his pants at his ankles, spelling his name in the river. Probably thirty folks stood in a circle, waist deep in the river, around Pastor John. In his arms he held a screaming lady who had her hands raised. He dunked her three times, and each time she came out of the water screaming a garbled "Hallelujah!" After the third dunk, Pastor John led her over to Amos, who helped her up out of the water and gave her a towel.

She was shorter but bigger than Amos. She hugged him and kissed his cheek, tears pouring off her face, then went on to hug about thirty other people who must have been family and friends. These people really liked each other. Pastor John kept dunking people, and Amos stood by with a huge grin, ready to help. Some people Pastor John dunked once. Others twice. Some three times. And one man he dunked four times. I guess he really needed it. The fourth time, Pastor John held him underwater for close to thirty seconds, at which time the guy really started waving his arms. Pastor John brought him up, hugged him, and passed him to Amos, who gave him a towel and set him next to a woman who offered him a comforting shoulder.

Dunking those thirty people took a little over an hour, because Pastor John was good at this. I think he enjoyed it too. And he made it fun for everyone. Any time he took someone's hand, he'd relate chapters from his or her sordid past to the others in the group. He always ended it with an encouragement about how that person had climbed up from sordid to surrendered. When he finished talking, the congregation members would clap and throw their arms up, and he'd go to dunking.

This was no sprinkling. Pastor John splashed water everywhere, and everybody got wet. The last person to go was a child, maybe nine or ten. Pastor John took the little boy in his arms, held him close, and nuzzled his nose. When the boy said he was scared to go in the water by himself, Pastor John went under with him. He went under three times, and when he came out the last time he held the boy high in the air. The dad waded over and gently took his son from Pastor John as he let him back down in the water.

With the baptism over, Pastor John prayed. The group in the water held hands, and the group out of the water held hands or stretched their arms out over the ones in the river. Pastor John prayed for those he had baptized and for those who needed baptizing and then asked the blessing on the food.

Pastor John could pray. And it wasn't a posturing thing, as if he were trying to one-up those around him. Something about it was different. It was personal, powerful, and real, as though he were talking to somebody right there in the group.

When he finished, everyone climbed out of the river and made a mad dash for the tables. All at once, as if someone shot a gun, the women fell into place, pouring sweet tea, passing plates, and piling them high with chicken, rolls, and slaw. They had done this before.

Within five minutes, all two hundred people had food and drink and places to sit. Behind me I heard a stick crack.

"Professor, I brought you a plate." I was leaning against an oak tree, peering through the small stems of one of Maggie's favorite plants, resurrection fern. It's a funny little fern that grows out of the cracks of the bark, spends most of its days brown and crinkly only to soften up and turn green at the first sight of rain. I pulled my nose out of the fern, and Amanda offered the plate a second time.

"Hi, Amanda." I looked for Blue, who was licking Amanda's ankle. *Thanks, Blue.*

"You look like you could use some food."

"No, really, I'm not hungry."

From the other side of the picnic tables I heard, "Don't let him lie to you, Amanda. Give him the plate. He'll eat it. He's so hungry now, he don't know if he's got a stomachache or a backache." Amos waved a chicken leg at me and smiled a greasy "I'm-eating-a-chicken-leg-and-liking-it" smile.

Amanda offered me the plate, piled high with a sample from every bowl, and then handed me a Styrofoam cup overflowing with tea. "We've only got one flavor, and I hope you like it sweet."

The plate probably weighed five pounds, but I took it. Blue sidled up next to me and started sniffing the underside of the plate.

"I saw you when you pulled up," she said. "I thought you'd come."

"Oh." I didn't know what else to say. My first reaction was to drop the plate and disappear, but I was stuck. Amanda led me to a table near her father, and I started nibbling at some chicken, trying not to inhale it.

Pastor John wasted no time. "I understand you are my daughter's professor."

"Yes, I am."

He stuck out his hand. "Good to see you, son."

"I don't think I ever told you, but you did a nice job at my grandfather's funeral. Thank you."

"Your grandfather was as fine a man as I've known. Did more talking with his hands than his mouth. That's always made an impact on me." Pastor John looked back toward the steeple and waited for my reaction.

"Yes, he did on me too," I said, taking another bite of chicken.

"Now, about you being her professor." Pastor John's tone caught me all of a sudden. "Amanda seems to have a lot of homework here lately."

There was something behind his smile. The last thing I wanted was a temperamental and public conversation with the parent of a student. Not today.

"I hope so," I said, chewing.

Pastor John raised his eyebrows. "What, to give my child busywork?" He clasped his hands and rubbed them together. "To tell her what to think?"

Pastor John's eyes were penetrating. I should've run for the truck when I had the chance. I was in over my head, and I knew it. Mrs. Baxter's chicken wasn't tasting so good anymore.

"No, sir. That is not my intent."

His eyes, switching between his bifocals, his normal lenses, and the space above his glasses, wandered over my face. Then he leaned his face into mine and said, "Well then, son, what is your intent?"

Maybe it was hunger. Maybe it was fatigue. Maybe I just didn't care. Whatever it was, my answer was a silver bullet. I shot it into my target with the expectation that it would do damage. I put my plate down, wiped off my mouth, and fired.

"My intent, sir, is to help her learn how to think better. To help her question what she thinks by *how* she arrived there. To equip her with the tools to consider and process. If I can do that, her writing will take shape soon after." I sipped my tea, swallowed a mouthful of chicken, and said, "That is my intent."

I picked up my plate again and dug around for a chicken leg. Maybe it was because I needed to remind myself, but before he could ever open his mouth, I pointed at him with the chicken leg. "Sir." I paused. "Pastor John, to be honest, I'm not looking for an amount of work. I hate to grade papers, and I don't slap little silver stickers on passing quizzes. I'm looking for a process. I'm interested in *how* Amanda gets from here to there. And to be brutally honest, I don't really care where she starts or where she finishes. That's your job."

With my voice echoing off the river, I began to notice how quiet it had gotten, how everyone was listening to me, and how much I had said. Being tired and hungry does strange things to a person.

Pastor John sat back, took off his glasses, wiped them with his white handkerchief, and looked at me through his now-naked eyes. He smiled, nodded his head, and muttered, "Huh-huh," as if he was talking to somebody I couldn't see. Then he slapped me on the knee and said, "Son, welcome back. You let me know if you need anything." He stood up and put his hand on my shoulder. "And Professor, I miss your grandfather. Seeing you reminds me of him. And it's a good remembrance too. I think he'd like it very much."

Everybody had long since quit talking and was listening to

the two of us. I guess our voices carried a good bit under those oaks.

"Son, you give my child all the work you want to. If she doesn't give you what you want when you want it, you let me know." He patted me on the shoulder and started making the rounds to check on his flock.

Amos got up quickly, brought his plate, and sat down next to me. "Listen here, you little squirt. I didn't bring you out here to put that doctoring mumbo jumbo on my pastor." He smiled and pointed his own chicken leg in my face. "You got to learn to tone it down."

"What? I say something wrong?" My face was covered with chicken grease.

"It wasn't necessarily what you said as much as how you said it. And the fact that you said it at all. All that bit about 'process' and 'your job.' You should have heard yourself."

"Amos, you're half the reason I got this job. Now, are you going to let me do it, or do you want to do it for me?"

"Naw." Amos slipped into his southern drawl. "I think you got it covered there, Professuh."

"Good. You arrest people, and I'll teach them how to think so that you don't have to arrest them."

Amos got up and said, "I'm going back for more. You eat all you want. Talking all uppity like that probably worked you up a pretty good appetite." Amos wiped the smear off his lips and then turned and hollered, "Amanda, make sure that boy eats 'til he can't move."

Before thirty minutes passed, Amanda had handed me two

more topped-over plates. I felt like a tick and had to unbutton my jeans. I knew I gained eight pounds right there in that folding chair. Blue too.

The crowd thinned, and I helped Amos clean and clear tables. We carried them inside the church and stacked them against the wall in the narthex. As I was heading to my truck, Pastor John thanked me for my help, and Amanda gave me two more plates wrapped in cellophane and spilling over with food. I guess those folks were trying to tell me something.

On the top of the first plate she had written *Professor* and on the second *Blue*. Along with the plates, she handed me a milk jug of sweet tea. At this point, I had drunk so much tea and had to pee so badly that I nearly gave it back. Thinking better of it, I tucked it under my arm, and Blue and I headed for the truck. I drove until I was out of sight, then pulled over next to where the river bumps up next to the road. I got out, ran to the bank, yanked open my shorts, and peed for a minute and fifty-five seconds. A new personal record.

I drove in the drive and heard Pinky grunting, squealing and kicking the inside of her stall. When I had filled her trough, she grunted at me as if to say, "Took you long enough. Where you been?"

Nighttime and crickets found me rocking on the front porch, thinking about Maggie, my class, and how uncomfortable I had become in my own house. Home was quiet, and I didn't feel like walking inside. I was unable to put my finger on it, and my skin began crawling as if it were covered with poison ivy. Then it hit me. A stranger, silent and invisible, had moved into my home, taken Maggs's place, and begun to rearrange everything that was sacred to the both of us. Everywhere I turned, Memory had already been there.

I raced inside and searched the house but never got closer than the tail-end of her shadow. When I finally cornered her in the bathroom, I slammed the door and screamed from the hallway, "Pack your bags and get out! I don't want you here. Not today. Not ever!"

I had never lived with, much less slept with, any other woman, and I wasn't about to start now. "Maggie's coming home! You hear me? I said she's coming home."

I slammed the screen door, and Blue and I walked through the cornfield to the river.

*chapter fourteen*

Junk mail was spilled around the base of the mailbox when I got around to opening it the following afternoon. I dug it out and stuffed it in my arms like firewood. Buried in the back of the heap was a conspicuous envelope. The VISA bill.

I hated that thing and moaned every time I saw it. I'd been paying it down since I took Maggs on that little surprise trip eighteen months ago. She had always wanted to do two things: fly to New York City and see *Riverdance*. It so happened that *Riverdance* was premiering in New York at that time, so late one night, after Maggs had gone to bed, I did some searching on the Internet and ended up booking flights, room reservations, and tickets.

I was busting at the seams to tell her, but managed to keep it a secret for two weeks. When the alarm went off that Friday morning, I poked her in the ribs and said, "Honey, pack your bag. Plane leaves in three hours."

Maggie lay there and pulled the covers back over her head while I showered. When I came back, I grabbed the covers at the foot of the bed and yanked.

She jerked up and said, "Dylan Styles, you know this is my only morning to sleep in. Now go away and leave me alone." Her hair was going everywhere, and she had a big sleep mark imprinted in her left cheek. She slammed the pillow over her head and motioned to the light switch.

So I pulled the *Riverdance* tickets out of my pocket along with the plane tickets and slipped them under her pillow. That got her out of bed.

We spent the weekend in New York City and saw the show from the third row, front and center. I had as much fun watching Maggie's face as I did the show. The next day we walked the streets like Dumb and Dumber, strolled through Central Park, toured Ellis Island, stood at the foot of the Empire State Building, and rode the elevators to the top and waved at the Statue of Liberty. Maggie loved every minute of it. Fourteen hundred and sixty-nine dollars later, we came home.

I opened the envelope, and the number at the bottom of the page said I had paid for the first twenty-four hours. Now I needed to pay for the second. I tossed the bill on the floorboard and bumped the stick into drive.

I drove past Pastor John's church, onto the hard road, and

up the hill at Johnson's pasture, where I crossed the railroad tracks midway. I made it into town just as Frank, the owner of Frank's Hardware, taped a "Back in Ten Minutes" sign to the front door.

Ten minutes is about the time it takes to drink a cup of coffee, so I headed across the square, bought a paper, and sat down in the corner of Ira's Cafe. Just as I slid into the booth, Amos saw my truck and parked his squad car. He pointed his toothpick at me and walked through the front door.

"Morning, Ira," he said to the lady cooking eggs behind the counter.

"Mornin', sugar. You sit down there with Mr. Quiet, and I'll be there in a minute."

Amos slid into the booth across from me. "Hey, buddy, what's up?"

I pointed across the square to the hardware store. "I'm waiting on Frank so I can buy bolts for the harrow."

Amos looked over his right shoulder. "Frank left another 'ten minute' sign?"

"Yup." I rummaged through the money section of the paper.

"How's our girl?" Amos asked.

"Same. I'm going there now. Soon as Mr. Back-in-Ten-Minutes finishes helping Ms. White with her latest emergency."

"That's the trouble with this town. Everybody knows your secrets."

"Tell me about it."

Ira walked up to the end of the table and kissed Amos on the cheek. "What you gonna have, sugar?"

Amos looked at me. "I just love the way she calls me 'sugar.'"
Then he looked up at Ira. "Give me three over medium. No,
four. I'm hungry today. A couple of biscuits and some of that
good honey that George steals from his neighbor."

A guy wearing a white T-shirt and flipping pancakes
hollered over his shoulder, "They're my hives."

Amos turned and hollered back. "Yeah, but the bees are
eating from his flowers."

George hollered again. "At least that's what he told the
judge. I can't control where my bees go. It's not like I can
train them."

Amos laughed.

Ira turned to me. She was a fixture in this town and had
worked at this cafe for as long as I can remember.
Consequently, she knows everybody and everything about
everybody too. If you tell Ira something, you might as well
announce it on CNN, because the world of Digger will soon
know about it. She was also the most colorful person in town,
and everything she wore always matched. Shirt, skirt, shoes—
all the same color. She looked like a walking color swatch.
Today she was lime green.

"Good morning, Ira," I said.

"Good morning, honey. How you doing, Dylan?" She
leaned down and gave me a big wet kiss across my forehead.

"I'm fine. Thank you," I said, wiping my forehead.

"You don't look fine. You look like somebody peed in your
cornflakes." Did I mention that Ira was brutally blunt and
had spent ten years married to a sailor?

"Thanks, Ira. I'll just have a biscuit, please."

"Okay, honey. Y'all give me a few minutes. I got to make some more biscuits."

Amos and I small-talked for ten or fifteen minutes, until Ira showed up with a plate of ten or twelve eggs and another plate of about a dozen hot, steaming biscuits. She slammed down both plates, poured two more cups of hot coffee, and did not leave a check on the table. She looked at me.

"Dylan, don't you get your butt out of my booth until you and Mr. Cue-ball here eat everything that I've put on those plates. You understand me, mister?"

"Yes, ma'am," I said. There was enough food on our table for five people.

Amos smiled, picked up a fork, and split a biscuit. "Well," he said, stuffing a buttered, honey-dripping biscuit into his mouth, "I think I made *America's Scariest Police Chases* last night."

"What happened?" I piled eggs on a biscuit.

"Well, I pulled this guy over for speeding about ten o'clock, and he decided he didn't want to be pulled over. He was driving a big, four-door Lexus. Before I knew it, we were going about 120 down I-95. Then he hops the median and starts racing down the back roads at the same speed. Mac at the motor pool said this morning that I just about burnt up the engine and definitely ruined a good set of tires. Anyway, this guy bangs his Lexus around a good bit and then parks it in the middle of Old Man Packer's duck pond. You should have seen that thing fly through the air after he hit that hay bale."

Amos stuffed some more eggs into his mouth. "The driver managed to swim out and spent last night in jail, but his car is totaled. Some people amaze me. There I was, just giving the guy a hundred-dollar speeding ticket, and he hauls off and wastes an eighty-thousand-dollar car and a night in jail. Not to mention what Judge Hand will do to him when I give my report. This is a crazy world we live in, Dylan."

"What'd he say when you pulled him out of the pond?"

"Nothing. He just stood there looking at eighty thousand dollars' worth of splash and bubbles. Never even loosened his tie. Looked like a respectable fellow too. I handcuffed him and placed him in the back of my car. When I asked him why he ran, he gave me some lip about how the police were always picking on him. I asked him if he thought seventy-two was too fast in a fifty-five zone. And you know what the guy said?"

"No. What'd he say?"

"He said, 'It depends on the person.' I said, 'Sir, the law is no respecter of persons. It is what it is.' He didn't like that. Got real quiet. Then he started talking about his lawyer, and anyway, he's in jail, and I'm here eating breakfast. How come you're not saying much?"

"'Cause I'm eating my fifth biscuit."

Amos smiled with honey dripping off his chin. "They're good, aren't they?" He pointed his butter knife toward the kitchen. "She's sweet as pie and can cook like nobody's business, but that woman can cuss like nothing I've ever heard. I guess thirty-odd years waiting tables in this place with that guy will do it to you."

"Tell me about it."

After forty-five minutes, Frank reappeared in his window, fixed his hair in the reflection, peeled the sign off his door, and unlocked the bolt.

I nodded my head. "Frank's back."

"All right. I got to go. Judge Hand is expecting me. I'll pay Ira. You hug Maggie for me."

"I'll do that."

And it was at that moment that the guilt set in. Guilt caused by the fact that for almost forty-five minutes I had not thought about Maggie, or the death of my son, or the fact that my wife was a vegetable in the hospital, eating from a tube and urinating into a bag.

The guilt landed on my stomach like lead. I walked out the front door, turned right down the alley next to Ira's Cafe, and vomited five biscuits, six eggs, and a pot of coffee. I wiped my mouth on my shirtsleeve and steadied myself against the brick wall. A second wave coursed through me, further emptying my stomach. I wiped the messy tops of my boots against my jeans, drove to the hospital and forgot why I needed to see Frank.

I slipped quietly into Maggs's room, and Blue jumped up on the bed, nestling his nose in at her feet.

"Hey, Maggs," I whispered in her ear. I would have given the farm to hear her voice.

"Hello, Professor," Amanda whispered as she walked into the room and interrupted the silence.

"Hi."

"I won't be but a minute." She checked Maggs's feeding tube and then began to tiptoe out. Just as she was about to disappear behind the doorframe, she turned around and whispered, "Professor, I won't be in class tomorrow. Doctor's appointment. I left you a voice mail at home, thinking I might miss you here. See you tomorrow afternoon, maybe."

"Okay. Thanks for letting me know."

Amanda left, and the silence crowded in again. Blue whimpered, as if to say, *Look, man, say something. She needs to hear your voice.*

I took hold of her hand. "Maggs, I miss the sound of your voice." That's when it hit me.

Voice mail.

I picked up the phone, dialed as fast as the rotary phone would let me, waited four rings, and then she picked up.

"Hi, this is Dylan and Maggie. Sorry we missed your call, but leave us a message and we'll call you back. Talk to you soon. Take care."

I quickly dialed back, wedging the phone between my shoulder and ear, dialing with one hand and holding Maggie's with the other. Blue crawled across the bed, put his front paws in my lap and licked the phone, whimpering. After the eighth time, I set the phone in the receiver, rubbed my face, and stared out the window.

*chapter fifteen*

I DISMISSED CLASS, GRADED QUIZZES FOR ALMOST an hour, then packed my bag and slipped out. Crossing the yard to my truck, I got curious, so I wandered over toward the fence. The football team was practicing on the far eastern side of the field. I threw my bag in the back and walked through the gate toward the scrimmage. I didn't necessarily want to see it as much as I wanted to smell and hear it.

As I was walking, I heard a voice behind me.

"You singing, Professuh?"

I turned around to see Russell towering over me like Goliath.

"Who, me? No, I'm just, uh . . . " Okay, I lied.

Russell smiled. "You was singing, Professuh." His eyes widened, and a grassy, sweaty smile cracked his face.

"Not really," I dodged. "Who do y'all play this week?"

"Professuh, that singing sounded good." Russell raised his eyebrows and tried not to smile. "Sing some more."

"Russell, I can't sing my way out of a wet paper bag."

"My daddy loved to sing. He liked blues and old hymns. Sang both so much he got 'em mixed up all the time. One minute he'd be singing 'bout a girl he once knew, the next it was the coming glory." Russell's smile came back, and he raised his eyebrows once again. "And you still ain't answered my question, Professuh. Was you singing?"

"Russell, it's 'Were you singing.'"

"Okay, Mr. Professuh, sir." Russell had little quit in him. "Were you singing?"

"Yes, I was," I admitted, my eyes scanning the practice field.

"I thought so. Now, what was you singing?"

The last thing I wanted was a casual conversation with Russell. In class is one thing. Out of class, that's another. Students can't differentiate. Pretty soon, they start wanting to have out-of-class discussions in class. At that point, the idea of you as teacher, and them as students, hops on a ghost train and flies south. Never to return.

"Russell." I gathered myself. "I was singing a song my wife, Maggie, used to sing to our son before he was born."

"How's it go?"

"Russell, aren't you supposed to be out there somewhere, hurting somebody?" I pointed to the field.

"Professuh, you ain't answering my question." He put his hand on my shoulder.

Russell has a contagious smile. About like Pastor John's. It absolutely destroys any walls you throw in its place. You could rebuild Jericho, and Russell's smile would bring it crumbling down.

"Russell, let me put it to you this way," I said, looking at his hand on my shoulder. "There ain't no way in God's green earth I'm singing you a lullaby." I stepped up toward the fence, crossed my arms, and kept my eyes on the scrimmage, appearing intent on the action on the field.

"Professor," he said in his best English, "'Ain't' is not a word."

I laughed. I walked back toward him, stepping over pieces of wall as I went.

"Professuh, you don't laugh much, but when you do, it's a good laugh. You oughta try it some more."

*What is it with these kids? I'm walking around here half-naked tripping over wall rubble.*

Russell continued, "So how's that lullaby go?"

"No."

"Now, Professuh." Russell started talking with his hands. "They's no need to start getting huffy. We jus' having a friendly conversation, and you was about to sing me a song."

"Russell, go away. Go hit somebody. I'll see you in class."

"I ain't gonna do dat, Professuh. Been hitting people all day. That's how come I'm standing here. 'Cause I'm good at it, and all those boys over there ain't. Now come on, I heard it when I walked up here."

"How's your term paper coming?" I asked.

"Professuh, don't change the subject. We ain't in school. This is football, you see." Russell used his hands to paint along with his words. "In case you ain't never seen one, that's a field. That's a ball. This is grass. These are pads, and this is sweat. School is over there, and this is here. Let's keep 'em separate." His smile grew bigger. "Now are you gonna sing, or am I gonna bring this up in class? I am bigger than you, and . . ."

"Yes?" I said. "And what? I can flunk you in two shakes."

"I'm waiting." He tapped his size-fourteen cleats on the grass.

Every time I stood in Russell's presence, I noticed how big he was. He stood maybe seven inches taller than me, weighed at least 290 pounds, and had very little fat. Maybe 8 percent. With shoulder pads, he was huge. I was glad I didn't have to tackle him.

"If you ain't in there," the coach hollered, tobacco juice oozing out the corner of his mouth, "or standing on the side-line, I want you on a knee."

I sat down on a nearby bench, and Russell took a knee. He faced the scrimmage, one ear trained on the coach and one on me. He knew how to look as though he were paying attention. Sweat was pouring out of every pore, and Russell was in his element. Heat, pads, pain. Paradise.

I gave in and sang.

I sang Maggie's sweet lullaby, and maybe I wanted to hear it too. At first I murmured, barely above my breath, but Russell would have none of that.

"Professuh," he said, keeping his eyes pointed toward the

field, "that don't count. I can't hear you." He cupped his hand to his ear.

So I sang it for real, as if I were singing to Maggie's tummy. I finished my song, blinked away the glisten, and looked down at Russell, expecting chiding.

"Professuh," Russell said, strapping on his helmet, "you awright." He buttoned his chinstrap and didn't look at me. "You awright."

I don't know if he looked away because he didn't want to see the water in my eyes or didn't want me to see the water in his.

"See you in class, Russell."

"In class," Russell said with his back toward me.

I heard the second snap of his chinstrap, and Russell jogged off. Man, he was big. Powerful too. Whatever his folks fed him, it worked. There's no telling how much it cost to feed that kid when he was coming up.

I walked off the practice field, pulled the door of my truck closed, cranked her up, and headed for the hospital. As I was driving over the old tracks, I glanced back across the field and spotted Russell. He had rejoined the scrimmage, tackled the running back, and was now holding both the ball and the running back's helmet. The running back lay on his back, dazed, shaking his head, surrounded by three trainers.

Minutes later, I caught myself humming.

*chapter sixteen*

I DISMISSED CLASS AMID A PUDDLE OF AFTERNOON sweat. It was now almost October, but the lazy summer haze was hanging around, winning the battle against the cooler breezes that made a strong charge in the evening, but beat a retreat during the day. With every class, I kept threatening to buy a window unit and blow some AC into this place. If I did, I'd bet my truck that the introduction of that window unit would change the seating chart. All my kids would be crowding around that thing—even Koy.

On her way out the door, Amanda glanced at my arm, looked down her nose, and shook her head. "You better let me clean that again." She left without another word.

I rolled down my sleeve, stuffed my hand in my pocket, and began packing my bag. As I was leaving, I almost stumbled over Koy, who was still seated. She had her hands folded in front of her mouth and looked as though she wanted to say something. I decided to help her out.

"You were quiet in class today."

"I'm quiet every day."

"True." I smiled and waited for her to say something else. I wasn't going to drag it out of her.

"Professuh." She lifted her book bag into her lap. "I write a lot, and, uh, I was wondering if maybe you'd look at this for me. Tell me whether you think it's any good."

I walked over and leaned against the desk next to hers. "Sure, I'll look at it, but don't take me as the sole measure for whether or not it's any good. I may say it's great when others think not. And I may say it stinks when it doesn't. I'm just one opinion, and unfortunately, I like what I like. Know what I mean?"

"Yeah, me too." Koy reached into her bag and pulled out a well-worn journal. This book had seen some time. She handed me the journal reluctantly and walked out of the room.

The pages were worn, tattered, and on them she had written thousands of words. I slid it into my backpack and turned to leave. When I did, I noticed Koy standing back in the doorway.

She turned slowly, pointing at the journal, and said, "Professuh, that's . . . that's me in there." She looked away, then turned and faced me. Her right hand came slowly up to her face and removed her glasses. Beautiful green eyes stared out at me. An emerald surprise.

*Why would someone try so hard to hide something so beautiful?*

She stepped forward, took a deep breath, and said, "Can we keep me between you and me?"

"Koy." I reached into my backpack and pulled out the journal. "If you're asking me whether or not I will keep what I read in this journal inside me and between us, the answer is yes. Absolutely. But trust? Trust is another matter. It's a choice. It's earned. It's something I don't do with everybody. Am I trustworthy? You have to decide that. Not me. It's your call. And if you ask me to read this journal, you're trusting me."

She stood motionless a minute, looked at the floor, glanced down the hall, put her glasses back on, tugged at her handbag, then walked over to me, grabbed the journal out of my hand, and left without a word.

Maybe I was too hard. Maybe not. Who knows? I do know this: most people, myself included, are at their most vulnerable in a journal. They pour it all out. Sometimes a journal is the only ear that will listen, or at least the only one that you want to talk to. So we talk until our hand can write no more and then, spent, we fall off to sleep or go to class or get back to work or whatever it was that we were escaping from in the first place.

I WENT HOME, PIDDLED AROUND THE HOUSE, AND THEN decided I'd drive to the hospital after the late shift had settled down. I was surprised when I found myself instead curled up on my front-porch swing, watching the sunrise light the corn tassels. Last thing I remembered was watching the wind make waves out of the corn rows.

Squinting in the morning sun, I saw that on the floor below me lay Koy's journal with a note on top of it.

*Professor, I didn't want to wake you. Sorry about yesterday. Please read. Koy.*

I percolated some Maxwell House, returned to the swing with a steaming cup, resisted a tug to get to the hospital, and started on page one.

By noon I had read the whole thing. Mostly poetry and short vignettes. Scenes of her life. No beginning. No ending. Snapshots absent a context.

When I finished, I had one question: why in the world was this girl in my class? Koy was good. I'm not talking about "she has good style" or even "control of the English language." Koy had a gift. The real deal.

Sitting there on my porch, holding that girl's mind and heart in my hand, I could only think of two real possibilities. Either she was a gifted genius unchallenged by school, sort of a Bill Gates with a pen, or something had happened to her. Something violent and sudden had taken away the tenderness and replaced it with the ice-queen demeanor and sunglasses.

What I held in my hand reminded me of a feeling that I had had several times in grammar school and rarely since. It was that awe mixed with incredulity that I got in Ms. Edward's music class while studying Mozart. Now I had it with Koy. How could someone so young produce something so fine and grown-up?

I put the journal down and sipped my coffee, which had long since grown cold. It was horrible. Maggie loved cold coffee. She used to pour a cup in the morning, let it sit a few hours, and then pick it up just before lunch. Sort of a midday caffeine hit. I never did figure that out. Why would anyone purposefully drink cold coffee when she could have it hot? I sniffed the top again, realized it had sat dormant for more than three hours, brought it to my lips, and sipped again curiously. The cold dregs swirled around my tongue and fell down my throat. I noticed a different taste and once again felt the cold hammer of loneliness slam me against the porch.

THE THERMOMETER OUTSIDE READ NINETY-EIGHT DEGREES, and not a single cloud dotted the clear blue sky. I walked through the hospital doors wearing a long-sleeved black T-shirt, Blue at my heels. All was quiet. Maggie lay in her room, a solemn sleeping beauty. Someone had recently brushed her hair and painted her fingernails. I checked her feet to see if they were cold and noticed that the same person had painted her toenails as well.

Maggie always slept wearing socks. She hated cold feet. Without them she put her feet on my back or stomach, depending on which side I happened to be sleeping at the moment. Blue licked her feet, rubbed his cold nose against her fingers, sniffed her hair, and lay down at the foot of her bed.

Maggie looked as though she were sleeping. Her expression didn't mirror the doctor's dooming comments about "permanent damage." About "never waking." We were now through the 50 percent range and well into the 25 percent chance of recovery. A few days ago, he shook his head and said, "Dylan, I'm just being honest. Prepare yourself."

But she didn't look like what her chart said she was. She looked like my wife on Saturday morning. She looked like she was about to wake up and float with me downriver. I walked into the room, picked up her chart out of the sleeve on the end of her bed, read the doctor's illegible comments, opened the window, pitched it as far as I could, and watched it flail into the reflection pond three floors below. They don't bar the windows on the rooms of vegetables. Not much danger of their jumping out.

I kissed her forehead. She was warm. She smelled like Maggie. I whispered, "Hey, Maggs, it's me," and sat down. She didn't move. I didn't expect her to. It's just that every time in our life that I whispered, "Hey, Maggs," kissed her forehead, and put her coffee on the table next to the bed, she woke up, turned on her side, put her head in my lap, took a deep breath, and said, "What do you want to do today?"

Maggie was a pretty intense sleeper. Sometimes I'd get up in the middle of the night, and her hand would be sitting upright on her forehead as though she were thinking or had forgotten something. Whatever she was thinking about, whatever she had forgotten, it had wrinkled the skin between her eyes above her nose. I'd lean over, pull her hand down to her side, kiss her gently, and place my hand on her forehead. She'd relax. The skin would ease, go soft, and the wrinkle would disappear. When I didn't wake up, and she spent most of the night in that tense wrinkle, she'd wake and her neck would be screaming with pain. I knew it was only evidence of her depth. Maggie is a simple complexity. A paradox. Meaning between extremes.

I put my head down next to Maggie's and breathed. It was the first time in our married life that she let me share the same pillow. I wanted to smell her. Hear her breathe. Listen to her feet shuffle under the sheets. I wanted to be with my wife.

I'm not talking about the sexual thing. God knows I could. I'm a man. This is my wife. I love her. But after the delivery, the hemorrhage, the blood, and what the doctors had to do, even if she woke right this minute, it would be months before that was physically an option. And then there's the emotional aspect. Maggie's strong, but not that strong.

No, I'm talking about that sweet thing that happens when you open your eyes and realize in the dim daybreak of dawn that your wife has nudged her head next to yours and that you're now breathing air she breathed. That sweet thing that happens when you realize this and then close your eyes and feel that soft rush of her breath tickle your eyelashes. The sweet thing that happens when, after feeling that soft rush, you doze, each breathing parts of the other's air.

About dark, long after my stomach started growling, Amanda walked in the door, pulling a cart.

Blue looked up from the floor and perked his ears.

"Hello, Professor. Hello, Miss Maggie. Hello, Blue." She stopped next to me, grabbed my left arm, and started pulling back the sleeve of my T-shirt. I winced and jerked it back, but Amanda would have none of that. "Professor, if you don't give me that arm, I'm calling in the doctor, a couple of really big nurses, and your deputy friend. So we can either do this the easy way, or we can do it your way."

I extended my arm.

My T-shirt was stuck to my flesh. Small circles of pus and serum seeped through the fibers of my shirt. Amanda took my wrist in her hand and started methodically cutting and peeling the shirt away. After about the third pull, I realized how much it hurt. My arm was raw meat.

While I winced, Amanda spoke to Maggie. "Now, Miss Maggie, don't worry. I'm taking good care of this arm until you get to where you can. At least when he's in this hospital. I can't speak for him outside of here, but in this hospital, I'll take good care of him. We need to get his arm healed up. From what I can tell, he's not real good at taking care of himself." Amanda looked at me. "He keeps picking at this thing like he's trying to get rid of something." She turned to Maggie again. "So it would help us all out if you'd just go ahead and wake up before this arm gets to where he can't use it anymore."

She finished bandaging my arm, held out her hand, and said, "Swallow this."

Shortly thereafter, I dozed off. About two in the morning, Amos tapped me on the shoulder and said, "D.S., let's go get some coffee."

Blue licked my ankle as I wiped my eyes and cleared the drool from my chin. I was groggy, but whatever Amanda had given me had worked. I kissed Maggs and put my hand on her forehead.

"See you tomorrow. Thanks for letting me share your pillow. I promise, if you wake up, you'll never have to do it again."

Amos and I walked out of the hospital and crossed the street to the all-night diner. It used to be a Waffle House that had long since gone out of business. Now the sign above the door read "Al's Diner, Open 24 Hours." I've never been there when Al wasn't working the grill. When that guy slept, I'll never know.

Amos and I sat down and ordered coffee, and I placed three orders for scrambled eggs.

"How is she?"

"Same."

"What's this business with your arm?"

"Huh?"

"I said, why do you keep doing whatever you're doing to your arm?"

"Oh. I just goofed it up working in the pasture."

"That's not what your nurse said."

"Yeah? What does she know? She wasn't there."

"She says that every time she sees you it's worse, and now you're trying to cover it up. That's why she's bandaged it like that. So you can't make it any worse."

"Amos, it's three in the morning. Can we talk about something else?"

"How's class?" he said without a break.

I looked up. "Shouldn't you be home sleeping or working or something?"

"I am working."

"My tax dollars are paying you for this time?"

"How's class?"

"You don't quit, do you?"

"Not when it comes to you." Amos smiled, his white teeth shining in the dim light of the diner.

I rubbed my eyes. "It's probably a good thing too."

"Have you figured it out yet?"

"Figured out what?"

"Amanda."

"Amos, would you quit talking in code? It's about three hours past my ability to translate."

"Have you figured out Amanda Lovett?"

"What's there to figure? I've got an attractive, kind, pregnant preacher's daughter sitting in the front row of my class, and she also happens to be my wife's nurse. Yes, I've got that figured pretty well."

"Yeah, but have you figured how that attractive, kind, sweet, unmarried daughter-of-a-preacher got pregnant in the first place?"

"No. I haven't spent much time on that."

"You probably thought she was just another statistic."

I rubbed my eyes and stared out the diner window. "Amos, please come to a point. Just about any point will do."

"Six months ago, Amanda Lovett was kidnapped, driven seven miles from town, and tied to a tree deep in the Salkehatchie.

She was then raped by at least two men, maybe more. Six days later, they dumped her on her daddy's lawn. You need me to draw you a picture?"

That was picture enough. "No, I got it."

"That girl, the same girl that bandages your arm, brushes your wife's hair, leaves a towel for Blue, and brings you orange juice in the morning, was beat up and left for dead. She was also impregnated." Amos sat back. "This is a small town, and word travels fast, but you Styleses have a tendency to keep to yourselves. Always have. Now . . . " Amos pointed his toothpick at me. "You want the answer to your next question?"

"Yes."

"Well." He tongued the toothpick to the other side of his mouth. "I could tell you, but you need to hear it from her. Ask her sometime. "

"Amos, did you bring me to this one-tooth establishment to tell me this?"

"Yup."

"Why?"

"'Cause you need to hear that there are folks in this world who got lives just as bad as yours. Life ain't fair, and welcome to earth."

"Thanks. I feel much better just knowing that."

I paid for the coffee and eggs, and Blue and I left Amos talking with Al. When I cranked my truck, Garth was singing a duet with Martina, but I turned it off and rode home in silence, except for the rhythmic sound of a nail in my tire hitting the blacktop.

# chapter seventeen

FRIDAY NIGHT WAS THE BIGGEST GAME OF THE
year, according to Marvin. This was "The Rivalry." Every
school has a nemesis, and Digs's was South Carolina Junior
College.

Blue and I walked up to the fence next to the track and
stood parallel with the goal line. The bleachers were filled
with kids, and because dogs make some folks nervous, I put a
leash on Blue. He looked at me as if I had lost my mind.

"Sorry, pal. It's just for an hour or so."

I leaned against the fence and looked up at the clock. It
was the third quarter, and Digs was beating SCJC by a touchdown, 27-20. From what I had heard in the classroom, Digs

had speed and a decent quarterback, SCJC had a running back named Thumper, and both teams had defense.

The Digger defense was on the field, and Russell was lined up on the far side as defensive tackle. SCJC snapped the ball, and the quarterback rolled left—to Russell's side of the field. Russell ran over the offensive tackle and sacked the quarterback for what would have been a twelve-yard loss had the quarterback not fumbled the ball.

Players scrambled everywhere trying to pick up the pigskin. The stands erupted again in a wave of arms and a roar of penny-filled milk jugs. Out of the heap, Marvin came up with the ball and began running down my side of the field. His arms and feet were a blur. When he passed me, his face was a picture of gums, teeth, and unadulterated joy. He crossed the goal line twelve yards ahead of the nearest player, spiked the ball, and did some dance I had never before seen. Then Russell picked him up and they, and the rest of the defense, paraded to the bench. Score: 33-20.

I was saying something to myself about fast feet when I heard, "Hey there, Professor."

I didn't need to look. The seductive voice gave her away. I turned and said, "What? No sunglasses tonight?"

Koy reached up and pulled her sunglasses down from their perch atop her head. "How's that?" she said.

"Much better. I almost didn't recognize you."

Digs kicked off and tackled SCJC on about the twenty-two.

"So, what are you doing here?" Koy asked.

"Watching a football game," I said, pointing to the field.

"Don't most people do that from the stands?"

"Yeah, but I thought it might be too much for Blue. You know—all the noise."

"Oh," she said with a skeptical expression. She knelt down and rubbed Blue's head. "What's your story, Professor?"

"What do you mean, what's my story?" I asked.

"I mean, what's your story? Why's a good-looking, upstanding guy like you teaching a loser class like ours?"

"You think you guys are losers?"

"Come on, Professor. We're all adults here."

"Well, I used to teach some, had a break in my farming, and this class came along. I saw it, applied, and they accepted me."

"That ain't the way I heard it."

"It ain't?"

"No, it is not," she said in her best imitation of me. "Way I heard it was that you was found 'bout half dead in a cornfield by your buddy, the deputy, who I saw somewhere here tonight." She tilted her head, looking out over the field, and put her finger to her lips. "You know, he carries a big gun, and he ain't too bad-looking. Anyway, your wife knew you could teach, and he knew you can't farm. So the two of them signed you up and stuck you in this class with the rest of us losers."

I nodded. "All right, now that you know most of my story, what's yours?"

Koy picked her glasses off her nose and tucked them back on top of her head. "Professor, I'm just playing with you. You look like a sore thumb out here. You're about the only white person in this smelly armpit." She waved her hands across the crowd. "I thought maybe you could use some friendly conversation."

"Is that what this is?" I said, smiling.

"Oh, you ought to hear me when I'm unfriendly." Her right hand played with her earring.

"I'll pass. I like the friendly."

"Good." She moved up, rubbing shoulders with me, and rested her chin on her hands over the fence. "So what's the deal? Why are you here?"

"I like football. I wanted to see if Russell and Marvin are really as good as Marvin keeps telling me they are."

"Believe me, they're better. Up there, in that box"—she pointed to the press box above the stands—"are about sixteen scouts. The guys on the roof above them are the reporters who call the game. They kicked them out of the press box to make room for all the scouts."

I scanned the rooftops and wondered about Russell and Marvin's futures. Three years from now their lives, and lifestyles, would be very different. I turned back to Koy. "My story is simple, Koy. My wife and I moved back here after graduate school. I couldn't get hired as a teacher, so I leaned on what I knew—farming. But, as you so aptly stated, I'm not much of a farmer. Not yet, anyway. So, for a lot of reasons, my wife, with a little help from my friend Amos, signed me up to teach this class. And here I am."

"Professor, tell me something I don't know."

"All right."

It was fourth and seven. SCJC had the ball on Digs's forty-yard line. They handed the ball to Thumper, who lowered his head and shoulder and rambled for eleven yards. First-and-ten on the twenty-nine. At the snap, Marvin rushed in from his corner position to support, but like a lot of corners with good feet and little desire to butt heads, he tried to arm-tackle and strip the ball. He probably learned that from Dion, who could actually do it. After Thumper ran through Marvin and gained seven more yards, Marvin got up, buckled his chinstrap, and headed for the sideline. Guess he needed a breather. Russell, not needing a breather, stood in the huddle, waiting on the next call.

"Koy." I looked down. "You're goofing off, and your work shows it. What's in your journal is far better than what you produce in class. Why the difference?"

She blinked and batted her eyelashes. "Because school-work don't mean nothing."

I nodded. "You're right, but you've got a gift. And you're wasting it.

"Yeah, but . . . "

"But what?" I asked.

She put her head on the top rail of the fence and gazed out across the field. "Professor, I swear, sometimes you don't seem too bright when it comes to people. Can't you see? Look around you. This is Digger, South Carolina. I'm never getting out of here. I'm stuck in this cesspool, and you know it. Why you think they call this place Digger?"

"They call it Digger because you can dig yourself into or out of a hole." I paused. "And getting out of here is your choice. But it's not going to happen if you keep giving me half-completed work and a half-committed attitude. You don't do that in your journal."

Koy looked away and put her sunglasses back down over her eyes. "Yeah, well . . . I'm digging, all right." She stepped away from the fence. "I'll see you, Professor." She walked off the way she came: alone and at a distance from the stands.

Two minutes remained in the game. Thumper had rushed for over two hundred yards, but I don't think many of those yards were gained against Russell's side of the field. Digs was still up by ten points and looking pretty good. But a lot can happen in two minutes.

SCJC snapped the ball. The quarterback took a seven-step drop and threw deep down the far sideline. Marvin was in man-coverage and timed his jump well. He intercepted the ball on the ten, took a few lateral steps, and headed back up the sideline, where the free safety made a couple of good blocks and freed things up. Thumper took an angle and was just about to blindside Marvin when Russell decapitated him. Marvin took three more steps and was gone. Ninety yards.

He started dancing at about the ten. Danced all the way into the end zone and threw the ball through the goalposts. The referee threw the flag for excessive celebration, but Marvin didn't care. He danced all the way to the sideline, where every player and coach high-fived his hand or slapped his helmet. He went over to the bench, jumped up, raised his arms to the crowd, and started the wave. People were jumping and pennies were spilling all over the place. Come Monday, I knew he'd be a handful.

# chapter eighteen

M Y SCREEN DOOR SLAMMED, AND AMOS BOUNDED
into the living room, where I sat in the dark listening for an
echo of Maggie's voice. It was mid-November, Canadian winds
had blown in an arctic front, and the temperature had slipped
to twenty-three degrees. I don't understand weather patterns
all that well, but arctic front or not, it was butt-cold. The
weatherman said it would drop another three or four degrees
before the night was out.

Next to me were a pair of old Carhart overalls, hip waders,
and my headlamp. Amos didn't say a word. Just popped his
head around the corner, saw me, nodded, and turned back
toward the door. I grabbed my stuff and threw it into the back

of his truck. While I waved my hands across the heater vent inside the truck, one thought occurred to me. Winter had come, and Maggie would like that.

I turned to Blue and held up my hand like a stop sign. He laid down on the couch, let out a deep breath, and wouldn't look at me. The silent treatment. "Not tonight," I said. "Don't want you getting hurt." He whined and dug his wet nose beneath the sofa cushion.

Willard's parking lot was full by the time we arrived, crammed tight with trucks, dog boxes, blaze-orange vests, baseball caps advertising farm equipment, hip waders, chewing tobacco, Carhart overalls, and coffee cups now used as spit cups. Mr. Willard's thermometer, hanging on the gas pump, read twenty-two degrees, but that probably accounted for a little bit of wind chill.

A few weeks ago, Amos said he bought his dad some new insulated hip waders for this year's season. Amos parked his Expedition next to his dad's old Ford. His father walked over to him, running his fingers up the elastic suspenders. "Moose, I love 'em. Best I've ever owned."

"Glad you like them."

Mr. Carter put his hand on Amos's shoulder, and the two walked ahead of me toward Mr. Willard's store. Mr. Willard saw us coming and opened the door with a smile. Then he hung the "Closed" sign over the suction hook in the middle of the window.

His coffeepot was almost empty after Amos and I filled our mugs and a beat-up green thermos that looked as if it had rolled one too many times around the back of somebody's pickup. Back outside, Mr. Carter banged on the side of an empty Maxwell House coffee can for attention, then climbed atop the dog box wedged in the bed of his truck. He zipped up his coveralls, pulled up his collar, shoved his hands in his pockets, and began.

"Howdy. Now y'all come in close. That's better." His voice was blowing smoke, it was so cold. "It's too cold to yell. And Jim, don't stand too close to my exhaust. I don't want you passing out again. I don't want to hear any excuses from you when we get in the Salk."

Mr. Carter smiled, Jim shuffled his feet, and everybody laughed.

Jim Biggins, who is just what his name implies, owns a junkyard, but come winter, he supplies most of Digger and even some of Charleston with firewood. In seven years he's never run out of wood, and neither have the folks in Digger. He sells it cheap, and Jim has kept a lot of people warm long after their gas has been cut off.

A few years back, he had just come off working a double because the Weather Channel said South Carolina would experience a hard freeze. Once he got home, he pulled on his coveralls and came coon hunting. We got inside the swamp, and Jim just couldn't hold off the sleep any longer. No amount of coffee would change that. Just about the time the dogs treed a coon, Jim slumped over and fell asleep at the base of an old cypress, curled up like a baby.

Jim is about six foot six, dresses out at three hundred

pounds, and is the strongest human being I have ever known. There was no way we could tote him out of the swamp. So Mr. Carter and the rest of the boys continued hunting while Amos and I hung out in the swamp for a few hours, letting Jim nap. We made a fire and sipped coffee, and when Jim woke, he stood up, shook his head, and apologized. We walked out of the Salk about an hour before daylight. Since then, he's never let me pay for firewood, and I've never run out. Somehow every year it just shows up.

Towering over everyone from his perch in the back of the pickup, Mr. Carter addressed the crowd like the chairman of the board at the annual stockholders meeting. "I'd like to welcome everybody to the first coon hunt of this year." He eyed the full moon and cloudless sky. "Looks like we got us a good night."

Coon hunting in Digger is a religion, something passed down from father to son. Amos's dad has had the best coon dogs in the state for years. He's been winner or runner-up of the Greater Salkehatchie Coon Gathering for twelve of the last fifteen years, and he breathes coon hunting. It could be blowing forty miles an hour outside, treetops blowing right off the trees, but come first freeze of the year, Mr. Carter would load five or six of his best hounds and head to Mr. Willard's store.

Participation here is by invitation only, and Mr. Carter is selective. If you get invited, you better be able to keep up, and you better not have a problem walking ten or fifteen miles.

Mr. Carter prides himself on dogs that can hunt all night

and on into the next day. His dog kennel is a real operation. Twelve kennels raised four feet off the ground. Every dog has its own box, automatic waterer, and food bowl. Once a month Mr. Carter drives to the Wal-Mart distribution center and loads up his pickup with about eight or ten seventy-five-pound bags of Alpo. Twelve dogs can eat a lot of food, and they can get rid of it too. Every morning Mr. Carter cranks up his pressure washer and hoses down the concrete into a holding area, where he shovels the muck into a five-gallon bucket and dumps it into a hole that he dug with his front-end loader. In fifteen years, he's pretty well dug up his whole pasture, but he's got the greenest grass of any farm in Digger.

In almost twenty years, he's lost only one dog to snakebite, because he trains them to stay away from snakes. In springtime he waits for the weather to warm up and catches a rattler or moccasin crossing a road or slithering along some bank somewhere. He tapes its mouth shut and then puts both the snake and the dog into a closed space and buckles a shock collar on the dog. I'm not talking about a pet-supermarket bark collar that sort of tickles the dog into thinking that it ought not to sniff the snake. His collars do what they advertise. They shock. They aren't inhumane, but they're strong enough to straighten all four legs and bring a dog off its feet. He calls it electroshock therapy. Mr. Carter used to threaten to put one on Amos and me when we were kids, if he thought it was needed. As a result, we didn't let him know about all the trouble we got into.

With the dog and the snake in the same space, he would

let the dog do what it naturally did. Sniff. But every time the dog got close to or sniffed the snake, Mr. Carter lit him up with that collar. "Watch this," Mr. Carter would say. The dog would pace back and forth, looking at the snake out of the corner of its eye. The snake would coil up and silently watch the dog, wishing that its mouth weren't taped shut. The dog, not knowing that the ropy-looking thing in the corner of his kennel wanted to kill it, walked over, sniffed, and attempted to place the snake between its teeth. Just about the time the dog's teeth touched the snake's skin, Mr. Carter mashed the big red button in the middle of the 2D-cell radio control in his hand. The dog yelped, jumped three feet off the ground, straightened all four legs, and returned to the opposite corner of the kennel, whining, never to sniff a snake again. Curiosity cured.

One year a fellow in Charleston called Mr. Carter and gave him a real stubborn dog named Gus. Gus was, and still is, cross-eyed as a goat and dumb as a brick. By Mr. Carter's account, the previous owner was tired of messing with him. To cure his stupidity, Mr. Carter caught a six-foot diamondback and put him in the kennel with Gus. Dumb Gus immediately went to sniffing, and Mr. Carter shocked—three times. Finally Gus got the picture. That collar just about killed him, but Gus is still alive and has never been snakebit.

Mr. Carter kicked the dog box to quiet one of his hounds and turned again to face the crowd at his feet. "Glad y'all could make it. John Stotton said he could not be here tonight 'cause Emma is feeling a little under the weather, but he promised to make it this weekend. Pastor John had a wedding over in Charleston. And"—he looked at Amos—"son, who am I forgetting?"

"Sam," Amos whispered.

"Oh yeah, Sam Revel said he's got some business in Columbia. All send their apologies. Butch Walker and his boys said a few of their milking cows got loose, but if they can join us, they'll be along shortly."

Every year we all compete to see who can come up with the best lighting apparatus. There's a science to it. You have to consider three things: weight, longevity, and candlepower. John Billingsly won last year's pat on the back with a one million candlepower Q-beam mounted to his chest, powered with a backpack full of four lithium ion batteries converted from an Apple laptop. John works in computer sales, and rumor has it that he's threatened to increase this year's output to two million candlepower. John doesn't understand overkill. He's the guy in town who trades his own computer in every three months whether he needs to or not, and the back of his toilet is full of magazines that tell you all about the latest computer technology. John even writes for some of them. A lot of school kids in Digger have benefited from his "used" models. Anyway, when he stepped out of his truck for coon hunting, he looked like a walking lighthouse.

Mr. Carter moved to the front of his dog box, eyed the crowd, and pointed to John Billingsly. "I think we can pretty well agree that John here is this year's hands-down winner in the light category. John, you outdid yourself again."

John smiled earlobe to earlobe, and four or five guys patted him on the back.

"Anybody with bad eyesight, stay close to John. But be careful; he looks like a walking runway light, so be wary of planes looking for a landing strip on the outside of the Salk."

After the laughter quieted, Mr. Carter continued. "Gentlemen, we haven't hunted the south end of the Salk in almost three years, so tonight I thought we'd drive that direction. Any objections?"

Mr. Carter's authority is never questioned. This is his show, and everybody knows it. Nobody spoke.

"Good. Now, Jimmy," he said to a man in faded green Carharts. "You still got that mangy female, Sally?"

"Yes, sir," Jimmy answered.

"Well, good. She seems to work real well with Badger, so we'll let the two of them out first. Now, y'all know that the first catch of the year is a training coon. It's not a keeper. So any of you that might be a little weak in the stomach ought to hang back once we get to the tree. Everybody agree?" Mr. Carter folded his hands and lowered his head as though checking off a mental list. "The CB's on channel seven, and if the reception is bad there, we'll go to fourteen. Everybody got a partner?"

One fellow in the back raised his hand. "No, sir."

"All right, Frank, me either. You're with me. Anybody else?" Nobody spoke. At that, Mr. Carter bounced off his dog box onto the tailgate and hit the ground at a trot. Sixteen truck engines started at one time amid a cloud of white exhaust and the pang and smack of glass-packs. Mr. Carter's old Ford slowly led the procession out of the parking lot.

That scene would make a great commercial. Represented there were about fifteen models and years of Ford and Chevy's best work trucks, all in varying degrees of worn out. All we'd need is a Bob Seger, Alan Jackson, or George Strait song, and we'd fit right in with Monday night football.

The commercial proceeded down Highway 42 until we got to McSweeney's Fork, turned right down South Salk Road, and drove four miles to Gunter's Hole, where we eased under the huge live oak limbs bordering the edge of the swamp.

Around Digger, the Salkehatchie is mythical. Everybody knows the stories. Confederate gold. Lost lovers. Indians. World War II German spies. Vietnamese foot soldiers. Eighteen-foot alligators. You name it, it's buried there. Somewhere beneath the slow-moving black water, the hundred-foot cypress trees, the hanging moss, and the swamp stench, there's a story to go along with most every idea you could have about a swamp. If you can think it, it's probably already been mythified.

Every coon hunter in the Salk is required to have two things: a radio and a partner, the idea being that if you get lost, at least you'll be able to talk to folks on the outside, and you won't be lonely. It happens about once a year. Rarely does anybody spend the night in the swamp, but several times they've walked out some ten or fifteen miles from where they walked in. The swamp itself is forty square miles of the exact same thing. Landmarks are difficult to make. Nobody "knows" the swamp, not even Mr. Carter. He's pretty good around the edges, most of us are, but we know our limits. Amos and I are as good as anyone. We've dug for a lot of Confederate gold in our days, even built a few *Swiss Family Robinson* forts in the cedars, but even we know where our experience stops and the swamp takes over.

And one more thing. When the sun goes down in the Salk, "dark" takes on a whole new meaning. It may be clear and starlight bright outside, but you step one foot inside that swamp, underneath the canopy, and it's a different story. No matter how familiar you might be with a particular area of the swamp, when dark comes, you turn around, try and find your way out, and things look real different. No matter how well you've marked it, orange surveyor's tape, breadcrumbs, or what, the darkness will make you doubt.

At Gunter's Hole, Mr. Carter unlatched the box doors, letting Badger and Sally catapult off the tailgate. The two bounded off into the darkness. We stood outside in the cold, engines idling, feet shuffling, listening to single barks like submarine pings as they faded a half mile, then a mile, then a little more. Talking was over. If you needed to communicate, you used hand signals, or worst case, you whispered.

Mr. Carter does not tolerate talking while he's listening to Badger. Varying tones are more difficult to pick up the farther he gets from the edge of the swamp. After a few minutes I could tell no audible difference in Badger's bark, yet a smile began to crease Mr. Carter's face. I had learned long ago that Mr. Carter's face could tell me far more than Badger's bark.

One second after Mr. Carter's crease reached a full smile,

Badger broke into an all-out hound wail—a totally different bark. It sounded like a cross between death and ecstasy, telling Mr. Carter that its nose had found what it'd been sniffing for. Mr. Carter had his hand on the dog box, so when Badger broke, he unleashed the second latch, and five dogs disappeared like four-legged ghosts into the swamp. The only trace of the dogs was the deafening chase bark. All the hunters cut their engines and hit their hunting lights.

Mr. Carter looked at me and said, "D.S., grab my Winchester."

I did. As kids, Amos and I had shot a dozen or so raccoons, more than a hundred squirrels, and a thousand aluminum cans with Mr. Carter's Model 61 Winchester. I knew this rifle.

A coon-dog fight is a brutal thing, and the coon usually wins if you aren't careful. That's where Mr. Carter comes in. He's seen many a blind dog following a coon fight, and he hates to see his dogs hurt. Even Gus. Grabbing a handful of dog leashes, Mr. Carter immediately sloshed into the swamp, following the dogs.

The mossy grass was frozen and crunchy, and a thin layer of ice covered the floor. Amos and I filed behind him, as did everyone else, and we slipped into the swamp with seven dogs, at least one raccoon, and about seven million candlepower of artificial light, thanks in large part to John Billingsly and the rest of the coal miner convention. We lit up the underside of the canopy like a runway. Wherever we looked was bright as day. Wherever we didn't look was an abyss.

One more thing about the Salk: you don't want to step where you haven't first looked. We followed Mr. Carter, who, despite his seventy-four years of age, moved pretty well. As the barking got louder, his pace quickened. After twenty-two minutes, we neared the tree, and Mr. Carter was almost running. Ice and black water were splashing everywhere.

Reaching the tree, he immediately tied up Badger and handed Sally to Jimmy, because if he didn't tie up Badger, the other dogs would never fight that coon. Gus, maybe, but the young dogs didn't have a chance. Badger is vicious when it comes to coons, and he never shares a fight with another dog. If he finds the coon, it's his to fight with. Go find your own coon.

Having tied up Badger, we backed up and started our laser light show in the trees above us while Gus and the four younger dogs stood against the base of the tree, barking. You'd think spotting a coon in a tree would be no big deal. Just shine and light up two orangish-yellow eyes. But old coons didn't get to be old coons in the Salkehatchie by being stupid. After a few minutes, Amos spotted a hole in the canopy where the moon was shining through. A rare sight. Rarer still was the fact that it was shining through silver-gray hair. The coon was sixty to eighty feet up, perched atop a short cedar limb, looking somewhere between scared and comfortable.

Amos turned to me, looked as if he was about to ask me a question, and then held out his hand, into which I placed his dad's Model 61. At Mr. Carter's command, all the hunters cut their lights, save one. His. He shined, and Amos shot. An effective tandem. Amos hit the coon exactly where he intended—square in the left rear hindquarter—and it started falling.

You'd think that a wounded coon that just fell forty to eighty feet, with the air knocked out of it, probably suffering a couple of broken ribs, maybe even a concussion, wild-eyed-scared, and facing six or eight bluetick hounds, would roll over and give up or just lie there and die.

Not hardly. The coon hits the ground, bounces three to four feet, swings at the first three dogs he sees, and takes five eyes with him. Young dogs usually get hurt because they stick their noses too close to the coon's reach.

We can meet, shake hands, pat backs, sip coffee, pull on hip waders, hang an assortment of lights around our necks, reach the swamp, release all the dogs, trek to the foot of a two-hundred-year-old cypress, and the thing on the back of everyone's mind is not the lights, the dogs, the chase, or even getting lost in the swamp, but the coon—and what he will do when he hits the ground.

No matter which way you slice it, if the dogs tree the coon, chances are that the coon is going to get the worse end of the deal. But for every one time we catch a coon, he makes nine escapes. I'm amazed at that thing that happens between a coon that's escaping and a hound whose job it is not to let him escape. Nature versus nature. A bluetick hound has the best nose on the planet, but a coon is one of the only animals that washes its food, and it can climb trees taller than Jack's beanstalk. I have walked away from the base of many a cypress tree, knowing full well there was a perfectly good raccoon at the top of it. We simply couldn't see it. The fit have a tendency to survive.

This coon bounced off five or six limbs on its way down and

landed with a thud. When it hit, it bounced, hissed, bared its teeth, swiped, landed again, and launched into Gus, whose crossed eyes straightened for a split second. He dodged the swipe, hunkered, sprang, and locked onto the coon's head, taking a good cut in the neck.

Fight over.

Two of the younger dogs each grabbed a hind leg and began chewing. The other two went for the body. The coon, half-dead from its descent, a quarter more from Amos's shot, and an eighth more from Gus's locked jaw, used its last eighth and took one final swipe at the dogs closest to him. Both took a good cut across the nose, and Jake was cut pretty deep around his right eye. Mr. Carter watched in quiet but ready judgment, taking notes and considering his training.

Gus sank down in the mud and laid both his front paws over what was left of the coon, which had long since stopped breathing. His locked jaw had not moved from where he first sank it. Mr. Carter told Gus to "release," which he did, and the coon lay motionless amid a circle of dogs, men, and blood-smeared sheets of ice floating in the water. Mr. Carter gently poked the coon in the eye with his rifle barrel to see if it blinked. If it did, he'd pull the trigger.

The air smelled of peat moss, coon, and dog. In more than twenty years of coon hunting, I had never looked away. But tonight the sight of blood, flesh, and a corpse was too much. Some blood had hit me in the face and dribbled down my cheek. I wiped it off and studied my fingers. The blood was red, warm, and sticky. The cold air quickly caked it, causing it to stiffen on my face like paint. It seeped into the cracks of my palm and the wrinkles in my wrist. When I wiped my face a second time, I caught a whiff of it.

"You coming, pal?" Amos asked.

"Yeah, just a second."

Amos took a handkerchief from his back pocket, dipped it in the swamp, and said, "Here, this'll help."

The water was cold, clean, and smelled of cypress roots. I scrubbed my face with Amos's handkerchief, then knelt to dip it in the Salk and rinse it out.

"Keep it," he said, nodding his head.

I dipped and rinsed it twice more. The water dripped off my face and made small ripples that raced around my legs as I squatted in the water. I closed my eyes and shivered as the cold took its place. I dipped my hands into the water and splashed my face. The water ran off my cheeks and down my neck. Some of it dripped back into the Salk and rippled about me. I stood up, exhaled a big white cloud of cold air, and wiped my face with my sleeve.

When I looked around, Mr. Carter and the procession were almost out of sight, and John Billingsly was bringing up the rear. Amos stood a few feet off, studying me quietly. Wrapped in the Salk, with the smell of swamp water sweetened with coon blood and dog sweat rising up around us, Amos said, "Hey, pal, you okay?"

The moon was high and bright now, glistening off the water like a spotlight. I looked down, saw my dark and distorted reflection, and spoke.

"The doctor told Maggs she could start pushing. She pushed, and I counted. Around three, the baby's head showed. Not all the way out, just where I could see the top of it. Then the doctor's face turned white. His eyes looked like half-dollars, and he ordered a nurse to go get some machine.

"Maggie looked at me with tired eyes. I tried to comfort her, but I had no idea what was going on. The doctor told Maggie to keep pushing while he put this suction thing on my son's head. A minute or two later, my son's head popped out. It was all smashed and blue.

"Maggie couldn't see it, but she could see my face. I don't know what my face said, but whatever it was, it probably wasn't what Maggie needed. At that point, two nurses pushed me aside and started pushing down on her stomach, trying to force the baby out. I held Maggie's head in my arms. She was tired. Real tired. The nurses kept pushing, and the doctor was barking orders everywhere. People were running all over the place. I heard a big gush and splash, and the doctor handed my son to a nurse.

"The doctor was tugging on the cord that was still inside Maggie. Blood was pouring out. Maggie's eyes closed, and she went limp."

One of the dogs barked somewhere, quickly answered by another farther north.

"On a table next to the wall, the nurse and doctors kept working on our baby. Pumping his chest, putting this mask over his mouth. He was blue and limp. Maggie's eyes opened again, she saw him, how blue he was, and . . . started crying.

Then her face went white and her eyes rolled back in her head and she threw up all over. That was the last time I saw her eyes open."

Amos shifted uneasily, and his lip quivered as his feet sank further into the muck below.

"A doctor came flying into the room, tying one of those masks around his face, and pushed me out of the way. I crumpled in the corner, lying in Maggie's blood. One doctor injected something into her arm. Another one tried to stop the bleeding. I felt numb. Maggie's blood pressure plummeted. Then I heard the paddles of the resuscitator and the doctors yelling, 'Clear!' My son's arms flew straight up in the air. His body bucked and then fell still and limp. The delivery doctor was sewing like crazy. After a few minutes, the doctors pulled their masks off and looked at the clock. They wrapped him in a blanket. Nobody even bothered to wipe off all the white stuff. I never held him. They didn't offer, and I didn't think to ask.

"Maggie stabilized a little bit. I stood up and noticed my hands. They were stiff and sticky, and so was my face. I leaned over Maggie. She had vomit in her hair. I grabbed a towel and wiped her face and cheeks and around her ears. I propped her head up on a pillow and tucked her hair behind her ears. The doctor just kept watching her monitor."

The tail end of the light parade had completely disappeared, allowing the darkness to return and silently surround us. I strained my eyes for any glimmer of light but saw none. The night grew thick, the canopy pressed in, and I felt alone.

"Somewhere about midnight on the second night, I fell

down. I woke up in a bed next to Maggie. The nurse said some big, bald-headed deputy sheriff, who had been in the hall for two days, picked me up and put me in bed next to Maggie. The doctors said that Maggie lost about half her blood. My son's head was fourteen centimeters in diameter and his stomach was eighteen. He weighed eleven pounds four ounces. I guess you know the rest."

We stood there for some time. I don't know how long, but it was long enough to get really cold.

Finally, Amos held up his hand and stuck three fingers in the air. Chin high, lip quivering, he whispered, "These three remain."

I nodded, and we walked out of the Salk.

Amos and I drove home with his heater on "scorch." The digital thermometer on his rearview mirror read eighteen degrees, and the coffee in my thermos was lukewarm and tasted like aluminum.

Pulling into the drive, Amos asked, "Do I need to worry about you?"

I shook my head.

"You sure?"

I nodded again.

"Hey." Amos put his hand on my shoulder. "Hug her for me."

I pushed the door closed, walked up the steps, and listened as Amos's tires crunched the frost on my gravel drive.

# chapter nineteen

"PROFESSOR?"

I raised my head, and the sunshine blinded me. An odor of urine, Pine Sol, and Maggie hit my nose pretty quickly, reminding me what my life smelled like. Through fuzzy, dry eyes, I recognized Amanda, who sat next to me unwrapping the bandage on my arm.

"Good morning," she whispered. "Sorry to wake you, but class starts in an hour, research papers are due today, and I thought you might want to eat something." She pointed to the table behind me. Eggs, sausage, and toast sat steaming. "But not until I put a new wrapping on this."

"Thanks. It feels better."

Amanda pulled off the gauze and studied my arm. "Looks better, too, but"—she eyed me with suspicion—"I think we'll keep it wrapped another week. Just in case."

I nodded.

Amanda pointed her finger as if she was about to say something; her brow wrinkled as though she was thinking real hard. Then she pointed back to the food. "Blue already ate his. It's cafeteria food, so it's not great. But it's hot, and that's worth something."

"Thanks," I said, turning away and wishing for a toothbrush.

"Professor." She patted my arm. "This might scar—for life. You did a real number on it. I told the doctor about it, and he said you either need to leave it alone or get used to wearing long sleeves in public."

"What else did the doctor say?" I said looking at the bandage and letting my nose filter the air of Betadine fumes.

Amanda hesitated. "He said that you need to quit trying to rub the skin off your arm, and for me to tell him if you don't."

I nodded and looked back at Maggie. Without looking at Amanda, I said, "Amos told me about you getting kidnapped." I paused. "I didn't know." I looked up at her. "I'm sorry."

Without batting an eye, she said, "Me too." Then she laughed. "I'm sorry 'most every day."

"Why?" I asked. "Because of the baby?"

"No! Heavens, no." She tilted her head and patted her tummy, and her eyebrows drew close together. "It's not his fault, Professor. He didn't have anything to do with it. Two wrongs don't make one right." She tilted her head further, as though she couldn't understand the look on my face. "I'm sorry for those guys, whoever and wherever they are. They may not ever have to face me, or my dad, or even Big Amos, although I hope he catches them, but one way or another, this life or the next, their time will come. God knows. And to answer your next question, no, I don't hate them. And I certainly don't hate this little boy here."

"But . . . " I didn't know how to ask it.

"But what?" She smiled. "Yes, Professor, if you need to hear me say it. Remember, I'm training to be a nurse. They did what they could to make sure that I would not get pregnant, but my body didn't know I wasn't supposed to get pregnant. By the time they got me to the hospital, my body had already done what it was made to do."

I wanted to ask the next question, but I didn't have to.

"No, Professor. That was never an option. Not because of my dad, or his church, or anything like that. There was no pressure there. I made up my own mind. And no, I don't have some crazy wish to be one of the single mothers that I read about in the paper. I have no desire to become a statistic. At least, that one. I had hoped to do this the traditional way." She smiled again. "You know: a wedding, white gown, handsome man, and then the child thing. But . . . " She shrugged her shoulders. "I'll have to wait on that. He's out there. He's just got to find us."

She walked up next to the bed and patted Maggie's feet.

"Can I ask one more question?" I asked.

"Sure. I've been doing all the talking."

"You don't seem mad."

"Professor, that's a statement, not a question."

I smiled. "Okay, why then? Why aren't you standing out there on the front lawn, shaking your hand at the sky?"

Amanda shook her head. "Professor, God knows how I feel. I tell Him all the time." She raised her eyebrows and smiled. "How do you think I made it this far?" She looked out the window.

"I spent a few weeks pretty mad. We argued. I screamed a lot. But what good is it going to do? Yelling won't make me un-pregnant, won't catch those two guys, and won't give me back what I lost. Maybe it's my daddy in me, but I think that if we could give God a choice, He'd prefer that we scream and argue rather than say nothing at all. And believe me, Professor, I've done my screaming." Amanda stood and put her hand on her hip. "Now, it's time to do my living. Although—" She batted her eyes and smiled slyly. "I keep the lines open."

She was quiet for a moment, then stuck her point-making finger in the air. "Professor, you didn't ask, but I'm going to tell you . . . at least this is what I'm banking on. If God is who He says He is, then He's big enough to handle my ranting and raving." She paused again. "And all my questions."

I held Maggie's hand and kept my mouth shut.

Amanda patted Maggs's foot again, turned, and walked to the door. "Professor?" she said.

"Yes?" I looked up at her.

"I probably talk more than I should, but you asked." She smiled again, placing one hand on the door and resting one leg, bending it at the knee. "What I really want to say is this: I'm just talking about me. I know other people have had tough times, too, but you asked, and I told you."

I heard a shuffle, and when I looked up, she was gone. Blue licked my knee, and the plate of steaming eggs, sausage, and toast began to smell real good. Maggie's feeding bag was half-empty, so we ate in silence.

At a few minutes before nine, I kissed her forehead, checked to make sure her socks were pulled up, folded Blue's blanket, and left for school. Walking down the hall, I realized how thickly Amanda had wrapped my arm. It looked like a billy club. Judging by the size and thickness of the bandage, it'd take thirty minutes just to cut it off.

*chapter twenty*

THANKSGIVING WEEKEND I WAS ALONE, PARKED ON
the front porch and sniffing the air for the smell of turkey.
There was none, only a lone fireplace somewhere south of my
rocker. In my lap sat my students' research papers, which they
had placed in my box by 5:00 PM the day before. My hope was
to grade them over the four-day break and return them the
next week, allowing the students the remaining three weeks
of the semester to rewrite and make corrections.

In teaching my previous seven classes, I had developed a
method for reading papers. I thought it helped bring fairness
to the whole process. When starting a paper, I didn't look at
the name until after I'd given it a grade. Also, I read each one

twice. The process helped keep me honest. Sometimes, if I'm familiar with a student's topic, then I know whose I'm reading, but most times I have no idea.

Rocking with the rhythm of the corn, my eyes were focused on four particular research papers. They stuck out not because of their poor quality, but because they were good, real good. Even excellent.

After the second read, I was still impressed, but I had some suspicions. Then I looked at the names. No way. Not this year, not these guys, not anytime soon. I finished reading the rest of the papers a second time and spent Sunday and Monday thinking it over.

The answer was simple, but that was just the problem. *Do I question four students about their papers, accuse them of plagiarism, and hope I get a confession? I'm the teacher, that's my job. I think they're guilty. No, I know they're guilty. It's a nonissue. They're gone. It's out of my hands. School policy.*

It's not that easy.

Some students think that the teacher is paid by their tuition and consequently owes them something—as if showing up to class is admirable and completing assignments is optional. They're not all like that. I do have real students, the kind you hope you discover. Because that's what teachers do. We discover, or uncover, kids.

I spent the weekend thinking about my fibbing four. They weren't even discreet about it. A voice inside my head told me that it is not uncommon for a student to sue a teacher for such an accusation. It happens.

To be honest, there were two voices inside of me. One said, *Just give 'em back. Forget it. You really don't care. They're only cheating themselves. It's their future. You've got enough on your plate.* The other said, *Wait a minute, what are you doing?*

That second voice was the tough one. I fought it. *Hey, I'm just an adjunct. These kids will never see me again. All they want is a grade, and all I want is to get out of there and pay my bills.* But I knew that wasn't really true.

I sat on the porch, rocking, reading, and making absolutely certain. It wasn't too hard. In sum, I had four papers and four lives handed to me on a silver platter.

MY STUDENTS FILED INTO CLASS, AND I HANDED OUT THE papers, all except the four. I looked at those students and said, "Your papers were really good. Actually, they were great. You four hang out after class. I'd like to talk to you."

That was enough to quiet them for the remainder of class. Not one uttered a single peep. Marvin chewed on his lip, Russell looked out the window, and Eugene and Alan shifted their minds into high gear.

Class ended, the rest filed out, and my fib-four sat mumbling and tongue-tied in front and around me. They tried to pass over the uneasiness.

I said, "Guys, your papers were great, which is why you're sitting here. I want you to tell me about them."

Marvin spoke up. "Well, ain't you gonna give 'em back?"

"No, not yet. I want to ask you some questions first." I had the papers in my hand and was nervously but slowly shuffling them like a deck of cards.

"We'll get to that," I said. "Eugene, let's start with you."

Eugene was intelligent. He had a good sense of humor but was also curious and usually made a good contribution to my class. I liked him. It was evident that people respected him, because they listened to what he had to say.

Eugene tossed his head, slipped down in his chair, and gave me his best attitude-look, which said, *All right, but I ain't done nothing wrong.*

"Eugene, tell me about your paper. I'm impressed. It's really good. Just tell me about it."

"It's been a long time since I wrote it. I don' remembuh much. Whatchoo wanna know?"

He threw the slang in to get over his uneasiness, I knew, because he could pretend to speak like a Rhodes scholar when the urge hit him.

"Well, just tell me where you got the idea."

"I don't remember, but I asked you a few weeks ago if I could write about these two poems, and you said I could."

"I remember. All right, how about this: explain your thesis." Silence.

"Well . . . explain your conclusions?"

"I don't know. It's been a long time since I wrote it." Whenever Eugene's mouth moved, his hands followed. His hands were starting to come alive as I asked him more questions.

The others began to get uncomfortable as they wrestled with how they might answer these same questions.

"Well . . . tell me what poems you used. What are the titles?"

"I can't remember, but one is about a ship and the other is about. . . ."

"Who is the author?"

"Dickinson, um . . . Emily."

"Good. Now, why these poems?"

Silence.

"Okay, you hold on to that. I'll come back to you."

Eugene breathed, but it was not an easy breath. His head was turning, and I could see that entrepreneurial side kick in. He was thinking about how he could make a deal.

I turned to Marvin. "Marvin . . . "

I had learned a few things about Marvin. He was the most highly recruited freshman Digs had ever signed. He'd probably enter the draft at the end of his sophomore year. If he stayed healthy, he could go all the way. Aside from football, he had a great sense of humor, always made me laugh, and I enjoyed having him in class.

About six weeks ago, I was in midlecture, and Marvin was gabbing away with anybody who would listen. I stopped in the middle of a sentence, looked him square in the face, and said in a tone he had not heard before, "Marvin, what's the one thing all great cornerbacks have to have to play in the NFL?"

Real quick, it got pin-drop quiet. Marvin laughed, cocked his head back, and said, "Quick feet, they all gotta have quick feet." He looked around the class, proud and looking for support for what he knew was the right answer. Eugene gave him a high-five. He leaned back in his chair.

I said, "No, there are a lot of guys who can run a 4.3 but aren't in the NFL. It's not quick feet."

Marvin sat up.

I turned back to the class and said, "Can anybody help Marvin? What is the one thing that all great defensive backs have to have in order to play in the NFL?"

It was quiet in my classroom. Then slowly students chipped in, "Good hands," "Size," "Like to hit," "Good eyes."

"Nope," I said, "that's not the one thing." I looked back at Marvin.

He looked up, slouched a little, and said kind of quietly, "They gotta listen."

"That's right, Marvin. Dion Sanders was one of the greatest to play the game not because he ran a 4.2, but because he knew how to listen. Marvin, I want you to learn to listen in my classroom. You with me?"

Since then, Marvin has listened more than he has talked. He's even asked a few questions. Now I looked at him, but he never gave me the chance to ask the question.

He pointed at his paper. "Professuh Styles, I wrote my papuh."

"Okay, then tell me about it. What's your thesis?"

"I don' remembuh, but I wro' my papuh." Like Eugene, he was using slang to cover up what he couldn't hide.

"Okay, here, on page one." I opened his paper and pointed to the first paragraph. "You talk about necromantic lust. What is necromantic lust?"

"Necromani' whut?"

"Ne-cro-man-tic lust. You use it right here in this sentence, which, I think, is your thesis."

Marvin squirmed, kind of flung his head, half-grunted, and slouched.

"Okay, here." I pointed again. "You talk about Aristotelian philosophy. That's a pretty broad topic, so let's just talk about his metaphysics."

"His meta-what?" Marvin's voice got high-pitched.

"His me-ta-phy-sics."

Silence. The other three were motionless. The heaters in the room were really working. On top of that, I noticed that my heart was pounding at a pretty good pace. Any louder and they'd be able to hear it. Somebody's foot shuffled on the dusty floor.

"Professuh Styles, I wro' my papuh, I jus' can' remembuh ri' now. But I wro' dit."

"Okay, then let's start over. What's your thesis?"

Silence.

"What's your conclusion?"

Silence.

"What's your title?"

Deathly silence.

"Okay, you think, and I'll go on to Alan."

Alan was always early to class. Always did his homework. Never caused a problem. Asked some pretty good questions and never talked out of turn. Even raised his hand. He braided his hair into about ten braids and wanted to go to work with his brother when he got out of school. I liked him.

He looked like he came up tough but also looked like he came up honest.

Alan's paper was the only one of the four that struck me as slightly different. There was no way he had written it—the language was too clean—but I did believe that he had typed it.

"Alan, tell me about your paper."

He launched into some of the specifics of his paper, relaying to me the highlights. Three minutes later, he finished speaking and rested his hands on the tabletop. His eyes told me he wasn't guilty, but they didn't necessarily say he was innocent either.

"Okay, what does this word mean?" It was a scientific term, and I can't begin to remember how to spell it. I had no idea what it meant. Neither did he.

"Okay, how did you organize your ideas?"

Silence.

"Okay, where did you get this information?"

"In a book."

"Well, you don't cite it, so how am I to know where it comes from? It's obvious that you've done some good research here. Your language is clean, but I just don't know where you got your ideas."

Alan must have had a poor grammar-school experience, because his written use of the English language was horrendous. Judging by his prior two essays, I know there was no way on God's green earth that he had written a single word of this, other than his name.

When I first read his paper, I saw quickly that he had given me what he thought I wanted. What he didn't realize, what none of them realized, was that I would work with each person from his starting point, not mine. They didn't know that. And they sure didn't want to believe it. Maybe that was my fault. Maybe that was the reason the five of us weren't down in the department chair's office right then.

"Okay, what does this sentence mean?" I read the sentence and then looked at him.

"Well, it mean dat de thing dey talkin' 'bout der is only foun' in space, and when it mix wit d'other elemen's, then it have dis effect." Alan was no dummy. He had a good head on his shoulders, and he knew his topic. He understood what was said; he just could never say it the way it was written.

"Then why not tell me like that rather than the way it is written here?"

Alan's eyes got real big, and he pointed at the paper. "Dat souns bettuh. And you'da graded me lowuh lik' you dun on de utter papuhs."

"Well, if that's the case, then who said it? I don't know, because you don't give anyone credit for saying it."

"I say it."

"Well, the way you just explained it and the way you wrote it here are two very different things."

Alan was quiet, and his forehead wrinkled.

"Okay, you hold on to that, and I'll go on to Russell."

At this point in the year, Russell had become my favorite. I know I'm not supposed to have favorites, or at least I shouldn't admit it. But Russell was a leader. Had it written all over his body. He was soft-spoken, kind, funny, curious, he cared about my class, and until now, I think he liked me.

"Russell, tell me about your essay." By this time, Russell knew the drill.

"Well, it's 'bout television and its impac' on kids."

"Great, tell me more."

Russell thought, and then he said, "Well, my sistuh helped me do som' research."

"That's fine. I told you to get help if you needed it. Now tell me more about your paper."

Silence. Eugene and Marvin had had just about enough of this, and their attitudes were feeding off each other. Eugene piped in, "I wrote my paper a long time ago, but I wrote it."

"Okay, while Russell is thinking, we'll start over. Eugene, tell me about your paper." I went through the whole thing again. And yes, I was more worried and more scared. I was losing, or at least getting nowhere, which was losing. I was also getting somewhat mad.

Finally I put the papers down. "Guys, does anyone in this room have anything he wants to tell me? Anything at all?"

The silence was thick. I started over.

"Eugene. Tell me about these two poems. What kind of analysis do you perform?"

Silence. But their nonverbal communication spoke volumes, and a consensus was beginning to develop. I could tell they had realized that if they all ganged up on me, they'd have a better chance of getting out of this than if they just covered themselves.

Eugene sneered at me. "Professuh Styles, it's been a while, so I can't remember it right now, but I wrote my paper." He pointed his finger in my face. "I wrote my paper." He laughed uncomfortably, sat back, and slouched as if he had had the last word.

I turned again to Marvin. "Marvin, let's talk about your paper. Where'd you get your ideas?"

Marvin slumped, threw his head in a show of disgust, grunted again, and looked out the window.

"Alan, can you give me a good reason why the language and organization in this paper are so different from your first two papers?"

Silence.

"Russell?"

I put the papers down on my desk, and their eyes followed. I looked out the window, then at them, and I asked one more time, "Does anyone in this room have anything at all he wants to tell me?"

They knew. I knew that they knew. And they knew that I knew that they knew.

Stalemate.

I looked at each one, not knowing what to say. Finally I picked up the papers and said, "Guys, you know what I call this." No one allowed his eyes to meet mine.

"You know what the university calls this."

Still quiet.

"Eugene, what do you call this?"

Eugene sat up. "Professuh Styles, I don't know, but I wro' my paper. I need this class to graduate. And I know I wro' my paper." Eugene was reaching. He wanted to deal.

I looked at Marvin. "Marvin, what do you call this?"

"I wro' my papuh."

"Alan, how about you?"

"I . . . I typed my paper."

Then I turned to Russell. "Russell, what do you call this?"

No movement. No talking. No breathing. They had consensus, and I had nothing. They could win, and they knew it or at least thought it possible. If everyone kept quiet, they had me.

I put the papers back down on my desk, looked back at Russell, wondered if I should play the only card I had. Very quietly I said, "Russell . . . what would your dad call this?"

Russell shook his head, closed his eyes, and said, "Aw, man, why'd you have to go there?" He wiped his big hand over his face, closed his eyes again, and looked down in his lap. His massive shoulders slumped, he took a deep breath, his chest expanded and contracted, and he looked me straight in the eye. "He'd call it cheating."

Checkmate.

Marvin and Eugene deflated like balloons. Alan sat quietly.

I nodded. "Thank you. That's what I call it too."

I sat on my desk, my legs dangling off, and they sat slumped in their chairs, looking at me. Long seconds ticked slowly by.

I turned back to Russell. "You need to know before I go any farther that you just showed more honesty and more integrity than I've seen in a long time. I have no respect for what you gave me, but for what you just said, well . . . I thank you."

I slowly turned to Alan. "Alan, what do you call this?"

He sighed, raised his eyebrows, and said in a meek, honest, willing voice, "Cheating."

I turned to Marvin, who had slumped farther in his chair. He could not believe that Russell had just given in. "Marvin?"

"Cheating." His eyes never touched mine.

"Eugene," I said as I turned.

"Cheating." Eugene tossed his head in disbelief. But behind that, his eyes showed relief. He was ready to pay the piper, but I knew he'd still accept a deal.

Going into this, I knew that to have any recourse at all, I had to have a confession. Full and clear. The problem with the game I had just played was that I had no idea what to do with the pieces. School policy is immediate expulsion.

*Immediate expulsion.* I tossed the idea around in my head. It's not that I thought the policy wasn't fair or just, but it seemed complicated that an adjunct professor should have that much control over one person's future. On the other hand, the only reason I had such control is that the four of them had given it to me. If I did what I was supposed to do, Marvin and Russell would lose their athletic scholarships, Alan would never be the first in his family to get a college degree, and Eugene would always be one class away from graduating.

At that moment, part of me wished I had just given them grades and turned the things back. The other part of me believed that the best I could do for them was march them down to the chair's office. But if I just washed my hands of them, what did that further? Hate? Maybe.

So I turned to them and said, "I'm just curious. If you guys were me, what would you do?"

The deal maker spoke first, before anyone else screwed it up. "I'd just let us rewrite it. I mean, you know." Eugene raised his hands, palms up, and his eyes got real wide.

"Yeah," Marvin chimed in.

"I can do that." I nodded. "Sure. But that sort of washes over the real issue here, which is respect." I waved the papers in front of them. "What you guys gave me disrespected me. You thought you could slip it by me. You also thought you could be lazy and get away with doing nothing. That's dissin' me. And I'm not willing to wash over that. So you're not gonna just 'rewrite it.'"

Marvin, seeing his chance, spoke up with his best display of attitude yet. "Well . . . you always make us feel like we can't write for you. You make us feel like what we write ain't good 'nuff."

Before "nuff" had rolled off his lips, I jerked my head at him and said, "Marvin, don't bring that victim-mentality stuff into my classroom. I've stayed after class, I've helped you rewrite essays, and I've come in here every day and taught you with respect. I'd be willing to stack my class up against any other class you've got. I treat you the way I'd want to be treated, and you know that. So I don't want to hear any lip about how I've made you feel like you can't write for me. You got lazy. That's all there is to it."

"Well, you made fun of me," Marvin said.

"Made fun of you? When?"

"The day I walked in wearing sweatpants, and you made fun of me."

"What'd I say?" I had no idea.

"I don't know. You said that I looked like I just got out of bed or something."

Then I remembered. He was right. I had said it. Although he had looked like he had just gotten out of bed.

I thought for a second. "Marvin, you're right. I did say it, and if it hurt your feelings, I'm sorry, but my insensitivity does not justify this." I held up his paper. "Marvin, I've seen you play football. You take your licks and walk like a man on that field. So start walking like a man in my classroom."

I turned back to Eugene. "I can't just 'let you rewrite it.'"

Eugene knew I was right. He had a good sense of right and wrong. All of them did.

Marvin found his attitude again. "Then you already made up yo' min', haven't ya?"

"No, I haven't. I have no idea what I intend to do."

"You aw'ready decided."

I'm no Freud, but clearly Marvin needed someone to believe in him, and he was testing me.

"Guys, before I go any further, you all need to know what I think about you. Win, lose, or draw, you need to know what I think."

I looked at Eugene. "Eugene, you're smart, people look up to you, they listen to you, and they respect what you have to say. I like having you in my class. You ask good questions."

197

I turned to Marvin. "Marvin, you've got a great sense of humor. You make me laugh, you're easy to be around, and I enjoy listening to you. I also enjoy watching you play football. You've got real God-given talent. You might even have what it takes."

"Alan, you're always on time, you ask good questions, and you contribute to my class as much as anyone. That's worth a lot. On top of that, folks around here say you can build or fix pretty much anything, and you've already built four cars from the ground up. That's a gift too."

Then I turned to Russell. "Russell, people like you, they look up to you, they listen to you, and they will follow you because you're a born leader. I have a lot of respect for you, not for what you gave me, but what you told me. And you don't need me to tell you this, but any idiot can see that if you stay healthy, your football career will continue long after college."

I waved my hand across all of them. "You guys need to know this. It makes me sick that you'd hand me these papers, expect to slip one past me, and then still expect me to treat you with respect." I got quiet.

After a long moment of silence, I said, "Here's the deal. I really don't know what I'm going to do at this point, but you've got a choice. You can walk down the hall, tell my boss, Mr. Winter, that your professor has wrongly accused you of plagiarism, and bring him to class on Thursday. Or you can write an apology stating that you plagiarized, cheated, and disrespected me and that you're sorry. You've got two ways to get back into my class: bring Mr. Winter or bring a written apology. That's all."

I got up off the desk, turned my back, and put my things together. They slithered off their seats and tiptoed out, never saying a word.

I drove home, my head pounding, wondering what I could have done differently. *Was I too easy on them? Too tough? What will they remember from today?*

At nine-thirty the phone rang. To be honest, I was expecting that. I also needed it. "Hello?"

"Yeah . . . uh . . . Professuh Styles, this is Russell."

"Hello, Russell."

"Uh . . . Professuh . . . I just wanted to call an' tell you that I'm sorry for what I did. I disrespected you, and I'm real sorry." He took a deep breath. "I just wanted to tell you that."

I don't know why, but at that moment I thought of Charlie Bucket returning the Everlasting Gobstopper that he stole from Willy Wonka. As he laid it on the desk, Wonka's hand slipped up, covered it, and he said, "So shines a good deed in a weary world." I've always liked that.

"Thank you, Russell." I tried to sound reserved. "I haven't made up my mind what I'm going to do yet."

"Yessuh, well . . . I just wanted you to know I was sorry."

"I'll see you Thursday."

"Yessuh."

I hung up the phone. I knew that Russell lived in the athletic dorm, and that meant that Marvin couldn't live too far from him. I wondered how long it'd be before I heard from him. The phone rang two minutes later.

"Hello?"

"Um, uh-uh . . . is dis Professuh Styles?"

"Speaking."

"Professuh Styles, this is Marvin."

"Hello, Marvin."

"Yeah . . . um, I just wanted to call and apologize fuh dizrespekin' you and treating you the way I did." Marvin was scared. He was also sincere. I had not heard this in his voice before.

"I appreciate it, Marvin." I left it at that. I wanted him to sweat, and I wanted him to worry. I wanted them all to worry. To feel the weight of it, right down to the last minute. Is that wrong? What's worse? Causing them to feel the full weight of it, or no weight at all?

"I'll see you Thursday."

"Yessuh."

To be honest, I had hoped that those two would call. Eugene and Alan were good guys, but Marvin and Russell had heart—at least a different heart. Their calling said they knew that they had really screwed up. I needed to know that. It also said they were worried. I needed to know that too.

Thursday came, and my foursome walked in early, more or less together. Each one placed a neatly handwritten note on my desk. I didn't read them but placed them in the cover of my roll book and waited quietly for class to begin.

Judging from their four faces, two days of uncertainty had worked.

Class ended uneventfully, the other students left, and I shut the door. The four of them sat uncomfortably upright in front of me—eager, attentive, and scared. Hands folded in front of them, they looked like the pocket-protector club. I picked up the notes, read each one slowly, and put them next to me when I finished.

"Okay, here's the deal. School policy is that I take this evidence before the dean, at which time he will immediately expel you."

The guys tensed up, and their faces blanched.

"But I'm not going to do that."

Each face relaxed.

"And because I'm not going to do that, here is your option. Each of you is going to write a new essay. The question is simple: What is plagiarism, what is integrity, and can you have the second and do the first? The highest grade you can expect to receive is a C." I raised my eyebrows. "So, if you write an A paper, you get a C. Write a C paper, and you get an F. That's the deal. Take it or leave it."

Eugene was the first to speak up. He nodded and looked to the others. "We made our bed, now we gonna have to lie in it. That's fair."

Marvin said, "Well, I can't write no A paper, so I might as well quit now."

I said, "Marvin, you do what you want to do. But there's one more part to the deal: all of you have to accept. If one says no, then I go to the chair."

Everybody looked at Marvin. Especially Russell.

He ducked his head. "I'll write the essay."

"Alan?" I asked.

"Sounds fair."

"Russell?"

"Yessuh, soun's good to me. Real good."

Marvin spoke up. "How long you want it?"

"Whatever it takes."

"Ooh, dat's the worst kind." He threw up his hands. "When you want it?"

"Well, I know you guys are playing a big game down in Florida this weekend, so I don't imagine you'll have much time between now and Monday." I looked at the calendar on my desk. "Today is Thursday. I want it in a week. If that's not enough time, then bring what you've written, and we'll work on an extension. Believe it or not, I remember what it's like to play football and study."

Russell spoke up. "You played football, Professuh?"

"I did."

"What position?"

"Tailback and"—I looked at Marvin—"corner."

He laughed.

"Marvin, I've seen you play. You've got speed. Good speed. Maybe even good enough speed. But I had one thing you have yet to develop."

"Yeah, I know," he said, holding out his hands. "Thinking. I got to think bettuh."

Russell wasn't done with me. "What happened?"

"Injury."

"Bad?"

"Bad enough," I said. "If I wanted to keep walking, I had to quit playing. That was my choice."

"That's a raw deal," Marvin chimed in.

"That's life, Marvin. It is what it is." I collected the papers. "Guys, you've got a week. And I don't want you getting any help on this one. I want independent thinking."

They grabbed their books and stood, not knowing what to say.

Marvin was the first. He stuck out his hand. "Thanks, Professuh Styles." His hand said thank you twice as hard as his mouth.

"You guys need to know something." I looked at Marvin and Russell. "You two have something I never got. You've got a full ride to do what you do well—play football. I walked on and never made it. You have. If I ever hear of you doing anything like this again, I'll pull this file, walk into the dean's office, and you're gone. And you two, Eugene and Alan, same goes for you. If I ever hear of the two of you getting in any trouble . . . ever . . . this'll be on the dean's desk first thing. It'll be kind of like a criminal record that only I know about, and it'll follow you until you leave this place. You game?"

They all nodded.

Marvin looked toward the door and then shook his head. "That means I got to clean my stuff up."

Eugene stepped up, stuck out his hand, and said, "Thanks, Professuh Styles."

Marvin was next. He stuck out his hand again and smiled

earlobe to earlobe. He would never admit it, but he hated conflict. "Appreciate it, Professuh Styles."

"Thursday, Marvin."

Then Alan. "Yeah, thanks, Professuh Styles."

"Thursday, Alan, and . . . you're welcome."

Finally Russell. He was breathing a lot easier, and his shoulders had relaxed. The thought of not having to tell his mom why he had lost his scholarship and been kicked out of school had hit him square in the chest. His eyes were watery. He looked down on me and said, "Thanks, Professuh Styles. I really appreciate it. Thanks a lot." His big paw wrapped twice around my hand; he could have crushed it if he wanted.

"You're welcome, Russell."

Russell turned to leave.

"And Russell, I meant what I said."

He nodded and left before the tear trickled out of the corner of his eye.

From the hallway, Marvin turned around. "Yo, Professuh Styles. Can I still pass yo' class?"

"That's up to you, Marvin. Mathematically, it's possible. But if I were you, I'd do some thinking on this essay. Think of it this way: you've just picked off a pass, but there's ninety yards between you and the goal line."

"Yessuh." Marvin smiled, performed his best Heisman pose, and skipped down the hall.

They left the building while the faint echo of my different drum resonated off my classroom walls. I had played my best, and Maggie would be proud, but I felt empty, not full. I guess that's because playing your drum only has meaning when you share it with someone else.

It was late when I got home. I walked into our bedroom, slipped off my boots, and left them in the middle of the floor where they didn't belong. Blue hopped up on the bed and shoved his nose under Maggs's pillow while I brushed my teeth.

Turning out the light, I noticed the glisten of Maggs's perfume bottle tucked behind my shaving cream on the sill of the bathroom mirror. I lifted the bottle off the sill as if it were holy water, turned out the light, and walked to my bed. I set the bottle on the bedside table, slipped off the cap, put my head on the pillow, closed my eyes, and breathed.

*chapter twenty-one*

TUESDAY MORNING THE SUN WOKE ME, AND FOR some reason I did something I had not done since the delivery. I walked into the nursery. I don't know why. Prior to that day, I had no reason, but that morning was different. I walked in and grabbed the baseball glove and football out of the crib. I tucked them both under my arm and walked outside into the field.

The corn was now very much dead, and the weeds had pretty much taken over. It was a couple of weeks to Christmas, and my crop was a long way past hopeless. Midway through the field, I spooked a deer that snorted at me and crashed out through the other side. I made it to the graveside and stood there quietly. A wisteria vine had crept over from Nanny's grave and started growing across my son's granite marker. I have no memory of my dad, but that didn't stop me from wanting to play catch with him most every day of my life. Sometimes, after Maggs would go to sleep, I'd slip out into the stillness of the night with my glove and play by myself.

My favorite movie is *The Natural*. I can't tell you why, there's just something about it. And yes, I've seen it a few times. Maggie makes—or made—fun of me when I'd plug in the VCR and sit down for the umpteenth time to watch the last scene of fireworks, the shower of sparks, and my favorite scene, the last two seconds. Robert Redford and son stand in a wheat field and throw a baseball back and forth while Glenn Close stands stoically to one side. I like that scene because maybe baseball is more than a game. Maybe football is too. Maybe each is a tether that links father to son before puberty and rebellion pry them apart.

Looking down at the grave, I set the football inside the baseball glove and laid them on top of my son. The thermometer at the house had said it was cold, but I never felt it.

LATER THAT AFTERNOON, I DISMISSED CLASS, AND EVERYONE filed out. I turned around, and Koy still sat in her seat. Her glasses covered her eyes and hid her face. She hadn't been in class for two weeks—since the football game—and she knew she owed me some sort of readmit. No readmit and five absences. That's bad. The school requires me to fail anyone who is absent three or more times without a valid readmit. The look on her face said Koy was either scheming or didn't know what to say or where to begin. Probably both.

I broke the silence. "Hello, Koy. You were quiet today."

"Professuh," she started, "I don't have a readmit for missing the last two weeks."

"Koy," I said, coming around my desk and leaning against the front of it, "you know policy." I crossed my arms. "Why not?"

"'Cause they don't give readmits for where I been."

"Why not?"

"'Cause they don't." She looked out the window.

"Koy, that doesn't help me." I leaned forward. "Can you tell me where you've been?"

"Yes."

"Well?" I said quietly.

Koy stood. She was unusually dressed: a long, loose-fitting denim jumper, turtleneck, and boots. She usually wore tight, flashy clothing that revealed more than it concealed. Not hussy stuff, but attractive, revealing clothing, which said maybe more than she intended. She walked to the front of the class and hung her head. That was unlike her too. She stood directly in front of me, her face about a foot from mine. Taking off her glasses with her left hand, she stretched out her right hand and opened it. She uncurled her fingers, and resting in her palm was a crumpled and sweaty piece of paper.

I opened it and read the name of the business silently. *Hillcrest Women's Clinic.* Across the bottom, written in pen, was *$265.00. Paid in Cash.*

I fell back against the desk. The paper was heavy, and I wanted to lay it down. My hand grew hot, and I looked at Koy. Her eyes were red, borderline bloodshot. For a few minutes we stood in the quiet. She offered no excuses; I asked no questions.

After several minutes of silence, I whispered, "Are you okay?"

She nodded, smeared the tears across her cheeks, covered her eyes with her glasses, and walked out of my class. The only sound was the smack and slide of her heels on the old wooden floor.

I walked to the window and watched her open her car door and start the engine. She puttered off, and I sat down next to the window, wrestling with the weight of that receipt.

*chapter twenty-two*

I WEAR COWBOY BOOTS MOST ALL THE TIME. THEY'RE me. No, they're not the most comfortable shoes ever made, but there's something about them. If you ever start, you'll understand. I grew up watching John Wayne with Papa, so my first pair of shoes was a pair of Dingo boots. Once I outgrew them, Papa had them bronzed and used them for bookends for Nanny's cookbooks. They're in the kitchen now.

Currently I have six pair, seven if you count my barn boots, and Maggie hates every single one. She only tolerates one pair, a pair of black Tony Lamas made out of Brahma bull hide. Good-looking. She bought them for me. The rest are a hodgepodge of whatever I could find on sale. They're old and beat up, and most are in need of new soles. If she could, Maggs would pitch them all—or use them as pots for her plants. She'd prefer that I wear nicer "dress shoes" when I'm out in public, so I compromised and showed her the Tony Lamas that I had been eyeing.

Maggs can flare a temper when she wants. When she gets fed up or frustrated with me, it usually comes back to the boots. "Dylan Styles, you are not John Wayne. This is not a dude ranch, and you are not a cowboy." Then she puts her hand on her hips and mutters to herself, "I married the Marlboro man."

If I came home looking like the cover of *GQ*, or a model for Polo or Johnston Murphy, Maggs would have my head examined. Just 'cause a shoe fits does not mean that you wear it. You have to ask if it's the shoe you want to wear.

The same goes with jeans. I wear Wranglers. The kind with the tab on the right rear pocket. Maggie can't stand them. She likes Levis. I keep telling her that Levis are made for people with low waists and funky-shaped bodies. Wranglers are made for real people with real bodies—people who wear boots.

I bought Maggs a pair one day, rubbed some dirt on them to make them look worn, and then slipped them into her drawer. She was getting ready to go work in the barn and pulled them on without knowing it. She got them buttoned and made it all the way to the coffeepot before she squealed, "Dylan Styles! You sneak. What is this?" Then she tripped over her heel trying to get them off.

I convinced her to wear them, but it wasn't easy. Now she only wears them when she's cleaning out Pinky's stall or working in her garden, but I did catch her going to the store in them one day. I didn't say anything, though, because if I did, that would have been the end of it. She'd have taken them off right there and never worn them again. Sometimes it's best to be quiet when you're right.

That was about two years ago. They look pretty well worn by now, but I think if she was honest, which she'll never be when it comes to those jeans, she likes them. They might even be her favorite pair. In my opinion, they fit her great. Lord, do they fit her. But she'll never give me the satisfaction of admitting it. Funny how that works.

A WEEK HAD PASSED, AND MY FIB-FOUR OWED ME PAPERS.

Marvin walked into class first, sat down, and began blowing into his hands. "It's cold as Siberia in here."

He was right. Winter had come on quickly.

Just before the bell, Koy walked in and quietly took her seat. Glasses on.

I lectured on the need to comb one's writing to get rid of filler and get the most out of one's words—to find some happy medium between Hemingway and Faulkner. They were half listening.

Class ended, my foursome dropped their papers on my desk with ear-to-ear smiles, and everybody filed out.

"Koy, may I see you?"

She looked my way, took a few steps, then stood at my desk as the rest of class departed.

"Have you thought about what you'll do when you leave here? Have you thought about getting a four-year degree?"

"Some," she said, offering nothing further.

"Well, in case you do, I took a few of your works, specifically a few assignments and a few journal entries, and sent them to the chair of the English department at Spelman."

"You did what?" she demanded, taking off her glasses.

"Koy, Spelman is a great school. It might be a good fit for you."

"Professuh, that stuff is personal. I thought you said you wouldn't show it to anyone."

"You're right. I did. I broke my word."

"Professuh. Why? I thought I could trust you." Koy put one hand on her hip, and her eyes filled with tears.

"Koy, you can trust me to believe in you. And I believe you have a gift. As it turns out, so does the chair of the English department at Spelman. This envelope explains that. Spelman gives a few writing scholarships every year to promising students. Scripps-Howard gave them a bunch of money, and it seems they want to give you some of it."

She took the envelope from me and read the letter. Twice. "Is this for real?" she asked with disbelieving eyes.

"Every word," I said, smiling.

Koy was silent for several minutes, reading and rereading the letter. Then, as if shot out of a cannon, she jumped up and kissed me square on the lips. "Oops, sorry, Professor. I didn't mean to do that." She kissed me on the cheek, grabbed her backpack, and ran out of class, screaming at the top of her lungs.

Two seconds later she ran back into the classroom, gave me a great big bear hug, kissed me on the cheek again, and disappeared. I heard her run across the lawn beneath my window and up to a group of girls crowding around the soda machines. After a few seconds of hysterical, noisy speech, they started jumping up and down, hugging her, handing the letter back and forth, and dancing as though they'd struck it rich in the Sierra Madre. I stood at the windowsill and wondered how long it'd been since I'd even felt like dancing.

# chapter twenty-three

IT WAS FRIDAY, AND ONLY ONE WEEK OF CLASS remained. I slipped on my boots and whistled for Blue, who was chasing a jackrabbit down a corn row, and we hopped in the truck. I hadn't been up to see Bryce in a few weeks. I needed to pay him a visit.

Bryce and I don't ever talk about what happened with Mr. Caglestock. We never discuss investments or money or anything of the sort. I just check in on him.

I skirted town, passed the amphitheatre, rambled a few more miles, rounded the corner, and bumped the gate of the Silver Screen, which as usual was locked and chained. I left my truck and picked my way through the trees to the fence just like ten thousand kids before me.

On Friday and Saturday nights, that place used to be the center of the world of Digger. One side was Sodom. The other was Gomorrah. I pulled the fence up, Blue and I slipped under, and we hiked the drive to Bryce's trailer. I'll never understand, and it'll never make sense. Bryce can afford to buy all of Digger, yet he lives in a trailer. At least nobody will ever say that he's reckless with his money.

At the top of the hill, approaching the ticket booth, I heard somebody inside banging on something. After a few more whacks, Bryce appeared with a hammer, a screwdriver, some Liquid-Plumr, and a car battery.

"Howdy, Bryce," I said, backing up.

Bryce took one look at me, said "Dylan," nodded his head, and walked back to the shed next to his trailer. Any greeting other than my name and a nod would be excessive coming from him.

Bryce was actually dressed that day. Which is always nice. Every time I climb that driveway, I prepare myself for the image of his naked frame. Not a pretty sight, but one you'd better be prepared to see if you're going to come up here. Today, he was wearing cut-off fatigue shorts, a T-shirt that used to be white, combat boots, no socks, and apparently no underwear. The hole in the back of his shorts gave that away. But let's praise progress where we see it. Boots were progress. The fact that they were laced up and almost polished was nothing short of miraculous.

"How're you doing?" I asked.

Bryce walked into his shed, dug around for something,

and began throwing odd tools and objects over his head. "Hand me that torch, would you, Doc?"

I handed him the flashlight, and he disappeared deeper into the shed. I don't know how Bryce knows about my education. I've never told him, and we certainly don't travel in the same circles. In the last eight years, I think Bryce has really only spoken to me, Maggie, and Mr. Caglestock. But one thing about Bryce, he may play the ex-marine out-there bagpipes-playing drunk, and he may be, but he knows a heck of a lot more than folks outside of his private hell give him credit for. Sometimes I wonder who's crazy—Bryce or the rest of us?

He came out of the shed holding an enormous fuse and sweating profusely.

"What's that for?" I asked. He had left behind all the other tools except the Liquid-Plumr, which was now looped through his belt and carried like a holster.

"Projector." Bryce stomped past me in a perfect military march toward the projector house.

"Oh, I see." Bryce had something on his mind, and no amount of conversation from me was going to distract him. "Well, then, what's the Liquid-Plumr for?"

Bryce stopped, looked at the bottle hanging from his belt, and appeared to be thinking pretty hard. "Oh, that," he said, and started marching again. "That's gasoline."

"What's the gasoline for?" Sometimes you have to keep at Bryce.

"Well"—Bryce reached the projector house and began

climbing the steps to the projector room—"if this fuse don't work, I thought I'd set it on fire."

"Oh," I said. "Can I help with the fuse?"

"Nope." Sweat was pouring off his forehead. His hands were dripping wet, and the chance of electrocution seemed pretty good. "I got it."

It was apparent that Bryce had not been drinking that day. He was far too lucid. Which was good, but also bad. It made for better conversation but usually ended up in an explosion, a fire, or both. If he didn't get some beer in him quickly, flames were a certainty.

Bryce slapped the fuse into a box on the wall and lifted the breaker switch. The projector reel turned, and Clint Eastwood appeared barely visible on the screen. He was lighting a short cigar and looking at the camera through squinted eyes under the brim of a weathered hat.

"*Good, Bad, 'n' Ugly,*" Bryce said, pointing to the screen. "I was smack in the middle, when the ugly guy death-marches Clint into the desert. Then, whammo, the fuse blows and hacks me off something fierce." Bryce spat. "Took me three days to find the second reel, and then the fuse goes blowing on me. That really chaps my hide." Bryce rubbed his fingers along the handle of the jug hanging from his belt.

"Yeah," I said. "I can tell."

"Well, how 'bout a beer?" he asked.

"No, thanks," I said, holding out my hands. "I'm on my way to town. Just wanted to say hi."

Bryce looked at me out of the corner of his eye. "Well, if you change your mind, *Rio Lobo* is showing tonight."

*Rio Lobo* is a John Wayne classic and squarely positioned in my top five. Bryce knows this. He must have wanted some company.

"Thanks," I said, nodding my head. "Blue too?" Never assume anything with Bryce.

Bryce looked at Blue, nodded affirmatively, and marched back toward his shed.


AT THE HOSPITAL, EVERYTHING WAS NORMAL. IF YOU CAN ever call a hospital normal: people walking around in white coats, poking needles in other people, or cutting them open and either putting something in or taking something out. Don't get me wrong. I'm all for hospitals, but think about it. In what other environment do we allow strangers to do the stuff they do to us at hospitals? Where the words "drop your shorts" or "take your clothes off" are not perverted or sexual, but routine? Everything from sawing the top of your head off to checking your prostate to removing a cancerous lump to inserting silicone in a breast. If a Martian came to earth, he'd have a lot of questions about hospitals.

Blue walked with me to Maggie's room and jumped up on the bed with her. He licked her face and hand, then curled up next to her feet. A nurse I did not know walked by, stuck her head in, eyed Blue, and was about to say something, but

I gave her a look, and she quietly disappeared. They had quit bugging me about Blue weeks ago.

Maggs's hair was combed, her sheets and socks were clean, the window shades were pulled to half-light, and Blue's bed was unfolded and spread in the corner. On the table was a cup of crushed ice. Not for Maggie, obviously. For me, the habitual ice chewer.

Amanda again. *Nothing gets past her. How does a girl, almost nine months pregnant, working the night shift, with ankles swollen to the size of grapefruits, do all this? I don't get it.*

I sat next to Maggs for an hour or so and brought her up to date. I told her the latest about Bryce, the farm, and class, and as I did, her breathing sped up. Her lips tightened and then relaxed. It wasn't labored or fretful breathing, but excited breathing. I told her, "Semester's almost over, and DJC hasn't fired me yet. Some of my students are starting to write pretty well." I looked out the door toward the nurses' station. "Amanda has come a long way, and this other girl, Koy, has a real gift. A born writer. My football players? Well, they're just like me when I took that class."

Her breathing skipped, the right corner of her mouth quivered, and her right index finger pointed and then relaxed. Blue laid his head across her leg, and I continued holding her right hand with my left.

"They turned in their term papers almost two weeks ago, so we'll be busy this week. I gave them a few days off to work on their last assignment. Some of them deserve it. Others, well . . . "

Maggs and I sat in the quiet, and I watched her chest rise

and fall with every breath. Her breathing was quiet, but deep, and her nostrils flared with each rise of her chest. She has a beautiful nose. I patted her stomach, which, the doctors say, has healed, and rolled my chair down to the end of the bed to put cream on her feet. Her nails were immaculate. I rubbed her feet, slipped her socks back on, and slid my hand beneath hers. Her right index finger flexed again, and this time it didn't relax. I sat a few minutes watching her finger. Her breathing sped up, and her forehead wrinkled. After a few minutes, her finger went limp and breathing slowed. I looked at her face, and the wrinkle had half disappeared.

I'm a shower person myself, but not Maggs. She has a thing about baths. If we could afford the hot water, she would soak for hours, draining and refilling the tub several times. Maybe it's a woman thing. I went into the bathroom off Maggs's room, shut the door, ran some warm water into the sink, and soaked a washrag until it was just north of lukewarm. Then, careful not to disturb her IV, catheter, or the plethora of electronic nodes, I bathed Maggie. I don't know if that's right or wrong; maybe I just wanted to see and touch my wife. Whatever it was, I know that if the roles were reversed, I'd want her to do the same for me. I'd want my wife's hands on me. I'd want to know she was there, thinking about me, and her hands could tell me that better than anything else she might do.

Every afternoon the physical therapy team, made up of two nurses who look as though they ought to be teaching an aerobics class, spends thirty minutes flexing and stretching Maggs's limbs. Sort of like an involuntary yoga class. Their purpose, while good, is to slow the inevitable atrophying of Maggs's muscles.

My purpose was a bit different. I just wanted her to feel my touch and know I was right there, holding her. "Maggs," I whispered, leaning my nose against her ear, "you can wake up anytime you want. Even if I'm not here. You can wake up anytime."

I toweled her dry and kissed her forehead on the wrinkle, and her finger flexed around mine again, like a promise. I stroked her hand, her finger relaxed, and Blue and I tiptoed out the door.

I SPENT THE AFTERNOON WORKING ON THE TRACTOR, which really needed Bryce's Liquid-Plumr. Not to start it, but to set it on fire. Late in the afternoon, the mailman came and left me a nice present in the form of the property tax bill.

Sundown arrived and found me idling back from the river on the tractor, pulling a trailer full of wood. I had cut a load, not because Jim Biggins had failed to provide his yearly supply, but because the weatherman said we would need all we could find. I stacked it outside, showered, and the moon reminded me of Bryce, so I grabbed my coat and headed out.

Blue and I slipped over and under the fence and found Bryce sitting in a beach chair, watching *Rio Lobo* and surrounded by empty beer cans.

"Hey, Doc. Have a seat." He threw a can of Old Milwaukee at me.

I chuckled. Why in the world a man that rich would buy beer that cheap just killed me.

Bryce stood, stumbled a little, grabbed a rusty beach chair, spread it for me, set it next to his, and then threw me another beer. I had yet to sip the first one.

It was early in the movie, and the Duke was buying a drink for two Confederate soldiers just released from a Union prison. Bryce held his beer high, garbled something inaudible, ended it with, " . . . John!" and chugged whatever was left in the can. He tossed it behind him, popped another top amid foamy spray, and then sat back comfortably.

It was cold, probably thirty-eight degrees, and Bryce had not changed clothes since I left. Or added any, for that matter. From the looks of things, he was working on his second twelve-pack and doing a good job of it too.

The movie reeled on. The Duke made it to Blackthorn, had a barroom brawl, picked up a girl who fainted. After some classic-John conversation, which was short on verbiage and long on body language, the Duke, a French-Mexican called Frenchy, and the girl headed out after the bad guys to Rio Lobo. Along the way, they stopped at an Indian burial ground where they cooked dinner, drank what was left of their Apache herb tonic, and called it a night.

Bryce was right there with them. When it came time to switch the reels, he was in no shape to do it, so I climbed the steps, switched the reels, fed the tape, and sat back down in my chair.

Bryce was out cold. Both literally and figuratively. It would take more muscle than mine to haul him to his bed, so I grabbed a few blankets from the trailer, covered him like a cocoon, and sat back in my chair with my third beer. The temperature had dropped some more.

The movie ended, and the methodical whacking and slapping of the end of the tape in the projector room woke me. I climbed the stairs, cut the machines off, and considered heading to my truck, but instead sat back down in my chair and found the moon. It was moving around in some pretty wide circles but finally stood still when I put one foot on the ground. The night was clear, my breath showed like cigarette smoke, and Blue was curled up next to me to get warm. Surprisingly, Bryce was a quiet sleeper. You'd think a guy like that would snore like a jet engine, but he was quiet as a mouse and sleeping comfortably. Another lesson from Vietnam, I suppose.

"Blue?"

Blue's ears perked up. I scratched his head and neck, and he dug his front paws under my leg.

"What do you think about all this business?"

Blue raised his head, looked at me, then laid his head on my thigh and took a deep breath, putting one leg on top of my thigh as if to hold me down.

"I'm not going anywhere."

He dug his paw back under my leg and nestled his nose in between his front legs.

# chapter twenty-four

DECEMBER 23. OUR ANNIVERSARY. THAT SEEMED LIKE another life and two other people. I had split a lot of firewood to buy that diamond for Maggs.

I've never met Maggs's mom, because her parents divorced when she was eight and Maggs hadn't talked to her since she was twelve. Her dad was a hard nut to crack. Loved Maggs, and me, too, I suppose, but he always looked askance at me. I don't think he ever figured me out.

When I went to see him and ask his permission, he sat across from me at his desk in a white shirt and power-red tie and said, "Yes, D.S., you may marry her. Absolutely. But I worry about you guys. It's a tough world out there, and you've never really decided on a career. How will you provide for her? Sometimes . . ." He paused. "I wonder if you have the fire in your belly." Two years later he died.

With the money I saved splitting wood, I bought a diamond, then found an old platinum setting at an estate sale a few weeks later. I had a jeweler put the two together and put it in a little box.

On a late summer night, Maggs and I walked down to the river under the moon. It was hot, but I was cold, and she could tell I was a little tongue-tied. We made small talk, but I was useless. Finally, on the way back through the cornfield, my palms were sweating so badly that I had to do something. I didn't know how to start. Mr. Stupid. I reached in my pocket, grabbed her hand, tried to say something and couldn't. So I just knelt down. Right there in the middle of the cornfield.

She giggled. I opened the box, and she lit up like ten thousand fireflies.

"Dylan Styles!" she screamed. "Where did you get this? Did you pick this out by yourself? What have you been doing?"

I gently took her hand again, as if I could calm her down.

Tears filled her eyes and she nodded. "Yes."

I slipped the ring on her finger, and to my knowledge, the only time it ever came off was on our wedding day. And that was just so I could put it back on her.

We walked back down to the river and sat on the bank, talking about life. Where to live. How many kids we'd have. Their names. What kind of flowers she'd plant in the yard. That was one of the happiest nights of my life. The next morning, as the sun came up over the river, we were still sitting on the bank, talking.

Finally we walked back through the field and called Amos. He said, "Well, it took you long enough."

We married six months later. That was nine years ago today.

MAGGIE WAS SLEEPING WHEN I WALKED IN. BLUE NUDGED her hand and then took his place at the foot of the bed. I wheeled the chair around to the right side of the bed, on Maggie's left. I sat and held her ring hand in my hand. It was the first time I had sat on that side of the bed since the delivery. I don't know why. Never gave it much thought. Just habit, I guess.

I gently slid my hand under hers and began rubbing her hand. Maggie's long, beautiful, slender wrist didn't look right wrapped in a hospital tag. I opened my pocketknife, Papa's yellow-handled Case, and cut the tag off. I stroked her fingers and turned her wedding ring in circles around her finger as we sat in the silence. Turning it, I noticed something wasn't right. The diamond didn't sparkle. I angled it to get it under the light, and still no glisten. It was as though the diamond had gone dead. Looking closely, I saw that a red film covered the top and sides of the diamond. Maybe the back too.

I slid her wedding ring off her finger and ran it under some hot soapy water. As I washed it, little flakes of blood caked off and splattered the sink below. I grabbed Maggs's toothbrush from the drawer beside her bed, loaded it with toothpaste, and went to work. Then I rinsed the ring under water that was so hot it was painful. Having scrubbed and rinsed, I dried it off. There was no need to hold it under the light now. I sat down next to Maggs, gently held her hand, and slipped it on her finger.

"Maggs." I gently placed my finger on the wrinkle in her forehead. "Maggie." The wrinkle disappeared. "I know you've got a lot going on in there, but I need you to listen for a minute. I need you to wake up. Let's go home. You and me. Let's get up and walk out of this place. Whatever happened is over." I paused.

"It's lonely at home. See . . ." I rolled up my sleeve, tore off the bandage, and placed her hand on my arm. Her fingers rested on the scab and scar of my left forearm. The wrinkle returned. "Honey, I need you . . . I need us."

I laid my head next to her hand, kissed her finger, and closed my eyes. "Baby, I can't get to where you are. So you're going to have to get to me."

# chapter twenty-five

CHRISTMAS EVE DAY WAS COLD AND OVERCAST
and looked like snow. It was probably just one or two
degrees below thirty, but who was counting? I think the
wind chill was a good bit lower.

Maggie loves Christmas. Our house always showed it
too: wreaths, candles, stockings, the smell of evergreen.
And she never let us get away with a fake tree. Last year we
put so many strands of lights on the tree that when it
came time to undecorate it, we couldn't. We ended up
taking off all the ornaments, leaving seventeen strands of
lights on a six-foot tree, and hauling the whole thing
out to the hard road for pickup. A thirty-four-dollar tree

and fifty-four dollars' worth of lights. Maggie saw it no other way.

"You can't have a tree if you're not going to put lights on it."

"Yes," I said, "but honey, we don't have a Christmas tree. We've got a fire hazard at the cost of about five dollars a night. Between now and the time we take it down is about $150."

She laughed, batted her eyelashes, and said, "I know it, but it's Christmas."

The "but it's Christmas" statement really cost us. And shopping? I swear, if the Taj Mahal were on sale and Maggie knew of someone who really wanted it, she'd figure a way to get it. I can hear her now, "But it was only $90 million. That's half off!"

Our house was always neat, but I did my best to dirty it up. I'd leave underwear on the floor, the toilet seat up, the toothpaste cap off, books right where I left them, shoes where I took them off, pantry door open. Not Maggie. We'd cook dinner, and she'd have all the dishes cleaned and put up before we ate. The kitchen looked as if we were never there. Sometimes at night, I'd get out of the bed to go to the bathroom, and I'd be gone maybe thirty seconds. When I got back, the bed would be made up.

Papa and Nanny's house isn't much. Take away my romantic descriptions, and it's basically an old farmhouse with creaky floors, a built-in draft, bowed ceilings, a rusted roof, and forty layers of cracked and peeling paint. But that didn't stop Maggie.

Our front lawn looked like Martha Stewart stopped by on

her way south. Plants everywhere. Colors? Honey, we got colors. And smells? If you get downwind, you almost can't smell Pinky. Maggie's thumb is so green you can take dead branches, give her half a cup of water, some mystery juice that she cooks up out in the barn, three days, and whammo! Blooms. I have seen that woman take dead fern, I'm talking crunchy-in-your-hand dead, and in a week's time it needs splitting and transplanting.

Maggie's absence from our home was more evident than ever on Christmas. I had built no fire, and I didn't intend to. No need to accentuate the obvious. The yard was in disarray. Weeds were rampant. The house was a mess. Laundry was, well, like the weeds. If I didn't know any better, I'd say a bachelor lived in my house.

The wind beat against the tin roof, and somewhere outside Pinky was making noises. Blue was curled up by the fireplace, whimpering.

"If you're gonna keep that up, you can go outside," I said.

He placed his front paw over his nose and looked at me out of the corner of his eye. His tail was still.

I needed to go to the hospital, but this day was harder than others. I showered, dressed in clothes I had worn several times, and headed out. Blue met me at the door and waited while I pushed against the screen. He knows better. Blue and I got into a cold truck and headed for town. Driving past the Silver Screen, I naturally thought of Bryce. I needed to stop in. "After Maggie," I muttered to myself.

We parked at the hospital, which was more or less deserted,

and headed in. Maggie was in her room, right where I left her. In the air I smelled Amanda's perfume. What was she doing, working on Christmas Eve?

I stood next to Maggs's bed and held her warm, beautiful, elegant hand. Lately, I've sat less and paced more. Or stared out the window talking over my shoulder. Maggie understands. I couldn't sit still at home. What makes me any different here?

Standing at the window, I heard footsteps behind me. Amanda was getting pretty big, and her walk had turned into a distinct shuffle. She was well into the full-blown pregnant-woman waddle. Which is beautiful.

I have experience with only one pregnant woman. I mean, experience that really counts. And I couldn't say this before, but few things are more beautiful than my pregnant wife was as she stepped out of the shower or stood in front of the mirror and asked me if I thought she was fat. Nothing was ever more alluring to me than the sight of my wife carrying my son. If you've never loved a pregnant woman, then you can't understand, but if you have, then you do, and you know I'm right.

I didn't turn around. "Good morning, Amanda."

"Good morning, Professor. Merry Christmas to you."

I turned and looked at her. "You look nice. New dress code for working holidays?"

She was wearing casual clothes, not the hospital issue I had grown accustomed to.

"Oh, I'm not working. Just stopped in on the way to my Mammy's." She paused. "My grandmother's."

"I got it," I said, turning back to the window.

"Professor, you got any plans for today?"

"Now, Amanda." I held out my hand. "Don't you start scheming. Blue and I are spending Christmas Eve right here with Maggie. The last time you schemed, I ended up embarrassing myself in front of your dad and his entire church. Not today. I'm parking it right here. But thank you for whatever you were scheming." I smiled.

"Professor," she retorted, "you didn't embarrass yourself." Her eyes showed excitement. "Daddy's been asking me to invite you to church. He said he wishes you'd come back."

"Yeah, so he could preach that fire and brimstone right down on me rather than just let it filter through the windows and drift a few miles down the road? No thanks. Your dad's a good preacher and a good man, but I'll pass."

My voice grew soft, and I turned back to look at Maggs. "Your father doesn't need my doubt in his church. Neither does your church."

Amanda's face said she realized she was getting nowhere. She opened Maggie's bedside drawer and took out a brush. She gently stroked and brushed Maggie's hair. As she did, it struck me how much Maggie's hair had grown. Maybe an inch or two.

"Where'd the brush come from?"

"Oh, I bought it. Got it at the dollar store." Amanda didn't look up.

I fumbled in my pockets and pulled out a handful of loose bills and change. "How much was it?"

"Professor." Amanda looked straight up at me and put her

hands on her hips. "It's Christmas Eve. You don't pay people for the gifts they give you." She dropped her head and continued tending to Maggie.

I sat down next to the bed and slipped my hand under Maggie's. Amanda eyed my Bible.

"I see you brought along something to read. Kind of dusty, isn't it?"

"Yeah, that's what happens when you don't read it," I said, looking at the drab cover.

"Umm-hmmm," she said, as if she had a follow-up statement but decided to keep it to herself. She finished her brushing as snow began to fall outside. Heavy, thick flakes started sticking to the windowpane.

We sat in the quiet for a few minutes. "How you doing?" I asked. "I mean, with the baby and all. What do the doctors say?"

"They say he's big, and I'm little. Say I ought to think about a C-section. So I'm thinking about it. I'm not opposed to the idea. I'm just not sure I want a zipper on my stomach." Amanda made a motion across her stomach and smiled.

I laughed. It was the first time I had laughed in Maggie's room. Amanda too. We actually giggled. It reminded me of Maggie.

Outside, the snow fell more heavily. Inside, the silence hung warm and easy. Not talking was just fine with all three of us. After a while, Amanda stood up from her chair and quietly slid it back against the wall.

"Professor, you take care of Miss Maggie." Standing in the

doorway, she turned to me. "And Professor?" Amanda's eyes searched my face and bored into the back of my head. "You don't have to be celebrating Christmas to talk with God."

I nodded. Amanda left, and Blue and I continued to sit with Maggie. After an hour or so, I rang for the nurse.

"Yes," she barked over the intercom, as if I had interrupted her nap.

"Umm, do you know where the Bible talks about the birth of Jesus? You know, Mary, Joseph, 'no room in the inn,' the wise men?"

"Luke 2," she said promptly.

"Thank you," I said, wondering how in the world she knew that. I thumbed for Luke, skipping over it twice, and turned to the second chapter.

Maggie had told me that her dad read the Nativity story to her when he tucked her into bed on Christmas Eve. Holding up the thin pages to the light, I read the whole thing aloud to her. When I finished, the corner of Maggie's closed right eye was wet, but her breathing was slow and easy.

Maggie was at peace. I placed my palm on her flushed cheek and felt the warmth of her face. For another hour, Blue and I sat quietly with her, watching snow fall on oaks and old magnolias. When I stood up at last to look out the window, snow covered everything in sight.

It was ten o'clock when I left. I squeezed her hand and kissed her gently. Her lips were warm and soft. One orange light lit the parking lot and cast an odd glow into the room.

"Maggie," I whispered. "All this . . . it's nobody's fault. It

235

just is." I brushed her nose with mine. "I love you, Maggs . . . with all of me."

Blue and I walked down the quiet hallway. A light shone from the nurses' station, but that was about it. The night nurse was reading the *Enquirer* and munching on a bag of cheese puffs.

While I was walking down the hallway, it struck me for the second time that I had actually laughed in Maggs's room. Amanda and I both had laughed. It felt good too. Maybe, under all that haze of sleep and heavy eyelids, Maggs just needed to hear me laugh. The last time I had really laughed was a few hours before we went to the delivery room—just moments before the bottom fell out of my life.

As I was walking out through the emergency room, I passed the counter where they kept the scanner crackling with police and ambulance activity. It served as mission control for the emergency room. For the waiting room, it provided some sort of entertainment. Over the static, I heard Amos's calm voice saying he was just west of Johnson's Pasture and headed to the hospital with somebody.

That was nothing unusual. During the week, Amos made almost as many trips to the hospital as he did to the jail. I used to tell him, "You know, Ebony, if things don't work out with the sheriff's department, you'd make one jam-up ambulance driver. You already know the entire lingo."

He never thought that was too funny. There it was, Christmas Eve, and he was probably transporting some drunk who had had one too many at a Christmas party, gotten in a fight, and needed a few stitches. Put me in Amos's place, and I'd have thrown the sucker in jail, slapped a Band-Aid on his face, and let him sleep it off. Not Amos.

If he was west of Johnson's Pasture, that meant he was east-bound on 27 and would be at the ER in about ten minutes. I didn't feel like answering any of his questions tonight, so Blue and I walked through the electric doors and onto the sidewalk. As I did, my feet flew out from under me, I went down, and I almost cracked my tailbone. A solid sheet of ice covered the pavement. Pulling myself up by the flagpole, I cussed, rubbed my butt, and hoped nobody had seen my tumble. Especially not Miss Cheese-puff. Blue stood a few feet away, watching me with suspicion.

The parking lot was empty when I started my truck. Even in this cold, the old girl cranked without a hitch. The older she gets, the more oil she burns, but Chevy made a good truck in this one. The fuel gauge was bumping on E, but I had enough to get home.

We pulled out of the hospital, I touched the gas, and the rear end of the truck slid out from underneath me, spinning us around 180 degrees. "That's twice," I whispered to myself. "Better take it slow."

Three miles out of town, I plowed slowly west on County Road 27. Several inches of snow blanketed the blacktop, and the temperature had dropped to twenty-eight degrees. With both hands on the wheel, and keeping an eye out for haz-ards, I let my thoughts wander. In front of me awaited an empty and cold house on what would have been our first white Christmas. Behind me lay Maggie. And in between, there was me.

A lonely place.

I wasn't in any hurry, so I dropped the stick into low gear and spun up Johnson's snow-covered pasture. Cresting the hill, I coasted down the other side, letting the engine RPMs act as my brake. About midway down the hill, I approached the railroad crossing, where eighty years before Chinese immigrants had laid railroad track for the Union Pacific.

The snow was spreading over the windshield like a blanket. I flipped the wipers to "high" but still couldn't see anything. As I bumped over the tracks, a light caught the corner of my eye. I was only going about five miles an hour, so I slowed to a stop on the other side of the tracks and rolled down my window. Looking down the hill in the direction of the light, I strained my eyes against the cold sheet of white that was biting into my face. The flash looked like a taillight, but down there was no place for a taillight, much less a car. I guess that's why it caught my attention.

I started rolling up the window when the wind swirled, and I caught a break in the snow. This time there was no mistake. It was a taillight, at the bottom of the ditch about five feet off the ground. That meant the car, or truck, or whatever was connected to it, was upside down with its nose in the ditch. I pulled to the side and left the truck running. Blue's eyes followed me out, but he kept his nose muzzled under his forearm and didn't budge from the passenger's side floorboard.

Stepping into the snow, I pulled the collar up on my jean

jacket, crossed back over the tracks, and stood in the emergency lane of the eastbound traffic. The taillights were sticking up in the air, creating a small red halo effect around the car. On the snow beneath it were the scattered remains of what looked like blue plastic police lights that were once strapped atop the car. Leaning sideways, I read the upside-down reflective letters on the back of the car: Colleton County Sheriff's Department.

I hit my butt and started sliding down the bank. I had intended to scoot down to the car, using my heels as a brake, but the cold and wind had turned the snow-covered bank into a sheet of ice.

My descent was fast and painful. I couldn't stop, slow down, or veer to the left or the right. Midway down, I hit a small embankment that tossed me head over heels and sent me tumbling like a human snowball. Gaining speed, I passed Amos's car and shot headfirst into the ditch. The splash surprised me, but not as much as the cold water. After a millisecond, the only thing I wanted was out.

I planted my boots in the muck below and reached for the bank. Pulling at snow and frozen grass, I kicked my toes into the bank, pushed up, and reached for the window frame of the car. The car was resting on the edge of the ditch, and every window was shattered. A few more inches, and water would have been pouring in. Dragging myself up on the bank, I didn't have time to think about being cold because I bumped the body of what appeared to be a big, limp man lying in the snow. When I found the face, it shocked me.

"Amos!"

His glassy eyes were looking at me. He was wet, and his face was a blood-soaked mess. Surprisingly, he was not shivering. Without saying a word, he slowly lifted his left hand, clicked on his flashlight, and pointed it through the driver's window. The light was swaying back and forth, and I could tell he was having a hard time staying conscious. Hanging upside down in the passenger seat was a mangled mess of long, black, wet hair. Amos's drunk party-goer, no doubt.

"All this for some drunk . . . " I grabbed the flashlight and scrambled around to the other side. As I did, the car slid an inch or two further into the ditch, and water started seeping in, filling what used to be the top of the car. I shined the light into the bloody and swollen face of the passenger. Her eyes were closed, and her arms were hanging limp down below her head. Brushing away the hair, I slowly tilted myself sideways, trying to see who I was looking at.

Amanda.

"Amos! What the . . ."

I don't know how long she had been hanging there, but her face looked blue and puffy in the light. The passenger's window was also blown out, and little pieces had cut her face. Glass was everywhere.

If she wasn't dead already, Amanda needed to get out of that car, because in a few minutes her head would be underwater. I reached up, put my hand around her throat, and felt for a pulse. It was slow and weak.

"Amos?" I said, scampering back around the car.

His eyes were still closed, and he hadn't moved. His breathing was slow, shallow, and apparently painful, 'cause he winced every time he tried to breathe too deeply. If I had to guess, I'd say he had two or three broken ribs.

Looking inside the car, I saw that the air bag hung deflated, and the steering wheel was bent where both his hands had been. In the back, Amos's workout bag was sitting on the ceiling-cum-floor in an inch of water. I pulled it out and looked inside, where I found a set of gray sweats. I wrapped the sweatshirt around his head and propped it up with some snow.

Amos looked at me through two glassy eyes that kept rolling back behind his eyelids.

"Hey, buddy," I said, tapping his face, "stay with me."

Like his face, Amos's uniform was splattered with blood, and the gray sweatshirt had begun to spot red. To make matters worse, I was starting to notice the cold, and my fingers were getting pretty numb and close to useless.

I grabbed the radio off Amos's shoulder and punched the talk button. "Anybody . . . HQ . . . anybody . . . this is Dylan Styles." I closed my eyes to think. "I'm at the railroad tracks at Johnson's Pasture. Amos had a wreck."

*What road is this? Come on, Dylan, think.*

"County Road 27. We need an ambulance! Now." I dropped the radio and grabbed Amos's head with my left hand. "Come on, buddy, focus."

The dispatch crackled. "Come again, Dylan. This is Shireen. Come back, Dylan."

I grabbed the mike again and mashed the transmit button.

This time I shouted, "Shireen, send an ambulance. Amos is hurt bad. So is Amanda Lovett. Railroad tracks on 27. Shireen, get an ambulance."

Shireen said something, but I couldn't hear it because I was too busy pulling on the passenger door. It was jammed. I gently patted Amanda's cheek. "Amanda." I patted harder this time. "Amanda, help's coming. Hang in there. Help's coming."

There was no response. Reaching for her throat again, I felt for a pulse. Still there, but no improvement.

The snow was still falling heavily. By the looks of the car, they had flipped over several times. I needed leverage to get Amanda out, so I checked the trunk, which was dangling open. I yanked out the tire tool, shoved it into the door crack, and leaned hard against it. The door still wouldn't budge, but the car did. It slid another inch or two into the water. I leaned harder and Amanda rocked in her seat belt, waving her hands back and forth in the air below her head.

"Come on! Open!" I leaned into it with everything I had. "Please don't do this to me." The door creaked and moved another inch and stopped. As I pushed, the car slid a foot farther downhill, pulling me down into the water with it, where once again the cold took my breath away. When I stood, water was covering Amanda's hands and was mid-thigh on me. I dropped the crowbar on the bank, placed one foot on the side of the car, and pulled against the door handle.

Nothing.

Growing frantic, I started banging on the door with Amos's crowbar. My fingers were frozen, my footing was bad, and I was running low on options and time. I began swinging the tire tool as hard as I could. On about the sixth whack, it slipped out of my hands, ricocheted off the frame, and spun through the darkness. Splashing in the water a few feet away, it was gone. I was now almost waist-deep in water with nothing to pull on, no footing, and I was losing control over my muscles.

Looking back inside the car, I could see Amanda's hands covered in water that was bubbling up against the top of her head. I don't know if it was the sight of Amos, cut and bloody; the sight of Amanda, blue, limp and unconscious; the thought of my wife, lying in that bed for four months; the thought of my son, lying in a cold, dark box; or the thought of me living in the middle of it all, but somewhere in there, I came apart.

It began low and guttural. Pretty soon it was angry, violent, and all I had. The snow had been beating against my back, so I turned to face it.

"Where are You?" Swinging at the snow, I fell chest-deep into the ice and water. "Huh? Where? You may be in that river watching over a baptism, and You may be hanging on the wall and watching when those numb people walk down and eat and drink You in every steeple-topped, vine-encrusted, pigeon-drop palace around here, but where are You now? For six days You left Amanda stripped and tied to a tree, You left me alone in a puddle on the delivery room floor, and You aren't here now!"

I kicked the water and screamed as loudly as I could. "Why won't You answer me?"

The wind picked up, and the snow fell harder. "Don't You

hang up on me! Nuh-huh. Not now, when I've got Your attention. You want my attention? You want my belief? Is that what You want? Not until You get in this ditch!"

I stood up in the water. My clothes were stiff, wet, and covered in ice. I leaned my head against the car, breathing heavily, and closed my eyes. The snowfall had stopped and the moon appeared over my shoulder, casting my shadow on the water below me. Listening to my own wheezing, I stood weakly, close to broken, and hanging by a thread. "Lord," I whispered, "I need You in this ditch."

The car gave way, slid another foot, and partially submerged Amanda's head. I opened my eyes. "That's not helping me."

I lifted her head forward and gently pulled her shoulders toward me. Her eyes flickered. I pulled on her arms, but she didn't move, and I couldn't reach up across her stomach to unbuckle the seat belt. I reached into my back pocket, pulled out Papa's knife, fumbled to open the blade, and then cut the seat belt across her chest. The lap belt held, so I reached up, hooked under it, and pulled. I knew I was taking a chance, but I didn't have many others. Amanda's limp body fell forward, and she groaned. I pulled her arms and head out the driver's side window, but her stomach was too big. I cradled her in my arms and rested my face against hers.

"Amanda? Help's coming. Help's coming."

Her eyes opened and closed.

"Amanda? Amanda?" I gently slapped her face, and her eyes opened, but her pupils were everywhere. "I can't pull on you. You got to kick yourself out of this car. Move your legs. Come on. Help me get you out." I cradled her tighter and tugged until she groaned. "Help me, Amanda. Please help me."

I slapped her face again. Harder this time. She groaned, tried to move her legs, groaned again, and then her eyes closed and she let out a deep breath.

"Nuh-huh. Not you too! Don't you breathe out on me like that's your last breath." I dug my feet into the muck below and pulled as hard as I could. I placed my mouth against her ear. "Amanda, you do not have my permission to die in this ditch. You hear me? I know you're in there. You do not have my permission."

I pulled again.

"Amanda, open your eyes. D'you hear me? Talk to me. Please don't let this happen."

Amanda hung limp in my arms. Losing my grip, and slipping further in the ditch, I bear-hugged her head and shoulders and rocked her back and forth in the car. Her hips slid, and something gave way.

"That's right. That's right."

Amanda's petite frame slid through the window up to her stomach. She groaned, and it was then that I realized that her stomach was rock hard.

"Amanda," I whispered in her ear again, "I'm going to turn you and slide you out this window."

She groaned, but I turned her anyway. Her sweater caught on some glass, ripped, and exposed her stomach. I dipped down into the water and lifted her shoulders and head up.

Her eyes flickered again. I lifted, pushed, pulled one more time, and she slipped out of the car and into the water.

Sliding out, all of Amanda's weight drove me down into the water. My feet lost their grip, and the water rose around my shoulders and my neck and then wrapped its cold fingers around my face and head. Pulling at me, it swallowed my head and ears. My head submerged, and I shouted under water. It was an eerie, muted explosion of anguish. I heard the swish of the water above me, felt the weight of Amanda's limp body on my outstretched arms, but my left hand told me that Amanda's head was out of the water. For an eternity, I fought the ice and water to hold her above my head, while struggling to get my feet under me. In fear, and involuntarily, I sucked in a lungful of water.

I kicked my feet into the muck below and caught something solid. Maybe a rock or a root. My legs shot us out of the water, and we landed on the bank. I was coughing, gasping, screaming for air, and Amanda lay on the ground, limp, lifeless, and without expression.

I tried to drag her up the ditch, but she was too heavy. I took off my coat and feebly wrapped it around her, but she wasn't shivering.

Resting my arm underneath her head, I leaned down and placed my face close to hers. Through the moonlight, I saw that she was open-eyed and crystal-clear focused on me. Her eyes startled me.

"Professor?" she whispered.

"Yeah . . . yeah. Hey, I'm here. Right here."

"My son."

"Don't talk. We got to get you to the hospital. The ambulance is coming." I looked back up the bank for those headlights.

"Professor . . . my son." Amanda gritted her teeth. "He's coming."

I looked down, placed my hand on Amanda's stomach, and felt the contraction hit. She groaned.

"What, right here?"

Above me, coming around the back of the car, I heard movement. Expecting Blue, I looked up, but it was Amos crawling to me with the sweatshirt still wrapped around his head. "Amos! Get to the road! Stop the ambulance!"

"Not coming," Amos whispered. "Road's too iced over. Sending a four-wheel drive, but it'll be twenty minutes 'fore he gets here."

"But she's having this baby now!"

Amos looked at me, leaning against the bank and breathing heavily, and said, "I know." He had regained his focus. "We were sitting in church when her water broke. We were on our way to the hospital when we hit the tracks." He tossed his head in the direction of the road. "Guess we're delivering that boy right here."

Amos closed his eyes and breathed as Amanda's stomach went soft again. She opened her eyes, they rolled back, and her head fell limp to one side. The left side of her head was cut, swelling, and bleeding a lot.

Amos grabbed my arm with his right hand and jerked me

down on top of him. His eyes were three inches from mine. Through clenched and bloody teeth he said, "Dylan, you got to deliver that boy right here." He winced. "D.S., this is your time, your minute. You hear me? I can't help you, but I can talk you through it."

He opened his arm toward Amanda and slid down next to her. "D.S., place her head on my chest."

I did what he said.

"In my trunk is a wool blanket. Wrap it around her."

I reached into the open trunk and grabbed the blanket. Then I slid off Amanda's underwear, the middle of which was soaked a deep red, and wrapped her, as best I could, in the blanket.

"Can you see the head?"

I shined the light. "No, not yet."

"How far apart are the contractions?"

"I don't know . . . a minute. Two at the most."

Just then Amanda's stomach tightened, she grunted, and her limp legs stiffened.

Opening his eyes, Amos asked, "That one?"

"Yes."

"How 'bout now? Can you see the head?"

I looked again. "Sort of. I can see something." I shined the light again. "Yeah, I can see the top of his head."

"All right." Amos wrapped his right arm over Amanda's chest and cradled her to him. Talking in her ear, he said, "Amanda, baby, I know you can hear me. I know it hurts. I know everything in you hurts, but you the only one can do this. Can't Amos or Dylan do this for you. You got it?"

Amanda made no response.

"Good, don't talk. But when it hurts . . . you push."

Amanda's stomach tightened, she groaned louder, her legs tightened, and the baby's head came through the canal.

"Head's out, Amos." I caught Amanda's son's head in my fingers, and a warm, slippery, sticky liquid coated my hands.

It was no longer cold. The moon broke through from behind a single cloud, cast a shadow on the three of us, and glistened off the snow. I didn't need the flashlight to notice the blood.

"Make sure the cord isn't wrapped around his head."

"How? What am I looking for?"

"Just run your finger around his neck and tell me if you feel a cord."

Shoving the flashlight in my mouth, I looked for a cord. I held the baby's head with my left hand and felt for the cord with my right.

"No cord," I said around the flashlight.

"Good," Amos said. "All right, Amanda, one more. This boy's coming right here. This is it."

Amanda's stomach tightened, she groan-coughed, and the baby's right shoulder slipped out.

"Amos, I got a shoulder."

"Gently, Doc."

Amanda's breathing was labored, and she was moaning.

"Make room for the other shoulder. Don't be afraid to use your hand. Make room. Pull if you have to, but not on the baby. You know what I mean. You've seen this done before."

I nodded. I ran my finger along the baby's back, slid my fingers in between Amanda and the baby, pulled gently outward, and the baby slid out. A wet, gooey, warm baby landed in my hands. Pulling him to me, I saw that he was blue, limp, and silent.

"He's out."

Amanda let out a long, deep breath.

"Is he breathing?"

I stuck my ear against his face.

"No."

Amanda whimpered.

"D.S." Amos raised his head, and the veins in his neck showed in the moonlight. "Get him breathing." His tone was urgent. "Put your mouth over his nose and mouth, and breathe into him. Breathe a full breath, but don't force it."

I cradled Amanda's son in my arms, placed his mouth and nose in my mouth, and breathed.

"What's happening?" Amos asked.

Again I pulled the baby's mouth to my cheek. "Nothing."

"Do it again."

I did. "No good."

"Take three fingers and compress his chest. Think of it like you're pushing on a roll of bread and you don't want to push through. Just mash it down."

I did.

"Anything?"

"Nothing."

Amos's eyes showed fear, and he kicked the ground beneath him. "Slap him."

"What do you mean, 'Slap him'? Where?"

"Slap the kid, Doc! Just slap him!"

I smacked Amanda's son on the bottom. He jerked, sucked in a deep, gargled breath, and screamed at the top of his lungs.

Bathed in the moonlight, we sat listening to Amanda's newborn son. It was, quite possibly, the most beautiful sound I had ever heard.

Amos nodded, "Nice job, Doc. Nice job." His head fell back against the bank, his eyes closed, and there, in the middle of all that, Amos smiled.

I grabbed the sweatshirt off his head and placed the baby on Amos's chest. Shining the light on the bank, I found my knife, cut the cord midway between Amanda and the baby, tied a knot, and wrapped the baby tight inside the sweats. Amos's big hand cradled the child while his right arm covered Amanda.

"Amanda, honey," Amos assured her, "this boy's fine."

Kneeling in the snow between Amanda's legs, I looked down and noticed the dark, sticky flow. "Amos, I got a lot of blood."

"How much?" Amos asked.

I shined the light. "It looks like Maggie."

His brow wrinkled. "Can you get us to the hospital in your truck?"

"Maybe, I'll check." Scrambling to the top of the hill, I found my truck quiet. No exhaust was coming from the pipe. It was dead as a doornail. I turned the ignition and mashed the accelerator to the floor, but she had seized up and wouldn't turn over.

Sliding back down, I whispered, "It's dead."

"Dylan, you got to get us to the top of this hill. That truck'll be here soon."

I carefully took Amanda under the arms and pulled her toward the top of the hill. Beneath her, the snow trailed red. Digging in his heels, Amos inched upward with his right arm and held the baby with his left. His head was bleeding again. As Amanda and I reached the road, I heard the low whine of gears and saw headlights climbing toward us. As I lay there in the road, in a pool of blood, holding Amanda's head in my arms, two men jumped out of the truck and ran toward us.

They quickly placed Amanda on a stretcher, wrapped two blankets over her, and slid her under the topper of the pickup. One of the men took the baby from Amos and then helped him to his feet, holding him steady. I crawled into the truck next to Amanda, and one of the medics handed me the baby. The other man grunted, lifted Amos into the truck, and laid him down on the other side of Amanda.

The first man looked at me and said, "Do you know her name?"

I nodded and said through my chattering teeth, "Amanda Lovett."

Just before the driver shut the tailgate, Blue jumped in with us. The man ran around to the front of the truck and jumped into the cab. We could hear the radio exchange through the open window between the cab and the back.

"HQ, this is 716."

"Go ahead, 716."

"Shireen, we're inbound with four. I need a blood type check on Amanda Lovett."

"Did you say Amanda Lovett?"

"That's affirmative." The driver paused. "And Shireen, tell 'em we need lots of it."

As our speed increased, I realized that the driver, whoever he was, was pushing the limits of what the snow and ice would allow. A dim light inside the topper shone on Amos's eyes. He was looking at me. He didn't say a word, but his eyes flashed to Amanda and back to me. She was entirely limp.

I shook my head. Amos's right hand came up and grabbed hold of Amanda's. The baby was quiet and still in my arms. His face was shiny and puffy, and his eyes blinked open and shut in the dim light. He appeared to be comfortable, and thanks to Amos's sweatshirt, mostly dry. A whitish paste covered him, and he was sticking long fingers in his mouth. The little guy was as bald as a cue ball.

In a few minutes we reached the hospital. The truck stopped; somebody raised the window, lowered the tailgate, and a woman in a white uniform appeared. She reached for the baby, I extended the boy to her, and she disappeared behind two sliding doors and into a host of people.

Two men pulled Amanda from the truck. They placed her stretcher onto a gurney with wheels and disappeared between the two electric doors. Pastor John and Mrs. Lovett met them at the door and ran along behind them.

The doors to the emergency room were crowded with people. Two large men dressed in blue smocks jumped into the truck, grunted "One, two, three," and lifted Amos onto a stretcher, then briskly rolled him through the sliding double doors while holding a towel on his head and shouting his vitals as they ran.

Back in the truck, I was shivering so hard that my head was bobbing back and forth, and I could not stop my teeth from chattering. Two more nurses climbed into the back of the truck, grabbed me under each arm, and lifted me onto a stretcher. They rolled me inside, down a hall, past a room with a lot of shouting and bright lights, and into a tile-covered room under a stream of a warm shower.

"Can you stand?" one of them asked.

I nodded.

They lifted me off the stretcher and set me on my feet. I was bent half over, my head hanging and my arms pressed against my chest. Warm steam filled my lungs, and warm water crawled down my back.

I stood.

One nurse worked to cut off my clothes while the other prepared some sort of IV and a breathing mask. "What hurts?" the first nurse said.

"N-n-n-nothing."

After five minutes in the warm water, he looked up from his cutting and asked again, "What else hurts?"

"E-e-e-everything."

He nodded. "Good. That's good."

# chapter twenty-six

I WOKE UP AND TRIED TO MOVE, BUT DOING SO WAS strangely painful. I ached everywhere, and a hundred nicks and cuts stung most every inch of my body. Clarity came easy in the morning light. I was in the room with Maggie, a patient now myself. Lying there, I remembered Papa kneeling next to Nanny. One strap of his overalls had slid off his shoulders, pushed down by the weight of a broken heart. His big, callused hands were holding hers—tenderness cradled in the palm of might.

I looked over at Maggs, closed my eyes, and said, "Lord, I'm begging You. Please don't take her away from me."

"Merry Christmas," I heard from the foot of my bed. I

looked up and saw a nurse dressed in white. She was not the answer I was looking for.

"How do you feel?"

I had forgotten it was Christmas morning. "Poorly."

"That's to be expected."

"How's everybody else?"

"The baby is fine. Deputy Carter is pretty banged up. A few head lacerations, but he says he'll live. Amanda Lovett is in ICU."

"Will she live?"

"We've given her six units of blood. But whatever you two did out there is the reason she's still here."

The nurse left, and I pried myself off the sheets. My boots lay on the floor, but the paramedics had cut them off last night, so they were useless. Maggie would have liked the sight of that. I unhooked my IV, grabbed another hospital gown from the shelf next to the closet, and threw it over my shoulders. I still felt cold, so I pulled another blanket out of the closet and wrapped it around myself. I took three steps and knew immediately that I needed some pain medication, quick. Hunched over, I walked down the hall, and a nurse behind the counter ran around to stop me.

"Sir, you really need to get back in bed. What happened to your IV?"

She put her arm around me, trying to guide me back to my room. I stopped and looked at her. "Amos Carter. Where is Deputy Amos Carter?"

She pointed. "He's at the end of the hall."

I aimed my face in that direction and said, "Let's go see him."

"But sir, he's sleeping."

"Then I'll just have to wake his lazy butt up."

She shadowed me to Amos's room, supporting me the few times I stumbled, and told another nurse to page the doctor. When I walked in, Amos was lying in his bed with an IV similar to mine. I pulled the metal stool on casters next to his bed and eased down on it. Thinking she had me cornered until the doctor arrived, the nurse left me alone with Amos. His room was lit only by a single dim fluorescent tube on the ceiling. His bald head was covered in a patchwork of stitches. It looked as though someone had played tic-tac-toe on his forehead.

"Amos?" I whispered. "Amos."

His mouth opened. "Hey, buddy."

"You okay?"

"Feel like I been rode hard and put up wet."

"What hurts?"

"Nothing right now." His eyes darted over his shoulder. "Thanks to that bag."

"You gonna be all right?" I asked.

"I'll walk out of here." Amos paused. "Dylan?"

"Yeah."

"You did good last night. Real good." Amos coughed and closed his eyes. "You hear what I'm saying?"

The doctor snapped his heels together and entered the room. I slid the stool back and stood to meet him.

"Mr. Styles, you really need to get back to your room. You are in no condi—"

"Amanda Lovett," I interrupted him.

"What?" he said.

"Amanda Lovett. Where is she?"

He frowned and put one hand in his pocket. "I don't suppose you're going to listen to me, are you?"

"Please, I just want to see Amanda Lovett." I wrapped my blanket tighter around me and raised my eyebrows. "Three minutes is all I want."

"Dylan, when you came in here, your body temperature was eight-six. Do you know how close . . . ?"

I straightened, which was painful, and for the first time I looked him squarely in the eyes.

He thought for a moment. "And after Amanda, it's back to bed?"

I nodded.

"I have your word?"

"You do."

"Come with me, please." He led me down the hall to a wheelchair. "Will you at least sit?"

"Thanks," I said and gingerly sat in the wheelchair.

Heels clicking on the sterile floor, he wheeled me down the hall, around a corner, and down another long hallway. After he punched in his code on the keypad, he steered me through two doors marked with lots of red reflective tape and ICU on the door. I have to admit, I was thankful for the ride. Outside of Amanda's room, Mrs. Lovett sat on a bench, her eyes closed and head resting against the wall. Inside, Pastor John knelt next to Amanda's bed, holding her hand with both of his and resting his head on the mattress. He looked asleep, but I knew better. This was a vigil.

The doctor checked my pulse and then left me at the foot of Amanda's bed. The tiny red flashing lights from Amanda's heart monitor bounced against the walls of the room. The continually expanding and contracting blood-pressure cuff around her right arm breathed in and out audibly, almost like an invisible presence. Amanda's eyes were shut, and she looked blanched and exhausted.

Pastor John spoke first. "It was a few hours last night before they could stop the bleeding." He lifted his head and looked at Amanda. "It seems my grandson's shoulders were larger than the space God gave him to come into this world. Soon after you arrived, half your class lined up to give blood. The other half arrived an hour or so ago."

He wiped away tears. "They gave her six units last night and two more this morning. She hasn't been awake since she's been here." He looked at me. His eyes were bloodshot and sunk deep in his head. He looked as if he could crack at any minute.

I shuffled to the opposite side of the bed, where I pulled up a chair, sat carefully, slid my hand under Amanda's, and rested it in my lap. This was the same hand that had brushed my wife's hair, slipped clean socks on her feet, painted her fingernails, changed her IV, bathed her, and checked her pulse. For a few minutes, we just sat there in the quiet.

I had done the same thing with Maggie a thousand times.

But Amanda's hand came alive, gripped mine, and held the grip. Behind her eyelids, she knew I was holding her hand, and in return she held mine.

Pastor John raised his head, and his eyes grew large and round. Tears filled the corners. When I looked up, Amanda was looking at me. Seeing his daughter's eyes open, and a faint smile bending her lips, Pastor John dropped his head, and his shoulders quivered.

"Professor?" Amanda whispered.

"Yes, Amanda."

"I heard you talking to God last night."

"Is that what you call it?"

"I do." She nodded slightly. "You sounded like Job."

Mrs. Lovett tiptoed into the room and stood beside her husband.

"I'm not sure Job used that kind of language," I said.

"From where I was sitting," Amanda continued, half-laughing, "I heard the whole thing." She closed her eyes again. "And I got to be honest."

"What's that?" I asked, knowing she had baited me and was about to tell me what she really had in mind.

"You were wrong about one thing." She pulled my hand to her chest, bringing my face just inches away from hers. "He was in that ditch with us last night. Just like He spent six days tied to a tree with me." She tilted her head and whispered, "How do you think I made it through?"

I shrugged.

"Professor, I'm not that strong."

I dropped my head and looked at the white in the palm of her hand. "Maybe."

"Professor?"

I looked up as a tear dropped off my lip and landed on my hand. "Yes, Amanda."

"You weren't alone in that delivery-room puddle of blood. He was there. Covered up with it, just like you. You were never alone."

I wrapped my hospital gown tightly around me and shuffled down the hall to the sobbing and grateful hysterics of Pastor and Mrs. Lovett. A nurse informed the ICU waiting room that Amanda Lovett was awake, and it erupted in a chaos of hugging parishioners and friends. Most of my students were there. Marvin and Russell stood next to the waiting room door, drinking Coca-Cola and looking at me. The tape across the insides of their elbows almost made me laugh. The blood of two athletes, flowing through Amanda's veins, would speed her recovery.

A hush came over the room as I walked through the sliding doors. Russell stood first. He met me at the door, opened his arms, and bear-hugged me, lifting my feet off the ground. Marvin raised his Coke can, nodded, and said, "Morning, Doc." His wide grin told me he was having fun.

When I arrived on Maggie's floor, my faithful nurse was waiting for me, and the doctor was on the phone. I entered Maggie's room and found Blue curled up in a ball, sleeping peacefully on his blanket. Beneath the window, Maggie lay angelic and perfectly still. I dropped my blanket and lay down next to her.

"Sir, you really shouldn't do that," the nurse said hastily.

"Lady," I said gently, my wife in my arms, "go away."

She left, and for the first time in four months and thirteen days, I slid beneath the covers and fell asleep next to my wife. Drifting off, holding back the sleep and fighting the medication, I felt Maggie's warm breath on my nose.

A few hours later I woke up to a clear, dark night. No snow falling. I don't know how long I had been asleep, but they hadn't moved me. And more importantly, they hadn't moved Maggie. They had replaced my IV and pumped me with some more fluids.

I lifted my head and looked at Maggie. I admit it, I expected her to be looking back at me. To be honest, I expected to wake up and see her eyes wide open and as crystal clear as the moment they wheeled her down to delivery.

They were not. She was sleeping quietly, and beneath her eyelids, her eyes were moving back and forth.

Maggs was dreaming.

I'm not quite sure where, but from someplace deep within, where the scabs are hidden, where the doubt can't go and the scars don't show, I began to cry. I couldn't hold it anymore, so I buried my head against Maggie's chest and cried harder than I have ever cried in my life. My sobbing brought the nurse running. She stood by the bed a few seconds, covered me with a second blanket, and left.

# chapter twenty-seven

THE NEXT MORNING, MAGGIE AND I WOKE IN EACH other's arms. Or rather, I woke up holding her in mine. For a while, I just lay there with my arm across her tummy. She had no choice, so I extended the moment as long as possible. I took her socks off and felt her cold feet rest on my legs. It was the first time I had ever willingly let her do that. After a while I sat up, covered her with my blanket, opened the closet, and rummaged through the clothes that I had left over the last four months. Dressing in the early morning light, I noticed that my hands were cut, scabbed, and sore up to my shoulders. I guessed the medication had worn off. I pulled out the IV and walked to the side of the bed.

"Maggs," I whispered. "I've got something to do. Don't go anywhere." Blue got up off his towel, stretched, and looked at me with a where're-we-going look on his face. I told him to sit, which he did. Then I held my hand out and whispered, "Stay." He lay back down, rested his head on his foreleg, and cocked his ears toward me. "Take care of Maggs. I'll be back." He stood up and looked at Maggs. I said, "Okay," and he hopped up on the bed and curled into a ball by her feet.

Pulling on a jacket, I walked out of Maggs's room and down the quiet hallway. A light shone from the nurses' station, but that was about it. The nurse was reading the *Enquirer* and munching on a new bag of cheese puffs.

"Merry Christmas," I said, realizing I was a day late.

She turned the page and never looked up. "It is? What's so merry about it?"

At the end of the hall, they had admitted an elderly lady with pneumonia. She'd been there two days and they said she'd make it, but her lungs were pretty full, so she would stay awhile. Anyway, her room looked like a floral shop. She must have been one of the pillars of some community, because her room was a blooming jungle. They brought in tables from the cafeteria just to give her more shelf space. Her door was cracked open, so I walked down the hall and silently entered. She was sound asleep.

I grabbed the biggest bunch of flowers I could find. It was a tropical arrangement at odds with the snow outside. In the greenhouse her room had become, she'd never miss it. I set the attached card inside another arrangement, whispered, "Thank you," and pulled the door closed behind me. Walking back down the hall, I set the flowers gently on top of the *Enquirer.*

The nurse put down her bag of puffs, licked the orange cheese off her lips, and studied the bouquet. Cocking one eye, she looked up at me over the top of her glasses. I just stood there, smiling, with my hands in my pockets. Careful not to disturb her lipstick, she dabbed the corners of her mouth with a napkin, moved the flowers to the corner of her desk, and kept reading.

"Hope you have a nice day," I said, rocking on my toes and heels and running my fingers through the change in my pocket like an old man in church.

"Umm, hum."

I leaned over the counter and tried again. "Hope those cheese puffs don't instep-clog your arteries, causing a massive heart attack right here when you're working so hard."

She took a deep breath, folded her flabby arms on the table, and slowly looked me up and down, this time through her glasses. Leaning back in her creaking chair, she folded her hands and considered whether to call security or just give me what I wanted. Finally, she relented. "Merry Christmas, Mr. Styles."

I turned to walk away, but she stopped me. "You going home?" she asked. I nodded, wondering where this was going. "Well, you can walk if you want to, but I'm headed that way. You might as well come along." I stared at her, hands in my pockets, remembering the sight of my truck stranded on the roadside. "Well, don't just stand there," she said. "Let's get going."

I followed her downstairs and out into the parking lot. At

the curb, her Buick Century idled up alongside me. She leaned over and unlocked the passenger side door. Between us sat the half-eaten bag of cheese puffs.

We pulled out of town, retracing the same route I had driven the night before. The air in the car was warm and easy.

Little snow had melted, but the roads were clearer and everything had a wet, glistening look to it. We made it to the railroad tracks, pulled off on the shoulder, and saw where the tow truck had fetched Amos's car and my truck. Only drag marks remained.

Pastor John's church was bathed in white, and in spite of what I had said, the blanket of snow really was a beautiful sight. Another mile and we drove into my drive and around the back of the house.

I opened the door and squatted down, resting one hand on the seat and one on the door. "What's your name?"

She smiled, tapped the name tag pinned to her shirt, and raised her eyebrows. It read, *Alice May Newsome. RN. Serving for 38 years.* She looped her finger beneath her seat belt and readjusted it. "My friends call me Allie."

"Thank you, Allie."

She nodded, rolled up my window, and quietly drove away.

I WALKED THE TREE LINE AROUND TO MY SON'S GRAVE AND down to the riverbank where the sunshine shone warm on my back. When I got to the sandy bank of the river, I stripped down to my birthday suit.

There I stood—a part-time teacher and sometime farmer, showing the first signs of weather and wrinkles, married to a woman who might never wake up, teaching dropouts, wrestling my pride, and looking into a future in question. I couldn't see beyond that second. But for the first time in a long while, I felt a smile on my face. I was standing on that bank like an idiot, smiling. Smiling! Yeah, it was cold, but I wasn't too worried about it. I had been colder.

The flow of the current was about normal when I stepped in. And the water was warmer than I thought it would be. I waded down to waist level and let my toes hang off the lip of the swimming hole where Maggs had taken her swan dive. Down there, the depth dropped to about twelve feet. I looked up at the bluff to my left and thought about our waking up in the middle of the late-summer night and walking hand in hand to the edge. About her stripping down, about her slender calves, graceful arms, the small of her back, about her soaring through the moonlight like Tinkerbell. Arms wide, feet together, her skin like porcelain. Then splashing into the black water, only to surface and let the water drip off the sneaky smile that spread across her face.

I saw us lying on the bank, watching the stars, while the warm, wet water pooled around us. I saw us walking back to the house, her shoulder tucked under mine. Swinging my cold hands, gently skimming the top of the water with my fingertips, I thought about that a lot.

Then I thought about my son, not too far from here, and

how the wisteria had grown across his grave. How the blooms were dead and gone but would be back.

Then I thought about the ditch and the night before. Deep down I was conflicted—an even mixture of fear and peace. Fearful, because maybe Amanda was right. And at peace because I hoped she was. If He had been there all along, then my doubt had no home and would be turned out. I realized that was what took me there, to that place, and it was the reason I was standing in the water.

I stepped off the ledge, took a deep breath, and buried myself in black water. The current swirled around me and pushed me to the bottom, where it held me while small bubbles rose from my nose and mouth, tickling my closed eyes. I saw Maggie, bright lights, the delivery-room floor, my son's face, doctors screaming, and Maggie crying. I hovered above my son's tombstone and the tops of the cornfields. Blue licked my face; Pinky grunted; the tractor idled; the river slid by, bubbling with yellow urine; Pastor John wiped sweat off his face; the railing creaked; Amos's bald head shone; the church bell rang; and Mr. Smiles beckoned.

Trembling, I rose, fell forward, and bit the bitter bread. I stood sweating in my classroom beneath the fans. Koy stared blankly through dark sunglasses, Russell and Marvin danced at football practice. Mr. Carter held forth atop his dog box, I walked the Salk, smiled at moonlight shining through silver hair, sat with Jim Biggins, rocked on the front porch, put my hand in the buzzard hole, saw a man in a dirty kilt with a chestful of medals, felt condensation running down a cold beer, stood in a deserted parking lot, laughed at Mr. Cagle-stock's bow tie, and heard the echo of John Wayne's voice.

I was in the library studying, writing my dissertation, eating take-out, selling my guitar, and wearing cowboy boots and faded jeans. I was on the front row of the amphitheatre, sitting in moonlight and listening to the wind filter through the pine trees.

Back at the splintery railing, Pastor John offered the cup to Amanda. "Baby, this is . . . " and then he offered it to me.

I sipped, and it stung my throat.

Standing next to Maggie's bedside, I heard her laughter, dialed voice mail, saw Blue lick her feet, slipped socks over her cold toes, saw Amos standing in the hall, touched the wrinkle on Maggie's forehead, sat with Amanda while she cleaned and dressed my arm, and felt Maggie's fingers gently touch my scar.

I swallowed.

It was dark and black on the bottom of that river, but above me light cut through the water like sunshine after the rain. That's when I knew. He was there. He was there all along. I pushed off that sandy bottom. Breaking the surface, I opened my eyes, looked downriver, and as far as I could see, the bank was white. On it, the sun shone brilliantly.

Standing in shoulder-deep water, I stopped to look at myself. I mean, really look. I studied my water-logged hands and the red scar on my arm. I marveled at my pale skin mottled with blue veins and goose bumps from the cold. And for the first time in a long time, I was clean. No blood. No blood anywhere.

# chapter twenty-eight

ON SUNDAY MORNING PASTOR JOHN'S CHURCH WAS alive and kicking when I drove by. To say it was loud would be an understatement. Blue and I were headed home, which was a mess, so I spent the day cleaning the house. Blue passed most of the afternoon staring at me as if I had lost my mind. Next I moved on to the barn, where he trailed behind me in disbelief.

Pinky was as protective and mean as ever. I threw some corn to her, and she grunted, crapped, and kicked the door of the stall. At the end of the day, Blue and I hopped on the tractor and idled under the oaks and along the river. Blue loved the tractor. We drove to the edge of the river, cut the engine, listened to the wood ducks fly overhead, and watched the sun disappear.

Back at the house, I cooked a dinner that looked a lot like breakfast. I'm not much good at anything else; Maggie could tell you that. Six eggs, an entire package of bacon, and some toast. I devoured it and then washed it down with percolated Maxwell House. The front porch was quiet except for the creaking of my rocker—a sound Maggie loved. Before me, moonlight bathed the cornfield, and a silent breeze waved through the rows of dry cornstalks.

I was starting to heal. A lot of the nicks and cuts were closing up, and the soreness was mostly gone. I guess people are like that. We scar, but in the end, we heal.

Amos didn't know it, but I had borrowed his Ford Expedition. I had my truck, along with Amos's squad car, towed to Jake's Jalopy Auto Center, one of those places where you can get most anything done. He'll fix your car, or better yet, sell you another if he can't. Consequently, he sells a lot of cars. I finished my coffee, slipped on my running shoes, and figured it was time to go get Amos. He'd probably had just about enough of that hospital.

I crossed the dirt road and pulled into Amos's drive, grabbed a duffel from his bedroom, packed him some clothes, and turned on a few lights to make it look welcoming. I would have cleaned up, but unlike the bachelor across the street, Amos kept a pretty tidy house.

The hospital was relatively quiet when I arrived. Maggs was asleep, as was Amanda, and the baby was sucking the nipple off a bottle held by Mrs. Lovett. The doctor, standing at the nurses' station, looked up from a clipboard and waited.

I waved. "Evening, Doc."

"You here for him?" he asked, pointing to Amos's room.

I nodded.

He considered that for a moment, then whispered something to a nurse. Looking back at me, he said, "Drive slowly. He'll be sore for a few days."

Amos was waking up when I walked into his room. I sat down and propped my feet up on his bed. "How's the head?" I asked.

"What happened to your boots?"

"They ended up on the emergency-room floor. A nurse cut them off me when we came in." I looked back toward the nurses' station. "So, what does the doc say?"

Amos shifted under the sheets. "He says I'm lucky to have been wearing my seat belt and even luckier the air bag inflated when it did. A couple more days in here, a week or so at home, and I should be up and about."

I threw his duffel on the bed, and his clothes spilled out.

"I was hoping you'd bring that," he said.

Amos stood gingerly, gained his balance, and said, "Man, this room is spinning." He leaned on me, I helped him dress, and we walked out of his room.

Amos looked at me. "I want to see Amanda before we go."

We exited the elevator onto the recovery floor where they brought people from ICU. Amanda was horizontal, but her head was propped up, and her eyes met ours when we walked into the dim room, empty except for thirty or forty flower arrangements.

"Hey." Amos sat down and gently took her hand.

"How you feeling?" Amanda whispered. "They say your head really put a dent in the steering wheel."

"Yeah, that's what happens when you have a hard head." Amos held his rib cage and tried not to laugh. "I'm okay," he said, "but I'm still taking a few days' vacation."

"You've earned it."

"What do they say about you, baby?" Amos asked.

"Well, I broke a few ribs, cracked my pelvis, suffered a concussion, and lost a lot, if not most, of my blood, but I'll mend. I'll probably spend a few weeks in here. The folks in Daddy's church and my classmates who gave blood have been just great. I don't think I can breast-feed, but we'll see." She smiled and looked out into the hall. "If I can get him away from Momma for two seconds, I might give it a try."

Amanda turned to me, careful not to move too quickly. "Hey, Professor."

"Hey there. How's your boy?"

"He's been here most of the day. Momma just took him down the hall to give him a bottle and walk him around a bit. She thinks he doesn't like being cooped up in this room." Amanda laughed. "I keep telling her that it's a lot bigger than where he's been the last nine months."

"You given him a name?" I asked.

"Yup," Amanda said, proudly raising her chin. "His name is John Amos Dylan Lovett. We're not sure yet what we're going to call him, but Daddy's already calling him 'Little Dylan.' Momma said that's all Daddy could talk about this morning in church. 'Little Dylan this,' and 'Little Dylan that.'"

Amos and I looked at each other and then back at Amanda.

"Are you sure you want to name a child that? I mean, he's liable to get in a good bit of trouble with a name like that." I paused and nodded. "I did."

Amos chipped in, "Still do."

Amanda pointed at the bedside table. "See for yourself. Even says it on his papers."

"Sure enough," Amos said, smiling. He read the photocopy and then handed it to me.

"Professor." Amanda looked up at me. "I asked Miss Maggie, and she didn't seem to mind. I hope it's okay with you."

I nodded and smirked. "It's okay with me. You name that boy anything you want."

Amos squeezed Amanda's hand. "Amanda, honey, I've got to get home, get in my own bed, stop the world from spinning, and get some sleep. I'll check in on you in a day or so. Soon as the world settles down."

Amos and I walked through the door and toward the exit. "That is one tough girl, Amos."

He nodded. "Woman. Tough woman. And I hope that kid never gets in trouble in school. 'Cause he'll have one heck of a time spelling his name on the chalkboard."

We walked out into the parking lot, and Amos noticed his Expedition. "Nice truck," he said.

"Yeah, well, the current owner is laid up and won't need it for a few days."

"How bad is yours?"

"Jake said I burned up the engine. When I get time, I'll go down and talk with him."

I dropped Amos off under a full, clear moon that cast long, beautiful shadows over the trees and his house. I went home wrapped in a warm, peaceful cloud of relief and reflection. So much had happened, I needed to kick back and absorb for a while. I sipped Maxwell House on the front porch, and Blue lay on the floor next to me, listening to the rocker. About midnight, I grabbed my coat and walked out into the cornfield.

Walking through the rows, I held out my hand and tapped each dry stalk as if I were numbering the posts on a picket fence. Papa would have plowed it under by now. After ten minutes, Blue and I walked out the other side, wandered down the side of the pasture, and paused underneath the big overhanging oak, where I sat down quietly with my son. His grave was covered with acorns and snaking wisteria, so I lifted a vine, brushed off the acorns with the palm of my hand, and blew the dirt off the tombstone.

The breeze filtered through the leaves above, bounced off the river, and swirled around my collar and back through the corn. It was gentle, cold, and quiet. And that was good.

# chapter twenty-nine

ON DECEMBER 30, THE WEATHER WAS BITTERLY cold and overcast as I walked down the drive to check the mail. It had been unusually cold in Digger this year, but this was getting ridiculous. Amos had borrowed his Expedition from me and driven to town to get some groceries. Since the accident, a bunch of women from his church had cooked him casseroles, pies, meatloaf, roasts, and more pies, but he had eaten all that already, and Amos wasn't one to let himself go hungry. I decided to spend the morning by myself, but when Amos got back with his truck I'd drive in and check on Maggs.

The chill wind whipped around my boxer shorts, dropping the temperature from real cold to even colder and persuading me to move quickly. I was standing by my mailbox, freezing and stuffing mail under my arms, when a Chevrolet Lumina with the words *Mike's Courier Service* on the side screeched to a halt behind me. I dropped the mail and turned to see who had just scared three years off my life. A sixteen-year-old kid, with more zits than cream could cure, hopped out.

"You Dylan Styles?" He was holding an envelope and waving it in my direction.

"I'm Dylan," I said, jogging in place and wondering if the hole in my boxers was open.

"You're hard to find. I been driving around these dang boondocks for an hour and a half. How do you live out here? This is Egypt." He shook his head and threw the envelope at me. Without another word he hopped back into the car, gunned the engine, spun the tires, fishtailed, and disappeared.

I jogged back to the house, dropped the mail on the floor, and took the letter over to the sofa by the fireplace to open it. It was printed on watermarked paper, embossed at the top, and signed by my boss at the college, Mr. Winter.

*December 27*
*Dear Dr. Styles,*

*Your teaching performance and student evaluations are exemplary. As a result, the DJC Board and I are pleased to offer you a one-year contract extension for this coming school year. We would be delighted to have you join our staff on a more permanent basis. If you so desire, please sign the attached, keep a copy for yourself, and return the other to me at your earliest convenience. I am available at any time if you wish to call.*

*Happy New Year.*

*Sincerely,*
*William T. Winter*
*Chair, English Department*
*Digger Junior College*

I scratched my head and looked down at Blue, who was studying me and pointing his nose toward the wind.

"Well, I'll be." I pointed to the letter. "Looks like I might get to teach after all. Go figure."

Blue hopped up on the sofa, put his head in my lap, and rolled over, sticking his stomach in the air. I leaned back, propped my sockless feet on the coffee table, and thought how much I liked the sight of my drum perched atop the mantel. I thought Maggie would like it too.

*chapter thirty*

By midafternoon, Amos hadn't showed, so I thumbed a ride to town with the contract in my pocket. I wanted to show it to Maggie. I stood in the cold for forty-five minutes before anyone passed me, but an hour later, the second car stopped. The driver was a young guy making his way to a party. He was eighteen and driving a 1979 Pontiac Trans Am. The same thing Burt Reynolds drove in *Smokey and the Bandit,* although my new friend had made a few alterations to the engine.

"Yup," he said, stroking the gearshift, "this one here's got the small block fo'hundr'd. So I bored it, stroked it, polished it, threw in some angle plug heads, a solid lift cam, couple of eight-sixties, and then I run the exhaust out through some three-inch headers and a couple of glass-packs. She's loud, but she'll dang near fly. I figure I'm pushing a little over fo'hundr'd hos'pow'r. On top of that, I took the rear end out of a seventy-two 'Vette and locked her down pretty tight. Lowered my gears to around fo'eleven."

I could barely hear him, but I believed him. He hit the accelerator and pinned me so hard against the seat that we were going eighty before I could lift my head up. It was the loudest, fastest car I had ever ridden in. He could burn rubber in all four gears, and he was all too happy to show me. The dashboard was a cockpit of gauges, switches, and flashing lights. I don't know how he saw the road over the thing sticking out of the hood.

We drove the remaining twelve miles to town in about seven minutes. We were going so fast at one point that when I opened my eyes, the dotted yellow line in the middle of the road looked solid. I tried to thank him when he dropped me off, but he couldn't hear me over the exhaust. He said he was on his way to the gas station, so I gave him the three dollars I had been saving to buy my dinner. I would have given him more, but the only other thing in my pocket was the next year's contract, and I didn't know how that could help him.

Maggs was serenely beautiful when I walked in. I married above myself. *Lord, that is one good-looking woman.* I sat down next to the bed and held her hand in mine. A familiar feel. Her fingers had been more active since Christmas. I even think she squeezed me once, but it was hard to tell. Maybe it was only more of that involuntary spinal activity that the doc-tor told me not to get too excited over.

I squeezed her hand anyway. Every time I sat down in that chair, I squeezed her hand three times. That meant "I love you." Maggs knew that. Throughout our dating and married life, three squeezes of any kind always meant "I love you." And the person getting squeezed squeezed back either two or four times. Two squeezes meant "Me too" and four, "I love you too."

When I squeezed her hand that day, Maggs squeezed me once. No, it wasn't two, three, or four squeezes, but it was a squeeze. And don't tell me that was some spinal reaction. That was a soul thing. I told her about the contract, and her eyeballs began rolling back and forth behind her eyelids, and her breathing picked up. I sat there laughing. Laughing at the thought of a college hiring me to teach on a regular basis.

As I was sitting in Maggs's room, somebody knocked on the door. I kissed Maggie and cracked the door. It was Koy.

"Hello, Professor. Sorry to bother you, but I wonder if I could talk with you."

"Sure," I said. "Give me a minute." I covered Maggie's shoul-ders with the blanket, made sure her socks were pulled up on her feet, turned out the lights, and closed the door behind me. Koy and I walked down to the coffee machine; I poured myself a cup and offered one to her. She shook her head.

"Um, Professor." She took off her glasses and looked around behind me to see if anyone else was listening. "Do you still have the, um . . . the readmit I gave you?"

"I think so. I think it's in my roll book at home. Why?"

"Well," she said, fumbling with her glasses. "I was wondering if I could have it back." She looked at the ground and waited for my response.

"Sure, you can have it back." I paused and looked closer. She looked as though she hadn't slept in a few days. "Koy, are you all right?"

"Yeah, I was just wondering if I could have it back. That's all."

"I'll bring it to school next week. I've got to turn in grades."

"Well," she stuttered, "I-I was wondering if I could have it sooner."

"Only if you don't mind coming to get it."

"I don't mind," she said quickly.

"I won't be home until late tonight, but if you come by tomorrow, I'll be there most of the day."

"Thanks, Professor. See you tomorrow."

Koy left, and after a minute I slipped out a side exit. I didn't want her to see me walking home, and I sure didn't want her to offer me a ride. The sight of a teacher and a student alone in a car has led to more than one accusation. Home wasn't that far away. I'd walked it before.

I was about three miles from the hospital when Amos came flying up behind me. He pulled alongside. "Thought that was you."

I climbed in. "Man, am I glad to see you. It's getting cold again."

"Amanda's going home tomorrow," he said. "Pastor John stopped me in the grocery store and said they were releasing her in the morning."

He dropped me off at the end of the drive, so I turned up my collar and walked through the pitch black with my hands in my coat pockets. When I got to the porch, somebody with sunglasses was sitting on the front steps, resting her head in her hands. Like the courier service guy, she scared another three years off my life.

"Koy?"

"Sorry, Professor. I couldn't find a light switch."

"Well, the sun will be up in about eight hours."

"Yeah. I thought maybe I could get that readmit tonight."

She looked cold, but not from the temperature, and she sounded as though she'd been crying.

"I'll get it." I walked inside, turned on the porch light, got the receipt, and walked back out on the porch. I handed it to her, and this time she did not take her glasses off.

"Thanks, Professor."

"Koy?" I said. "You don't have to answer me, but why do you want it?"

"I j-just want to keep it," she stammered and walked backwards to her car. "Thank you, Professor." She closed her door and slowly drove out of the driveway. It was eleven when she left.

I went inside, rubbed Blue between the ears, and poured myself a cup of milk. Standing on the porch, stargazing and sipping some sweet, creamy milk, I watched as a northwest breeze picked up and flapped through my corn.

My dry and very dead corn.

I polished off the milk and grabbed a match from the mantel. At the edge of the cornfield, with the wind blowing behind me, I struck the match and lit the stalk in front of me. It sputtered as the wind caught it and almost went out. I cupped my hands around the dead leaf and gave it another chance. In under two minutes, the fire was raging. I stepped back, crossed my arms, and watched it spread across twenty acres, quickly turning the field into a single, huge, roaring blaze.

Amos saw the flames and came running out of his house. He ran up my drive in his socks and grippers, dodging sparks and flames and breathing hard. He shouted above the crackle and roar, "Ivory, have you lost your mind?"

I stood there watching the glow and lost in the flames.

"No," I said, as the fire reached the road and began to die. "Actually, I'm just starting to get it back."

Amos shook his head and started jogging back to his house. I heard him mutter to himself, "Blasted idiot. All that education and he's still dumb as a brick. Burn my house down . . ."

I stood there long enough to watch the fire die and feel the cold return. Then I skipped back inside, lay down on the couch, and for the first time in several months, slept peacefully in my own house.

# chapter thirty-one

JAKE POWERS OWNS JAKE'S JALOPY. ASIDE FROM
being the only auto repair shop in town, it's also the only car
dealership in Digger. You might say he's got a monopoly on a
very small market. His selection is a hodgepodge of nearly
new and very used cars and trucks . . . mostly very used. Not
a single car on the lot is still under extended warranty, much
less factory warranty.

The place reminds me of the Island of Misfit Toys. How
Jake has managed to stay in business this long is the Eighth
Wonder of the World. And it's not as if he can sell. I think
people go there because they feel sorry for him, his mealy-
mouthed wife, and his four pitiful-looking kids. Actually, the

whole pitiful thing is probably a marketing ploy. He's probably a mastermind when it comes to yanking a customer's chain.

I was a perfect case in point. I had made up my mind that I was going to Walterboro to buy a real car, the kind with zero miles, when I remembered the billboard that showed the happy Powers children sitting on Mom and Dad's lap. Underneath, the caption read, *Come to Jake's Jalopy. Your purchase will help me feed my kids.*

It's pretty well known that if you want something reliable, something with a warranty, something that won't leave you stranded, you better get to Walterboro. But if you're in a fix, and you're a sucker, a Jake's jalopy will do. I wasn't really in a fix, but I didn't feel like haggling with a Walterboro car salesman, and besides, Jake had my truck. Maybe I could interest him in a trade. To be honest, I had an idea of my own. I also remembered that Jake worked holidays and would be open on New Year's Eve. So I headed out the drive and began walking to Jake's.

After a seven-mile jog-walk with Blue at my side, I turned in the lot.

"Hey, Jake."

Jake stepped between me and the gate before I could change my mind and leave.

"Hey, Dylan, how are you doing?"

Jake and I graduated high school together, and he's always been a little slow on the uptake. Truth is, he does have a child with some special needs, and he's good to his family. He works all the time, and the lot is always open. During Christmas, many people get their trees there. He'll hold as many trees as your wife wants to look at without batting an eye. Then he'll give you a fresh cut, load it on top of your car, tie it down, and wish you a Merry Christmas, which he genuinely hopes you have.

"I'm fine," I lied. The truth would take too long. "How's my truck?" I asked.

He shook his head. "Cooked. Engine's burnt slap up. It'd cost you more to put a new engine in it than what the truck is worth."

This was where Jake usually started trying to sell you something on his lot. But I knew this going in, so I just listened. Besides, he wasn't the only one scheming.

He continued, cocking his head as if he were doing me a favor. "I might could give you more in trade than you'd ever sell it for."

"Well, what do you have?"

Jake smiled, and behind his eyes I could tell he was doing the math. Old Jake thought he had me. But months ago I had seen a truck in the back of his lot that had piqued my interest. When mine burned up, I had the excuse I was looking for.

He slid a tattered three-by-five card from his shirt pocket and looked through the bottom of his glasses. "Let's see . . . " He scanned his card. "With a family and all, you probably need something like . . . " He squeezed his chin between his fingers. "Like this van here." He pointed to a Chrysler van at the front of the lot, parked beneath the row of flapping red, white, and blue flags.

287

It would take a bigger sucker than I was to leave there with that thing. I pointed to the back of the lot and said, "Uh, Jake, what about that truck?"

Jake looked up from his card and said, "Oh yeah. *That* truck."

We both gazed at the faded orange Ford pickup, covered in leaves and parked against the rear fence.

"Wow. You know how to pick 'em, Dylan." He slapped me on the shoulder as we walked to the back of the lot. "That's a '76 Ford F-150, four-wheel drive, no doubt. It's got about 140,000 miles on it, but the engine was just rebuilt and it's only got eight hundred miles on the new one, transmission, and rear-end."

Jake took off his glasses and kind of looked around before he continued. "Dylan, I know I sometimes sell some less-than-stellar stuff, but to the right owner, this is some decent trans-portation. I mean, the bed is rusted and duct tape covers some of the tears in the seats, but as for reliability?" Jake quietly patted the hood of the Ford. "I think this may be one of the more reliable units on the lot."

In this particular instance, Jake was probably telling the truth.

"It's got a four-sixty with a couple of small modifications. I think it dynos at about four hundred horsepower." He squinted his eyes in the sun. "Is that too much for your needs?"

"No." I tried not to smile. "I can probably make do."

"Okay, um . . . The gauges work pretty well, and the tires . . . " Jake kicked the tires. "They look pretty good. They're a little big for my taste, but you own a farm, so they might come in handy." He rested his hand on the top of the tire that came to the middle of his thigh. "How 'bout twenty-five hundred?"

Jake was reaching. He must have been having a tough month. The thing wasn't worth fifteen hundred. Not to anybody.

Except me.

He interrupted me before I could reply. "Nope, I tell you what, I'll give you five hundred for your trade and take fifteen hundred, but that's just 'cause you and me got some history."

I shook my head. "Jake, you're too good to me." I rubbed my hands together, as though I were doing the figuring in my head. Good thing Jake couldn't read my mind. I'd have paid ten.

"Will you take three?"

"Well, all right, I can cut it to a thousand, but . . ." Jake scratched his head. "What did you say?"

"I said I'd feel bad if I took her for less than three thousand. This is a classic, and you and I both know it. You're just doing me a favor 'cause we've known each other so long." I slapped Jake on the back and handed him my driver's license.

His eyes doubled in size, and he looked at me as though I had lost my mind.

"Dylan?" He collected himself. "Umm, yeah, let's go inside and get started on the paperwork."

While he was sitting at his desk, Jake's smile grew. The smile alone was worth three grand. The truck was just the icing on the cake. Or at least that's what I was going to tell Amos when he gave me a hard time about buying this truck from Jake.

I reassured him. "Yeah, Jake, I really do appreciate your kindness. I know you're an old pro, and you know cars. I also know that you've always been good to the people who come in here. You've done a lot of good in Digger. 'Specially come Christmas, or when folks just need some help."

Jake squinted again as if he wasn't quite sure what was coming next. "I have?" he asked. "I mean . . ." He cleared his throat. "I have. Thanks for noticing."

"Listen, we all do," I lied again.

Jake handed me the key and said, "I'll hold the title, of course, and send it to you in about twenty-four months. If that's okay with you."

"Sounds good. Hey, tell Liza and the kids I said hello."

Jake looked as though he'd just seen Elvis. He nodded, and I climbed up in the truck.

Finally, a four-wheel drive. I hit the starter, and it rumbled into a slow idle. Ahhh. It's a truck thing. If you don't understand by now, you might as well quit, because you never will.

As I was putting the stick into first, an older, hunchbacked, black woman pulled into the lot. She opened her squeaky door, climbed out of her car, walked over to Jake, and pulled out a neatly folded wad of bills. I overheard her say, "Mr. Jake, that's my ninth payment. I've got six more to go before it's paid for."

I waved at Jake. "Hey, good to see you, pal," I said. "And thanks for taking such good care of all us Digger folks. This beats Walterboro any day."

Jake scratched his head and turned his attention to the lady. "Miz Parker, you're real good about paying me. You're here every month just as soon as your Social Security check comes in. Let's just call it even. I've earned my money on that car."

"But Jake," she protested, bobbing her head, "I still owe you close to three hundred dollars."

"Yes, ma'am. Two hundred and forty-seven, to be exact." Jake put his arm around her and led her back to her car. "And maybe you know of some people who might need a car one day." He smiled. "Don't you have a bunch of kids?"

"Honey." Mrs. Parker put her hand on her hip. "I've got nine of 'em, and if any of them buys a car anyplace but here, I'll beat them like a redheaded stepchild." She reached up, clutched Jake to her big sagging bosom, and kissed him square on the mouth.

I pulled out of the lot with Blue sticking his head out the passenger's window to catch the breeze. I switched on the broken, scratchy radio, and Blue and I hummed down the highway to the sound of mud tires in need of alignment. I was in love.

I probably should have driven straight home, but I didn't. Instead, we filled up, something that, were it not for dual fuel tanks, we would have to do often. Then I eased her into first. Jake was right, that vehicle was not underpowered. Someone had modified that thing at some point. We left Digger with the windows down, and I pointed the hood toward Wherever, which is just south of Whocares. Blue and I wanted the wind in our faces. Maggs wouldn't have minded. If she'd been able, she'd have told me to get out of the hospital anyway. The sun disappeared around Charleston, so we turned south and headed down low country roads around Walterboro.

In need of some new boots, I stopped by the Western World in Walterboro and browsed the aisles. It didn't take long.

They were on the top shelf and just about jumped off at me when I walked by: Olathe Mule Skinners. Tough brown leather, medium toe, double welt, double-thick leather sole, medium heel, eleven-inch shank. They looked like the boots that Dean Martin wore in *Rio Bravo*, and when I slipped them on my feet, my search was over. I loved them. Maggie would not.

I turned to the attendant. "I'll take them . . . And yes, I'd like to wear them out."

He picked up my running shoes with two fingers, wrinkling his nose, dropped them into the box, and closed the lid. I paid the cashier, but not before buying two new pairs of Wranglers. Something Maggie would never let me get away with.

I walked out smiling like a cross between an artificial redneck and a wannabe ranch hand. But I was smiling, and that was not something I had done a lot of those last few months. Crossing the parking lot, I stepped in a puddle on purpose, and then Blue and I loaded up and I backed out of the parking lot.

My smile stopped me when I looked in the rearview mirror. I pushed in the clutch and sat there looking in the mirror at my face. After I recognized myself, we headed northwest up toward Columbia, and then south along a bunch of back country roads and some small towns that had grown up around cotton, peanuts, and tobacco.

Blue fluctuated between sticking his nose out the window and curling up in a ball on the seat next to me. He sniffed everything between the two locations. His nervousness told me he wasn't quite sure what to make of me or this truck. I rubbed his ears and he settled down, finally putting his head on my lap. I sat with one hand on the wheel and the other on the windowsill. Occasionally I'd look in the rearview mirror just to see my smile, trying to get used to it. If Maggie were here, she'd have been smiling, too, and it was that thought that kept the guilt away and the food down. Without Maggie's smile, I'd have never made it out of Jake's parking lot.

Just before dark, we were rumbling along some back road that was an irregular patchwork of dirt, hardtop, and potholes when something caught my eye. A side road with my name on it. Blue and I slipped off the hardtop and down the wet, grassy, low road with cypress trees so large that Maggie, Amos, and I all together couldn't reach our arms around them.

We idled for maybe a mile or so and then pulled up onto a sandy riverbank. I parked and let Blue smell the bushes. Hopping up on the hood, I crossed my legs in front of me, took another look at my boots, then tilted my head back and watched the sun go down over some no-name creek in some forgotten part of South Carolina through the limbs of a cypress tree that few humans had probably ever taken time to notice. I lay there for quite a while, humming a Randy Travis song.

The sun disappeared, and the cypress limbs took on a shape and character of their own in the dark. Blue whined. I turned the truck around, and we pulled back out on the hardtop. I don't know how many miles we drove that night. Maybe three hundred. We were gone five or six hours, but it sure didn't feel that way. Time is like that in Digger. It stands still for some people.

We pulled back into town about nine o'clock. It was dark,

cool, and clear, and I could have driven for three more days. I still had five or six good songs in my head that could have kept me busy all night. Turning onto the drive, I laughed because it occurred to me then how much Maggie would have hated this truck. If you looked up the word "redneck" in the dictionary, you might see a picture of my truck. But she'd love that I love it.

I rounded the house and parked it next to the barn, then placed a pan beneath the engine so that tomorrow morning it could tell me if it was leaking oil. New engine or not, it was an old truck, and old trucks burn oil. It's just part of their language. You drive one long enough, and you begin to speak it. I lifted the tailgate and heard light footsteps on the gravel behind me.

"What is that?" Amos asked, pointing at my faded orange beauty.

"This," I said, still smiling with my hand affectionately resting on the tailgate, "is heaven."

Amos pushed his baseball cap back on his head and looked at me skeptically. "Please don't tell me you bought that thing at Jake's."

"Yup," I said, rubbing my hand over the rusted tailgate.

"What'd it cost you?" Amos said with his hands on his hips.

"I'm not saying. All I'll say is that Jake cut me a fair deal, and I agreed to pay him every month for the next two years."

"Dylan." Amos tilted his head sideways. "Did you pay that boy more than his asking price?"

"Now, Amos, what makes you think I'd do a fool thing like that?"

"Just answer my question."

I looked into the bed of the truck. "The purchase of this vehicle was a private financial transaction between Mr. Powers and me . . . "

Blue lay in the back with his paws covering up his eyes.

". . . the details of which I am not at liberty to discuss."

"Dylan, you are dumb as dirt!" Amos turned and walked down my drive, shaking his head.

I walked inside, grabbed the jar of peanut butter and a bagel, and then walked back outside, where I put down the tailgate and sat in the bed of the truck with Blue.

After Blue and I finished off the jar of peanut butter, I went back inside and put on my PJs. Which meant taking off my new jeans and leaving my boxer shorts on. I built a fire and sat down, flame-watching with Blue. An activity he was fond of and something we had done a lot lately. While I was mesmerized by the flames, it dawned on me that I needed to get the mail. I walked down the driveway to the mailbox in my boxers. It was cold, but who was gonna see me? This is the boondocks. You heard the man: "Egypt"!

I opened the box, fished around in the dark, and pulled out two envelopes. I walked back up the drive, and by the porch light I saw that the return address on the first read *Thentwhistle*. As I ran my finger beneath the tab and tore open the letter, the hair stood up on the back of my neck and sent chill bumps down my arms. I'd been expecting it, and no, I had no way of paying Maggie's bills other than mortgaging the farm. I opened the letter, prepared for the worst.

*Dear Mr. Styles,*

    *It is my duty to inform you that the current bill for your wife's complete and ongoing care since her admission is $227,753.87.*

The size of the number took a few minutes to register. I looked across the farm, Nanny's house, Papa's fields, and I knew I had to let it go. I could never make payments on that type of mortgage. Life was about to become real different. I read on:

    *Secondly, and it truly is with great pleasure that I inform you: Hospital administration has just notified me that an anonymous donor has unexpectedly paid your bill in full and requested that all future bills be forwarded to an address other than yours for the duration of Maggie's stay with us. If you have any further questions, or I can be of any help at all, please call.*

        *Respectfully,*
        *Jason Thentwhistle*

    *P.S. Dylan, I sincerely regret the timing of our previous conversation and wish you and Maggie all the best.*

It took me about a half a second to determine the identity of the anonymous donor. That was just like Bryce; his actions always spoke louder than his words. And get a load of old Thentwhistle. Maybe he wasn't as smug as I'd accused him of being.

The second letter was less formal and addressed to *Professor.*
I recognized Koy's handwriting.

*Dear Professor,*

*I leave tomorrow for Spelman. I can start classes in the
spring semester. I never thought I'd get out of this cesspool.
Now that I'm leaving, it ain't all that bad. I did a lot of
dying in Digger. Lately, I've done some living too. Living
and dying—it's just a choice.*

*One thing I do know is that death is wrapped all around
you like a blanket. You've been dealt a terrible hand, and in
spite of it—or because of it—you live. You're the livingest
person I ever met. When you walk around, something inside
you seeps out of your pores and screams, "I'm alive!" and
"I'm not dying today!" It's electric, and people feel it. They
know you're coming around the corner because something in
them rises up to meet whatever it is that you got.*

*I can't quite put my finger on it. Maybe it's hope, maybe
it's love, but those words fall down. They don't describe that
thing that is you. I wish I could talk with your wife, because
I think maybe she knows. Maybe she's got the secret—the
key—and then maybe I'd know.*

*I hope you don't mind, but I went to see your wife last
night. I walked into her room with the lights off—the light
of her heartbeat bouncing off the wall—sat down next to her
bed, held her hand, and let my tears fall into her fingers.*

*Professor, I swear, so help me God, if I could I would walk into that hospital room, take off my skin, and give her me, I would. I'd strip before the devil himself, but life doesn't work that way.*

*My insides hurt pretty bad when I think about that clinic, what I did to my little girl, and what fate did to your son. That won't ever go away. There will always be two tombstones. But here today, right now, I'm living, and you did that. I was carrying a whole bottle full of pills, and I didn't eat them because you turned the corner, walked up to me, and breathed life into me when I didn't want any air. All I wanted to do was swallow.*

*Professor, you don't know it, but you introduced me to me. This life needs people who stand in the ditch and argue with God because the rest of us are either too scared or too proud. I don't really like all I see in the mirror, but I'm beginning to think that the girl behind the glasses is worth digging into. Maybe I'll take them off one day.*

*Koy*

I folded the letter and placed it back in the envelope, and I realized that I was still standing on the porch in my boxers. I went back inside and sat by the fire with Blue, where I reread the letter five times. When the coals grew powdery white, I slipped on my new boots, grabbed my sleeping bag, and walked out to the truck. I cranked it, left the lights off, and idled down to the river. After parking on the bluff, Blue and I hopped in the back and curled up in my sleeping bag. I couldn't count the stars. My eyes wouldn't let me.

# *chapter thirty-two*

I SHOWERED AND SPENT MOST OF NEW YEAR'S DAY on the porch. Thinking. Sleeping some. Rocking some. I missed Maggie's black-eyed peas. I don't know if I missed the peas themselves, the smell, the anticipation and taste of the peas, or the sight of Maggie wrapped in an apron, covered in flour and messing up the kitchen. Anyway, something was missing.

It may seem odd, and it was, but all day I had been thinking about Pinky. Once I got my nerve up, I got off my rocker, jumped down from the porch, and figured it was time to fish or cut bait.

I grabbed my bucket, filled it full of corn, and stepped into the stall. Pinky immediately grunted and banged against the opposite side.

"All right, girl," I said, teasing her with the bucket, "isn't it about time you and I got to know one another?"

Pinky snorted, crapped, smeared it across her buttocks with her tail, and kicked her stall.

I closed the gate, put the corn bucket down next to me, and squatted some fifteen feet in front of her. "I mean, think about it. How long have I been feeding you? Three years? Maybe four? Haven't I always taken care of you? Look around you." I pointed to her latest litter of twelve little pigs, only two weeks old and all vying for a chance to suckle. "Look at all that I've let you do. This place is full of pigs, and that's all because I feed you. You're a sow-shaped Hoover. All you do is eat."

I patted the bucket and sprinkled two or three kernels of corn in front of me. "Today is a new day. You and me, we're getting friendly." I patted the bucket again. "So come over here, and let's shake ears, or snouts, or whatever it is that people and pigs shake when they're getting friendly. I'll rub you 'tween the ears."

Pinky grunted and blew snot out her nose.

"Nope, that's not good enough," I said, wiping my face with my shirtsleeve. "That will not do. I'm talking about a full down-the-back-of-the-head-and-ear-rub. Snorting won't get it. Now get your big self busy, and come on over here."

Pinky swaggered back and forth and desuckled a couple of little ones. They were as filthy as she was. I needed a pressure washer. And the smell? Horrible.

"All right, you can swagger all you want, but you are not getting one kernel of this corn until you come over here and apologize for being so dang mean and ugly to me." I twisted a kernel of corn back and forth between my thumb and index finger. "And don't think grunting and blowing your nose in my face is going to get it, 'cause it ain't, as my students say. I ain't meeting you halfway. You got to come all the way, and I got all day. So, when you get hungry, I'll be squatting right here. It's your call."

Pinky banged her shoulders against the side of the stall, and her nose got wide and showed wet.

"Come on." I held the corn in the palm of my hand.

That pig then lowered her head and charged at me full speed, detaching six piglets from their faucets and flinging dirt everywhere as she charged. A half second later, all three-hundred-plus pounds of Pinky, led by her snout, hit me in the abdomen and rocketed me against the side of the stall. My head hit the top beam of the gate, the room blurred, and I found myself lying flat on my back, looking up at the rafters.

When my eyes opened, I was shoulder deep in pig crap. It was in my hair, and I think, in the cracks of my ears. Sitting up, I heard somebody outside the stall. I lifted my head, looked through the boards, and saw Amos rolling on the barn floor, holding his stomach.

"Oh, stop! Don't make me laugh!" Amos's black face looked almost red, and tears were streaming out the corners of his eyes.

I sat up in the middle of Pinky's stall and flung my fingers to get the clumps of manure and hay off them, and then cleaned out my ears. Inside the stall, Pinky finished her triumphant, tail-up victory parade, then walked over and began sniffing and licking my face. Looking at me eye-level, she nudged my leg with her nose, dug a little hole with her hoof next to my leg, and lay down in the hole. With a loud sigh, she laid her head on top of my thigh and released a deep, snot-blowing breath. Twelve little pigs then surrounded her, and consequently me, and began fighting for a teat.

Amos pulled himself off the ground and lifted himself up by the rungs of Pinky's stall. Wiping his eyes and catching his breath, he said, "D.S., you know . . . " He began laughing again. "You know you're covered in pig crap?"

I looked down, patted Pinky on the head, picked up one of her little ones, and held it like a kitten. "Yeah, well . . . clean don't always look it."

Amos rubbed his eyes again, still chuckling, and said, "Well, Mr. Greenjeans, when you get cleaned up, and I think that's probably a good idea, maybe even a priority, there's somebody at the hospital who wants to see you."

Accountants, doctors, and other constipated pains-in-the-butt came to mind. "Who?" I said, wrinkling my brow. "If they want to talk about the bill, I just got a letter from Jason Thentwhistle . . . "

Amos held his chin in his hands. His eyes looked down on me, and his teeth showed pearly white. Then his bottom lip quivered, and he broke into a smile.

MY SPEEDOMETER WAS PEGGED AT JUST OVER ONE HUNDRED miles an hour as I jumped the railroad tracks on my way to the hospital. The engine was whining as all four tires came off the ground on the other side of the tracks.

Amos followed in his Crown Vic, flashing blue lights, tooting his horn, and shouting over his PA system, "Slow down, you fool!"

Blue lay sprawled and whining on the floorboard, covering one eye with his paw. When I turned the corner and crested the hill that led up to Bryce's trailer, Bryce stood piping at his gate in full regalia, decked out with all his ribbons. He stood, feet together, red-faced, and blowing for all he was worth, but I was going too fast to hear what he was playing.

The hospital was a zoo when I arrived. I bounded up the stairs, tripped on the top step, and slid three rooms down on the janitor's nicely waxed floor. Blue jumped over me, disappearing down the hall and into Maggie's room, where a crowd stood looking in. I began to raise myself off the floor, but the sound stopped me—a sound that I had heard only once in almost five months.

The last time I had heard Maggs's voice, she was crying and screaming, "No, God! Please, no," as the doctor pulled the sheet over my son. Now I sprawled paralyzed on the floor, listening. The voice that had said "I love you" ten thousand times, the voice that said "Dylan Styles!" the voice that whispered "Let's go swimming" had cracked back into the world and filled my empty soul.

Moments before, I lived in a world where wisteria snaked across my son's grave as he rotted beneath a cement slab; where Vietnam Vets inhaled beer to help them forget the day they wiped Vicks salve in their noses so they wouldn't have to smell the bodies as they zipped up the bags; where a no-good farmer bathed in a cornfield but couldn't wash the blood clean; where snow fell on iced-over railroad tracks; where used-car salesmen robbed old women with inflated prices and double-digit interest rates; where little boys peed in the baptistry and pastors strutted like roosters; where evil men tied innocent girls to trees, stripped them, raped them, and left to them die; where students cheated and burnt-out professors scribbled useless information on sweat-stained chalkboards and couldn't care less; where not-so-innocent girls paid $265 for scar tissue; where the most precious thing I had ever known lay listless, scarred, childless, and dying in a nondescript hospital room in the armpit of South Carolina.

But then came Maggie's voice.

I looked around and found myself in a world where wisteria blooms in December; where a Scottish piper sings through his pipes; where used-car salesmen open car doors for little old ladies; where pastors dunk themselves with scared children who emerge clean and hungry; where students say, "He'd call it cheating"; where not-so-innocent girls carry receipts in their pockets and write books that will be read by Oprah; where a no-good professor bathes in the river, burns dead cornfields, and basks in moonlight and flames; and where my wife speaks.

I now lived in a world where the dead danced.

I walked into my wife's room, and there, under the window and glowing like the sun, lay Maggie—her big brown eyes meeting mine for the first time in so many months.

Breathing heavily and fumbling with my hands, I didn't know what to say. *Where do I start? Am I the same Dylan that she fell in love with, and is she the same Maggie? How deep are the scars? Are we the same us?* Standing there in my new boots and covered in pig smear, I didn't know who to be until I knew where she was. I needed Maggs to tell me who to be—because that would tell me where she was, and most importantly, who we were.

I closed the door, knelt down next to Maggs's bed, and watched her cracked lips quiver. I slid my hand beneath hers and searched her eyes, aching to know and be known. She blinked a lazy blink, tilted her head, and smiled.

# afterword

IT WAS MIDNIGHT WHEN WE HEARD THE PIPES. WE crawled out of bed, slipped on some jeans, and walked hand in hand along the tree line. Standing under the overhang of oaks, next to my son's grave, was Bryce, decked out in full military regalia, ruddy-cheeked and blowing so hard the veins on his neck stood out like rose vines. He was somewhere in the middle of "It Is Well with My Soul" when we walked up. A gentle breeze skirted along the bank and fanned over us as we stood facing the river. Our long shadows ran down to the river and disappeared into the water.

Without a pause, Bryce slipped into "Amazing Grace." The music went through us like the morning sun, warm and glowing. As the last hollow note of his pipes echoed off the river and faded into the distance, Maggs walked over and kissed him on the cheek. Bryce stood rigid, heels together, at attention, his eyes fixed on the horizon. He was wearing a green beret, his military dress shirt, and a chest spangled and twinkling with medals. Everything, from his hat to shirt to kilt to socks, was clean, pressed, and worn for the first time in a long time. Without saying a word he turned, began blowing, and disappeared like an angel into the darkness. As we stood underneath the canopy of oaks, the pipes faded away downriver.

Maggie slid her hand under mine and tugged on my arm. The air was cool, but nothing compared to the previous year. I stood on the bank while she ran in front of me and climbed the sandy bluff. In the moonlight, she stripped off her jeans and stood silhouetted against the moon, which formed a halo around her body and threaded her hair with silver. I watched, waist deep in the water, mesmerized. Enchanted. The slender calves, the small curve of her lower back, the graceful shoulders. She skipped to the edge and took a swan dive off the bluff, splashing into the water a few feet away from me. The ripples lapped against my stomach and brought chill bumps to my skin. When she broke the surface, and that black water dripped off her nose and ears, a sweet and sneaky smile creased her face.

Half a dozen wood ducks soared overhead, brushing the tops of the cypress trees with their wing tips. An owl hooted low and hauntingly; farther north along the river, a lone bluetick hound sounded a single lonely ping somewhere in the Salk. A mile south of us, the sound of singing, pungent with joy and ripe with smiles, rose like a flume of steam from Pastor John's church steeple. Maggie and I swam close together, swaying with the slow rhythm of the river while the echoes of voices showered down on us like a warm summer rain. Beneath it all I had only one thought, one need.

*Lord, I'm begging You. Please give me sixty-two more years with this woman.*

# *acknowledgments*

SOMEWHERE IN DECEMBER OF 1995, I BEGAN THINK-
ing about this story. I was driving through one of the bridge
tunnels in Hampton Roads on my way to UPS, where I
worked in the early morning preload. It being the Christmas
season, I think we had to clock in before 3 AM. It may have
been earlier, but I've tried to block that out. I had been in
graduate school at Regent University, and in order to remain
focused on school, I had suppressed my stories for so long
that they had begun to rebel and bubble their way to the surface. Cream does that.

Let me interject one thing—my graduate school experience was phenomenal. One lightbulb after another clicked

on and lit my path. I wouldn't trade it for the world. Three men in particular contributed to this, and I am greatly indebted to each—Doug Tarpley, Michael Graves, and Bob Schihl. Guys, thanks for a seat at the table. My hat's off to you.

At any rate, I remember driving through the tunnel and could hold it back no longer. Remember the grammar school project where the kid pours the vinegar over the baking soda in the papier-mâché volcano? As I was nearing the bottom of the tunnel, one scene erupted and flashed across the screen on the back of my eyelids: a man standing in a ditch, screaming at God. I knew he was cold, alone, and at the end of himself. Much like Crusoe, he was shipwrecked, a castaway in need of Friday to rescue him off the island. *The Dead Don't Dance* grew from that early-morning flash, or hallucination, as the case may have been. In later drives, mostly through the back roads of South Carolina, I saw a beautiful girl and somehow knew her name was Maggie, a handsome black man who looked like Mr. Clean with a badge, and a farmhouse with a rusted tin roof—one I knew well.

The path from idea to trade paper has been, as with other first novels, a graveled road marred with washouts, blind corners, stop-and-go traffic, and U-turns. Yes, I've worked hard, early mornings, late nights, stoplights, but that is the least of it. Many writers work hard. I, and this book, are in large part a product of other people's unselfishness. People who gave me a chance. Who believed in me. Without them, I'd not be here, and you'd not be reading this book.

I won't backtrack to my youth, but I need to start by thanking one of the finest writers I've ever met: John Dyson. John worked for *Reader's Digest*, writing some 160-plus articles and more than twenty-three books over a three-decade career. He's a writer's writer, a true craftsman and wordsmith. Not to mention a pretty good sailor. I won't bore you with the story, but John was instrumental in my first work as a writer. You know that process of smelting, where the silversmith heats the silver and removes the dross? John did that to me. Painful too. Somewhere in that furnace, he taught me what good writing looks like, and maybe more importantly, sounds like. Somewhere early in our work together, he told me "Charles, an editor is one who walks back through the battlefield and shoots the wounded." He was right, and true to form, came with both barrels blazing—though, in my case, that's not always bad. As a dwarf running among giants, I stand with one foot squarely atop John's broad shoulder. John, thanks for allowing me the view, for letting me whisper in your ear and ask the same irritating questions over and over, and for not brushing me off your lapel.

While one foot is resting on John's shoulder, the other is balancing on the tall shoulders of Davis Bunn. About two years ago, I had come close to my wits' end. I had finished the book, bought the *Writer's Guide* like all writers are supposed to, and sent out a couple hundred dollars' worth of manuscripts and postage to as many agents and publishers as I could find. Soon my mailbox began filling up with some of the nicest letters of rejection I've ever received. Each one was so kind and so completely rejecting that for about eight months, I quit going to the mailbox. During that time, Christy would walk in, drop the letter on my desk, kiss me on the cheek, and say, "You're not a reject to me." It was little consolation.

At any rate, Davis—who's written some sixty-plus novels—attended a party in D.C. and got cornered by my well-meaning but not-to-be-refused grandfather. Looking for an exit but hounded by my mercilessly pestering grandparents, Davis relented and broke his never-read-a-first-novel rule. A few days later, he invited me to lunch, where he fed me a sandwich, made two quick phone calls, and befriended me. Something I was in need of. When I got home, I had received two e-mails and one voice-mail asking to see this manuscript. A week later, I had an agent. And six weeks later, a publisher.

Granted, I'd not have had those if the work couldn't stand on its own, but Davis helped open the door. One I'd been bashing my head against. Maybe he recognized the flat spot on my forehead, and it reminded him of his own. Davis is a true professional who's taught me much about this business, how to navigate it, and what to do when the storms come—because they will. Davis, thank you for the view, the conversation, the friendship, and for relenting.

Davis led me to the office of a true statesman, one of the real patriarchs in this business, Sealy Yates. Sealy introduced me to a young bulldog in his office named Chris Ferebee. Chris read my novel over the weekend and called me on Monday night. "Charles, I'd like to help you get this book published."

It took me a few minutes to recover from that phone call. I'm not sure my neighbors ever have. Chris made a few suggestions,

I made a few corrections, and six weeks later, Thomas Nelson offered to publish my work. Chris, you're a true counselor, sounding board, ally, and friend.

Chris sent my work to an editor at Nelson named Jenny Baumgartner. Jenny read it and offered to buy me breakfast at this pancake restaurant in Nashville where they serve these fantastic buckwheat pancakes. We struck up a conversation, and not long after, Nelson bought this book, and Jenny became my editor, and maybe more importantly, my advocate at Nelson. Jenny has a great eye for fiction, a remarkable ability to take something good and make it better, and a unique talent to communicate all that into a form that even a writer can understand. I am also indebted to the team around her: Jonathan Merkh, Mike Hyatt, and Allen Arnold. To the rest of the team at Nelson and the many people that I've never met who have worked so selflessly, from designers to salespeople, please accept my sincere thanks.

Throughout this eight-year roller-coaster ride, my family and friends at home have helped me maintain my perspective and keep me off medication, and out of a room with padded walls.

Without getting too sappy, I'd like to thank: Johnny and Dave. True brothers. When I scraped my knees, you guys—at different times and in differing ways—picked me up, brushed me off, and helped me strap my helmet back on. My in-laws, Alice and O'Neal. Thank you for your encouragement and for not disowning me when I said, "I'm working on a book." My sisters, Grace, Annie, and Berry. You all read my stuff and told me it was good even when it wasn't. Thanks for lying to me. Keep it up. My grandparents, T.C. and Granny. When you asked to read my work, I was a bit worried that you'd find it foolish. "All that education and he's doing what?" You didn't, and what's more, you became two of my best cheerleaders. Thanks for cornering Davis. Mom and Dad. Thanks for your sacrifices, for loving each other, and for teaching me to run with reckless abandon and then letting me do it.

Our boys—Charlie, John T., and Rives. Thanks for running in here and hugging my legs or asking me to play catch or go fishing or build Legos or wrestle at regular intervals. I needed it. Still do. Always will. Most importantly, thank you for praying for my books. This is proof the Lord really does answer us, and I think you three had a lot to do with it.

Christy. Phew! I'm worn out. How about you? Ready for a vacation? You've earned it. Anywhere you want to go, just as soon as we pay off the credit card. How you kept your sanity through ten years of marriage, graduate school, three boys, and my dreams is a mystery. You amaze me. People ask me how I created Maggie, but I didn't have to look very far. She was walking around my house, digging in the yard, tucking in my boys, whispering in my ear, holding my hand, and sticking her foot in my back. Thank you for believing in me and hoping with me, because I know there were many days in this process when I was less than lovable.

Lord. What can I say that You haven't already heard? Thank You for this, for the people I've listed, and for hanging in there with a guy like me. My cup runs over.

*The Dead Don't Dance*

# READING GROUP GUIDE

1. The river is a powerful image in this novel. Both literally and figuratively, Dylan must choose to fight against the river or allow it to carry him where it wishes. What does the river symbolize in this story? How does Dylan finally come to terms with it?

2. Blood also plays a symbolic role in this story. What does it represent? How is it different from or similar to the role of water?

3. One review refers to *The Dead Don't Dance* as "a classic example of God-haunted Southern literature." Very similarly, Flannery O'Connor's writing is often referenced as a "Christ-haunted landscape." How is the South portrayed in this novel? Why does Southern literature lend itself so easily to being "God-haunted"?

4. What is the meaning of the title? Discuss the theme of dancing and identify how "dancing" plays an integral part in the meaning of the story.

5. Discuss Dylan's attitudes toward education and teaching in the novel. How and why do they change? What affect does this have on Dylan's identity and his own self-image?

6. Much like Jacob in the Bible, Dylan wrestles with God as he searches for answers to the questions that fill his soul. How did wrestling with God change Jacob? How does it change Dylan?

7. Every time Dylan returns from the cornfield, his arm is raw. It is soon covered in scabs and he continues to cover it up with long sleeves. What is he doing to his arm in the cornfield? Why is he doing it? Why the mystery surrounding it?

8. After eating breakfast with Amos at Ira's Cafe, Dylan realizes that he has not thought about Maggie for forty-five minutes. Overwhelming guilt descends upon him. What does this story imply about nature of guilt and its relationship to tragedy?

9. What role does Bryce Kai MacGregor-the naked, bag-pipe playing, movie-loving millionaire-play in this story?

10. What roles do Dylan's students play in his life? Why is it significant that Koy is such a poor communicator in person but such an articulate poet and letter-writer? How does the students' plagiarism mirror Dylan's inner conflict?

11. When Dylan tells Amos, "I see colors, not structure," how does this statement summarize the differences between the two men? How do their personalities complement each other?

12. Describe Dylan's faith. How do his interactions with Pastor John and the AME church affect him? How does Amanda impact Dylan's beliefs?

13. Dylan says, "I drive an old pickup because I understand it." How does this statement characterize Dylan? When he purchases a used truck from Jake's Jalopy Auto Center in Walterboro, why does he offer Jake more money than the truck is worth?

14. Dylan explains, "The Salkehatchie is mythical. Everybody knows the stories. . . . If you can think it, it's probably already been mythified." Why is it significant that the violent coon hunt takes place in "the Salk"? What impact does the hunt have on Dylan?

15. Though Maggie stays in a coma for most of the novel, how does her character generate a "presence of absence"? By the end of the novel, do you think the relationship between Dylan and Maggie has changed? If so, how?

*Maggie*

FOR CHRISTY
—*who stood beside me and believed.*

*chapter one*

SOMETIME BEFORE DAYLIGHT, I HEARD IT. INCHES FROM my face, it sounded like a mouse sliding a saltine across a wooden floor. Seconds later, it sounded like the horn section of a symphony, tuning up. Then like cat purring lazily in the sun. And finally, like a woman who'd been in a coma for several months and was regaining the muscle tone she'd lost in her throat.

It was one of my favorite sounds—the sound of sweet dreams, the sound of contentedness, the sound of my wife next to me—the sound of Maggie sleeping. At that moment, she was sacked out and snoring like a sailor. I lay with my eyes closed, playing possum, listening and smiling because she'd die if she knew. *"I don't snore!"* Unconsciously, I had paced my breathing with hers, making sure to inhale deeply enough and to exhale slowly enough.

Moonlight filled our bedroom with a hazy grayish-blue, telling me the moon was high, full, and shining like a Milky Way spotlight on Maggie. I watched her, lingered there, and milked the Milky Way. Most nights she flopped around like a fish tossed up on the beach; then, on into morning, she'd settle down a bit and start spreading out horizontally. Now she lay sprawled across the bed like a snow angel, hogging all corners as if she'd grown accustomed to having the bed to herself. My left cheek barely hung on the edge of the mattress, and not a single square inch of sheet covered me, but I could not have cared less. If I ever do, somebody ought to beat me into next week. Her feet told me she was wearing socks, her neck told me she was wearing Eternity, and her arms told me she was wearing me.

All the world was right.

Around four in the morning, Maggie flung herself sideways, stretched like Blue, and then reencircled me like an octopus. When she settled, her hair draped across my chest like tentacles, mingling into me. Maggie's hair had grown well past her shoulders. Long and shiny, it was made for shampoo commercials. Mine, because of the coming summer heat and what would be long hours atop the tractor, was cropped relatively close, exposing my neck to the sun, dust, and dirt. When Maggie cut it, she had nodded in approval, reminding me that my grandfather would have nodded too.

She tucked her nose up close to mine, where her breath filled my lungs either before or after mine had filled hers. Her chest rose and fell in an easy rhythm, and her skin was warm. Making sure she could not be uprooted, she hooked her right leg around mine like a boat anchor, stretched her right arm across me like a bowline, and then drove her right hand into the mattress like a tent peg.

Reluctantly I untangled myself and slid out from beneath the pegs. I pulled the covers back over her bare shoulders, tucked the hair behind her ear, and walked to the kitchen to put on the percolator. Blue followed, stretched, and stood at the screen door, his nose pressed against the latch. He knew how to flip it open, but with Maggie around he'd grown lazy and now waited on me with an air of expectation.

I looked at him, and his ears dropped. I pointed toward the bedroom. "Hey, pal, *she* was in the coma. Not you. Let your own self out."

Blue whined, nosed up the latch, and disappeared off the porch.

While the percolator coughed and sputtered—the sweet sounds of my addiction—I stepped out onto the porch under a clear sky and onto the stage of my life. Judging from the thick black figures silhouetted against the dawning skyline, several turkeys roosted in the trees that lined the river and towered above our son's grave. I couldn't see it, but unless something really bad had happened to the world, the river flowed silently beyond those trees, filling the earth—or at least most of South Carolina, and me—with life.

Before me spread the rows of corn, silent sentinels, six feet tall and swaying in rhythmic, military unison under the quiet whisper of the spring breeze. As my eyes adjusted, ten thousand shades of black reflected off the cornstalks like slender hands waving toward heaven. Papa once told me that farmers are the choir conductors for heaven. It took me a few years and several hundred hours atop the tractor to understand what he meant.

From my perch on the porch, I could almost read the brass plaque that squatted below the roses—my testament to Maggie's "Yard of the Year." I stared and shook my head because I was smiling at a post-coma memory. Something that, at one time, I wasn't sure I'd have again.

The evidence that Maggie was alive, breathing, and back home spread around our house like an English garden. Camellias, roses, gardenias, wisteria, iris, anthurium, agapanthus, and even orchids bloomed in every patch of earth not covered by grass, porch, stepping-stone, or house.

I sniffed the air and walked to the side of the porch, looking over the tips of the cotton rows that had come up thick and bulbous. It was only May; it'd be late June before we saw any blooms. And, like everything in life, that depended on the rain. Waist-high now, they would be the last plants to show their color. And I'm not talking about the cotton; I'm talking about the little white flower that precedes the cotton, telling all the word that the white gold is coming, spring is over, summer has arrived, and the hard work is about to start. Judging by the buds, we were still a couple of weeks off.

I jumped, grabbed the porch rafter, and stood hanging and swaying from the truss. I looked at the cotton primed to erupt and paint the world with white flowers, and I marveled at the life I lived. Each day of my existence amazed me. I pulled up a couple of times, remembered that I wasn't as young as I'd once been, hopped down, skirted around the roses, and then stepped into the cotton—walking up one row and down another. The bolls slapped my thighs while the sandy dirt sifted up through my toes, reminding me of Charleston and our month at the beach. I looked up, closed my eyes—the stars still shining in my mind—stretched my hands across the heavens, and filled my chest with the night—yawning in his pasture was a farmer's delight.

Between the buds, the many and various flowers lighting up the house, and the smile that spread daily across Maggie's face, I noticed someone unusual, an old invisible friend, as I walked around my house. He had moved out just after delivery, but once he heard she'd come home, he did too. He had returned slowly—a flash here, a sound there. He'd been back a week when I finally cornered him in the barn. When I asked him to stay, he moved his things into the space above the ceiling fan and made his bed on the rafters.

I tried to make him feel welcome, because he brought with him the smell of gardenias and magnolia blooms, hot baths, cool sweat, and gut-busting laughter. He routinely tap-danced on the roof, sang in the rain, listened to Dean Martin and Frank Sinatra all hours of the night, and laughed for little to no reason. Each day, he'd flutter down off the rafters, or the ceiling fan where he enjoyed multiple revolutions, and light on Maggie's shoulder. Pretty soon, he went wherever she did. And that was good.

I walked back to the house, pressed my nose against the window, and gazed at Maggie sprawled across the bed just a few feet away. Her eyes were moving back and forth behind her lids, and her right index finger looked like it was writing in cursive.

Yes, life had thrown us a curve, but nothing short of death would dim her desire to have a child. You could tell it in the way she had repainted the nursery, the way she ran her fingers along the teeth marks on the railing of our secondhand crib, and the way she tapped me on the shoulder in the middle of the night when her clock told her it was time.

I suppose she was like most women. Maggie dreamed of the delivery, of the excitement of getting to the hospital on time, of timing the contractions, of her pushing and me cradling her head and helping her count. Of looking down across her swollen tummy at the doctor's face as he waited for our child's head to appear through the canal. Despite the pain, the sweat, and the blood, she dreamed of hearing his or her first cry, of being handed our child with the umbilical cord still attached, of watching me cut the cord, and then, finally, of pressing him to her pounding chest and feeling him breathe, suckle, and pull at her with tiny, wrinkled, God-fashioned fingers. She dreamed of watching his eyes open and being the first person he saw. She dreamed of needing, being needed, and giving unselfishly—something she was good at.

But I knew that she, my simple complexity, and the dream didn't end there. She dreamed of pulling that wet, gooey, covered-in-white-paste kid—who no doubt looked a lot like me—off her sweating, flushed chest and of passing him to me—of extending him across space and time and placing him in my shaking arms. She dreamed of watching my face light up as I cradled the son or daughter we'd made—of giving me that part of herself, a second time.

For me, the desire for a child had grown over time. Maggie had planted the seed, watered it, and then waited. I first recognized it as my own desire, distinct from Maggie's, some twenty months ago. It was the moment I placed my son's casket in the dirt down by the river beneath the oak. It was a strange and new feeling. Something unexpected. I didn't know what to do with it.

Yes, I felt guilty—what parent wouldn't—but I also knew I wanted to try again. I wanted to be a dad, and I wanted Maggie to be a mom. I wanted us to share the ups, the downs, the hard times, and the great times. I wanted to build a fort with our son or daughter, play catch, go to the beach and dig in the sand, laugh, wrestle, go fishing, teach him how to whistle, how to drive a tractor, and yes, I wanted to walk her down the aisle.

I cracked open the screen door and crept inside. I tiptoed down the hallway, making the floors creak, sat in my chair, pulled the door shut, and picked up my pencil. The single lightbulb fell out of the seams in the tongue-and-groove pine ceiling, dangling from a fraying cord a foot above my head.

My writing closet was exactly four inches wider than I on each side, and if I scooted my chair up to the bottom shelf, the door just shut behind me. I fell into my writing position, resting my head on my left hand and holding the pencil in my right.

*Since Maggie woke up, I . . .*

Wait. Stop.

Saying *Since Maggie woke up* amazes me still. Every time I say it, I think the clouds should part, a huge brass horn should descend, and God should give me five minutes to blow at the top of my lungs for all the world to hear before I shout, *"Hey, World! Maggie woke up!"*

Before me sat a three-hundred-page dilemma. Maggie had asked me to tell my story, and I had. From the night our son had died on August 15 to the moment she woke up on New Year's Day—some seventeen months ago. My sweaty palms rested on the pages as the two sides of me waged war. I stared at the words and knew the pictures I'd painted would reopen wounds that had not yet begun to heal. I also knew that opening those wounds would increase the sense of responsibility that she had yet to express but that was written all over her face every time we failed to talk about it.

On the other hand, I had never lied to Maggie about anything, and before me sat two versions.

Hers was the watered-down, G-rated version, which told enough of the story to satisfy her desire to know, and yet protected her from the R-rated version with all the ugly parts left in. The one on the right was the real story, the one I had written for myself—the director's take that would cut her to the core because it contained all my doubts and fears. I had written it because something deep inside me demanded that I rid my soul of the secrets that I kept there—those conversations with myself that I never voiced.

The discrepancies were simple: While I told her about the delivery and about our son's never crying a peep, I didn't mention her own screaming or my being crumpled in the corner covered in blood while the doctors worked to repair the damage to her body. While I told her about the funeral and Amos singing and the sun shining, I didn't tell her that I held the casket between my knees after we'd picked him up at the morgue, or that I buried the teddy bear with him, or that I had wished every day between then and the time she woke up and even some days since that Amos had just lowered my son down on top of me and covered us both.

While I did tell her about the fire I set in our dead cornfield, I did not explain the scar on my arm or how it got there. While I told her about watching movies with Bryce to pass the time, I did not tell her that there were nights I could not drive home afterward. And though I told her how I pulled Amos and Amanda out of the ditch that slippery, snowy night, I didn't say that I stood in the ice and snow and screamed at God, shaking my fist at heaven and daring Him to strike me down. Or that, when He didn't, I wished He had.

In Maggie's version, I told her about being in the hospital, how I had sat with her and talked with her. I told her that on most nights, when the halls were quiet, I'd rub her legs to keep the circulation going. I didn't mention that while the therapist had said ten minutes was all that was needed, I often massaged for hours. And I did not tell her that when Amanda came daily to change her gown, I helped so I could see my wife, touch her skin, and feel her warmth. I did not tell her how I bathed her, put socks on her feet when they were cold, held her hand beneath the sheets. I did not tell her that I slid my chair close to the bed and whispered in her ear, "Please come back to me."

And I didn't tell her that finally, for one reason or another, I had come to the place that, even if she never woke up, I could have lived without her—and now that memory, that ability to be alone, was maybe the greatest betrayal of all. I stared at my work and remembered something my grandfather said one night, "There's just one problem with pulling the wool over someone's eyes. And it surfaces whenever they take it off."

While I collected my nerve, both manuscripts had sat collecting dust. I had finished a week ago, but it had taken that long to muster enough gumption to do what I was about to do.

I pushed back from the desk, stacked the pages, and wrapped my version in a plastic grocery store bag. I knelt on the floor, opened my pocketknife, and pried up the single board that hid the cash box where Papa used to hide Nanny's jewelry when they went on vacation. It was about a foot square and locked relatively watertight. I lifted out the box, dusted it off, and flicked the lock. Inside I kept our birth certificates, the deed to the house, and a few other keepsakes. I laid the manuscript in the box, locked the lid, and slid the entire thing back into its safe place.

I licked my fingers so the bulb wouldn't burn me and twisted it off, listening to the sizzle of spit on lightbulb. I walked into our bedroom and leaned against the door frame, watching my wife sleep wrinkle-free and without torment.

I tiptoed across the floor and gently pushed her Audrey Hepburn hair out of her Bette Davis eyes. I knelt next to the bed and watched her. If she had any idea I was there, she didn't show it.

I whispered, "Maggie," and waited. No response. I whispered again. Finally I touched her cheek and said, "Honey?" She swatted my hand like a mosquito and flopped to the other side of the bed as if the bugs weren't biting over there.

And then I did something I'd never done before. I lied to Maggie. I laid her version on her bedside table, set a cup of coffee down on top, and crept out. Once an early riser, Maggie had awakened from the coma and found her internal clock reset. Now she was happy to sleep till ten thirty. Knowing that, I was pretty much assured that the coffee would be good and cold by then—just the way she liked it.

I slipped on my jeans and hat, made sure my writing closet was locked, and stepped into my boots. Then I hopped onto my tractor and dropped the harrow into the ground—something I'd seen my grandfather do five hundred times.

With a slight breeze cooling my face, I turned around in my seat, saw the deep cuts in the soil, and remembered something else Papa once told me. He had his pocketknife in one hand, scraping the fingernails of the other.

"Funny thing about farming . . ." He'd pointed out across the field with the tip of his knife. "To grow anything new, you've got to cut the soil and get rid of what remains of the old. I imagine if the earth could speak, it would tell us that it doesn't like that too much." He shrugged. "But life is like that. The past fertilizes the future." He snapped his knife closed, slid it into his front pocket, and stared at me with no expression. "Problem is, we have a tendency to forget that."

*chapter two*

When Maggie opened her eyes that New Year's Day some seventeen months ago, I felt like I could see again. The fog lifted off my soul, and for the first time since our son had died and she had gone to sleep—some four months, sixteen days, eighteen hours, and nineteen minutes earlier—I took a breath deep enough to fill both my lungs.

I knelt and placed her hand in mine, and the tears and tremors I'd been holding back bubbled up and out. In truth, I cried like a baby. She did too. A long time passed, but neither of us spoke. At least not with words. Besides, just what would I say? Where would I begin?

Finally she managed a hoarse whisper. "Missed you."

It took me a second. "Me too."

She swallowed and tilted her head. "How long?"

I shrugged and swallowed hard again, wanting to break it to her gently. "Couple of months." She patted the bed, then shook her head, the tears spilling down the lines of her nose. "I knew when you were here. Each time. I tried to wake up, but . . ."

She ran her fingers across the scar on my arm, a puzzled look appeared on her face, and she started to speak again.

I stopped her. "Shhh . . ." I placed my finger to her lips, and she reached for me.

But before I could hold her and let her hold me, I had to tell her. She had to know. "Honey . . . he didn't . . . I mean . . ."

She nodded. "I know." The lines around her eyes slanted downward, the need showing. "Where?"

I nodded out the hospital window in the general direction of our farm. "Down by the river." I bit my lip, trying to gauge her response. "Amos and I . . . we . . ."

She reached again, and this time I let her pull me toward her, her breath washing my face, her eyes searching mine. Her mind was working hard to get the words out of her mouth. "You forgive me?"

I shook my head. "Maggs . . . there's nothing to forgive."

She placed her hand behind my head, pressed my forehead to hers, and I knew that we were still "us."

Two weeks later, they told me I could take her home. Word spread, and even staff members who weren't scheduled to work packed the hallways to see her off and wish us well. Their faces and eyes suggested both a homecoming and a sending off. I'd have taken either one.

I pulled the truck around in front of the hospital, pushed the wheelchair into her hospital room, and for the first time since she woke up, wore something other than running shoes to the hospital. Maggie took one look at my feet and said, "Nice boots." She never did miss much.

"Blue picked them out."

She sat in the chair. "How's Pinky like them?"

"'Bout the same."

To much applause and too many cameras, I wheeled her out of the hospital and up to the side of an orange truck she'd never seen. She eyed the truck, then me, but didn't say a word until we drove off. She looked from hood ornament to tailgate and said, "Where'd you get this . . . thing?"

"Jake's."

She put her feet up on the dashboard, looked again at mine, and then leaned back against the headrest. "You mean . . ." She paused for effect. "Jake's Jalopy?"

I nodded.

She shook her head and reached for my hand. "I really am married to the Marlboro man."

I tried not to take my eyes off the road and not to smile. I almost managed.

My friend Amos, in his sergeant's stripes and black SWAT T-shirt, escorted us home in his Crown Vic—lights flashing, siren blaring. We ran all three stoplights between there and here. When we passed over Johnson's Ferry and by Pastor John's church, I didn't say a word. Maggs and I had a lot of talking to do, but neither of these was the place to begin. We came into the drive, and I circled the house around back.

Maggie put her hand on mine and nodded toward the big oak down at the river.

*That'd be a good place to start.*

I parked the truck in the shade and helped her out, and she stood next to the grave, propped between me on one side and her cane on the other. She knelt on the grave and kissed the stone-cold face of her son. Maggie's tears trickled off her face and filled the carved granite letters. When they mixed with the dust and dirt on the grave, she dipped the tip of her finger on the drops and traced the shape of a heart like she would on a fogged-up bathroom window. I think she'd wanted to do that for a long time.

We walked into the house and by the nursery door, where she just leaned against the frame and looked inside. She stood there a long time, then wandered through the rest of the house, saw my drum on the mantel, read some of the letters from my students. Then she walked to the barn, sat down in the middle of Pinky's stall, and laughed for an hour while Pinky and twelve little pigs all vied for a scratch between the ears. It was glorious, smelly fun.

It didn't take me long to figure out that we were two people on two totally different schedules. She was used to sleeping twenty-four hours a day, and I had grown used to sleeping only three to four hours a night. I also found that she wanted to be near me, my hand on hers, hers on mine, asleep on my chest, whatever—she didn't let me out of her sight. And that was just fine with me.

MAGGIE HAD CREATED QUITE A STIR IN THE MEDIA WORLD. I held the reporters at bay, but sometime in the first week of February they found us. Tucked away in our seclusion and protective bubble, the media attention became pretty intense. Everybody wanted Maggie's story. Finally I called in Mr. Clean, aka Amos, and we brought all the reporters onto the back porch and gave a group interview that lasted about three hours.

Blue lay instinctively at Maggie's feet and bared his teeth while Amos controlled the crowd and questions. When Maggie got tired, I gave him the nod, and he started ushering people and cameras off the porch. Given the size of Amos's biceps and the way his shirt looked shrink-wrapped around his torso, nobody argued. That night we watched ourselves on the six o'clock news, and that weekend we watched an hour-long special in Amos's den along with Amanda—his wife—and Li'l Dylan, who had taken a liking to sitting in my lap.

The next morning, I left Maggie sleeping and drove up the road to the long-since-closed drive-in movie theater that was now home to our reclusive, multimillionaire neighbor, Bryce. I hadn't seen him for about a month, but that wasn't unusual. Bryce didn't keep time like everybody else.

Finding no sign of him, I picked up a paper in Walterboro, filled up the tank, and drove home. When I saw our picture on the front page of the lifestyle section, I shoved the paper below the seat and figured we'd had about enough of our own story. Maybe Maggie could use a few days at the ocean.

We drove to Charleston, where I rented a house on the water for a week. When the owner saw Maggie, his bottom jaw dropped. In a European accent I couldn't place, he said, "Momma, come quick."

An older, baggy woman came to the door, wrapped in a shawl and loose-fitting slippers. Her eyes grew wide, and she said, "Oh my, it's . . . Miracle Maggie."

That was the first time we'd heard anyone call her that.

The people were so blown away by Maggie's story that they gave us the top-floor suite for free. Every morning when we woke, the owner would cook us eggs, toast, jam, and strong coffee. We stretched a week into a month, and between midnight walks on the beach and that woman's cooking, Maggie found her sea legs. By the time we left, her cane was collecting dust in the corner.

Our second week there, we went to a famous seafood restaurant not too far from the water. For decades all kinds of famous people had frequented the place, and when they did, the owner nailed a bronze tag at the seat to let later patrons know who had sat there before them. He put me in Pat Conroy's seat.

Just before we left, the owner approached us, held up a shiny bronze tag, and asked, "Do you mind?"

I smiled and shook my head, and we watched as he nailed MAGGIE STYLES into place. Eyeing his handiwork, he brushed it off, turned, and said, "Please come back."

We walked home through the historic district, returning to our room about midnight. Maggie propped one foot up on the sink and began painting her toenails.

I picked up a magazine. "You know, I'm pretty good at that."

She eyed her pinky toe. "Uh-huh."

I stepped out onto the balcony, reading by flashlight when something metal clamored into the sink, followed by a single scream. I poked my head in and found her leaning in close to the mirror, studying the top of her head. She frowned and dug through her hair with the tips of her fingers like a mother monkey with her young. Then she stopped dead, pulled apart her hair like a curtain, and looked at me. "Is that what I think it is?"

"What?"

She rolled her eyes upward. "That!"

I stepped toward the sink and looked at Maggie's hair under the light. "Ahhh . . ." I fingered out the single gray hair and plucked it.

"Ouch!" she said, eyes narrowing. I held up the hair and was about to say something cute, but she held up a finger and said, "Not one word, Dylan Styles."

*Yes, ma'am.*

For two more weeks, we strolled the streets, rode in horse-drawn carriages, and somewhere in there began swaying to the same rhythm. Somewhere in there, we started walking in sync.

WHEN WE GOT HOME FROM THE OCEAN IN THE FIRST WEEK of March, we walked down to our son's grave site, and there we heard the pipes. Bryce appeared, decked out in full military regalia, and stood blowing till his face looked like a spark plug. Maggie walked over and kissed him on the cheek, and with tear stained freckles, he faded away down the riverside.

We walked back to the house, and parked in the drive sat a brand-new red Massey Ferguson tractor. We walked around it like it was a snake, then decided it wouldn't bite us, and better yet nobody would accuse us of stealing it. Somebody had tied a case's worth of empty Old Milwaukee cans to the back and hung a sign from the rear of the seat that read JUST WOKE UP. On the front, an airbrushed sign read MAGGIE LOVES DYLAN. Corny, yes, but who am I to change Bryce? We spent most of the next day on that tractor, and Maggie drove the entire time.

Life in Digger had returned to some sort of normalcy. That is, if anything in Digger was ever normal. Love had returned. Smiles cracked the faces of once-cold hearts. And me? I could smell gardenias even when they weren't blooming, and seldom a day passed that I didn't walk to the river and palm the acorns and dirt off my son's tombstone.

*chapter three*

By mid-March, much of Maggie's strength had returned. As had her green thumb. Propped up on the front porch swing, she spent an entire morning sketching an aerial view of the house and designing the yard layout. The next morning, with plan in hand, she tugged on my arm, batted those trademark eyes, and said, "I'd like to buy a few plants for the yard."

She flashed her design, and I knew instinctively that the next step in this parade would be an expensive one. I also knew occupying her hands would free up her mind, giving her time to work through two hurdles we had yet to address. The first was children, and whether or not we could ever have one of our own. The second was trying to explain to Maggie what I'd done for four and a half months while she lay sleeping.

I looked at the yard, where I'd let weeds take over, then back at Maggie. "A *few* plants?"

She arched her eyebrows and said with a sneaky smile, "Well, maybe more than a few."

She pulled on a tank top, stepped into an old pair of bib overalls, laced up her running shoes, and stuffed her hair under a baseball cap. When Blue and I got in the truck, she was unconsciously tapping her foot and making notes on her list.

We reached the nursery and grabbed two flatbed carts and the assistance of a young guy with a "Can I help you?" look pasted across his face. Midway through the first greenhouse, I had serious déjà vu. Toward the end of the aisle, I figured it out. The wholesale baby outlet. Although this little trip promised to cost even more. And just as I had in the baby store, somewhere down the second aisle I quit counting and just said, "Honey, I think whatever that is looks great, and we probably need a couple of those."

She rolled her eyes, stuck her pencil up into her baseball cap, and put her hand on her hip. "You're not helping me."

To say she was task-oriented would be an understatement. Chances were good that if she kept at this current pace, we'd be putting plants in the ground by flashlight. And I didn't care. My grandfather had lived by a pretty simple philosophy that made good sense to me—*Happy wife, happy life.*

Sweat had begun to bead on her top lip, and an *I'm thinking* wrinkle had creased the skin between her eyes. The ripple effects of the coma had been many, but it had done little to dampen her intensity.

I prodded her. "No, seriously, we probably need a few more of those."

She pointed a crooked, double-jointed finger in my face and said, "You want to end up on the couch?"

"Only if you're there."

She turned and kept counting flowers. "Don't get your hopes up."

"Yeah." I spread out my arms and yawned. "That whole snow-angel thing probably wouldn't work too well on the couch."

She cracked a smirk, picked up a handful of dirt from a nearby pot, and threw it at me.

Unfazed, our young assistant smiled and held up every plant like a true professional. With each one, Maggie stuffed her pencil behind her ear and weighed the look of the plant, the color, the size, and the cost. Several times she put back a perfectly good plant because the price was too high.

I picked up on her process and sensed her growing disappointment at the expense. I could see the high prices were quickly diminishing her idea of what our yard would look like. She had come in here thinking Martha Stewart's garden and was walking out thinking Charlie Brown's Christmas tree. So I backtracked to pick up what she'd passed over. When I reappeared, she looked at me and whispered, "Dylan, we can't afford all that."

I looked at the cart. "You're right, but I'm married to a woman who spends twenty dollars on a Christmas tree and a hundred and fifty on lights."

Our assistant laughed and then, seeing we needed a minute alone, excused himself and disappeared toward a huge greenhouse at the back of the property.

"Maggs," I whispered, "I don't care what they cost, because—"

I looked at her. She had regained some of the muscle she'd lost in the hospital, and the chiseled tone in her face and jaw had returned. Her overalls were faded and baggy, but they couldn't hide her strong shoulders, lean arms, the way the sweat beaded on her temples and just in front of her ears, and the penetrating depth of her eyes. Maggie was still that complexity that found meaning and expression between extremes, and all that beauty was just starting to bubble back up to the surface. Like the flowers she tended, my wife was full of buds and on the verge of exploding with color.

"But, Dylan . . ."

Blue circled around us, wagging his tail.

"It's all right. Really."

"But how?"

"'Cause at the end of the day"—I held up my hands, dirty and green from loading pots—"we're living . . . and life is thick."

Our assistant returned, leading an older man who wore a straw hat with a hole in the brim. "This is Mr. Wilson, my boss."

The man extended his hand. "Merle, all my customers call me Merle."

Maggie turned, tried to wipe her eyes without being seen, and stood behind me.

"Hello, sir. I'm Dylan, and this is my wife, Ma—"

"I know who you are. I seen the papers." He smiled and blinked several times, then pointed around the nursery. "Anything you want, at my cost. And if you'd like, come with me."

He led us to an enormous greenhouse out back where it looked as though he did his own seeding and potting. The place was overgrown with mature plants. "This is where I bring some of my best customers and those folks who really know and love plants."

Maggie stepped inside, eyed the rows of his well-kept secret, and sucked in a breath of air large enough for a woman three times her size. When her head and shoulders slowly lifted, it looked as if someone had shoved an air hose into her spine and filled her up.

I extended my hand. "Thank you, sir."

He nodded and stepped backward out the door. "Jes' holler, if'n you need anything."

We filled six carts that would later require four trips in my truck to haul it all back to the house. Eventually, Merle just let me borrow his mulch trailer, which on the last trip I had them fill with about eight cubic yards of potting soil and mulch. I returned the trailer, then found him at the register so I could pay our bill.

While he totaled it, I noticed a pink orchid stretched out across the counter. "How much for the orchid?"

He smiled, cleared out the calculator, spat a stream of dark juice into a can behind him, and said, "Follow me." We walked around the back of the property, and he led me into a humid greenhouse filled entirely with orchids. "These are my favorites," he said. "I don't usually let customers in here, but . . . again, at my cost—whatever you want."

There must have been two hundred plants. As Merle explained the story behind several of them and told how to care for them, I made mental notes. When he finished, I bought fourteen. He totaled my order and laughed like a man who knew the pleasure of dirt beneath his fingernails. He followed me home in his van so the wind wouldn't damage the orchid buds, which were just days from opening.

I thanked him again, carried the orchids into the house, and then found Maggie out between the house and the barn surrounded by her plants. She was holding a watering hose set on high, and the spray spread out into a wide fan that was doing a pretty good job of soaking everything we'd just bought. I tipped back my hat and sat on the front porch steps, trying to estimate the number of planting hours I had coming.

She clamped the hose off and said, "Honey, how much did all this cost?"

I smiled and stuffed the receipt back into my pocket. "Let's just say we won't be going back to New York City anytime soon."

Her jaw dropped. "That much?" Then she smiled, looked at her plants, and said, "Well, this is better than *Riverdance*."

I scratched Blue's head and laughed. "Honey, you're weird."

She nodded, and then a sneaky look stole into her eyes. I tried to jump out of reach, but I slipped on the steps, tripped over Blue, and landed on the grass face-first. Maggie unclamped the hose and doused me in about three gallons of well water. By the time I wrestled myself free of Blue and out of the stream, Maggie was on top of me and showering my head with her fire hose. I grabbed her by the pant leg and wrestled the hose free.

When she realized she was about to get a taste of her own medicine, she howled, "Dylan Styles! I do not want to get wet!" But it was too late, and she didn't really mean it anyway. I held her by the bibs and poured ten seconds' worth of egg-smelling water down the back of her bibs. She squealed at the feel of cold water that had come up from almost six hundred feet below-ground and was now spilling out the bottoms of her pant legs.

It took us the entire next day just to set the plants where she wanted them, and another three to get them in the ground. The day after we finished, I drove to the hardware store and had a bronze plaque made that read YARD OF THE YEAR.

*chapter four*

AFTER TWO DAYS IN LABOR AND ONLY MOMENTS before delivering our son, Maggie's cheeks had become flushed as she lay in bed. She'd clenched my hand, watching the contractions under the haze of the epidural, and I watched her. I remember thinking that there in that place, draped in sweat, exhaustion, and the giddiness of expectation, Maggie had never seemed more alive.

Moments later she opened her soul and pushed for what seemed like hours. Physically spent, defying what I thought were the laws of physics, she did what only she could do, and then, as if his universe somehow collided with ours, he appeared. The doctor caught him, there was a gush of liquid, and the doctor never even hesitated. He rushed him to the table, spread him like a lab experiment, and started to work.

That's when the smile left Maggie's face. Blazing only seconds before, it drained out of her like light from a candle that had burned out its own wick. It dimmed, sputtered, and snuffed itself out. Only the trail of smoke and the threat of hot wax remained.

Maggie had never held him. She had never held her own son. Wide-eyed yet afraid to breathe, she'd watched as they failed to revive him. Then she watched as they pulled the sheet over his scrunched, blue head and recorded the time. That was one of the last images she'd seen before she went to sleep. The other was my face. When she woke up, he'd been in the ground for months.

For Maggie, the desire to have a child was like that. It was like breathing. It was as hardwired into her DNA as the sound of her voice, the look in her eyes, and the touch of her skin. Take it out and you might as well take the Maggie out of Maggie. But it was that very desire that had put her in the coma in the first place. I wondered how she'd see it from the other side, but if anything, it seemed that the coma had made the desire that much stronger. If I'd thought she was on a mission the last time, I had another thing coming.

Toward the end of March—having conquered the weeds—we returned to the hospital for her first female checkup.

Dr. Frank Palmer was a good man. Midforties, father of several kids himself, he was always running between soccer, basketball, or baseball games. His wife and his kids were his life. I liked him and admired him for the way he went about his doctoring. Let's face it, people's privates are private for a reason, but he spent his entire day invading other people's privacy. Somehow he managed to do it with class and respect for his patients. He treated Maggie like a niece or a cousin whom he was both comfortable with and protective of.

Following her exam, Dr. Frank pulled me aside while Maggie was getting dressed. He raised his eyebrows and lowered his voice. "You might want to exercise some caution for a while in what you two do together."

"Like?"

"Don't watch too many Hallmark movies, don't go to a baby store anytime soon, try to keep her away from anything that involves needing Kleenex, and—most importantly—try to keep her thoughts on the future, not the past."

I looked down the hall. "But I don't understand. She's not responsible."

He nodded. "We know that, but her emotions don't, and until they level out, no power on earth can reason with them."

Dr. Frank referred us to a reproductive specialist whom he'd heard was setting the world on fire. With referral in hand, we drove to Charleston and saw a female doctor with more degrees on the wall than anyone I'd ever met. Between medical school and residency, she'd been in training for twenty years. And judging from all the plaques and signed pictures of famous people, I knew we'd come to the right place.

Her nurses ushered us into the examination room, which was nice as examination rooms go. In fact, it was the nicest one I'd ever been in. Of course, it had the cold, hard examination table with the stirrups tucked up along the sides, but it also had some artwork on the walls, a few comfortable chairs, and even a couch along one wall, suggesting that they had worked to put their patients at ease.

As I was studying the room, a petite nurse with a ponytail so tight it was pulling back her eyes set a small plastic cup on the table next to me and said, "We'll need a sample." She pointed over her shoulder at the small sliding door that led from this room into what must have been a lab or something, and said,

"Just slide it through there when you're done." Then, as if she'd just asked me to record the time of day, she walked out and pulled the door shut behind her.

I eyed the cup. *Why would a fertility doctor need a urine sample from me? What good would that do them?* Confused and bewildered, I turned to Maggie, who, unable to hold it any longer, began laughing like a hyena. That was about the time I understood what the nurse meant when she said *sample.*

I looked around the room again and got a whole new understanding of the décor. I shook my head. "Is she serious?"

Maggie was laughing so hard she couldn't talk.

I pointed at the cup. "I'm not doing that."

Evidently Maggie had assumed I knew that when a couple visited a fertility doctor for help, the first test they performed was a sperm count. She slid the lock on the door, turned off the light, and sat down next to me. Swinging both her legs across mine, she hung her arms around my neck and pressed her forehead against mine.

"Hey, forget them. It's just me, and we can do this together. We're good at this."

I looked around, wiped the sweat off my face, and nodded. Sunlight broke through the cracks in the blinds and lit the dust particles that were floating through the air, settling on Maggie's skin as she changed out of her clothes. She slipped into a pink, flowery gown and then tiptoed across the room barefooted, took me by the hand, and led me back across the room to what I understood was the husband's couch. With my heart pounding inside my chest, the growing fear that someone was about to walk in that door, and my embarrassment evident, my wife did the one thing she alone could do. She made me forget about everyone but her, and she loved me.

A few minutes later, Maggie slid the sample into the lab and unlocked the door. I guess that sent a signal to the nurse, because she appeared pretty quickly after that. Maggie sat on the end of the table, knees together, her legs bouncing slightly on her toes. The nurse laid Maggie back on the table and prepped the equipment for the doctor, who walked in a few minutes later.

She was older, maybe midfifties, and looked serious. She extended her hand to me, then to Maggie. "Hi, I'm Dr. Madison."

She slid her hands into rubber gloves and, with little introduction, began a less-than-tender probing of Maggie's insides. When finished, she quickly inserted cameras into and over Maggie's tummy, taking pictures and studying the screen above her. Despite her limited bedside manner, I did not for a minute doubt her ability. She knew what she was doing and didn't have to prove anything to anyone. For that I was grateful.

Twenty minutes later, feeling a bit like two cattle in a stockyard, we followed the doctor into her office, where she sat across from us searching for an entry point into her results. After fifteen minutes of explanations and diagrams that I didn't really understand, I raised my hand and said, "Pardon me, ma'am, but what does all this mean?"

I could tell she was trying, but even Dr. Frank will tell you that medical school does not teach you how to deliver bad news. She closed her clipboard, took a deep breath, and let it out slowly. "I don't believe you'll ever—absent a miracle—have more children of your own."

She looked out the window, then back at us. "Sometimes I love my job. I really do. And sometimes, like today, I hate it, because despite all that I know and everything I've studied, modern medicine has its limitations."

Maggie swallowed, then asked, "What are my chances?"

Dr. Madison tossed her head slightly side to side. "One in several hundred thousand."

Shaking, Maggie stood, collected her purse, and waited for me to open the door.

Dr. Madison met us at the door and shook my hand. She looked at Maggie, who didn't look up. "I hope you beat the odds."

AS THAT MAY MELTED INTO JUNE, MAGGIE BOUGHT EVERY pregnancy book that Barnes & Noble offered or could order. Hoping to find something the doctors might have missed, one shred of hope, one single ray of light, she read everything she could get her hands on. Few of our activities or conversations weren't preoccupied with getting pregnant. Which was fine with me, but as the months ticked by, it took its toll on Maggie.

Each month, the start of her cycle was the hardest to take. And because cycles are just that, cyclical, I often knew it was coming. She'd return from the bathroom, retreat into the kitchen, pretend she was fretting over dinner, and try to hide the depression that crippled her face.

I'd order pizza, then take her by the waist and lead her into the den and onto the worn magnolia planks, where we'd imitate Nanny and Papa. Most nights, we'd dance into the morning. Our life felt like a school dance where the DJ kept starting and stopping the music without warning.

Some dances need to finish.

Then came August 15. His first birthday. We walked down to the graveside, Maggie carrying flowers. She knelt on the slab, wiped away the leaves and dirt, and kissed it. She placed the flowers on the grove, brushed her palm across his name, and painted our son's stone with her tears. Then, her lips just inches from his name, she whispered words that only a mother can.

She stood and slid her arm beneath mine, and we took a walk by the river. That's when she surprised me. She tugged on my arm and whispered, "Maybe . . . maybe we could . . . adopt."

I studied her face, her lips, the tilt of her head, and it didn't take a genius to see: just saying the word was painful. I'd thought of it months before, actually, but hadn't wanted to bring it up for fear of hurting her feelings.

But as I saw it, the hard part for us was actually making a baby, not wanting one or knowing what to do with it once we got it. So looking at the situation objectively, I thought adoption might be a good way to go. The more I thought about it, the more I liked the idea. Besides, how hard could it be? It certainly couldn't be any worse than what we were currently up against.

Or so I thought.

*chapter five*

CLASSES AT DIGGER JUNIOR COLLEGE STARTED THE first week in September, bringing me seventy-five new opportunities. After a week of learning their names and adjusting my seating charts, I drove with Maggie to the only adoption agency listed in the Charleston phone book. The receptionist filled us in on the general stuff, then handed us a three-inch stack of papers and said, "Fill these out and get them back to us."

Doing so took us a little more than a month. They wanted to know about our family, like, starting at Ellis Island, about any family diseases and addictions, about our relationship, our medical histories, how much money we made and how we spent it. Since we didn't feel we had anything to hide, we answered honestly. Maybe that was our mistake.

The written interview felt more invasive than Dr. Madison—but we didn't know what rigorous was until they called us in two weeks later for a follow-up interview.

The receptionist sat us down in front of two psychologists, Mr. Sawyer and Ms. Tungston, a man and a woman who looked like they had done this sort of thing before. They were looking at duplicate copies of our notebook of answers and, without much introduction, began firing questions. To say they were impersonal, sterile, and detached would be too kind.

Mr. Sawyer went first. Without looking up from his notebook, he pointed his pen at me and said, "How much money do you make?"

That struck me as an odd way to start, but okay, I could roll with the punches. "Well, sir," I said, waving my hand at the notebook in front of him, "I make $27,000 a year teaching and almost another twenty between my farming and the crop and pine-straw leases we have with—"

"So . . ." He studied his notes. "What do you think you'll make this year?"

"Well, sir, I'll make pretty close to, if not more than, what we've written there." I looked at Maggie and then back at him. "I think what you see there is a worst-case scenario based on—"

He shook his head. "Please understand, your income methods are rather unconventional and not too predictable by today's standards." He pointed to Ms. Tungston, then back to himself. "We, as a committee, want to avoid placing a child into a poverty situation."

We seemed to have a disconnect. I shook my head and almost spoke up when Maggie placed a restraining hand on my thigh.

"Sir, Dylan's a hard worker. You can look at him and tell that." She put her hand on my neck. "See, his neck's even red."

Neither smiled. Mr. Sawyer took off his glasses. "Just curious, how does a farmer end up with a Ph.D.?"

"My grandfather taught me to farm long before I took an interest in school." I shrugged. "Just something I wanted to do, sir."

Seeing an entry, Ms. Tungston turned her attention to Maggs. She tapped her notebook with her index finger. "Last year you spent four months in a coma after delivering a still-born child?"

Maggie nodded and gulped. "He would have been a year old in August." She put her arm around me. "We named him after . . ."

Ms. Tungston returned to her notes. "Did the doctors ever determine a cause?"

Maggie shook her head. "No."

"Was your coma related to the pregnancy?"

I spoke up. "Ma'am, the delivery was pretty rough, and, well, Maggie . . . hemorrhaged pretty badly, and . . ."

The woman paused, and her voice softened. "We often encounter mothers who have lost a child." She waved around the room. "That's how they end up here. Dealing with that takes time." She looked at me and back to Maggs. "Have you two dealt with this issue in your life?"

Maggie sat up straight. "Ma'am, if you're talking about the loss of my son, and four months of my, our, life, I'm working on it." She held my hand, her knuckles turning white. "We're working on it. Every day. But some hurts need more than just Band-Aids."

*Lord, I love my wife.*

Maggie's eyes had begun to water. Deep down I was starting to get pretty angry, but I knew that anything even vaguely resembling a temper would kill our chances altogether. I bit my tongue and tried to smile. Maybe this was all part of the game, and they were just trying to see what we were made of.

Mr. Sawyer continued. "As for transportation, we place a premium on safety. I see that you drive a truck?" His heavy eyebrows bobbed above his glasses and said more than his mouth.

Thinking we could use a little levity in the conversation, I said, "Yep. And if that breaks, we own a pretty good tractor."

No one seemed to get the joke.

"You realize that federal law mandates that you cannot put a child-restraint seat in the front seat of a truck?"

I hadn't thought about it, but I was quick on my feet. "Sir, that's no problem. I know this guy in Digger, and he can get us pretty much whatever you think we should have." I threw it back at him. "What would you prefer?"

He didn't like my asking the question, but he tossed out an answer. "We approve of the safety ratings on most major minivans."

I nodded and said nothing as I felt the water rising around my neck.

Then they threw in the bomb.

He scanned his notebook with incredulity. "You understand that this process can be rather expensive?"

I nodded assuringly, hoping that he wasn't about to say what I hoped he wouldn't.

"Given your financials, are you sure that you can come up with the $38,000 down payment en route to the almost $45,000 you will need to complete the adoption process?"

I knew these numbers and had given them considerable thought, but, like many things lately, I'd kept them from Maggie. She had enough to worry about. She looked at me in disbelief as I spoke quickly and with confidence.

"I've already obtained approval for a loan that exceeds that amount. Won't be a problem."

He looked as though he half-believed me. "From a reputable lending institution?"

I knew this lingo. "A+."

He made a note and said, "And you can fax me that approval form . . ."

I nodded and waited for the next question, though in my mind I had yet to answer his last. This was not going as I'd planned.

He lowered his eyes. "What's your collateral?"

"The farm."

"And if you default, what happens to that child's home?"

"Sir, I've never defaulted on anything, and I don't intend to now." I paused and stuck out my hand. "I give you my word."

Evidently he didn't place the same value on my word that Maggs or Amos or my grandfather or I did.

I continued, "We only have one credit card; other than some plants, its balance is nearly zero. And our monthly payment on the truck is less than $300." I pointed proudly at the truck in the parking lot outside the window.

Mr. Sawyer's eyes followed my finger. "You're making payments on that vehicle?"

"Yes, sir, it says so . . ." I tried to point to the financial tab of his notebook, but he waved me off.

"Never mind."

I admit, prior to walking in there, I had visions of Little Orphan Annies bottled up in run-down shanties with cranky Miss Hannigans browbeating them while they waited to be rescued by another Daddy Warbucks. But halfway through this interview, I thought, *If this is what it takes to adopt a child, then you can just keep Annie and her little dog too.*

It's a good thing he couldn't hear me.

Abruptly, they both stood. He pointed at me, and she pointed at Maggs. Both said, "Follow me."

Maggie gripped my hand, and I could see the doubt growing. I whispered, "Hey, no big deal. Forget her. Just answer like you're talking to me, and we'll be fine."

She smiled, or tried to, and we went behind separate doors. Thirty minutes later we emerged from our respective rooms, and I could tell by the look on her face that her interrogation hadn't gone much better than mine.

We drove home in relative silence. Maggie chewed on a fingernail and pulled her knees up to her chest. I stared out the window and wrestled with how and where to get the money.


THE NEXT MORNING I LEFT MAGGS A NOTE THAT READ "Back before lunch." I drove to Jake's and pulled into the gate, and he walked out of the trailer, smiling. I could tell by the look on his face that he was already thinking about his steak dinner.

I hopped out of the truck, shook his hand, and skipped the small talk. Walking quickly, I led him down the row of six minivans. "Jake, I need one of these."

His roadside marquee, lit with dozens of tiny lightbulbs, towered above us. JAKE'S JALOPY flashed intermittently with FREE FINANCING and NO MONEY DOWN.

Jake smiled and tried to slow down the conversation. He laughed and leaned back, sticking out his growing belly, and said, "Needing to upgrade to the old family car, eh?" He had changed the picture of his family just below the flashing sign. They had added another child, and everyone's face was a little plumper. Business was good.

"Jake," I said, eyeing the options, "think of this more as a lateral move. I need to trade my truck for one of these."

"Well, let's see." He pulled a three-by-five-inch card from his shirt pocket and began scanning the years, models, and prices.

I knew that he knew all those by heart, so I stepped closer, placed the card back in his pocket, and said, "My wife needs a car to take our child to and from school, the grocery store, and wherever else he or she needs to go. What can I get for my truck?"

Jake bit his lip, eyed the truck, then eyed his vans. Then he looked back to the truck. "Looks like you've taken pretty good care of it, but the depreciation on something like that is—"

"Jake," I said, lifting a hand, "at last count I've sent seventeen people down here to buy a car from you."

"You have?"

I began rattling off the names. His eyes grew bigger.

"Guess you have." He walked up to a white Honda minivan that was about five years old. He kicked the tire. "This one was owned by a woman who didn't never go nowhere. It's only got 40,000 miles on it, got meticulous service records, ain't never been wrecked, comes with a factory extended warranty and the highest safety rating in the industry." He looked at me. "For you—your truck plus $5,000."

I shook my head. "Jake, you don't understand. Think"—I cut the air with my hand moving side to side—"horizontal." I stuffed my hands in my pockets and let out a deep breath. "Adoption ain't cheap."

He stepped back. "You guys adopting? I thought Maggie was pregnant."

"Jake, that didn't work out like we'd planned. Work with me here."

"Your truck plus $3,000." He was getting closer.

"My truck plus $1,500."

"Two thousand."

I stuck out my hand. "Deal, but I don't want it on paper. I want you to take my word for it, and on paper I want it to look like I traded my truck for this thing."

His face grew contorted. "I don't understand. You want me to take your word?"

I nodded and led him to the trailer. "I want you to trust me to drive out of here in your van with nothing but a promise that I'll bring you $2,000 cash within the week."

Jake looked at me like I'd lost my mind.

I sat back, crossed my arms, and nodded. "Deal?"

Jake let out an exasperated, disbelieving breath. "I appreciate what you've done for me, man, but I can't—"

"Jake," I said, "I need a favor. And yes, I will bring you cash on the barrelhead before the end of the week."

He looked at me, raised both eyebrows, and held out his hand, palm up. I was talking his language, and I knew now that we had gotten through all the baloney.

"You'll put it in my hand."

I tapped his palm with my index finger and then curled his fingers into a fist. "Right there."

Ten minutes later, I cranked the engine in the white minivan. The corner of my rearview mirror told me it was seventy-seven degrees, which was not unusual for South Carolina in November. God didn't usually turn on the AC till January. I waved my hand back and forth across the vent. *Maybe the soccer-mom mobile isn't that bad after all.*

I drove out of Jake's lot, looked in the rearview mirror, and saw my truck parked in the lot, waiting on the next buyer. I shook my head and spat out the window. *No one on the planet will ever love that truck as much as I did.*

I fastened my seat belt, adjusted the air vent, and concluded—AC or not—that Honda couldn't hold a candle to either my old '72 C-10 or the '76 Ford I was now leaving behind. But if it would help Maggie and me qualify in the eyes of the adoption committee, I'd drive a horse and buggy.

From Jake's I drove straight to the office of John Caglestock. His secretary, Lorraine, stepped from behind her desk to greet me. "Hi, Dylan. You don't usually just show up without calling. Everything okay?"

"I just wondered if I might have a word with John."

She waved me to a nearby chair. "Let me check." She walked into his office and then out again ten seconds later, followed by John.

"Hey, Dylan, come on in." He shut the door behind me, and we sat at the small conference table across from his desk. I had come to John with my hat in my hand, and he sensed it. He also knew that as the guy who overlooked Bryce McGregor's affairs, I knew exactly how much money John and his firm had made off Bryce. And it was millions. So, while I needed John, John also needed me. I was banking on this.

John also knew I'd never ask him or Bryce for anything that wasn't really important, so if I was here, looking as though I needed a favor, well . . . he could read the writing on the wall.

I cut to the chase. "John, Maggie and I are trying to adopt a child."

He nodded, wrapped his glasses behind his ears, and settled them on his nose.

"I need $38,000 as a down payment, $45,000 total, plus I need another $2,000 to pay off the minivan I just bought. I wondered if you could . . ."

John didn't even blink. He touched the phone next to him. "Lorraine, please bring me my checkbook. Personal."

Two seconds later, she appeared in his office and laid the checkbook on the table. Ignoring my protests, he opened the book, scribbled, signed, and then tore out a check, made out to me, for $40,000.

I shook my head. "John, I can't. That's not why I came here. I need a cosigner at the . . ."

John punched the button again and said, "Lorraine, get me Richard at American National."

Two minutes later our phone beeped, and Lorraine interrupted. "Sir, I'm putting him through now."

John put him on speakerphone. "Richard, how are you?"

"Good, John. How're things?"

"Listen, Richard, I need a favor."

"Anything."

John looked at me, then at the phone. "A good friend of mine is going to come see you about a loan. He doesn't have much to show, but he's good for it, and I'll guarantee it."

"You want your name on the paper?"

"Yes, and he needs the money pretty quickly."

"As in, how quickly?"

John looked at me, and I shrugged.

"How about an hour? He's trying to adopt a child and needs to show that he's good for it."

This sounded like something John had done before, and it sounded like Richard, whoever he was, was in a position to make it happen.

"I'll have the paperwork ready when he gets here. How much?"

John spoke without blinking. "Extend the line to fifty. He probably won't use it, but I want him to have some room."

Richard murmured, "Uh-huh," and I could hear him scribbling near the phone.

John continued, "Thanks, Richard. If you'll courier me my end, we'll take care of it this afternoon."

"Will do."

John punched the speakerphone button and hung up. He looked at me, and I wanted to kiss him.

I stood up and shook his hand. "Thanks, John."

He extended his personal check a last time. "I'm happy to loan it to you myself."

I patted him on the shoulder and turned toward the door. "Thanks, John. You've done enough already. We're grateful." I took a step back and whispered, "Oh, and, John?"

He raised his chin.

"I need this to be between us."

He nodded and drew a horizontal line through the air with both of his hands like an umpire calling a runner safe at home plate. "Whatever you wish."

I drove out of the lot, made one quick stop at the Baby Superstore, and then drove to American National, where Richard, the bank president, met me at the door. I signed several pieces of paper, and within three minutes he handed me a checkbook for my own line of credit. The entire transaction didn't take five minutes.

I thanked him, left the bank, and then drove an hour back to Charleston, where I walked into the adoption agency and handed the receptionist a check for $38,000. She eyed it and quietly disappeared.

When Mr. Sawyer, the male member of the inquisition committee, appeared from his office wearing a rather confused look, he held the check out in front of him as if it were hot.

He was about to say something when I pointed toward the door. "Sir, if you would just follow me."

I led him out the front door and clicked the unlock button

on my key fob twice just to make sure he heard the chirp. I opened both side doors, cranked the engine, turned the AC on "snow," and pointed at the brand-spanking-new baby seat buckled in tight and proper in the backseat.

He looked at the check, then the van, and then back to the check. "I will say I am very impressed, Dr. Styles, but . . ." His face turned cold again. "I've got to be honest with you. We were more than a bit concerned about your wife's answers during her individual interview."

I turned off the car and followed him back inside. "Sir?"

He wiped the beading sweat off his head. "Have you ever considered getting Maggie professional help?"

"Sir?"

He looked at me. "A psychologist."

"You sure we're talking about the same woman?"

Once again, my attempt at humor had little effect.

He lowered his voice and eyes. "A stillbirth can be one of the most difficult hurdles a woman ever faces. Your wife might need professional help to deal appropriately with the trauma of the past."

The sound of my breath exiting me was like the sound of a helium balloon that had been untied. "Sir, I just don't understand." Maybe it was the deer-in-the-headlights stare that convinced him I was serious.

He loosened his tie and squinted through the glare of the window. "Dr. Styles . . ."

"Dylan, please."

"Dylan, in our experience, the loss of a child isn't something a woman simply 'gets over.' It takes awhile. Many think that adopting will fill the empty place that remains." He squinted again and tossed his head slightly. "Our work with several thousand mothers over more than two decades leads us to this conclusion."

I stared at him, trying to make sense out of what he was saying.

He tried to help. "Dylan, mourning"—he let the word roll off his tongue and hang there for emphasis—"is healthy. It is something that needs to take place."

"Sir, I don't mean any disrespect, but I think that's what we've been doing."

He nodded as if I'd just proved his point. "You might let that run its course and then come back and see us."

"Sir, you'll not find a home with more love than ours." I was losing, and I knew it. "Or a mother with more love than Maggie. Sir, I know."

He nodded. "If you wish to withdraw your application, you could return in, say, six months and reapply." He paused. "The committee would look favorably upon this."

"Sir, I just don't think I can walk into my house right now and tell my wife that I've withdrawn our application. In football terms, that's called 'piling on.'"

He extended his hand. "I understand. We'll be in touch."

I followed him to the door. "Sir, do you know when that might be?"

He stood in the doorway to his office and grabbed a handful of yellow slips that noted his missed phone calls. He riffled through them, registering a few, then considered me again. "The committee has not completed its evaluation, but when we do, we'll notify you in writing."

Knowing that answer would not satisfy Maggie, I tried to ask respectfully. I took a slight step forward and half whispered, "Is that two weeks or two months?"

He placed a hand on the doorknob and lowered his voice. "Months."

He shut the door, and I walked out past the receptionist. I didn't feel like being friendly, but I said, "Ma'am," anyway.

She looked over her shoulder and whispered, "Sometimes it can take a year or more."

I walked out and, not being too experienced with the key fob, pressed the wrong button, setting off the Honda's alarm. It honked, flashed, and woke up everyone for four square blocks. The only benefit was seeing Mr. Sawyer glance out his window. At least he knew the minivan came well equipped.

I arrived home shortly after lunch. Maggie was sitting on the porch with a bowl of pole beans between her legs. She had tied a bandanna underneath her hair at the base of her neck. Scarlett O'Hara had nothing on my wife.

Maggie saw the van, then me driving it, and jumped off the steps. "Something wrong with the truck?"

I opened the door and left the car running. "Not that I know of."

She put her hands on her hips. The wrinkle appeared between her eyes, and her lips tightened. She went from restful to ballistic in less than a second. She almost shouted, "You traded your truck!?"

I backed up. This was not what I'd expected. "Yeah, honey. We need to show an appropriate vehicle to the adoption agency, and—"

Her eyes narrowed. "Forget them. You loved that truck."

"You're right, I did, but—"

"Don't 'but' me. We can't let those people run our lives. They don't know us. They can't even begin to understand what we've got."

The wind had picked up the ends of her scarf and was blowing them around the sides of her face, tickling her cheeks. Her face was flushed and sweaty.

I shrugged. "Maggs, there will always be other trucks." Deep down, I knew this was not true.

She looked inside the Honda, sat on the seat, ran her fingers through the ice-cold AC, smiled, raised her eyebrows, saw the baby seat buckled in the back, and said, "And to think I was just starting to like that orange . . . thing."

We drove around for an hour, letting her get used to the steering with no play, the quiet accelerator, the lumbar support, the seat heater, the surround sound, the side mirrors with turn-signal flashers, and the leather seats. By the time we turned back into the drive, I think she'd all but forgotten my truck.

THAT NIGHT, AMOS SAW THE WHITE VAN AND DROVE IN TO check on us. He rolled down his window and took off his sunglasses. "Got visitors?"

Maggie clutched her stomach and doubled over, laughing.

He looked at me. "What'd I say?"

I shook my head. "No visitors." I kicked at the dirt and lowered my voice. "It's . . . ummm . . . Maggie's new car."

Amos looked around. "Where's your—?" Then it hit him. He smiled, covered his mouth, and then burst out laughing.

"It's not funny," I said.

As he pulled out of the drive, he was still laughing.

The following week I started getting itchy to hear from the agency. I watched the mail. Then I thought about the possibility of that letter not saying what I hoped. I'd never been very good at getting the mail on a regular basis, but starting that night, I made a point of getting to the mailbox before Maggs. Every day.

*chapter six*

I COULDN'T HAVE BEEN MORE THAN TWELVE THE DAY
I came home from school with my hands stuffed in my pockets and tried to tell Papa why the underside of my eye was
black and puffy. No, I had not thrown the first punch, but that
didn't mean I wasn't guilty. The shiner proved that. I sat on
the front porch and struggled with my story while Papa
cleaned his fingernails.

He knelt down and stuck his face about two inches from
mine. "'Almost true' ain't true," he said.

"Well . . ."

He held up a finger and led me around back to his work-
shop in the barn, where he picked up a six-foot bricklayer's
level and held it up for me to see the bubble. He leveled it,
centering the bubble, then lifted one end just slightly, sending

the bubble off plumb. He raised his eyebrows. "It either is, or it isn't."

EVER SINCE WE'D FINISHED UP WITH THE ADOPTION COM-mittee, I'd been trying to tell Maggie more about my four and a half months alone. But every time I tried, I got tongue-tied and twisted, adding more confusion than resolution. So one cold January day—nearly a year to the day that I'd brought her home—Maggs finally just put her finger to my lips and said, "Shhh." She took me by the hand, led me to the linen closet, and opened the door.

There I found three empty shelves—the bottom of which was desk-high—a rickety chair not any wider than my butt, ten yellow pads, and a coffee cup filled with No. 2 pencils.

She sat me in the chair and said, "Just write it."

I looked at the blank page. "But I don't even know where to start."

She shrugged. "Start with us."

I scratched my head, and she shut the door behind me. I sat there for a long time trying to find an entry. Just how do you tell a story like that? I mean, seriously, where should I start? Despite her tough exterior, Maggie's insides were eggshell frag-ile. Should I tell her everything? Let her know the depth of my thinking? Every event? The extent of my loneliness? How far back down into that pit should I lead her? Should I tell her there were times when I looked up and saw no light at all?

Maggs was walking a narrow ridge as it was—it wouldn't take much to push her off either side. Her emotional ups and downs had been difficult to anticipate or gauge. Dr. Frank said this was "to be expected," and I should just act as if nothing were out of line. I told him it was kind of like riding Space

Mountain at Disney World—a roller coaster that ran along a track at breakneck speed in pitch-black darkness. Not even the driver knew when the turns or flips were coming. Maggie couldn't quite seem to get her emotions in check, and when she did express them, she couldn't control them. She'd cry at the drop of a hat and laugh when things weren't funny, and once she started crying, it took her awhile to stop.

If I told her the whole truth about the four months she spent asleep in that hospital bed, I ran the very real risk of making her feel responsible. And with all the pregnancy and adoption stuff running through her head, no amount of explaining would change that. So I looked at the blank page in my new "office" and wondered if it wouldn't be better for selected scenes in the director's cut to end up on the editing room floor. So I closed the door behind me and began writing half the truth, excusing it by saying I loved her.

I hadn't done much writing since grad school, so it took me awhile to remember how. As a teacher, I had always told my students that when you face a blank page, the hardest part is getting started. So to help yourself out, write the word *The* and you're on your way.

I took my own advice, and once I did, things I'd forgotten returned. *Some things are so simple.* I think that's partly the reason Maggie sent me in there. Yes, she wanted the story, but she knew me well enough to hold off in the hearing of it until she was certain that I'd emptied myself of it—proving that therapy comes in many forms. Maggie still knows a lot that I don't.

Every morning I wrote for an hour. Memories surfaced and flashed before my mind's eye—the hospital, tear stained nights, never-ending days, loneliness so deep I thought I would drown—and maybe sometimes I wanted to. I flung open the doors of my mind, dug them out of their holes where I'd hidden them from Maggie, and pretty soon ten pads turned into twenty, and all the beauty and wonder—and yes, even ugliness—of my life stared back at me. The mirror told no lies.

Spring arrived, I turned in my grades, and I could tell she was getting antsy about the amount of time I'd been spending in the closet. When she saw me installing a lock on the closet door, she looked at me as though I'd lost my mind. She put her hands on her hips and said, "Dylan Styles! What are you doing?"

"Making sure you're not tempted."

"Tempted to do what?"

"Read my book."

"But you're writing it for me."

"Right, but I know you. And the thought of those pages just sitting in there waiting to be read is more than your sneaky little fingers can stand." I waved the brass key in my hand, then hung it around my neck and smiled.

She huffed and shook her head. "I can't believe you'd accuse me of trying to read something before you gave it to me."

I smiled and slipped on my John Deere baseball cap. "Believe it."

"Couldn't I just read a chapter or something?"

I pulled the cap down to shade my eyes. "Nope."

She threw a couch pillow at me. "I don't like you anymore."

I walked out, laughing, and let the screen door slam behind me.

She bounced another pillow off the doorjamb and yelled, "You're on the couch!"

"Maybe," I said over my shoulder, "but I'm taking my book with me."

Later that night, I came home and found her trying to pick the lock. "Hi there," I said, waving the key.

She jumped and dropped the screwdriver. "Dang you, Dylan Styles!"

Remember that *Waltons* episode about the house fire, in which John Boy had to choose between rescuing his family and rescuing his notebooks? I remember watching him stand helplessly as the flames climbed out of his attic window, and how much emotional strength it took him to rewrite his novel in the following months. The fear of his fiery loss made an imprint on me. I didn't want a house fire to wreck several months' worth of effort. So I double-checked the lockbox, making sure it was watertight, and the "safe" in my house was just that.

It had been eleven hours since I left Maggie the counterfeit. Sitting on that tractor for the better part of a day while she stowed away in the house, reading, gave me plenty of time to regret my decision. I pulled the tractor out of gear and rolled to a stop. I pulled off my hat, wiped my brow, and studied the storm clouds as they thundered in the distance.

In my mind's eye, I imagined giving both copies to my grandfather. Palms up, he walked into the kitchen where the light was brighter and hefted each like Lady Justice—balancing the scales. Feeling the difference, he squinted an eye and asked me why I had not centered the bubble.

*chapter seven*

THE AFTERNOON SUN BORED INTO MY BACK, REMIND-
ing me that not even Hades was hotter than South Carolina
between May and the better part of September. It was as if God
held a magnifying glass as big as the state in between us and
the sun, cooking us from the inside out.

The mixture of sun and heat can do crazy things to a man, especially when he's sitting atop a tractor. Gives a man a lot of time to
reflect. Rambling along the rows, dust and diesel fumes rising up
all around me, I often thought about the slaves and how they
managed. I don't think you can farm in South Carolina and not
wrestle with that; it is what it is. Most of the irrigation ditches that
drain the low country were hand-dug by black men and their sons.

I have never been able to settle that in my mind. Where in
history did one man convince himself that he could buy

another? I understand the spoils of war and taking a man's house after you've fairly whipped him on the field of battle, but men aren't made to own one another. I don't care if I owned all the tea in China; I could no more "own" Amos than I could walk to the moon. I'd die for him, but if you tried to sell him to me or anyone else, I'd probably shoot you.

One day when I was a boy—maybe in first or second grade—I got home from school and ran out to the field to climb up on the tractor with my grandfather. He was drilling seed into the ground, his hat tilted back, straw stuck between his teeth, and pretty soon he began showing me the ditches that the slaves had dug. They're hard to miss; you could drive a Buick down them.

Whenever Papa spoke of slavery, his top lip grew tense and he shook his head, as if something disgusted him. I asked him why somebody didn't just buy up all the slaves and set them free. He stopped the tractor, cut the engine, sat me up on the wheel well, and pushed back my ball cap. He said, "D.S., a long time ago, a man did just that. He gave all He had, bought up all the slaves, and set them all free."

That didn't make sense, so I asked, "Then how come there were still slaves?"

He leaned over the side of the tractor, spat through his teeth, and switched the straw to the other side. He looked a long way across the pasture—well beyond where it ended. "That is a question I have given much thought to. And"—he smiled—"when I get to heaven, that's one of the first questions I intend to ask Him."

Whenever I think about the slaves, or the Holocaust, or Columbine, or Amanda being tied to a tree, or my son behind me buried beneath a stone slab, I know that Satan is alive and well on planet Earth. And whenever I hear my wife's voice, feel her touch, listen to her breathe, or feel her skin on mine, I know that God is too.

While the wound on my forearm had healed long ago, the reminder it left was mounded like a Band-Aid stuck between my skin and muscle. Sometimes at night I would wake to Maggie's fingers unconsciously tracing the outline while she slept.

A lot of people have asked Maggie if she could hear us— could hear me—those many months that she was in her coma. I've never needed to ask that. Of course she could. Love has its own communication—one you can't prove in a court-room, in a lab experiment, or on a doctor's chart. It's the language of the heart, and while it has never been transcribed, has no alphabet, and can't be heard or spoken by voice, it is used by every human on the planet. It is written on our souls, scripted by the finger of God, and we can hear, understand, and speak it with perfection long before we open our eyes for the first time.

A tickling breeze ushered itself upriver, bringing with it some early wood ducks and a few welcome clouds, turning the unbearable afternoon sun into the bearable evening sun. The breeze swirled about me and cooled my neck, which had once again turned red, etched with the charcoal lines of dust and dirt packed into the crevices of my sun-spotted skin. The clouds rolled in, stalled overhead, graciously protecting me from the magnifying glass, and slowly squeezed out several large drops. Big as acorns, they splattered on the dusty soil, sizzled on the muffler, trickled between my shoulder blades, and ran down the lush green leaves of the cornstalks spiral-ing above my head. Those few drops were usually the early warning system that God was about to spray hell with ice water. Within moments, I couldn't see twenty feet in front of my face.

I pulled off my cap, faced up, let the cool and delicious downpour drench me, and drank what I could. I had not seen or heard from Maggie all day. Normally, she'd have found me by now. But given the little gift I'd left on her bedside table, I didn't expect to see her till along toward dark.

It was hard to hear over the thunderous clap of drops on leaves, but toward home, I heard a screen door slam, followed by the hollow pounding of bare feet on the back porch and then screaming. Not scared screaming, but "Where are you?" screaming. I stood up on the tractor seat, looked out over the corn, and saw Maggie, wearing a T-shirt and cotton under-wear, standing on the back porch, shielding her face from the rain with what looked like a stack of papers. She jumped off the back porch and started crashing through my neatly laid and quickly growing stalks.

When she appeared in the clearing, her hair was stuck to her face and her T-shirt and underwear were soaked clean through. The sides of her arms and long, thin legs were red where the cornstalks had slapped her, and the shirt stuck to her stomach. Her face was puffy, eyes red. And by the looks of her, she'd not been out of the house—or bed—all day. In her right arm, she clutched what remained of my manuscript. The rest of it had scattered like bread crumbs between us and the front door.

I stepped off the tractor and held my hat in my hand. Judging by her half-naked run across the pasture, my story had spurred something inside Maggie. I just couldn't tell how deep, or whether it was joy or anger. Both emotions are fueled by the same fire, and Maggie's face told me hers was raging. Then there was the deeper question: Could she spot the coun-terfeit without ever having seen the real thing?

She stood there, rain dripping off the ends of her hair, the lobes of her ears, the tips of her fingers, and cascading through the goose bumps on her thighs and calves. Her bare feet were caked with sand and mud, and so help me, with God as my witness and probably the cause, a Maggie-sized hole broke in the clouds and let through one ray of sun that, like a heaven-sized flashlight, lit the rain droplets on her skin like ten million diamonds.

*Lord, I love my wife.*

She walked up and leaned against me, her head to my chest. Then she dropped the pages in her hand, threw both arms around me, gripped me like a vise, and clung there while the sobs exited her chest. We stood there a long time. I wanted to tell her I had lied to her, but given the opportunity, I would do it again, so I said nothing. She wiped her face, brushed the hair out of my eyes, and tried her best to smile. She swallowed, fought for words, and then kissed me—her wet face pressed hard to mine. Finally she drew back and nodded. That was all she needed to say.

Since she'd been home, parts of Maggie's soul—down where her love lives—had been tied up in knots. Waking up from the coma didn't untie them; it just helped expose them to the daylight. We'd spent the last several months trying to get at each one. Sometimes we had to back up and start over, only to back up and start over again. But when you're untangling the rope that holds your anchor, you take all the time you need.

There in the cornfield, draped in rain, tears, tenderness, and uncertainty, her eyes told me that many of those knots had loosened. I'd like to think my story did that, but I imagine that was only part of it. The bigger part was the miracle that is Maggie.

That night we sat in the tub, floating in bubbles and laughter, soaking until our fingers grew white and prunelike while reading her favorite parts. Finally she just shook her head and slid up next to me. We sat there a long time, long enough for the water to get cold.

Awhile later, she stepped out, toweled off, took me by the hand, and led me across the room, where she hung her arms about my neck. I don't how long we swayed atop those magnolia planks, but somewhere in that dance, we lost track of time. Later, soaked in a sweet South Carolina sweat, she pressed her chest and forehead to mine and managed, "Thank you . . . for waiting for me."

I locked my hands behind her waist and tried to smile. "I'd do it again."

Outside, the ancient gnarled oaks, covered in Spanish moss and crawling with red bugs and resurrection fern, stood like silent sentinels guarding us from the world that began just beyond the edge of my tractor rows. The quilted patchwork of South Carolina that had sewn itself into the fabric of us, with soybean and watermelon, corn and kudzu, cotton and tobacco, hay bales and barbed wire, old tractors and hand-dug ditches, rivers and moonlight, sweat, blood, tears, tombstones, and worn magnolia floors, rose up out of the dirt and covered us like dew before the dawn. And where God had once doused us with the other end of the rainbow, now He painted us in starlight and all the wonder of the Milky Way.

EVIDENTLY MAGGIE'S EMOTIONS WERE IN TUNE WITH HER clock.

Early in June—six weeks later—I hopped off my tractor and walked up the steps, smelling worse than any man should but led by the smell of pot roast and the promise of gravy and a stack of biscuits. Maggie met me at the door in a turquoise-colored sundress held up behind her neck with a single spaghetti strap. She led me to the kitchen, where the table was covered in a white tablecloth, candles, my grandmother's silver, and a small package—about the size of a Cross pen box set—tied with a bow.

I looked at the table, sniffed my yellowing shirt, and said, "I'm not sure we can live with me right now."

She pointed at the seat and half closed one eye. "If you don't open that box in the next sixty seconds, I'm going to blow a gasket." She pulled my chair out, sat beside me, and set the small box in front of me. In the background, Celine Dion and Frank Sinatra were singing "I've Got the World on a String."

Maggie was one big fidget. She pushed her hair behind her ears, crossed her legs, uncrossed them, crossed them back, and then crossed her arms. I studied the box, then untied the bow and lifted the lid. Inside sat four small, familiar white sticks with four unmistakable pink lines—all pointing directly at me. They were lined up in a row and dated—one for each of the last four weeks.

I'll never understand how she kept it a secret.

I held the four sticks, their meaning slowly registering somewhere back in my mind and then hitting me like a lightning bolt to the brain. I looked at Maggie, then at her tummy and our child growing inside and nearly six weeks old. I hit my knees, stuck my ear to Maggie's stomach, pressed in, and listened, wondering if he was a boy or she was a girl.

I've never been a fearful man. That does not mean I've never known fear; God knows I have. There's no *S* pinned on my chest. I just mean it's not something that stays with me all day perched atop my shoulder and whispering in my ear. In the months after Maggie woke up, I wrestled—even battled—with a long litany of *what ifs* that scared me. But her waking every morning had put that whisper to rest.

But the moment I leaned in and listened, tasting the trickle of hope and wondering at the unfathomable enormity once again, that whisper echoed. It smelled like the air behind a trash truck, the soil in Pinky's stall, or the floor of the delivery room. Its breath alone could gag a maggot.

Whereas *hope* had returned only after I'd cornered him in the barn and extended an invitation, *what if* reached up out of the floorboards, threw his bags on the couch, and made himself at home without so much as a peep. And unlike *hope*, who was tidy and neat, *what if* was a slob, seldom cleaning up after himself, and made it his point to throw remnants of his life in every nook and cranny of the house. Polar opposites, *hope* never raised his voice, while *what if* never lowered his. Not compatible roommates, they charged the air with a tension that even Blue picked up on.

That night as we lay in bed and Maggie twirled her finger through both of my chest hairs, I closed my eyes and saw the giant patchwork that had enveloped us. Once perfect and without blemish, it had begun to fray along the edges.

Within weeks, it would be coming apart at the seams.

*chapter eight*

DAYLIGHT FOUND ME AT THE KITCHEN TABLE NURSING some Maxwell House, reading the paper, and trying to erase the constipated look off my face. My snow angel was still zonked out with Blue, and if the last couple of months were any indication, she'd miss breakfast and brunch entirely. Don't get me wrong; every moment Maggie slept meant energy stored in reserve, so on the one hand, I was grateful. On the other, we used to eat eggs, grits, and toast off the same plate.

Since Maggie could spot a fake—especially in me—a mile away, I was trying to find a legitimate reason to get out of the house before she woke up. The moment she walked into this kitchen, she was going to take one look at my twisted face and say, "You want to talk about it?"

After sitting a long while at the breakfast table, skimming both the business and metro sections of the Charleston paper, I was no closer to knowing how to answer. In fact, my mind was swimming in questions. All I knew was that the most precious person in my life, who thought I actually had something to do with hanging the moon, who—maybe more than anything in life—wanted to be the mother of my children, was wrestling with stuff way down deep in her soul and needed me more than ever.

I was right back where we started—I couldn't protect her, nor could I wave a magic wand and make life all better. And though her doctors had not mentioned it, *what if* had echoed back into my head. I might have been staring at the newspaper, but the headline my mind read was WHAT IF SHE HEMORRHAGES AGAIN? I stared at the columns and knew one thing for sure: there was no easy way around. Like it or not, we were going to have to live through this.

My skin was crawling, my heart was racing, I'm sure my blood pressure was elevated, and I had no defense. I needed some time alone.

The phone rang, bringing me my chance.

"Dylan, good morning. How are things?" It was Caglestock. "I'm calling about Bryce," he continued.

Usually that meant a stock transaction, but his tone of voice told me he hadn't called to talk about money. "We've had no contact with him in over a month. Neither have the couriers we've sent for signatures. You mind checking on him?"

"No worries. I'll phone you as soon as I know something."

I scrambled some more eggs, browned a few pieces of toast, and then slopped that, along with a spoonful of cheese grits, onto a plate that I covered with foil and placed in the oven. I left a note on the kitchen table, grabbed the keys and my FM scanner, and headed out.

The scanner was a small black digital radio, covered in buttons and a single antenna, which Mr. Carter—Amos's dad and chief of the Digger Volunteer Fire Department— gave to all department volunteers. Not much happened from Charleston to Walterboro and surrounding parts that I didn't know about.

The DVFD No. 1 is Mr. Carter's baby. He put it together from nothing. He even petitioned the state for a grant that built us our own firehouse and got us a couple of trucks and all kinds of gear. We handle mostly local calls, and in truth, we're support personnel for the guys who really know what they're doing.

They don't let me drive the truck yet, and I haven't saved anybody's life, but I do have my own suit, complete with helmet, boots, ax, and air tank. I've used the Jaws of Life twice, though only in drills, and they let me blow the horn whenever we're racing through traffic. That might be my favorite part. Amos says I'm the most obnoxious horn blower he's ever heard, but he can't complain because people get out of our way. Every time I put on my suit and go running out the door to meet the rest of the team, Maggie takes one look at me and falls on the floor, laughing.

To keep us up on the latest information and techniques, and give us an excuse to practice or drive the truck, Mr. Carter holds weekly safety meetings where we learn stuff we've never even thought about. He travels all around the state getting trained and certified, then brings all that back to us.

I slid the scanner into my pocket and whistled softly for Blue, who did not appear. I walked around the house and looked through our bedroom window and saw him cuddled up at Maggie's feet. When I motioned for him to load up, he laid his head back down and covered his nose with his paw.

I could hear Pinky snorting and kicking her stall in the barn, mad that I hadn't appeared earlier. I stepped into the stall, spread a bucket of corn, and offered to give her a scratch. She ignored me and crapped on my boot.

"Hey," I said, tossing her a kernel of corn and shrugging my shoulders, "I thought we had an agreement."

Pinky grunted, buried her nose in the dirt, and then flicked a shovel's worth of mud and manure high into the air, where it umbrellaed about me.

"Thanks," I said. "Love you too." I hung up the bucket, pulled the gate behind me, and showed my heels to Pinky.

As I backed up the van, the flash of the screen door caught my eye. Maggie came stumbling over the threshold, her hair sticking up and eyes half closed, wrapping my pajama shirt around her. She jogged down the porch steps and stepped up to the window. "You okay?"

I nodded.

"You sure?"

I lied again.

She narrowed her eyes and folded her arms. "You've been kind of quiet since last night."

I shrugged and stumbled for words.

She put a hand on my shoulder and then ran her fingers through the back of my hair. "Hey . . . it's just me. I know you." She grabbed my hand and laid it flat across her tummy. "We're doing this together, same as last time. I'll be the mommy; you be the daddy. Right?" She smiled and shrugged. "All except the little hitch in the delivery."

*I am such a pile of crap. How does a woman like that love a man like me?* I cussed myself and nodded. "Coffee's probably cold by now."

She tugged on my sleeve, pulling me closer. "Are you listening to me?" Her lips were warm and wet. "Dylan Styles, I'm not talking about coffee. I'm talking 'bout us. All three of us."

"Maggs." I took off my cap and made a pitiful stab at the truth. "I lost you once. I don't want to . . ."

She smirked. "Well, we should have thought about that"—she pointed to the window of our bedroom—"in there."

"I know, but . . ."

She held her finger to my lips and said, "Shhh . . ." Her eyes filled around the edges, and she shook her head. Evidently *what if* had been whispering in her ear too. And here I was worried about me. I really am a pile of crap.

The tears broke, and I opened the door and stepped out, wrapping her tight. "I don't know how you do it."

She whispered, "Because you love me—and because you're there when I wake up."

"Honey, I'll always be there when you wake up."

"You weren't this morning."

I laughed. "Well, I do like to get up before lunch."

She hit me in the chest. "That's not funny. I just need more rest than I used to."

We swayed a moment more.

"Caglestock called, said Bryce has been AWOL for a month."

Maggie wiped her tears and looked concerned. "You think he's okay?"

"Don't know, but I'm going to find out. I left you some breakfast in the oven."

"Doesn't taste as good when you're not there."

"Tell me about it."

## chapter nine

I IDLED THE VAN DOWN THE DRIVEWAY, STOPPED AT the mailbox, and then sat in the front seat flipping through the bills. Before me lay Amos and Amanda's house, where the front yard was strewn with kids' toys. Despite their best attempts to tidy up, the front yard looked as if it were hit daily by the same tornado. A red wagon, a tricycle, a small playhouse turned on its side, a sandbox missing most of the sand, a football, a kickball, and other odds and ends painted the picture that the proud grandparents had gone a bit overboard. Every time I mentioned to Amos that his front yard looked like trailer trash, he just shook his head and said, "In-laws. What can you do?"

"Evidently," I said, "you spread it all across the front yard, letting them know how thankful you are."

While Maggie and I had been connecting the straight-edged pieces of our puzzle, Amos had too. He had been promoted to sergeant and given command of a SWAT team that roamed all over South Carolina, focusing on narcotics. They gave him a new truck, new uniform, new pistol, and a new schedule. Thinking he needed a bit more change in his life, he'd married Amanda Lovett last June 25—Li'l Dylan's six-month birthday. Pastor John, buttons busting, performed his daughter's wedding ceremony before a standing-room-only congregation. I stood next to Amos, holding the rings, and looked out across the congregation—which looked a lot like a hat convention.

At Amanda's request, the reception took place on the river-bank—beneath the oaks. Knowing it'd be the last time they got to cook for Amos, the church ladies let out all the stops. From greens to chicken to roast to mashed potatoes to sweet potato pie to you-name-it, they covered us up in some of the best cooking I'd ever seen.

We ate until we couldn't see straight, then danced a little—something Amos has never been too fond of or good at—and then Amos and Amanda drove to the Outer Banks, where Amos said he intended to work on his tan. While Grandma Carter bounced Li'l Dylan on her knee, Amos and Amanda spent a few days at the beach. When they returned, Amanda moved in and quickly got rid of any remnants of Amos's bachelor days. Within a week, it looked as if he were the newcomer, not her.

A week or so after they returned, I was helping him take out the trash, and he held up a picture of Ted Williams. "How do you throw out a picture of the greatest hitter ever to play baseball?" He shook his head and pitched it into the trash can. "It just makes no sense to me whatsoever."

Having been through this very same gleaning with Maggie, I put my arm around him and smiled knowingly. "Brother, therein lies the secret."

"What?"

"*Your* favorites. Not *hers.*"

He nodded and said, "Yeah, I'm beginning to see that."

"Remember," I said, pointing toward the front door, "this is her house now. You're just lucky she lets you sleep here."

Six months later, there had come a single-pause-double-knock at our kitchen door—Amos's signature. The porch lightbulb was burned out, but when I opened the door and let my eyes adjust, Amos stood there giddy-faced and breathing heavily, as if he'd been running. The cold air turned his breath to smoke. Maggie flipped a switch, and the kitchen light bent around the corner, lighting his straight teeth and the whites of his eyes.

"D.S.! D.S.!" He was so excited he could barely speak. "D.S.! D.S.!"

"You already said that."

He jumped up and down as though he were skipping rope to an erratic rhythm. "Li'l Dylan's gonna get a brother."

My head was swirling with our own adoption process, and I didn't catch on too fast. I scratched my head, maybe even feeling a bit jealous. "You guys adopting?"

He shook his head and skipped faster, as if the person swinging the rope not only had doubled the pace but now was swinging two ropes. "No, dummy." He poked himself in the chest. "'Manda's pregnant."

I looked behind him and saw Amanda standing there with Li'l Dylan on her hip and a huge smile spread across her face. Maggie pushed me out of the way, gave Amos a huge kiss on the forehead, and dragged Amanda into the house, where they sat talking till long after Li'l Dylan's bedtime.

Amos and I sat on the front porch in the swing, and while Li'l Dylan curled up in my lap and napped, we sipped Coca-Cola and laughed at the changes in our lives. Close to midnight, Amos brushed Li'l Dylan's brown cheek and smiled. "He's gonna be a big brother."

NOW I SAT IN THE VAN, STUDYING THE YARD, AND FOUND myself lost in what-might-have-been dreams—a bad way to start the day. Minutes later, Amos turned into his drive in his black, state-issued Chevrolet 2500HD pickup. It was one of those "undercover" cars that comes complete with black windows and driver's-side spotlight telling everybody and their brother that the driver is a cop. He hopped out, waved, and started walking across his lawn toward the front door. Amanda opened the front door, and Li'l Dylan came crawling out, making a beeline for his daddy's black-booted feet.

I honked, pulled out of the drive, and tried not to remember that I was driving a minivan with a five-star crash test rating. I watched through my rearview mirror as the Carolina Cruncher, Mr.-Clean-turned-Mr.-SWAT, dressed in black fatigues and black T-shirt and carrying a SIG Sauer P226 in a hip holster, knelt down, picked up his son, and seamlessly transitioned into Mr. Daddy. I've seen a lot of beautiful things in my life, but that is one of the more beautiful.

I RATTLED THE CHAIN AT THE GATE THAT LED UP THE LONG drive to Bryce's drive-in. The chain and lock had been replaced and were, by any standard, huge. It looked as though he were protecting Fort Knox. I shrugged, pulled up the fence as usual, crawled under, and made my way toward Bryce's trailer.

Bryce had never been big on upkeep. Maintenance just wasn't in his vocabulary. As long as I'd been coming up here, not much had changed except the worsening condition of everything in sight. From the exponentially growing trash piles to the flaking paint to the bent speaker poles to the cesspool that Bryce called a trailer, the entire place was racing down one giant spiral toward uninhabitable. It was no wonder he never married. If Health and Human Services had ever come up here, they'd have condemned the place.

To say that Bryce was a pack rat would be kind. Problem was, he packed most everything in huge piles that dotted the landscape—gigantic mounds of twisted metal, car parts, wood scraps, and pretty much anything he'd ever used. His property looked like a bad marriage between a garage sale and a city trash heap. I never could tell the difference between what was trash and what wasn't. Bryce never bothered with that distinction.

When I crested the hill and exited the woods that once served as the parking lot for silver screen number one, I looked around and couldn't believe my eyes.

To start with, the piles were gone. Not a single scrap of trash could be seen. Anywhere. Except for one smoldering burn pile down the hill a few hundred yards, the place was spotless. The grounds had been mowed and edged, and every square foot of concrete had been blown or swept meticulously. And I don't mean the grass had just been *cut*. It had been cut, raked, then picked up and discarded someplace else. And not a weed grew anywhere within sight.

Everything that could be painted, starting with the three movie screens, had been painted, and now sat sparkling white. And that's another thing: there were now three screens. Two had been mysteriously rebuilt. In all three parking lots that spread out like a star from the concession/projector house, all the speaker poles had been repaired and evidently rewired. On closer inspection, the projector house, too, had been cleaned. I climbed the stairs to the projector room and what Bryce had fondly called the "film library." The several hundred reels of movies that had at one time been filed in a mound on the floor were now rolled up, sealed in round metal cases, labeled, and filed alphabetically on specially built shelves.

Outside Bryce's trailer, a clothesline stretched between two poles standing seven feet tall and sunk some forty feet apart. Four pairs of military-issue camouflage BDUs hung equidistant across the line along with three pairs of bleached white boxers and two pairs of tube socks. Each item was stretched taut between two clothespins and hung without a wrinkle. Everything smelled of detergent. On his front steps sat two pairs of black GI boots, sparkling like granite countertops.

I stepped inside the trailer, and the smell of bleach and Pine Sol hit me like a wave. I could have eaten off the floor. Outside the back door, the mop bucket had been turned upside down and leaned against the house. Next to it leaned the mop, which had quit dripping but was still moist.

I studied the trailer, my jaw at my waist. Bryce's bed was made, which astonished me because I'd never seen sheets on the mattress before today. Towels were hung in his bathroom, his toothbrush sat in the holder, the toothpaste cap was screwed onto the tube—which had been rolled from the bottom up— and his closet would have made Martha Stewart proud.

If I thought the bedroom and bathroom were amazing, the kitchen was a totally new revelation. New appliances, new linoleum, new exhaust fan, new bar stools at the counter, new silverware, new plates, new everything. The whole kitchen gave the impression that someone was actually using it—or could. I shook my head and then opened the fridge.

First, there was food. Real food. Vegetables, eggs, milk that was not cottage cheese, orange juice, fish, bottled water, Gatorade, chicken. Second—and this was the most glaring sight—there was no beer. Further, as I looked around the trailer and in the trash cans that stood orderly alongside, there were no beer cans—empty or full—anywhere.

But if the absence of beer was glaring, then there was one other absence that was as difficult to miss as the detonation of an atomic bomb. I looked around the trailer again and made sure. I looked behind doors, under the bed, through all the closets, and on the rack where they usually sat, bright, polished, and on display. Regardless, I found no bagpipes and no kilt anywhere.

I stepped out the back door and onto the porch. Scratching my head, wondering what in the world was wrong with Bryce, I saw a used foot trail that I'd never noticed before. It led into the woods on the back side of the hill where the drive-in sat.

I turned around to walk back into the trailer and noticed a glass frame encasing what looked like an aerial map. I looked closer and saw that it was actually two aerial photos. One was a photo of the drive-in proper, covering what looked like a distance of maybe a thousand square yards. The second looked more like a satellite photo that included Bryce's entire piece of property. I don't know how many acres or square miles it comprised, but I'd say the bottom of the map probably covered twenty miles, while the sides stretched up for closer to thirty. At the bottom was a little dot that looked like the drive-in, and at the top was the unmistakable Salkehatchie River. In between sat tens of thousands of acres of forest and swamp that few men had ever ventured into, much less through. It was a no-man's-land. It you wanted to hide, it'd be a great place to do it. It'd also be a great place to get lost if you were trying to hide and didn't know what you were doing.

I descended the steps leading off the porch and followed the trail out into the woods where the pines grew up like bean stalks. Another hundred yards and the trail led me into a clearing covered by about twenty gargantuan oak trees towering some sixty feet above the ground.

It was like walking into the Astrodome. The forest floor had been cleared for several acres, mulch had been spread along what looked like a running path, and along the perimeter of the canopy ran what looked like a fitness course. From tires to ropes to barbed wire to cable crossings over water holes to wooden walls that must be scaled to towers that must be rappelled, the obstacle course looked difficult by design.

To me, it looked as if the participant started by climbing over a sand hill covered in barbed wire, then over a hundred yards covered in hurdles, pipes, and tires elevated off the ground, then up a free-hanging rope that ended at a tower, where the then-exhausted participant must rappel down, only to climb along a tightrope that had been stretched between two trees some sixty feet apart. Falling would get you wet. Then through a series of ladders, up, over, and under a series of walls, around some pilings, and between some poles with seriously sharp points.

I had no idea how long Bryce had been working on it, but I guessed it had taken him months, maybe even a year, to complete it. The trail headed off into the woods far beyond my view, but I'd seen enough. I backtracked to the trailer and kept my eyes peeled.

I walked back through the trailer and noticed something I hadn't seen before. On the desk sat a manila envelope with "Caglestock" written in Bryce's handwriting on the front. I opened the envelope and saw that Bryce had signed in all the places where Caglestock's secretary had stuck the "Sign here" stickies. I stuffed the envelope under my arm and started back down the hill.

Toward town, I stopped at a pay phone and dialed our number. After six rings, the machine picked up. "Hey, this is Maggie and Dylan. Leave us a message, and we'll call you back."

After the beep, I said, "Hey, it's me. If you're there, pick up." When she didn't, I said, "Well, guess you're outside or something. I've got to see Caglestock and thought maybe we'd go together, get a bite to eat in—"

Just then, the phone picked up. Maggie was breathing hard. "Hey," she said, laughing and trying to catch her breath. "I was . . . in the stall." She tried to catch her breath again. "That pig has gotten big . . . Phew! She stinks too."

"Tell me about it."

"Did you say something about lunch?"

I smiled. "Something like that."

"I'll be waiting on you when you get here."

I paused. "You know, it'll take me about ten minutes to get there, and maybe . . . I was just thinking . . . well, you might feel better if . . ."

"I'm going now." The phone clicked silent, and I leaned against the pay phone glass, thinking of my wife, muddy and content in her overalls.

*chapter ten*

We arrived in Walterboro just after the lunch crowd had exited Ira's Café. Ira, decked out in turquoise blue, met us at the door looking like a color swatch. She hugged Maggie and gave me a huge wet kiss on the cheek, which I wiped with my sleeve.

She pointed her coffeepot at me. "You best not be wiping off my kisses. I don't give too many out."

"Take my word for it," a guy in the kitchen hollered. "She's telling the truth."

"Hey, Ira," I said. "Good to see you."

Ira winked at us, smiled, smacked her gum from side to side, and then adjusted her left bosom with the V in her elbow, kind of lifting it back into place. Evidently business had been good in the last year, because they were bigger, and she looked as though she was trying to get used to them getting in her way. She pointed us to a booth. "You just missed Amos, but sit down and I'll stir up some lunch."

We sat in our booth and watched the Walterboro lunch crowd scurry across the town square en route to their jobs or in search of the next pocket of gossip. Across the square sat the town hall and what looked like both Amos's truck and Pastor John's Cadillac.

Ten minutes later, Ira delivered a lunch that looked a whole lot like breakfast. A mound of steaming eggs, piping hot biscuits, fresh sweet cream butter, honey, and cheese grits. She even threw in a few slices of salty fried ham.

It took us nearly an hour to eat it all. We washed it down with syrupy sweet tea, and when I asked Ira for the check, her face became contorted.

"Look here, you little whippersnapper, you get cute with me and I'll take a broomstick to the side of your head." She looked down at my backside. "Among other places." She sloshed the coffeepot at me again. "Now, don't you come in here and start snapping your fingers at me. No, sir."

I left twenty dollars on the table and grabbed two toothpicks at the counter—one for now and one for later—and we walked out. While I picked my teeth, we stood in the center of the sidewalk, gauging our level of fullness.

Maggie turned to me and shaded her eyes from the sun. "You know, that sounds gross."

I pulled the toothpick from my mouth. "What?"

"That." She pointed.

I stuck the toothpick back in my mouth and kept picking while she watched my fingers work. Then she ran her tongue over her teeth, sucked through them, and looked up at me again. "Does it really work?"

I nodded and offered her my second toothpick. She eyed it, stuck it in her mouth, and started picking. Finally she mumbled something I couldn't understand and nodded.

We turned toward the truck and walked directly past the alley where I had vomited breakfast about a year and a half earlier. Vomited because I'd eaten a huge breakfast with Amos and then realized that I'd gone forty-five minutes without thinking of my wife lying in a coma at the hospital. I looked at the ground where I'd stood that day, remembered the feeling in my stomach and the splatter on my boots, and felt it return when I remembered that I'd cut that scene out of Maggie's version of my story.

She clenched my arm more tightly, and her eyes innocently searched mine. "You okay?"

I swallowed hard and lied again.

We backed out of our parking spot and eased around the corner, where Amos and Pastor John were just exiting the courthouse. I waved and pulled up along a No Parking zone, thinking they'd walk up to the window and act sociable, but once I got a closer look, their faces told me otherwise. When they reached the sidewalk, Pastor John patted Amos on the shoulder and said something I couldn't hear, then they walked directly to their cars.

Amos, dressed in SWAT black, looked as if he'd been up all night. The stubble on his face and head was at least a day over-grown, and his clothes were stained with salt rings where he'd been sweating. He looked tired and aggravated. He stepped up into his truck, pulled down his glasses, held an imaginary phone to his ear, and then pointed at me and drove off, quickly.

Pastor John opened his car door and stepped in, but I waved him out and tried to break the tension that was thick in the air.

"Pastor John!" I pointed toward Amos. "If that guy causes you any trouble, I know where he lives."

He halfsmiled and waved. If I thought Amos looked tired, then Pastor John looked like a man who'd spent three days walking through the desert without food or water. His face was drawn and his eyes bloodshot. He tried to smile again and cupped his hand around his ear as if he were having a hard time hearing me because of the other cars.

"You two okay?" I hollered.

Pastor John looked toward the courthouse, brushed some pollen off the top of his car with the flat of his palm, and said, "Son, I'm looking over my shoulder . . ." He took what looked like a deep, painful breath and shook his head. Then he slid into his seat, shut the door, and drove off.

Maggie raised an eyebrow. "What was all that about?"

I followed his license tag with my eyes and then saw him place a cell phone to his ear. "I don't know, but evidently whatever it was didn't go very well."

*chapter eleven*

I SAT IN THE OFFICE CHAIR, MAGGIE'S HAND ON MY knee, and fidgeted. We had come to make sure the pink lines weren't lying. I slid Papa's watch from my pocket for the fourth time since we'd sat down. I eyed the face, and it told me that Dr. Frank's office was overbooked and running behind schedule. It was a twenty-one-jewel, Hamilton railroad pocket watch, and if I kept it wound, it lost only two to three seconds a month. Nanny had given it to him as a tenth-anniversary gift, and I don't ever remember a day that he didn't carry it. When he died, I thought about burying it with him, but then I wound it, heard the ticking, and thought better of it.

Catty-corner to the hospital, the professional office building sat brimming with people. I looked out the waiting room window and across the parking lot toward the hospital. I spotted the window of Maggie's room down at the far end of the hospital and thought of all the times I had looked down from it. It didn't take me very long to realize that I liked the view from Dr. Frank's office better.

I looked around the office and took notice of all the pregnant women and their husbands. And not just pregnant, but busting-at-the-seams, could-go-anytime pregnant. I whispered to Maggie, "Why are there so many people in here?"

She looked up from her magazine and cocked one eye. "Why do you think?"

"I know that. But why now? I mean, last time we were here, the place was empty. Today it's packed."

She shook her head and put down her magazine. "You're killing me, Doc."

"What?"

She rolled her eyes. "Can you count backward?"

"Yes."

"Well, count nine months backward from June."

I used both hands, opening each finger. Messing up once, I had to start over. "October." I shrugged.

"Right." She closed her magazine. "What happens in October and November?"

"Monday Night Football?"

She shook her head and whispered, "It gets colder."

It took me a few seconds. "Oh."

A nurse walked into the room and called, "Maggie Styles?"

Maggie stood up, and all heads turned toward us. I stood and reached for her hand, but she smiled. "I'll be back," she whispered. "You can't really help with this."

She walked to the door, where the nurse handed her a small plastic cup with a screw-on lid. A few minutes later,

Maggie poked her head around the corner and motioned for me to follow.

The nurse led us to a small examining room and handed Maggie a gown. "It's less than flattering, but here . . . The doctor'll be here in a minute."

Maggie stood behind the curtain, stripped down to her birthday suit, and handed me everything but her socks. "If he wants my socks, he's going to have to ask." She came out, turned, and lifted her hair off her shoulders. "Tie me?"

I gathered the gown around her waist and watched goose bumps appear at the base of her back, along the outline of her hips, and on the backs of her thighs. When I messed up tying the third bow, Maggie shook her head slightly and whispered, "You did that on purpose."

Busted.

I said nothing, pulled fresh paper out of the roll on the table where her bottom would be, and then helped her step up onto the examining table. I stood alongside, holding her hand and looking at the stirrups folded out of sight. Maggie saw me staring and leaned over. "Hey, you in there?"

Busted again.

I had a few things on my mind. First, there was the physical side. Given what her body had endured both in delivery and in the atrophy of the coma, could Maggie handle the next eight months and what they led up to? Second, could she handle it emotionally? Eight months is a long time to wonder if those will be your last months on earth, and if you'll be leaving your widowed husband to raise an only child alone. Or, even worse, just alone. Maggie was strong, but was she that strong? I had my doubts. Both about her and about me.

Which brings me to my last issue. While I was uncertain about Maggs, I was relatively certain about myself. I knew beyond a shadow of a doubt that I was going to suffer hell until I knew the answers to the above.

While the knot in my stomach grew and ground against my nerves, the door opened and Dr. Frank walked in wearing an exasperated face. Given the state of the waiting room and all the hormones that came with it, I'd have looked that way too.

He sat down on the rolling stool and scooted up to us, taking in and then letting out an enormous breath. "Hey, guys. How're you two doing? You holding up?" He shook my hand and put his other appropriately on Maggie's knee.

We nodded.

"I guess I don't need to tell you what you already know."

Maggie tilted her shoulders. "So those little sticks really are telling the truth?"

He nodded. "They usually do."

She looked at me. I scratched her back and looked at him, not wanting Maggie to see into my eyes.

"Hey, it's a walk in the park from here," he said. "Just sit back and enjoy the ride. Your body will take care of the rest."

I never knew that one man's words could be so prophetic.

He inserted the earpieces of his stethoscope and spoke while he listened to Maggs's heart. "You picked out names yet?"

"Haven't gotten that far."

"You've got time." He paused and moved the stethoscope to her back. Maggie breathed deeply without being told. He examined her back and the muscles in her shoulders that had returned over the last year. "Maggie, you really are healthy. Whatever you're doing, keep it up, because you're looking great."

The nurse came back in and helped him slip his hands into two whitish rubber gloves that each made a distinctive *smack* as he pulled them tight. Maggie lay back on the table and placed her feet in the stirrups while the nurse covered Dr. Frank's fingertips in jelly.

I held her hand, noticed that Maggs had painted her toenails bright red sometime between last night and this morning, and then watched her wince as he examined her.

"I won't lie to you; you've got some pretty good scar tissue that will take some stretching." He pulled off his gloves, pitched them in the trash, and helped Maggs sit up. "So as the baby grows, understand that it will feel different from last time. Little aches and pains that will make you wonder. But that's normal. So take a deep breath"—which Maggie did— "and start painting the nursery."

He followed the nurse to the door and stood in the doorway, smiling at us. "I'm excited for you guys. I've been waiting for this day."

Maggie was beaming.

"But take it easy. No marathons. Just live your life. Get as much rest as you want, eat right, and make sure you take enough time for each other." He pointed at me. "Go on a date every couple of days, like it or not."

Maggs squeezed my hand. "We can handle that."

The nurse reappeared over his shoulder and looked at Maggie. "I forgot to weigh you. Come see me when you get dressed."

They shut the door, and Maggie wrapped a bear hug around me. We stood in the doctor's office several minutes just holding each other. Maybe everything was going to be okay. Maybe I was just being a little paranoid. Maybe . . .

A few minutes later we walked out the door, and Maggie headed toward the nurse and the scale.

Seeing his moment, Dr. Frank tapped me on the shoulder

and motioned me around the corner. "You want it sugarcoated or straight?"

I looked down the hall toward the sound of Maggie laughing with some nurses. "Straight up."

He lowered his voice. "Sometimes, when women who've suffered some type of trauma become pregnant, their bodies will reject it."

I leaned in closer, and he put a hand on my shoulder.

"If so, it's got nothing to do with you two. It's the body's natural reaction to protect itself. Honestly, I'm amazed it let you get this far this soon. But that is one strong woman. I know I'm not telling you anything you don't know, but the next few weeks are critical. No bumpy tractor rides, no car wrecks, no scary movies, no nothing that will shock her system and make it unconsciously want to shut down and protect itself."

He looked down the hall to where Maggie was stepping off the scale. "If you've ever protected her," he said, looking back at me, "now is the time to do it."

I shook his hand. "Thanks, Dr. Frank. We appreciate you. We'll keep you posted." When I turned and walked down the hall, the sweat cascaded down my back.

*chapter twelve*

EVERY MORNING WHEN MY GRANDFATHER WOKE, he'd sit on the edge of the bed and run yesterday's sock between his toes like a shoe shine. Once his toes were clean, he'd walk to the window and look out across the fields. Then he'd walk to his dresser, pick up his pocket watch, and wind it. He'd wind it slowly, adding tension to the spring with every turn, always stopping just one turn shy of too much. That was the trick. Too much and it would lock up, seizing internally, and that meant a trip to the watchmaker, but after years of practice, Papa had the feel for just right.

Maggie and I walked out of the doctor's office, underneath the magnifying glass and across the parking lot. Her face shining like a glow plug and her feet barely touching the ground, she bounced as she walked. Except for the long hair, she reminded me of Julie Andrews dancing atop the mountain at the start of *The Sound of Music*. And when she pulled her sunglasses down over her eyes and smiled at me, she looked like Audrey Hepburn in *Breakfast at Tiffany's*. I opened the van door and she climbed in, bouncing up and down on the springy seat like a puppy in the window of a pet store. Only then did she remind me of Papa's watch spring. Problem was, I didn't know where she stood in relation to too much.

Maggs put her feet on the dash, tucked her knees tight into her chest, smiled, and began pointing her finger. That meant we were going in search of something to eat. When we got there, her stop-sign hand would let me know.

Her finger led us to the drive-through window at Dairy Queen, where I ordered two large vanilla cones dipped in chocolate. Maggie wanted hers covered in sprinkles, so I passed it back through the window and shrugged, and the guy doused it with rainbow sprinkles.

Licking circles around our cones, we rolled down the windows and headed toward home. Maggie finished her ice cream before I'd eaten half of mine. She took a deep breath and slid her sunglasses up over her head, pulling her hair back behind her ears. "I think we can let the cat out of the bag now."

"You sure?"

She patted her stomach. "Well, pretty soon it's going to become obvious."

"Okay."

"Ooooh," she said, sitting up quickly and pointing at the grocery store, "pull in here."

I did as directed and parked in the fire lane while Maggie ran in, smirking. Minutes later, she ran out laughing, barely able to put one foot in front of the other. That's my Maggie, just cracking herself up.

"What's so funny?"

She pulled out a notepad, wrote "Guess what?" on the top piece of paper, and then pulled a baby bottle from her bag. She unscrewed the nipple, slid the note inside the clear plastic bottle, and screwed the nipple back on. She held it up, triumphant. "The message in the bottle."

I looked at the bag. "How many of those you get?"

She shook the bag and what must have been a dozen bottles. "Enough."

First, we pulled into Bryce's and parked at the gate. If he was around, we knew he'd want to know. Besides, Maggie really wanted to tell him. She grabbed a bottle and held my hand, and we tiptoed up the drive. The woods were quiet, and it was cooler beneath the tall canopy of oak arms that had overgrown the cracked drive up the hill to Bryce's compound. Where the limbs shadowed us from above, the roots had broken the asphalt and turned most of the hardtop into what looked like a road map of the United States.

When we cleared the trees, Maggie took in a deep breath and said, "Holy smokes! You weren't kidding. What happened?"

I shrugged. "No idea."

We searched the grounds, even the obstacle course, but found no fresh evidence of Bryce. Maggie looked around, shaded her eyes, and pointed atop the second screen. "You ever see that before?"

I looked up, and my eyes widened. The second screen had been rebuilt, larger than an IMAX screen—probably seventy feet tall. Erected across the top was, for lack of a better term, a crow's nest. Fed by a ladder and a metal walkway, it looked large enough for one man, and because of its position atop the hill on Bryce's property, it would give anyone up there a rather advantageous view of Digger.

I shook my head and shrugged. I didn't know much about military tactics or training, but judging from the level platform, and the length of it, the ladder leading up the side, and the idea that high ground is best, I started putting two and two together. Given Bryce's history, or what little I knew of it and the mystery that surrounded it, compounded with the stories I'd heard from Amos that rose out of his SWAT sniper training, I started to wonder. But I said nothing to Maggie.

Thinking he'd return to his trailer sooner or later, we left the bottle hanging from a string on the front door. We walked back down the hill, underneath the tentacled arms of the oaks and beneath the shade of the canopy. While our feet crunched dried acorns, I had a strange feeling that just because we hadn't seen Bryce didn't mean he hadn't seen us. This wasn't something I knew but rather something I felt—kind of like static electricity.

One question kept popping up across the backs of my eyelids: *Why?* I had now been here twice and was pretty sure Bryce knew about both trips, but he hadn't showed. Granted, Bryce had never been a very social person. He prized his own company, avoided most other human beings on the planet, and had no real friends to speak of. But for some reason, all that had changed when it came to Maggie and me. Especially Maggie. In fact, he'd made efforts to see us when he didn't have to. All that, coupled with the sight of Bryce's compound, put a wrinkle in the center of my forehead that Maggie would have seen had she not been working on her note to Amos and Amanda.

We headed toward home and pulled into their drive, and

my giddy wife hopped out and dropped a bottle in the Carters' mailbox. She climbed back in, propped her feet up, and kicked the dashboard.

"What'd the note say?"

She smiled and leaned her head back. "Dylan's got a secret."

*chapter thirteen*

AT 11:00 PM I HEARD A FAINT TAP ON OUR BEDROOM
window. When Amos is your neighbor, you learn to live with
these things.

I looked out the window and saw him motioning me toward
the front porch. Given Maggs's little gift we left in the mailbox,
I'd been expecting a visit. I covered Maggie, who had been
asleep since a little after nine, and stepped into my jeans. Blue
hopped off the end of the bed and followed silently behind.

When I slid open the door, Amos was sitting on the porch
railing, looking out over the corn. He didn't look at me, and
when Blue brushed up alongside the railing, he didn't seem
to notice. From the side, his face looked thin, and his eyes
were sunk back in his head. He pointed at the cotton. "It's
pretty in the moonlight."

I nodded and moved around the side where the moon lit the sweat on Amos's face and shone off the badge that hung on a chain around his neck. He looked tired. His waist was hung with all sorts of police paraphernalia: a SureFire flashlight, black, nonreflective; handcuffs; a retractable baton; his Kimber in .45 auto; several clips; and a few other odds and ends that I couldn't place.

I spoke softly. "You been up awhile?"

He nodded. "Couple of days."

"You want to talk about it?"

Amos shook his head. I walked inside, grabbed two cups and the pitcher of sweet tea out of the fridge, and returned to the porch. Pouring a glass, I handed it to him and sat on the railing next to him. Blue hopped up on the swing and pointed his nose at us.

"Thanks." Amos wiped his face with the fat of his palm and looked up at the ten trillion stars looking down on us. Then he looked at me. "You still got Papa's Model 12?"

I nodded.

"You remember how to . . . ?"

Amos trailed off, and I nodded again.

"You might think about . . . keeping it handy."

Papa's Model 12 was a pump-action Winchester twelve-gauge with a thirty-inch barrel and a full choke. The longer barrel and full choke gave it a tighter pattern at longer distances—good for shooting geese, turkey, or deer. According to Amos, it was reliable and gained in popularity with inner-city gangsters in the 1940s and 1950s. Starting in the '60s, law enforcement adopted it to clear houses and hallways, and in Vietnam, marines and Rangers alike used it in the tunnel networks.

What had started out as a hunting shotgun evolved rapidly into a rather potent self-defense weapon. The only difference between theirs and mine was that most of them had cut twelve inches off the barrel so the pattern spread more quickly. The sound of the pump action sliding a round into the chamber is definitely distinct. If you were breaking into a house and heard that sound somewhere in the darkness around you, it'd get you to thinking.

I looked at him. "Ebony, feels like there's a whole lot you're not telling me."

He nodded and glanced over his shoulder to where Maggie lay sleeping. "You two got enough to worry about right now." He stood, lifted his belt, and pulled his car keys from his pocket. "Just keep it close. You hear me?"

"I heard you the first time, but that doesn't mean I understand you."

He looked off across the pasture. "The sound alone might do you as much good as the business end of it." He grabbed his bag and started down the steps. Then he stopped, shook his head, and reached into the bag. He pulled out a small gift tied with a bow and set it on the railing. "Got this for you." He feigned a smile. "It'll come in handy."

He looked at his house across the street. "'Manda'll be over tomorrow with something for Maggie. She's over there now, dreaming up something."

Amos walked down the drive and across the street into his yard. I watched him dodge the toys and then disappear through the front door. His status among local and federal law enforcement had increased a lot in the last two years, and his broad shoulders carried a lot more than just the shirt on his back. And I loved him for it.

*chapter fourteen*

AMOS AND I WERE NINE, AND IT WAS SUMMER BREAK. We were dressed up like cowboys, walking through Dodge City while keeping our eyes on Boot Hill.

Marshal Amos had seen the bad guys run behind the general store, which looked a lot like our barn, so he told his faithful companion, Texas Ranger Dylan, and we slipped around back and ducked into Papa's soybeans. If we could corner them in the barn, they'd have to jump from the hayloft and we'd get them in the air on the way down. It was the fourth time this week they'd chosen that escape route.

Sure enough, they had climbed the ladder inside the barn and were already taking shots at us. That meant we had to face them. Man-to-man. Amos and I straightened the bandannas around our necks to keep the dust out, checked the caps on our pistols, and loosed the holster fob. We licked the sights on our carbines, and then we walked out of the shoulder-high plants, challenging all comers. We sprinted around the barn, dove into the sawdust, rolled, shuffled behind the Evinrude motor clamped to the motor mount, and aimed at the sun just cracking through the slats in the hayloft.

I looked at Amos, he nodded, and we came out blazing. Like Wyatt Earp at the OK Corral, and John Wayne in *True Grit*, we bit down on our bandannas like halter reins and started slinging lead. We worked the levers on our faithful Model 94 Winchesters and popped as many caps as our fingers would let us. When they were empty, we threw down our carbines, pulled both six-shooters, and kept pouring the lead at them. When the remaining two finally leaped from the loft, Marshal Amos squeezed off a fantastic shot behind his back, leaving him out of ammo and me to deal with the worst of the outlaw gang alone.

I stepped quietly, crunching dried hay, and when that notorious outlaw came swinging down the rope with a knife in his mouth and a pistol in each hand, I shot his hat off to blind him, then shot him through both hands. Amos and I handcuffed the entire gang, locked them in the jail (where chances were good they'd attempt a jailbreak tomorrow), and walked to the saloon for some sweet tea.

We never suffered from lack of imagination. We could shoot the same outlaw ten times, and he'd always come back meaner and nastier—which was just fine with us. Bring them on; we could get more caps. The fight of good versus evil got us out of bed in the morning, and the promise of another shootout sped us through our chores and out into the fields, where we'd lasso rustlers, rescue fair maidens in distress, and warn the stagecoach that the bridge was out.

And if there was one thing in this life that we spent hours dreaming about, it was a Model 69 pump-action Winchester in .22 caliber. With that in my hands, not a squirrel, raccoon, or armadillo in Digger would be safe. I had cut the advertisement out of *Field and Stream* and pasted it on the wall next to my bed. Amos had too. But the gun had a price tag of $129, and I was at least two summers away from being able to afford it.

Amos and I walked up the steps of the saloon just as Papa came walking out the back door. Before he could blink, and before I had time to think, I beat him to the draw and blasted him with both six-shooters. And it was there, with smoke trailing out of both barrels, that it hit me. Caught up in the moment and the game we were playing, I had just violated cardinal rule number one: *Never, absolutely never, point any gun, play or not, at a real person. Imagine all you want, but never in real life.*

Papa stuffed his hand in the open side of his overalls, half-closed one eye, chewed on his lip, and nodded us both inside. I dropped both guns out of fear of what was about to happen to my backside. He pointed to the kitchen table, where we unbuckled—*No guns at the table*—and then sat obediently. At minimum, he'd take my guns away for a few weeks, increase my chores, and tan my backside. At most, well . . . I'd rather not go there.

He picked up the phone and dialed Mr. Carter, and the two talked in hushed tones for several minutes. Before he hung up, Papa said, "You'll make the call?" He waited a second. "Good. We'll meet you down there."

Nanny had been shelling peas on the front porch, but she poked her head in when Papa appeared. Papa shook his head and waved her off with his hand. She returned to the porch, and Papa walked to their room; slid his wallet, change, and truck keys off the dresser; and then pointed us to his old, beat-up Dodge Power Wagon.

His failure to speak was a bad omen. My palms grew cold and clammy, and my stomach jumped up into my throat. The look of accusation and blame on Amos's face was almost more than I could handle.

We drove downtown in total silence. We had been warned. The time for talking was over, and I knew it. To make matters worse, my indiscretion was about to earn Amos a butt blister-ing too. The fact that he had not drawn would mean little to Mr. Carter. He was a part of it. The look on his face told me that idea had not been lost on him.

Papa parked the truck just off the town square and ushered us up the sidewalk and down another side street. At the first nondescript building on the right, he held the door and nod-ded us in. He still hadn't spoken a word, and his silence told me that I was in more trouble than I'd ever known in my entire life. In our house, guns—play or not—were respected. And when I fired off both caps at Papa, I hadn't.

The building was painted battleship gray, and the inside was very cold. The receptionist wore a sweater, which was odd given the fact that it was the middle of summer, and the whole place smelled like bleach and something else. Mr. Carter was sitting in a chair reading a magazine with his glasses on the end of his nose. When we walked in, he nodded at Papa and didn't say a word to either one of us.

We were dead meat. When their heads were turned, Amos glared and mouthed, "Nice going, butt head!"

The receptionist led us down a long hallway to a room that was well lit and looked like a hospital operating room, but without all the doctors and nurses. A man in blue scrubs met us in the back. He had a flashlight strapped around his head, but his apron looked like a butcher's. I remember thinking that if he was a surgeon, he sure was messy. With his hands covered in bloody white rubber gloves, he led us to a metal table, where a spotted white sheet covered what looked like somebody sleeping. The person's head was covered; I could tell his mouth was open, and I remember thinking it must have been difficult for him to sleep without feeling smothered.

About then it hit me that he might not be sleeping. Amos and I walked around the end of the table, and our eyes grew as wide as Oreos. The man's feet were sticking out from under the sheet. They were grayish-blue, and while the left pointed straight up, the right had sort of flopped over to the right. On his left big toe, somebody had tied what looked like a luggage tag. We walked around the other end, and Mr. Carter nodded to Papa, who nodded to the "doctor."

He set me on one side and Amos on the other, not more than six inches from the man's shoulders. Then he pulled back the sheet. He looked at both of us and then at the man on the table. "This . . . is what happens when you play with guns."

And I've never looked at one the same way since.

In the span of a millisecond, I learned that a firearm—no matter what kind—has one purpose: to kill. Period. No two ways about it. No matter what the movies teach you, and no matter how romantic the notion might be, if you point a gun at someone and pull the trigger, at the end of the day that person is dead. You can't pause, rewind, and replay. The blue man on the table taught me that.

Papa and I drove back to the farm in quiet, listening to the rhythmic sound of a pebble lodged in the tire tread. Back at the house, Papa was pensive. He returned to his tractor, where he usually did his best thinking. I started on tomorrow's chores, and when I finished those, I did anything I could think of that was helpful and would look as though I was paying penance. The thought of the whipping I was still sure of getting was a great motivator, and when Papa finally parked the tractor at a little after four, I had that barn looking like a showroom. Problem was, if Papa noticed, he didn't let on.

He hopped off the tractor and disappeared inside the house, and I stood just outside the door, waiting for him to call my name. With my heart pounding like a war drum, I stood against the frame and waited. A few minutes later he walked out the back door, kissed Nanny—who was drying her hands on her clean white apron—and then loaded back into the truck.

I couldn't quite tell, but Nanny didn't seem to have an angry look on her face. She almost looked as if she were trying to hide a smile. I wanted to ask if I could stay with her, but Papa cranked the engine and waved me into the front seat. This was not making sense. If he wanted me to suffer, he'd done the trick.

I opened the door. "Papa?"

He looked at me, his sun-wrinkled eyes bending downward at the edges.

"If I'm gonna get a whippin', I'd just as soon get it over."

He looked out the windshield, and when he looked back, I saw that his eyes had watered up. He patted the seat, swallowed, and nodded. He wasn't smiling, but he wasn't frowning either. Papa had something on his mind, and whatever it was seemed more important to him at the moment than blistering me, so I climbed in.

We drove back to town, something we rarely did twice in the same day. We parked on the street in front of the hardware store, and Papa led me between the aisles filled with garden tools and bolt bins and finally to the far corner of the store.

Mr. Steve, one of the four brothers who owned the place, was working behind the counter where they kept all the hunting and fishing stuff.

Papa leaned against the counter and extended his hand. "Steve."

Mr. Steve switched his cigarette to the other hand, brushed a few ashes off his shirt, and extended his hand. "Mr. Styles." He nodded at me and smiled. "Dylan."

Papa pointed his nose at the wall. "I've come to pay you what remains."

I looked at Papa, the confusion in me growing.

Mr. Steve nodded, smiled at me again, then looked back at Papa. "Yes, sir, eight months is a long time on layaway." He turned, walked to the only rifle I'd ever cared anything about, and pulled the Model 69 Winchester off the wall. My eyes grew as wide as bowling balls.

Papa pulled out a twenty-dollar bill and handed it to Mr. Steve, who punched the buttons on his cash register, pulled the handle, and stood back as the bottom drawer sprang open. He pulled out a single dollar, pulled the rifle off the wall, and slid the action downward, proving to both himself and Papa that it was unloaded. He handed it to Papa, who also checked it, and asked, "You want the box?"

Papa shook his head. "No." He looked at me and almost smiled. "It wouldn't last very long. Besides, we don't have very far to go." He hefted the rifle in his left hand, ever careful to keep the barrel down, then gently grabbed my left hand with his right, and we walked out while my teeth carved drag marks in the linoleum tiles.

Papa loaded me into the passenger's side and laid the rifle, barrel tip on the floor mat, next to me. My heart was pounding so hard I thought it would explode. He walked around, climbed in, and cranked the engine. He pulled his white handkerchief from his back pocket and wiped the sweat beading across his forehead. He methodically refolded it and then turned toward me. His face had turned serious again.

I swallowed, looked at the rifle, and swallowed again—afraid to hope. I saw now that Papa intended to hang this thing on the wall, where it would sit for two years, reminding me daily of my indiscretion. I'd have preferred a spanking. "Papa?"

Papa shook his head and put his hand on my shoulder. He thought for a moment, then said, "Yup, you messed up today, but . . . I did, too, when I was your age."

I almost smiled, then thought better of it. I wasn't out of the woods yet.

He lowered his voice. "I don't want to break the spirit of the kid in you; that's a precious thing." He took a deep breath. "But it's time we start making a man out of the boy I see before me."

That night, after we'd shot an entire box—fifty rounds—at more than our fair share of cans down at the river, Papa took me into the kitchen and laid the new rifle across the table. He sat me down and then laid down the law. His tone of voice told me that if I ever violated it, he'd take that rifle away for as long as I lived in this house.

"*Never* bring a loaded gun into the house."

"Yes, sir."

"Never point one at anybody—floor or ceiling only, unless you're shooting at a target and intend to pull the trigger."

"Yes, sir."

"Make sure of your target and what's behind your target. If you miss, what will you hit?"

I'd heard all this a hundred times before, but I wasn't about to interrupt him. "Yes, sir."

He sat back and patted the rifle, then pointed his finger at my face and inched his nose closer to mine. "Always, always, *always* treat a gun as if it's loaded, even when you know it's not."

"Yes, sir."

The kitchen smelled of Hoppe's solvent, Winchester oil, and Vicks mentholatum—Papa's choice of lip balm. Papa dipped the brass brush in the solvent, then ran it down the barrel, removing the gunpowder. Then he ran several quarter-sized, oiled white cloths down through the barrel until they came out looking as white as when they'd gone in. He brushed and oiled the action, the barrel, the trigger assembly, and finally the stock itself. Then he toweled it off so it wouldn't be too slick. When finished, the rifle lay on the table—clean, oiled, and empty. The thing that had filled my nights and days with dreams of heroes and grand deeds now lay on the table before me much like that man had.

Papa leaned forward. "You see that?"

"Yes, sir."

He paused, measuring his words. "By itself, that is harmless. Can't hurt a flea. The most dangerous thing about that . . . is you." He gently grabbed my hand and placed it on the stock. "You understand?"

I nodded. "Yes, sir."

"Does it scare you?"

I nodded.

He set me on his lap and wrapped his arms around me. I needed that hug. "Don't fear it—respect it." He smiled. "That way, you'll live to be my age, and older."

Later that night, the world seemed a lot bigger than it had when I'd woken up that morning. We were all sitting on the front porch, listening to the whippoorwill. Nanny and Papa swayed on the front porch while I stretched out across the top step.

"Papa?" The smell of his pipe wafted around us and filtered into the woodwork.

"Yes."

"You think it's okay with God if we have guns?"

Papa clinched his teeth about his pipe, pulled his yellow-handled Case Trapper from his front pocket, opened it, and began scraping his fingernails. Over his shoulder, nailed to the wall of the house, was a wooden plaque with the Ten Commandments etched onto it. He thought several minutes, nodded, and said, "I have thought a lot about that, and I think the answer is yes."

Knowing that he could quote each one by heart, I said, "Why?"

He didn't flinch. "'Cause not all men are good."

AMOS'S AND MY CHILDHOOD FASCINATION WITH GUNS HAD been killed that day, and that man lying cold and still on the stainless steel table took more to his grave than he intended. When I think back on it, it was one of the best lessons I've ever learned.

Amos asked me if I still had Papa's Model 12, and then asked if I remembered how to use it. I did. And he knew that I did. His question spoke volumes that both of us understood yet neither of us needed to voice. It told me that Amos had thought about it ahead of time, weighed asking me against not asking me, and asked anyway. And that, more than anything else, told me he was scared.

I looked toward the house, imagined the Model 12 leaning against the back wall of my closet, and tried to digest our conversation. I sat on the top step, leaned back, and noticed the small package perched above me on the railing. I lifted it, untied the silver bow that lay shining in the moonlight, slid off the lid, and found a child's pacifier.

With the pacifier lying on my left, Maggie asleep behind, Papa's Model 12 not too far away, uncertainty all around, our conversation swirling about inside me like smoke fumes, I sat in the middle and tried to make sense of it all.

When morning came, I still had not.

I stepped off the porch steps and walked around the side to the faucet beneath our bedroom window. The faucet had been running all night through a slow-leaking soaker hose that stretched through Maggie's vegetable garden. She had wrapped it around the base of a dozen or more tomato plants.

The window above gave me a clear view of Maggie stretched across the bed, tacked down at each corner. I smiled and tapped on the window. She didn't even budge. I tapped louder. She pulled a pillow over her head and waved me off. Blue rolled over and stuck all four paws in the air. I tapped a third time, and she threw a pillow at the window.

Laughing to myself, I reached down, turned off the dripping faucet, and froze. I studied the dirt path that ran between the house and the azalea bushes, and the closer I looked, the more unsettled I became. Footprints, lots of them, made by a barefooted person, covered the footpath.

As I followed them, I walked back and forth several times, finally coming to a stop beneath our window. Based on the length and depth of imprint, they were too big to be Maggie's and—I placed my bare foot inside the outline—too wide to be mine. I knelt, crawled around, and looked more closely. They couldn't be Amos's, because these had a defined arch and Amos was flat-footed. Maggie had been back here yesterday afternoon to turn on the faucet, but these prints covered hers.

All this told me two things: I didn't know what Peeping Tom had made these prints, and they had been made sometime between yesterday afternoon and this morning. I looked over to the porch where Amos and I had talked, just ten feet away, and felt cold.

*chapter fifteen*

THE PHONE RANG AND BROUGHT ME OFF MY KNEES.
I poked my head above the azalea tops and listened. It rang a
second time. Chances were good that a phone call this early
had to be Caglestock. He rarely slept—one of the self-inflicted
disciplines of managing Bryce's millions. "Hello?"

"Dylan, it's John." He sounded as if he'd been up awhile,
and based on the speed with which he spoke, as if he'd already
consumed a pot of coffee.

"Morning to you. How're things?"

"Good. Thanks for getting us those documents." Caglestock
paused. "Hey, Dylan, how much do you know of Bryce's past?
I mean, how much do you really know?"

I considered his question. "Ummm, only what you and he

have told me. Really, just the highlights. Bryce plays his cards pretty close to his chest."

John stalled. "Help me with that one."

"He only tells you what he wants you to know, or doesn't bother you with what he thinks you might not be interested in."

"That's my experience too. Which got me to thinking. We've done some digging, asked a few questions, and I wondered if you could come have lunch with us. Can you do that?"

"Sure. When?"

"Today." His tone had changed.

"Everything all right, John?"

"Don't know, but it'd be good if you were here. Still no word from Bryce."

I hung up the phone to the sound of Blue licking my toes and Maggie walking down the hall, covered in sleep. Her weight made the boards creak, and her calloused heels scuffed the bare floors. She walked up and leaned against me—sign language for "Good morning. Love you. I need a hug." Her hair was sticking in fifty different directions and floating on static electricity. If I hadn't known her, she might have scared me.

I hugged her, thought how warm she was, how soft her breasts felt and yet how firm her back had become, and finally, how perfectly she fit in the space between my shoulders.

"Who was that?" she mumbled.

"Caglestock. Wants me to have lunch with him."

She nodded, pulled the OJ from the fridge, and drank straight out of the jug. Then she pulled the bread out of the hamper, made two PB&Js, began eating one, and simultaneously started scrambling some eggs. While spreading cheese over the eggs, she ate the other sandwich. Every few seconds she'd take another swig from the OJ jug.

I leaned against the counter, hovering over my coffee mug

and watching. Maggs wasn't entirely awake yet, but in the last week or so, her appetite had become voracious. If something was edible and wasn't nailed down, she'd eat it.

When the eggs were fluffy, hot, and steaming, she ate them—directly off the skillet. She stood over the sink, scooped up a forkful, and blew across it. Not waiting long enough for it to cool off, she bit down, then stood with her mouth open trying to blow out the hot air. When she bit into a bite that was still too hot, she'd dance around a little like someone who'd swallowed a jalapeño.

Her short cotton nightgown fell an inch or so below the fold where her thighs met her bottom. Her long legs had begun to tan in the sun, and every day I marveled at the transformation. Her dance continued for several minutes while she polished off the eggs. After she'd cleaned the skillet, she peeled a banana and ate it in three bites. She washed that down with another swig and then stood holding the fridge door open.

She shook her head. "I need to get to the grocery store. There's nothing to eat here."

I raised an eyebrow and blew steam off my cup. "Tell me about it."

Eyeing the newspaper on the table, she pulled out a jar of pickles, sat down, and began reading the front page and fingering pickles into her mouth. She ate like a chain-smoker.

I tried not to laugh. "Honey, you want me to get you something to dip those in?"

She was reading the headlines and didn't pay me much attention. She shook her head, shoved another pickle into her mouth, and didn't look up. "No thanks."

I shook my head, kissed her on the cheek, and walked to the shower.

When I got out, I heard two women giggling and talking. The hyena laugh mixed with the muted snicker told me all I needed to know. I poked my head around the corner and saw Maggs and Amanda arm in arm, tears streaming down their faces, sitting on the floor of the den with a pint of Häagen-Dazs between them. Each was armed with a spoon and a handful of Kleenex.

"You girls okay?"

Amanda worked her spoon into the hard frozen ice cream and spoke over her shoulder. "Hey, Professor."

Despite the many changes in our lives and the multiple times I'd told her otherwise, Amanda just couldn't get past calling me Professor. By now, it had become a term of endearment.

"Hey, Amanda. How're things?"

"Good," she said, stuffing a spoonful into her mouth.

Maggs swallowed and pointed a loaded spoon at me. "You and Mr. Clean better get ready, 'cause dirty diapers don't change themselves."

I dressed, lifted our bedroom window, and, looking over my shoulder, quickly and quietly slid the long-barreled shotgun out and leaned it against the house. Blue looked at me as if I'd lost my mind.

Then I kissed Maggs, who'd decided to stay and talk children with Amanda, and waved to them both as I slipped out the back door. They had finished off the ice cream and were now standing in the nursery talking about window treatments. I walked around the house, grabbed the shotgun, slid it along the floorboard behind the backseat of my van, and idled out of the drive.

The air had turned hot, reminding me of things I missed. I turned off the AC, rolled down the windows, sped up, and remembered things I loved. The scanner sat beside me on the seat, crackling with numbers and codes that I was slowly learning to translate.

With sweat soaking through the back of my shirt, I drove the long way to town. It was Monday, Pastor John's day off, but when I drove by the church, his Cadillac was parked by itself around back. I looked in my rearview, saw nothing, and kept driving. A few more back roads and I drove by Bryce's locked gate. The chain and lock were still shiny with that just-off-the-shelf look. In the last year, confederate jasmine had grown across the gate and was now thick with fresh green leaves. It blocked any sight beyond the gate.

I drove by, felt the tug, and realized how much I missed seeing Bryce. I missed his deep, resonating brogue, his unshaven face, his reddish hair, his fat, burly chest, and our one-sided conversations that I seldom made sense of. I missed the sound of his pipes, his emerald green eyes, the taste of a cold beer shared in a Styrofoam cup. And, I'll admit, I even missed the comical look of him in a kilt or next to nothing at all.

Bryce was his own person, and to his credit, he didn't care what the world thought. There were times when I admired him for that. I didn't have time to stop then, but I told myself I would on the way back.

Lorraine met me at the door and led me to the conference room, where Caglestock introduced me to a man decked out in military dress and covered in medals.

"Dylan, this is Colonel Max Bates. He works in the Pentagon."

Colonel Bates wore a beret and a face that told me he'd seen more than his share of barrels pointed in his direction. He was in his midfifties and erect with a lifetime of military discipline. It seemed hardwired into his DNA.

The colonel extended his hand and nodded. "Dr. Styles,

good to meet you. John's told me about your friendship with Sergeant McGregor."

I shook his hand. "Yes, sir, Bryce is . . . well, he's someone I consider a friend, as much as Bryce is friends with anybody."

While we ate, Caglestock retold Colonel Bates of my friendship and working relationship with Bryce—how I handled his funds, how Bryce had given me power of attorney over most of his affairs, and how I tried to check in on him regularly.

The colonel listened, ate, and seemed to make mental notes. When Lorraine delivered a plate of chocolate chip cookies, Caglestock turned the conservation over to Colonel Bates, saying, "Max, I think it'd be helpful if you'd tell Dylan, tell us both, what you know about Bryce."

Colonel Bates swallowed, sat back, and thought for a moment. Finally he spoke. "Much of Sergeant McGregor's record is confidential. Top secret. Not even I, as his commanding officer, have enough clearance to read it, but since I saw most of it personally . . ." He shrugged and then shook his head. "When it comes to the psychological exams and reports, I won't have much for you." He picked a strawberry off the side of the cookie plate and ate it.

"Bryce Kai McGregor joined the Marines in 1970 for reasons I never did understand. Back then, he looked a lot like you. Clean-cut, full of life, innocent to an extent." Bates swiveled in his seat. "Maybe he was trying to earn his inheritance—I've seen it before. Rich kids wrestling with how to handle Daddy's money. We put him through the ropes, trying to get rid of him before he got himself killed, and he proved us wrong. The harder we made it, the better he did. It was like the kid had never been tested and had been waiting his whole life to be discovered. We laid him out at the range on the thousand-yard targets, and he dropped a few jaws. The kid could shoot like nothing I'd seen before or since. Boy had a gift." He paused, scratched his nose, and said, "And sometimes I wished I'd never discovered it."

He swiveled again. "Fast-forward a few years. Bryce, or Scotty, as he became known, was leading an elite team of specialists. Kind of like the Green Berets or Rangers, but more like what we now call the Delta Force. We didn't really give them a name, but we sent them any- and everywhere. Before Vietnam got so ugly, they'd been on missions all over the globe. And just as he did in training, the worse the conditions and the more impossible the mission, the more Bryce excelled. Fast-forward again to Vietnam, 1975, right at the end."

He paused again and chose his words carefully. "We had inserted Bryce and his team of eight in a place from which they were not expected to return. We told them that, we explained to them the value of the target, and we gave them the choice. They voted—unanimous. They were just like that." Bates teared up and shook it off. "For several reasons we lost radio contact. At the rendezvous, Bryce and his team never showed."

"Do you know what happened?"

He nodded. "I do—but that information is found in that part of the file I can't talk about." He folded his hands. "This is what I can tell you. Five months later, some three months after the U.S. had pulled out of Vietnam, I got a phone call. Three minutes later, I went straight to the top, we sent in two planes, extracted him, and brought the boy home—alone."

Bates took a handkerchief from his pocket and wiped his eyes. "I wished to God I'd never sent that kid in there. Of all of them, I should've . . . I knew he'd never leave a man behind. No matter the orders." He sat back, refolded his handkerchief, and stared out the window. "If you read the

whitewashed version of his record, you'll find a highly deco-
rated veteran who was and is missed by his country. If you read
the version you can't read, you'll find a one-man killing
machine, who's killed God only knows how many people, and
who, in the end, saw and had to do things that few men in history have ever been asked to do."

Silence spread across the room as the picture of Bryce,
passed out on his lawn chair before a John Wayne movie,
flashed before me.

Bates continued, his voice falling slightly. "We tried to reha-
bilitate him. Tried therapy, drugs, electroshock, you name it.
Anything we thought would help, we offered. Finally he left to
face his demons alone. I guess he's been facing them ever since."

"You make him sound like Rambo."

"I wish it were that simple."

Caglestock spoke up. "Would you describe him as having
post-traumatic stress disorder?"

Bates tilted his head and shook it. "If that were the extent
of Bryce's problem, I'd be jumping up and down. The military
can handle that. Bryce could too."

"If there's been a change in Bryce, why now?"

"If I knew the answer to that, I'd get my own talk show. In
my experience, men like Bryce are ticking time bombs. Some
just take longer than others to go off."

I didn't know what to say.

Bates looked at me. "I can see it on your face, so let me spell
it out. Bryce can kill you or any other human a thousand different ways with his thumb. Give him this pencil, and he can
kill you from the other end of the room. Give him a weapon,
and, well . . . if Bryce cracks or has already cracked, as we've
seen in a few others just like him, I don't think you're safe
going up to his place." He waited while the gravity of his words

settled in. "Actually, nobody within hiking distance is safe."

"What's hiking distance?"

He sucked through his teeth and calculated. "Bryce has covered a hundred miles without sleeping."

"What do you intend to do?"

He shook his head. "I can't tell you that. But if he contacts you, you'd do well to keep your distance. And under no circumstances should you take your wife or any other female up there."

"Why? I mean, what's the—"

He held out his hand like a stop sign. "If he's in the state I suspect he's in, the sight of a female might trigger some things you don't want to trigger." He sat back and placed both hands on his thighs as though he were ready to leave. "I've said enough." He stood and extended his hand. "I thank you for all you've done."

I nodded and shook his hand, and Colonel Bates walked out to the click of hard heels on tile floor. Caglestock led him to the door, said a few words in hushed tones, and then returned to the conference table, shutting the door behind him.

John took a deep breath as if he were still trying to digest the story. He poured us each a cup of ice water and sat back down. "What do you think we ought to do?"

I didn't hesitate. "I have no doubt that Bryce can kill me a hundred different ways from Sunday, but I'm leaving here, making one stop, and then going by to check on him."

Caglestock nodded. "You want me to go with you?"

I shook my head. "No. No offense, but I think I'd better go alone."

He nodded. "Call me if you run into him."

I stood to leave. "And if I find him, and call you, are you going to call him?"

I nodded out the window at Bates's car backing out of the parking lot.

Caglestock followed the red taillights with his eyes. "I don't know." He shook his head. "I don't know."


I DROVE THROUGH AN OLDER SECTION OF WALTERBORO AND passed the hardware store where Papa had bought me the Model 69 so many years ago. I parked along the street, grabbed Papa's Model 12 shotgun, slid the chamber slide open so that it not only was unloaded but also looked unloaded, and walked into the store—barrel down.

This would have seemed abnormal except that I carried it in my left hand, and folks were always carrying weapons in here. Vince, a crusty Korean War veteran and one of the best gunsmiths in South Carolina, worked here three days a week. Guys came from all over the South just to pass him their valuables across the countertop and hire his magic touch.

Vince had been working on firearms since the military taught him how in Korea. He could and would work on most anything, but he was partial to fine custom shotguns and double rifles. He also did all the custom work for most of the police and SWAT teams in two or three of the surrounding states. He and Amos were on a first-name basis, and because of that, so were he and I.

In the far corner of the store, the gun counter was usually dotted with men leaning against it like a bar. Mostly they talked about guns they wanted, or if they got tired of that, they talked about guns they had—which only led them back to ones they wanted. Vince seldom responded or initiated the conversation. He just nodded, lit another cigarette, and stared out the window of the store.

I walked up to the counter. "Hey, Vince."

"Dylan." He eyed the Model 12, and I passed it across the counter.

Vince, hanging the cigarette from his lip, took the shotgun and started looking it over. He worked the action, eyed the receiver, clicked the safety back and forth, slowly cracked the trigger, and then slid the action open once again. He said nothing, but the smile on his face told me he liked the feel of a fifty-year-old shotgun, and his eyes asked, *Can I help you?*

I looked over both shoulders and leaned closer. "I, uh . . . I think I want to change the choke on that."

The choke of a shotgun does just what it sounds like. It chokes the flow of shot. Think of a brass hose nozzle with a twist stream. Squeezing it down makes for a tighter stream. Opening it wide makes for a spray. What I handed Vince was a squeezed-down stream. What I'd come to get was a wide-open stream.

There was only one way to get this. I knew this, Vince knew this, and he knew that I knew this.

He eyed the tip of the thirty-inch barrel. "It's full now." He moved the cigarette from one corner of his mouth to the other. "With this barrel, even screw-in chokes won't make much of a difference."

Screw-in chokes were a development in late-model shotguns that allowed a shooter with a fixed barrel, or one shotgun, to screw in varying chokes to suit his or her hunting needs. The determining factor was the distance to be shot. In short, quail and skeet, usually close-in game, required a "skeet" or "improved cylinder" choke. Doves, a bit farther out, required more of an improved cylinder, while geese and turkey, sometimes shot from as far as forty or fifty yards, required a "full" choke.

I looked over my shoulder again and wrestled with what I wanted to say.

Vince read my face and asked, "You thinking about opening day of dove season?"

I shook my head.

He eyed the shotgun again. He knew no one in their right mind shot quail with a twelve-gauge, so he asked, "You taking up skeet shooting?"

I shook my head again.

He laid the shotgun on a velvet cloth laid out across the countertop. "You hunting something else close-up?"

I bit my lip and half-nodded. There was one choke wider than skeet. It was called cylinder bore and was used primarily by law enforcement. It gave the widest pattern in the shortest distance and really had only one purpose.

Vince looked at the shotgun. "Police and SWAT carry theirs down to fourteen inches." He ran his fingers along the blued steel. "But us normal citizens can't go below eighteen." He shrugged. "Unless you want to apply for a special permit, or your buddy comes in here and puts it on his books."

I shook my head. "Let's just go eighteen, maybe even eighteen and a quarter." I laid my hand across the barrel. "Legal, but . . ."

Vince picked up the shotgun again and interrupted me. "You sure you want to do that to this? They don't make them like this anymore."

I nodded. Given the right machinery, cutting off a shotgun barrel took about thirty seconds. Vince had the machinery that could cut, sand, and polish it.

He stubbed out his cigarette and said, "Give me about ten minutes."

I shopped the aisles and then returned to the counter as Vince was pulling off his black apron and oiling the shotgun. He handed it across the counter.

"I saw a lot of those in the war."

"What do I owe you?" I asked.

He shook his head. "Nothing. But if your greens or water-melon come in this year, I'll take whatever you got."

"Will do."

## chapter sixteen

I SHUT THE DOOR OF THE VAN, EYED THE NOW-shorter shotgun, and decided to leave it behind the backseat. I shuffled under the fence and up the drive. I smelled smoke and saw the white cloud wafting up just beyond the trees. When I cleared the canopy, a trash pile was smoldering not far from Bryce's trailer. It was mostly ashes and soot, meaning it might've been lit sometime yesterday.

I walked up to the trailer and knocked on the door. No answer. I walked around to what was now Bryce's film library and projection house. No answer. I walked around back toward the obstacle course and whistled, then I walked back to the trailer, pushed open the door, whistled inside, and waited. Nothing. I turned around. And almost peed in my pants.

Not three inches from my face stood Bryce, and it took me

a second or two to recognize him. He had lost weight. A lot of weight, maybe fifty pounds. He was chiseled, clean-shaven—both his face and head—and he wore military BDUs. They were camouflage, starched, and ironed to a crease. His black boots were polished to a mirror shine, and he carried what looked like an ivory-handled Colt 1911 in a shoulder holster.

He stood looking at me, studying my face and features as though we'd never met. While he studied, he reached into the pocket on his thigh and pulled out a pack of chewing gum—the kind with the little pockets protected by foil. He popped all twelve pieces out of the sheet of gum, tossed them into his mouth, and started chewing with great labor.

The smell of spearmint was overwhelming. Bryce chewed for several seconds, swallowing what was obviously extreme production by his saliva glands, and continued to study me while his eyes watered. When he had the gum in a manageable wad, he looked me over and said, "Dylan."

I stepped back. "Hey, Bryce."

His sleeves were rolled up and buttoned, exposing arms that were suntanned and rippling with muscle and veins. On the opposite strap of his shoulder harness he carried a large silver-handled, brass-butted survival knife. The thing was at least a foot long. The handle hung down toward his waist and could be slid from the sheath with a simple flick of the tab that locked it in place. Both the knife and the pistol were oiled and appeared to have had their fair share of use.

I eyed the weapons and Bryce, who was still chewing vigorously. Without a word, he turned with precision, hopped off the steps, grabbed a rucksack that I had not noticed, and hoisted it onto his shoulders. It was fully loaded, probably weighed a hundred pounds, and Bryce didn't even seem to notice it. He cinched down the straps and waist belt, nodded, turned toward the woods, and began what can only be described as a cross between a march and a jog.

"Bryce!" I managed.

He stopped, double-timed it back up the hill, and stopped once again just inches from my face. He was sweating, the vein along the right side of his brow was throbbing, and he looked magnificent.

"I just . . . we just . . . ummm, Maggie's pregnant."

Bryce stopped chewing, looked from me to the ground to the treetops and maybe to an image in his head. "Maggie?"

I nodded. His brow wrinkled a bit, then control took over once again. He stuck out his hand, and I took it. Or rather, he took mine.

I'd never felt a hand that strong. It was a vise. If he had wanted to crush mine, he could have. The muscles in the palm were thick and covered in callus. But like the rest of Bryce, his hand wasn't dirty. He was meticulously clean and smelled of deodorant and aftershave. He grasped my hand, shook gently, turned, and then disappeared into the trees. Within seconds, I couldn't even hear him walking.

*chapter seventeen*

AN HOUR LATER, I PULLED INTO THE DRIVE AND
idled around back. I admit, I was growing accustomed to air-
conditioning and cruise control—but the minivan couldn't hold
a candle to my truck. Maybe my identity was too closely linked to
some rusted metal and a few working parts, but the absence of
my truck had left a sour taste in my mouth. I missed it: I missed
the musty smell of sweat mixed with oil, the way it sounded when
I cranked it, the way it needed a few minutes to warm up in the
morning, the way I knew when to add to or change the oil, the
play in the steering wheel, the way the door sounded when I
shut it, and the sound the window made when I lowered it.

I put the Honda in park, shook my head to get out the bitter taste, and then imagined my wife strapping our son or
daughter into the child-restraint seat behind me.

It was late, and the sun had already fallen behind the trees. I grabbed my scanner—now my constant companion, since Blue seldom left Maggie's side—and stepped out of the van.

First thing I saw was Maggie sitting on the back steps with a large carving knife in one hand and a chunk of watermelon in the other. Her feet straddled a huge melon that had been whacked down the middle and already had most of the heart cut out of it. She had red juice smeared onto both cheeks and dripping off her chin. Her cheeks were so stuffed with watermelon that she looked like a chipmunk. Blue was licking the right side of her face.

I rested my foot on the first step and eyed the watermelon. "Where'd that come from?"

Maggie took another bite and smiled earlobe to earlobe. She took another enormous bite, squeezed juice out the sides of her mouth, and forced her lips into a funnel. She leaned back, lifting her heels off the steps, then lurched forward, spitting the seed high over my head and into the grass.

Blue jumped off the steps and started sniffing the grass. I wiped my face where Maggie had just covered me in watermelon puree. She pointed the carving knife out across our pasture toward Old Man McCutcheon's farm, which bordered ours.

Old Man McCutcheon was rather particular about his watermelon crop. Not only was growing watermelons a science that he studied; it was also something he protected—vehemently. And it had been this way as long as Amos and I could remember.

Sure, we'd stolen a few back in our day, but that ended with us tangled in an electrical fence after being spotlighted like two deer in the headlights. After McCutcheon cut the power and relieved us of the melons we'd been trying to steal, he sat us down in his kitchen, handed us the phone, and made us call our folks. And since stealing was stealing, that ended poorly too.

It would be years before we ventured back into his fields, and then only when we were certain beyond any shadow of a doubt that he and Mrs. McCutcheon had driven their motor home north for their every-two-years ten-day vacation.

Evidently Maggie had no such inhibition. She pointed the carving knife behind her. Stacked up like firewood sat five more watermelons just as large as the one she was currently dissecting. Given their size and weight, and what I knew of her size and weight, that meant she'd made no fewer than six trips across Old Man McCutcheon's fence and into his fields. One trip and you might get lucky. Two and you're tempting fate. Six and you're courting the dark side.

I smirked. "You go shopping?"

Her mouth was packed. There was no way on earth she could form a complete sentence. Maggie bit again, squeezing out more juice. "Uh-huh."

"Wow," I said, sitting next to her. "Must have been a long walk home from the grocery store, since I had the van."

Maggie's only reply was to lean back, lift her heels, inhale deeply, funnel her lips, and lurch forward again, sending the seeds out farther than the first. I looked closer and noticed that the ground was covered in shiny black dots. I got up and grabbed a melon, set it between my legs, and pulled Papa's yellow-handled Case Trapper from my back pocket. I slit the melon down the middle, cut out the heart, and buried my face in sweet South Carolina. Few things are better, and knowing she'd robbed Old Man McCutcheon made it all the sweeter.

By dusk, about the time the first of the wood ducks screamed overhead en route to their roost somewhere south along the river, we'd covered the grass in seeds, spit, laughter, and watermelon rinds.

It grew dark, and the fireflies lit up the night. They danced in silence over and in between the cornstalks, filling our eyes with wonder and lazy amazement. A gentle breeze ushered in and blew off some of the dust and heat. I grabbed a black plastic trash bag and began picking the rinds off the grass. The breeze shifted and swirled about the house, bringing with it an earthy smell and . . . the smell of smoke.

I stood, sniffed the air, and followed it toward the direction it had come from. Smelling smoke in the country was nothing new, but doing so on a breezy night like this, when the forest service never would have issued a burn permit, gave me pause. Then I smelled the unmistakable tinge of kerosene, which meant one of two things: a gas station had just blown up, or somebody's old house, made of heart of pine, also known as "fat lighter," was burning to the ground. Given the conditions and the absence of a gas station within ten miles of my house, I guessed the latter. When the scanner crackled five seconds later, it confirmed my fears.

I ran inside, jumped into my firefighting pants and boots, slid the suspenders over my shoulders, and ran back out the door, carrying my helmet and jacket and tripping over my own feet. Maggie was sitting on the porch listening to the scanner, and her eyes told me that the seriousness of what she was hearing outweighed the sight of me in my suit. She ran with me to the van and said, "I'll check on Amanda."

I threw my stuff in the back and took a long look south. The black billow of pine burning hot clouded the night sky, but it was the sight of the flames almost four miles away that really got my attention. I kissed Maggie, jumped into the van, slammed it into drive, and spun the front tires out the driveway. I turned onto the blacktop and nearly collided with Amos's truck as he spun sideways out of his own drive. I corrected and let him straighten out, and then I, too, punched the accelerator to the floor. I only looked down once, but when I did, the speedometer was pressing against the plastic somewhere north of eighty-five miles an hour.

We pulled into the parking lot that was swirling in red flashing lights and firemen running around like ants. I threw on my helmet and started toward the source, but the heat was so intense that we couldn't get any closer than the front steps of the church. Pastor John's Cadillac, parked right up front, had already been consumed by the flames, and when I looked up, the steeple was just beginning to fall. The collapse of the narthex sent a huge flash of flame and sparks out onto the men holding the hoses, all of which were trained on the base of the flames.

The fire must have started in the narthex, because not much of it remained. Based on the flames shooting out of the roof, half the pews were gone and the altar wouldn't be far behind. The church offices backed up to the rear of the church, and even in the darkness I could see smoke billowing from every orifice, window, or soffit.

Amos hit the ground running and tapped the first guy he found holding the hose. "Where's John?" he demanded.

The guy shrugged, and Amos took off for the back of the church. He returned a few seconds later, coughing, and grabbed an ax from the side of the ladder truck. With the ax spread between both hands, he disappeared again. I grabbed an air tank and a second ax and followed.

When I turned the corner, the flames reflected off the river and lit the shape of a man climbing out of the water. I couldn't see his face, and he was draped in something, but his eyes told me all I needed to know. He stepped out of the water as though he lived in it and began climbing the bank toward us. He was just a few feet away, but I didn't have time to wait or ask questions, so I put my head down and followed Amos.

Amos reached the door, braced his feet, and took one huge Paul Bunyan swing at it. The door literally came off at the hinges and flew backward into the smoke. Amos ran through the door into the smoke and disappeared. I lost sight of him, but he didn't have air and wouldn't last long. I followed.

I ran down the hallway, shouting, but couldn't hear or see him. The heat was intense, as was the sound of crashing timbers in the church and flames overhead. I'd never been in something this hot, but I knew we had a minute or so at best and a few seconds at worst. If Pastor John was in here, chances were good he was long dead from smoke inhalation—and if Amos didn't turn around right now, he would be too.

I ran down the hall toward John's office, turned right, and tripped on a body. I gathered myself, shone my light, and saw Amos's bloody face. A cross timber had come through the roof and hit him across the shoulder and back of the head. Pastor John's door was next to him and shut. I tried the handle, but it was locked. I kicked it, but it didn't budge. Smashed at it with the ax, and one hinge busted loose. Hit it again in the middle and loosened it again. Finally I swung as hard as I could and broke it free enough to wedge the ax in and hack it off the hinges.

I shoved the door out of the way and dragged Amos into the room, where the air was less smoky and a window AC unit was blowing outside air in. I figured that gave us about thirty more seconds. I heard another huge crash and jumped on top of Amos, covering him with my body, as sparks and flames exploded through the roof. I was hot inside my suit, and Amos wasn't wearing one, so I knew his skin had to be boiling. I shone my light around the office and saw no trace of John.

Time was up. If I didn't get Amos up and over my shoulder right now, we were both dead, because the roof was about to come in on us and I could barely see my hand in front of my face. I tried to lift Amos, then heard a cough and a thump behind me. I crawled around the side of the desk, and there lay Pastor John. His eyes were closed, his face had been beaten badly, his clothes were torn, his hands and feet were tied, and he was covered in blood.

I looked from Pastor John to Amos and back to Pastor John. I had time to get one person out of this hellhole before it swallowed us. I crawled over to Amos and slapped him in the face. *"Amos! Amos! Get up! Wake up, Amos!"*

He was as limp as a sack of potatoes and just as responsive. I screamed again, but neither man moved. I grabbed Amos by the strap of his shoulder holster and Pastor John by the ropes tied around his feet. I dragged both to the door, but the two of them were more than I could drag out. The smoke had gotten inside my air mask and was killing my eyes; the heat was so intense. I took another deep breath, grabbed each man again, and tried to pull them through the door, but the roof came in above me and something very heavy hit my helmet and sent me to the floor. I blacked out and tried to get up on my hands and knees, but the room was spinning out of control and looked upside down and backward. Something big and fiery had fallen across Amos, and the flames were starting to climb up his legs. I crawled across him, tried to stamp out the flames, but it was no use. Flames were all around us, and sparks were burning my skin around my collar and between my sleeves and gloves.

I threw the flaming thing off Amos, pulled Pastor John over next to us, covered Amos's body with mine, and cradled his head next to mine. I didn't know where the door was or used to be. I didn't know how I got in or how to get out, and the blow to my head had made me nauseous. I tried to control the urge to vomit but could not. When the first heave came, I started crying. I didn't want to go this way, and I didn't want Amos to either. I stood, made one last attempt to throw him over my shoulder. Then I took another look at Pastor John, and the tears came. How was I going to explain this?

I stepped over Pastor John, took one last look, and ran smack into Bryce. He was dripping wet, covered in a blanket that was also soaking wet, and in his arms he carried what looked like another. I grabbed him by the blanket, shouted above the roar of the flames, and pointed. *"Bryce! Pastor John!"*

Without blinking, Bryce lifted Pastor John over his shoulder, turned, and shoved me in a direction I didn't want to go, and we lurched through the flames together. When we came out the other side, we were standing in what used to be the hallway. Bryce pushed me again, and eight steps later we were running into the spray of the ladder hose that was falling down across the church. We turned through one last burning frame, jumped, and landed on the dirt outside Pastor John's office. I guess we'd just run through what used to be his wall. Amos landed on top of me, we rolled, and when I came to my feet, I saw that his pant legs were on fire. I was standing just a few feet from the river, so I picked him up, hugged him to my chest, and ran down the bank.

The weight of Amos's body pushed me down into the black, cool water. The hole was deep, much deeper than my six-foot height, and I had no footing. I threw off my helmet, wrestled myself out of my tank and jacket, and pushed Amos's head up and out of the water. I kicked hard, but my boots made it nearly impossible. I reached, grabbing for anything, knowing I needed air.

I pushed Amos as far as I could and then felt him yanked out of my hands with a force I didn't know existed in another human. Amos left the water as though he'd been propelled by an engine. My pants had filled with water, as had my boots, and they were pulling me down. It'd been a long time since I'd had any air, and I needed it now. I saw the flames beyond the water, reached toward them, and felt a powerful, muscled hand grab mine. Bryce lifted me from the water as if I were a feather and flopped me on the beach next to Amos, where I lay sputtering and coughing as the flames that had engulfed the church lit the beach.

I looked around and knew the paramedics were working on Amos. Looking up the hill, I saw them loading somebody onto a stretcher and wheeling him toward the back of an open ambulance. The guys fighting the fire had backed away and were now attempting to contain rather than extinguish. The church was gone.

A paramedic jumped across me and pointed a light in my eyes. I grabbed it and shone it toward Amos. I tried to reach for him to check his vitals, but the paramedic pressed my shoulders into the ground and said, "Hey, Superman, we'll take it from here."

I took one last look around, but Bryce was nowhere to be seen. Somewhere in there, everything went black.

# chapter eighteen

WHEN I CAME TO, AMOS WAS GONE. THE PARAMEDICS had my clothes off and were gingerly checking me for burns. Evidently I had escaped real damage. I'd been singed pretty badly, but I'd heal. They let me breathe some oxygen a few minutes to clear my lungs, but my tank had taken pretty good care of me. My throat was scratchy, my skin felt as if all the moisture had been sucked out of it, and in general I felt like a piece of smoked barbecue.

I walked up the bank in my boxer shorts and accepted a blanket from a paramedic who was handing them out. The ambulance carrying Amos disappeared down the road, and I knew I needed to collect Maggie and Amanda and then get to the hospital. I knew Amos had been breathing when we started out of the church, but after that, I wasn't so sure. And as for Pastor John, I wasn't so sure either.

I took one last look at the church, but there wasn't much to see. Nothing standing but some charred remains and a black residue that in the nighttime spotlight of the fire trucks looked like tombstones in a cemetery. I jumped into the van, pegged the accelerator, and wished for some Gatorade.

Amos's house was quiet and dark. I pulled into our drive and around the back of the house and parked the van. I ran up the back steps calling for Maggie, then came to a sudden halt. The screen door had been ripped off the hinges.

I stepped into the kitchen, which looked as though it had been hit by a tornado. The table sat upside down, two chairs were missing, and the other two lay on their sides in the hallway leading to our room. Pots and pans littered the floor, drawers had been pulled from the cabinets and dumped, and every utensil we had lay scattered like leaves around the room. What glasses we used to own now lay in ten million shards across the floor.

*"Maggie!"*

I tiptoed my way through the kitchen and stood in the den. My drum that had been sitting atop the mantel now lay on the floor with a kitchen knife sticking through the middle. The coffee table lay upside down, and the couch was turned on its side.

*"Maggs!"*

I ran down the hallway, dodging furniture, shoes, and lamps. Whatever had happened here, Maggie had put up one hell of a fight. I reached the door to our room and heard Blue growling. I turned the corner, and there in the corner sat Blue, crouched over the figure of Maggie, who lay crumpled on the floor in a bloody mess.

*"Maggs!"*

She was breathing, but her face was puffy and purple. Her lips were cut, her eyes almost swollen shut, and her shirt had been ripped off. Blue whined and nuzzled me, and he, too, was bloody.

I gently picked her up, bringing gurgled coughs and moans of pain from her bleeding mouth. She put one arm around me while the other hung limp. I carried her gently to the van and laid her down in the back. Blue hopped in and lay down next to her, careful not to nudge her. I climbed into the driver's seat, cranked the engine, and pulled out of the drive.

And then I saw the smoke trailing out of the soffit above Amos's kitchen. Shining through the window, a single flame rose up toward the ceiling. I looked down at Maggie's swollen and bloody face and shoved the stick into drive. I didn't let off the accelerator until we reached town.

I drove into the emergency room entrance and found one of Amos's newest deputies directing traffic. He tried to route me into the parking lot, and I almost ran him over. I pulled up in front of the double glass doors and opened the side door to lift Maggie out. The deputy ran up alongside me and shone a light in my face. When he saw it, and Maggie, he got out of the way and told others to do the same.

I put my hand on his shoulder and said, "Fire at Amos's house."

I lifted Maggs from the car and walked through the doors, Blue close on my heels. The receptionist took one look at me and immediately got on the phone. Two seconds later she punched a button and pointed, and the door marked Medical Personnel Only opened. I walked through and followed her to a brightly lit room that was filling up with nurses and techs. One nurse pointed at the bed, and I laid Maggie down gently.

I brushed the sticky hair out of her face, and she tried to smile. She said something, but I couldn't understand. I leaned over, and she tried to speak again, but she coughed, spitting blood. Finally she pulled me closer and whispered, "What took you so long?"

That's when the tears came.

*God, please take care of my wife.*

A nurse was cutting off Maggie's jeans, and another put her hand on my shoulder and led me away from the table. Amanda walked in then, dressed in flowery scrubs.

The nurse sat me down in a chair nearby and then returned to Maggie's bedside. When they finished cutting off her clothes, Amanda brought them to me and laid them next to my chair. She touched me gently on the shoulder and returned to Maggie.

I wondered about Amos and her dad, but her being here told me enough of what I needed. I picked up the clothes and studied them. The seat of Maggie's jeans was sticky, stained dark red, and under the light, I noticed that the tops of my arms were too.

THE STAFF GOT MAGGS COMFORTABLE, WASHED HER CUTS and nicks, gave her something to take the edge off, and put several pads beneath her. Then they rolled her down the hall for X-rays and a CT scan. Everywhere she went, Amanda went too. I sat in the room staring at the terrazzo.

A few minutes later they wheeled her back in, and I stepped up to the side of her table. Maggs had been crying, but she was doped up pretty well. Amanda, holding a fresh pad, nodded at me. I gently lifted Maggie's bottom off the bed and held her there while Amanda pulled off the old and put down the new. Amanda's face was pain-stricken.

I tried to speak. "When I left, your house was . . ."

She nodded but didn't take her eyes off Maggie. "I know."

Dr. Frank walked in soon after, spoke with the attending physician, and walked to the other side of the bed. A nurse followed, rolling what looked like an ultrasound machine.

They squirted a bunch of jelly across Maggie's tummy and then began waving the wand around her belly button. Maggs was having a hard time keeping her eyes open.

Amanda walked around the bed, tears rolling off her cheeks, and locked her arm inside mine. She stood next to me while Dr. Frank watched the screen.

The other nurses talked in hushed tones, and not even Dr. Frank said much. I heard a shuffling at the door and turned to see Amos standing in the doorway, wearing a hospital gown and leaning on a crutch. An oxygen mask loosely covered his mouth, while a nurse held an ice pack to his head. He looked as bad as I'd ever seen him. Some red-colored goo covered both his ankles and calves, and his head looked as though it had been hit with a bowling ball.

He shuffled over, sat next to me, held the oxygen mask close to his face, and breathed deeply. He coughed, breathed deeply again, and said nothing.

Amanda took the ice pack from the other nurse and held it gently on the back of his bald and blood-smeared head. He grabbed her hand, she squeezed his, and still neither one said a thing. Amos sniffled, bit his lip, and pulled the mask away from his face. His eyes were beyond red, and I noticed that his eyebrows and eyelashes were singed and had been mostly burned off. He breathed again. "I came as soon as I heard."

I thought for a minute. The room was mostly quiet. Whenever someone spoke, they did so in a reverent whisper.

People seemed to tiptoe around. I looked from Amos to Maggs and back to Amos. "Heard what?"

A tear fell off Amos's face. He pointed with the oxygen mask. "That . . . that Maggs was . . . was . . . is . . . losing the baby."

*chapter nineteen*

I KNELT NEXT TO THE BED AND BRUSHED HER HAIR behind her ear. Maggie's eyes were closed because they had given her something to relax her and help her sleep. They'd found at least three broken ribs and thought she'd do better if she could sleep eight hours or so. Her face was pale and bruised and still needed cleaning. I turned to Amanda and opened my mouth, but I didn't even need to ask.

Amanda brought some gauze pads and solution, and I gently cleaned Maggs's face and shoulders while Amanda washed her arms and legs. Amanda looked tired and worried.

I spoke softly. "How's your dad?"

She nodded and reached for my hand. "He'll make it. They'll keep him tonight, but it's just routine. Momma's with him now."

When we finished, I patted Maggie dry, covered her with a new gown and several blankets, and then lifted her again while Amanda changed the pad beneath her. It was spotted dark red and dotted with blackish clots.

Amanda rolled the pad inside itself, placed it in a bag, and looked at me with tears pouring off her face. Her bottom lip was quivering. Amos stood looking out the window, blinking a lot and crying.

Dr. Frank came in and pulled me aside. He was wearing jeans, running shoes, a team shirt for what looked like his kid's T-ball team, a white coat, and his stethoscope. He said, "Her injuries are many, but physically she'll recover. Whoever did this was pretty strong, but Maggie's tough." He tried to smile. "She's proven that." His forehead wrinkled with concern. "As for the pregnancy . . ."

He pointed at Amanda, straightening the pads beneath Maggie. "This will continue for another hour, maybe longer. Women's bodies do this at different paces." He looked as if what he was saying pressed down on his shoulders and made it difficult to breathe deeply. "We just have to wait it out." He sat me down, placed the clipboard on his lap, and said, "There's one other thing."

I tried to listen, but it sounded to me as if he were talking out of a barrel. The echo in my ears slurred the words, and all I wanted to do was cradle Maggie's head in my hands and tell her everything would be okay. We'd be okay. As long as she woke up, we'd make it.

Dr. Frank turned a pen over in his hand. "Has she been running a fever?"

I shook my head. "No." I looked at Maggie. Her temples were sweating, and yet her face looked pale. "Well, I don't think so."

"She has one now. Low grade. 'Bout a hundred. But based on her blood work, I think she might have had it awhile."

"What do you mean?"

He shook his head. "I don't think whoever did this"—he waved his hand across Maggie's bed—"did that." He pointed to the pad. "I don't think they're connected. The one might have brought on the other a bit faster, but I think the clock has been ticking and this would have happened, or was in the process of happening, anyway. I need to run some more tests."

He put his hand on my shoulder. "Let's get through tonight. We've got her on some antibiotics now, so let's worry about tomorrow, tomorrow."

Amanda dipped herself under Amos's shoulder and helped him limp out of the room.

When they got halfway to the door, I whispered, "Hey, Ebony?"

Amos turned.

"Your house was . . ."

Amos nodded, and they walked out, leaving me alone with Maggie.

The machines that I had come to hate were now monitoring her every movement, breath, and heartbeat. I sat next to her wanting to unplug every single one, scoop her into my arms, and disappear out the front door. I'd put in my time here, in these halls, these rooms. I had no desire to do it again. I whispered in her ear and laid my hand beneath hers.

After an hour or so, I checked her feet, then searched the room for some socks. I changed her pad and cleaned the backs of her legs and bottom. Then I straightened her gown, pulled up the covers, laid a second blanket across her feet and shins, and pushed the nurse's call button.

In a moment a woman's voice said, "Yes?"

"Hi, um, do you know if there are any socks around here for the patients?"

The voice hesitated, then crackled back over the speaker, "Honey, give me a few minutes. I'll find you some."

Ten minutes later I heard heavy footsteps and then a slight knock on the door. A familiar face looked in. "May I?"

It had been almost eighteen months since I'd seen her, working the nurses' station on Maggie's hall. She had cut her hair, lost a few pounds, and was wearing makeup. She grabbed the tip of her name tag and held it under the light so I could read it: ALICE MAY NEWSOME, SERVING 40 YEARS.

I stood, realized that it hurt to do so, and braced myself against the wall. "Hi, Allie. You look good. It's good to see you."

She hugged me and handed me a pair of socks. "Hey, honey, how's your girl?"

I shrugged. "She's tough, but . . ." I accepted the socks and gently tugged them onto Maggie's feet.

Allie had disappeared. In a few minutes she was back with a really hot cup of coffee, another blanket, and a pair of scrub pants.

"For you." She pointed at my clothes. "Thought you might be cold."

I looked down for the first time since being in the hospital and noticed that I was still dressed only in my boxer shorts and the socks I'd been wearing beneath my rubber boots.

JUST BEFORE DAYLIGHT, AMOS RETURNED. HE WAS LIMPING; his right calf and shin were wrapped in gauze and looked goopy with some sort of greasy brown medicine. All of it was held in place via some fishnet-looking thing.

His flip-flops, shorts, and aftershave told me he'd showered, and the small black duffel bag tucked under his arm told me he'd been by my house. He handed me the duffel, and it smelled like smoke.

Amos put his hands together and rolled his head around as if he were trying to pull the words out. "Last night, after we got here. Whoever they were, they came back to your house." He shook his head. "Your buddies got there within a few minutes, but . . . Some of the guys went back this morning and covered the hole in the roof with a tarp. You got insurance, right?"

I nodded.

He put his arm around me and pointed to the bag. "Thought you might want some clothes."

"Thanks."

"Your shower stuff is in there." He tried to smile, but he looked more anguished than happy.

I walked into Maggie's bathroom, pulled the curtain behind me, and tried to wash off the last twelve hours. I washed off the smoke and the sweat, and I scrubbed off Maggie's blood that had caked on my forearms, but the rest wouldn't come out.

I dressed in jeans and a T-shirt and walked back out into the room to find Amos standing guard over Maggie. The picture of our smoldering house was just starting to sink in. I wanted to know more. "How bad is it?"

Amos didn't look at me.

I tugged on his arm. "Hey."

Both sweat and tears were running down his face. "Let's get through this right here first."

I looked at Maggie and prayed to God the fire hadn't touched the nursery. "Where'd it start?"

Amos looked at me. He could tell I wasn't letting up. "Back of the house."

There were two rooms in the back of the house, ours and the nursery. "Which side?"

Amos raised his chin, his eyes glistening in the blue light of Maggie's machines. "Both."

I thought a minute, the anger bubbling. "Why? Why, Amos?"

A tear fell off Amos's face and landed on the sheet near Maggie's foot. "Why does somebody like that do anything? It's just meanness. That's all."

Moments passed in silence. I held Maggie's limp, hot hand and wrestled with disbelief. "How's your place?"

Amos shook his head. "Even the toys in the front yard are melted." He studied Maggie's face. "Did she say who did this?"

I shook my head.

Amos paused, letting the automatic blood pressure cuff expand, measure, and then deflate itself once again. "John said he didn't see who hog-tied him and set the church on fire. Said he was sitting at his desk, turned to grab a book out of his credenza, and then somebody whacked him on the head and turned out the lights. Next thing he knew, we were rolling on top of him and the room was full of smoke. Said his eyes were burning so bad and the roar of the fire was making so much noise that he didn't know who we were till we landed outside in the mud."

I looked at him. "You got any ideas?"

He nodded, stared through me, and said nothing. Then he looked at Maggie. "We should know more once Maggie wakes up." He walked to the door, turned, and looked as if he were replaying last night. "How'd you get us out of there, anyway?"

I shook my head. "I didn't."

Amos's eyes grew wider, revealing his confusion.

"Bryce did. Covered in a wet blanket. He threw Pastor John over his shoulder, and I grabbed the back of the blanket and followed him out."

Amos nodded. "I've got a meeting down at the station. I also got a call from Vince at the hardware store, said he wanted to talk to me. He said that you'd been in . . ."

I nodded and looked at the floor.

Amos stood in the doorway and waited while a few nurses passed in the hall. He lowered his voice. "You okay?" Even with all he had going on, all he was worried about, all the pain the burns on his legs were no doubt causing him, Amos was still checking my pulse.

"Yeah." I pointed at his leg and head. "You?"

He shrugged it off. "First degree. Nothing more. Give me a Band-Aid and I'm good. Besides," he said, smiling, "'Manda said the women from church are already dropping off casseroles and pies at her folks' house. You'd think I'd had a baby or something."

Amos pulled the door behind him and left me alone with Maggie. I pulled the chair up next to the bed, rested my head on the mattress, sank my hand beneath hers, and closed my eyes. In the dim light of the machinery glowing about her, the sick feeling of familiarity fell on me, and I did not like it.

*chapter twenty*

A COUPLE OF HOURS LATER, I FELT SOMEONE'S FINGERS running through my hair, gentle and soft. I sat up to find Maggs looking at me. Her eyes were heavy, her face flushed, and the monitor on the wall said her fever had risen to 101 degrees. Her breaths were short, and her face told me they were painful if she inhaled too deeply.

"Hey, you," she said, fighting off a shiver.

"Hey."

"I held them off as long as I could." Her voice was little more than a whisper. "I threw everything I could get my hands on, but . . ." She blinked, and a tear trickled off her cheek. "I just ran out of stuff to throw." She looked in the corner of the room where Blue lay, his tail tucked up under his back legs, his nose pointed at Maggs. "If he hadn't been there . . ."

"I got held up at church."

She nodded. "Amos told me. He was here when I woke up an hour ago."

Her face was still puffy, and her eyes had turned black and swollen. I wanted to touch her, but I was afraid I'd hurt her.

"Did you tell Amos what they looked like?"

Maggs shook her head. "He said he'd come back. But they won't be hard to spot."

"How's that?"

"Tattoos. They're covered." She tried to smile, but the cuts around her mouth and the swollenness of her lips made it difficult. I stood and kissed her. Her lips felt taut and swollen.

I tried to reassure her. "Amos has got everybody in South Carolina looking for them." I slipped my hand beneath hers and tried to change the subject. "Has Dr. Frank been in?"

She shook her head. "Not yet."

I stroked her hand and knew I needed to quit stalling. "Honey, you . . . we lost the . . ."

She placed her finger on my lips. "Shhh . . ." She nodded, and her bottom lip quivered. She tried to hold it together, but soon the sobs came. It was the most painful wail I'd ever heard pour out of another human.

Her cries brought Amanda running down the hall. She peeked in the room, saw me cradling Maggie in my arms, and quietly shut the door.

Maggie looked up at me. "I'm so sorry."

"Hey, hey, it's got nothing to do with you." I looked around the room, grasping for comfort. "We'll try again." I pushed the hair out of her face and brushed a tear off her lip. "We're good at that."

She reached up and clung to me. Her thin arms were shaking.

Maybe thirty minutes passed while she lay with her head next to mine. She closed her eyes, holding my left hand with both of hers. Eventually the tears dried, only to surface again like a rising tide.

I picked an eyelash off her cheek. "Honey, there's something else."

She looked up.

"Have you been running a fever?"

She tilted her head to one side.

"How long?" I asked.

"Four or five days. Just low, around a hundred."

"Why didn't you tell me?"

"I thought it was just a virus, thought it would pass. I didn't want you to worry."

I laid my chin on the bed and looked up at her. "You've got to tell me these things." I tucked her hair behind her ear. "No more secrets."

She smiled and nodded slightly. "No more secrets."

As the words slid off her tongue, my hypocrisy slapped me in the face.

She looked up at the ceiling and pressed her knees tight together, and her eyes welled.

I slid my hand behind her head. "Maggs."

She faked another smile. "Someday you're gonna make a great dad." The words slipped off her tongue, and the sobs came again. Her ribs made it impossible to mask her pain, so she cried harder and louder. The crying started in her toes, and her entire body shook beneath the sheets.

The sound brought Amanda running again. She checked the machine behind the bed, stepped under the single light, and slid her hand into Maggie's. She cradled the pale white hand in her brown, tender palm and checked the IV.

"Daddy wants to know if he can come see you."

Maggie nodded, and the tears continued to fall. Soon Amanda, too, was crying. Her tears fell onto the rounding top of her belly, and she brushed at them in embarrassment.

Maggie reached out, placed her palm flat against Amanda's tummy, and said, "How's everybody doing?"

Amanda smiled and nodded. "We're good. I just can't eat enough." She blew her nose. "I've never been so hungry."

A few minutes later, Dr. Frank walked in. He sat opposite us and laid his clipboard on the bed near Maggie's feet. "I heard you guys were having a good cry, so I thought I'd come join you."

Maggie held out the box of tissues and then nodded toward the call button. She sniffled. "If you run out, push that button."

"Yeah, I've been wanting to get one of those buttons at home, but I think my wife would kick me out of the house."

We tried to laugh, but we all knew we were just trying to delay the inevitable.

He looked at me, then at Maggie. "You should have passed everything by now." He pointed to the pad. "We'll keep this here today, but when you feel up to it, I think it'd be best if you got up and walked around some."

Amanda nodded and slipped out the door.

"When can I go home?" Maggie asked.

Dr. Frank checked the monitors on the wall behind her. "Tell me about this fever first."

"Four or five days, low grade. I just thought it was a virus."

"I want to run some more tests, try to get the fever down and get control of the infection. That means I might keep you a few days. You can't go home yet anyway—not until your husband cleans up the mess."

We were quiet for several seconds.

"Your lab results tell me there's something going on with

your blood that I can't get a handle on. I don't know what kind of infection or where it is, but it's a bugger, to say the least." He eyed the IV bag above her. "We're attacking it now with a broad-spectrum antibiotic, but I want to keep you where I can monitor you."

"What's a girl got to do to get something to eat around here?"

Dr. Frank scribbled on a notepad. "I'll have them send something up, but you only eat what I send up here. You got it?"

Maggie nodded and crossed her fingers across her chest.

He shook his head. "No kidding." He eyed the digital readout that listed her body temperature. It had risen to 102 degrees. "I need to monitor everything going into you until I get my hands around this infection. Deal?"

Maggie nodded and uncrossed her fingers.

He stood, patted her gently on the hand, and said, "I'll let you eat, then start the tests."

He stepped out, and Maggie put her head on my hand.

"Why don't you sleep some?" I said.

She closed her eyes and fidgeted around the tenderness of her ribs. Within a few minutes, she was asleep.


AFTER DINNER PASTOR JOHN CRACKED THE DOOR. HE pulled up a chair on the opposite side of the bed and patted Maggie's leg. We sat there in the darkness, waiting on Maggie to wake up. Thirty minutes later, she did.

Her eyes were glassed over, telling me the same thing as the machines on the wall. Despite Motrin, her body temperature hadn't changed. The fever was taking its toll.

She rolled her head toward Pastor John and smiled. He stood up, kissed her forehead, and sat back down.

Pastor John was in pain, but it wasn't physical. He patted

her leg again and said, "Maggie, I need to tell you a story." He pulled out his handkerchief, wiped his nose and the corner of one eye, and began.

"I wasn't always a pastor. When I was younger, more than twenty years ago, I fell in with three guys looking for trouble. Problem was, we were good at both getting into it and getting out of it. And because we liked what the money bought us, which was mostly an identity as something other than what we were, we stole anything we could get our hands on. Especially me." He let that sink in.

"I was smart, and gifted at being a thief." He shook his head, fighting the memories. "A couple of years later, our luck ran out." He smiled. "Maybe the Lord had had enough of our foolishness."

Tears rolled off Pastor John's face, and Maggie slid her hand out from underneath the sheets and grabbed his, pulling it close to her chest.

"We were put in jail, and somewhere in that cold cell, I got tired of lying. So I started telling the truth. Because of the way that works in the legal system, I got out early and they stayed in longer." He tried to smile. "The other guys weren't very happy with this. Evidently, they're still not."

He reached into his coat pocket and pulled out a stack of postcards held together with a rubber band. "Over the last several years, they've written me about once a month to tell me how ungrateful they are." He placed the cards back in his pocket, and his huge shoulders rolled forward. He unfolded his handkerchief, wiped his face, and then looked Maggie in the eyes. "I . . . Maggie, honey . . . I'm sorry."

Maggie reached out and hugged Pastor John. He cradled her and rocked her as she wept in his arms. He bit his lip and managed, "Some sins I'm still paying for."

We sat there a long time. Finally Maggie tried to sit up and said, "I'm sorry about your church."

Pastor John shook his head and looked out through the window into the moonlight. "We can build another building, but we might need some help with the steeple."

I nodded. "Yes, sir."

Pastor John leaned over and kissed Maggie's forehead. Then he stood and placed his hand on her head. He whispered, but not really to us. Finally he took my hand, spread it across Maggie's tummy, and covered mine with his. He looked at us both and spoke quietly, the weight of what he was saying pressing in on his voice. "In Isaiah God says, 'Fear not, for I will pour water on him who is thirsty, and floods on the dry and barren ground. I will pour My Spirit on your descendants, and My blessing on your offspring. They will spring up among the grass like willows by the watercourses.'" He walked over to the door, stood for a moment, and then slipped out.

ON TOWARD MIDNIGHT I HEARD A SOFT RAP ON THE DOOR, as though someone either was afraid to come in or was a southern gentleman of the sort who never barged in on a lady. It turned out to be the latter.

I opened the door, and a man dressed in a bright orange bow tie, white oxford shirt, starched khakis, and gold wire-rimmed glasses extended his hand. Jason Thentwhistle, hospital financial officer.

He pointed down the hall toward the nurses' station and doctors' cubicle. "If they want to run a test, or do anything at all, you let them. We'll work out the other side of it on the other side." He turned and walked about four steps.

I reached out and caught him by the arm. He looked at me guardedly, as one stranger would look at another.

"Jason, thanks for coming. We appreciate it."

He smiled, half nodded, and continued walking down the hall.

*chapter twenty-one*

BY MIDAFTERNOON OF THE NEXT DAY, MAGGIE'S body finished doing what it was doing and no longer needed the bed pad beneath her, so I helped her into the shower. It took awhile to get her cleaned up because she was bruised from head to toe.

She put on some hospital scrubs, and we took a slow and gentle stroll around the halls. Maggie leaned on me and hooked her arm inside mine. When we came to the large viewing window of the nursery, she leaned against the glass and stared at the six babies sleeping inside. When she pulled away, her tears slid down the glass and came to rest on the windowsill.

At dinnertime Amos walked in dressed in his SWAT gear, and despite the singed hair and skin, he looked as though he hadn't skipped a beat. In his hands were two chocolate shakes.

He walked over to the bed, set them down, and pulled two straws from his shirt pocket. "I checked with Dr. Frank. He said it was okay."

He knelt next to the bed and slid one huge palm under Maggie's shoulders. "How's our girl?" he asked. The assurance in his voice was worth a million dollars.

Maggie smiled lazily, physically tired and emotionally drained. She took a sip of the shake.

Amos put on his law enforcement face. "Maggs, I need to know who did this."

Maggie leaned forward while I adjusted the pillows behind her back.

"I've never seen them before. Two men. Black. Maybe late thirties, early forties. Both covered in tattoos. One guy had his shirt off, and his whole chest and back were nothing but tattoos."

"Could you recognize them?"

She nodded.

Amos pulled two pictures from his shirt pocket and held them in front of her.

Maggie looked at the pictures, sipped again, then nodded.

"Anton, as he likes to be called, and Felix became tattoo artists in prison. Now most of both their bodies are covered in ink—making them pretty easy to spot. They both look like that dude in *Moby Dick*." He snapped his fingers. "The one that was in the coffin."

"Queequeg," I said quietly.

Amos nodded. "Throughout their time in prison, they traded their services for information, which meant they were never too far from the pipeline. They kept pretty good tabs on John."

"Pastor John said he had three partners."

Amos nodded. "Third one's name is Whittaker. Nobody's

seen him. His name in prison was Ghost. Due to a sick twist in fate, overcrowding brought him two cells down, and the three got reacquainted. Oddly enough, that same twist brought a former Hollywood pyrotechnics expert next door to the twins, which would explain their newfound love of bonfires. From what investigators have gathered, the former partners became rather vocal about their post-prison plans."

"But why me? Why our house?"

Amos shook his head. "I'm working on that. Right now, I have no idea, other than you live across the street from me."

Maggie nodded and looked at me, then back to Amos. "Where are Amanda and Li'l Dylan?"

"Amanda's down the hall. Momma's got L.D. We're staying with them in town for a while."

"You scared?" I asked.

He looked at me, at Maggie, then back at me, and shook his head. "No. Not scared. Worried? A bit. Angry?" He spoke softly, as if he were talking to someone who wasn't in the room. His voice dropped and his eyes narrowed, telling me that one way or another, there would be a reckoning. "Yes."

*chapter twenty-two*

AFTER DINNER I DIMMED THE LIGHTS AND LEFT
Maggie napping in her room. Amanda had gone home for the
evening, but the on-call nurse had stuck her head in the door
and let me know she'd be checking on Maggie.

I knelt down in the corner of the room and scratched
Blue's tummy while he moaned and flopped his ears back. I
rubbed his muzzle and picked off the specks of dried blood
on the top of his head. I pointed outside. "You gotta go?" The
magnolia outside the window caught my eye. "Mark some old
territory?"

Blue tucked his nose up under a fold in the blanket, let out
a long sigh, and looked away.

I turned into our drive, aimed the headlights at the house,
and parked.

Shining my flashlight, I stepped through the door and noticed, above the smell of my burnt house, the unusual and lingering scent of cheap aftershave and lots of it. I checked the rooms, found the house empty, and then opened all the doors and windows, hoping the house would breathe itself free of the stench.

In the race to save the house, the screen door had been torn off, the back door broken off its hinges, and most of the inside sprayed with water under very high pressure. The water put out the fire, which had bubbled much of the paint, while the pressure behind the water peeled many of the blisters, making our walls look leprous.

From what I could see, most of the inside was wet and stained black. I walked down the back hall and looked overhead. The ceiling had caved in, exposing the rafters and pieces of hanging insulation. I made it to the doors that led into the bedroom and nursery, but there was no need to go in. Whoever had started the fire had evidently done so in both rooms.

The other half of the house—which included the kitchen and den—escaped everything but hose drag marks, overspray, and muddy footprints.

In our room the walls had burned to the studs, the furniture was nothing but soggy, charred cinders, the mattress on our bed was little more than a crumbling mess, and the ceiling and roof were gone. The motor for the Hunter fan that once hung above our bed now sat at an angle in the middle of the mattress, its wires sticking up like an insect's antennae. The moonlight shone through the blue tarp and gave the room an eerie blue haze.

I was afraid to look into the nursery, but I knew I had to. All the stuffed animals were little more than charred remains, and the rocker had all but disappeared. The crib sat at an angle, as if one leg were shorter than another. The books of nursery rhymes were crumbling and wet, and all the baby clothes in the closet lay in pieces on the floor, blackened scraps of cotton.

Between the two rooms, my writing closet, its door marred and bubbling from the heat, remained locked. I didn't know what it looked like on the inside. As for Maggie's orchids scattered around the house, they had not fared well. They were nothing but naked stems without bloom or petal.

I was standing in the kitchen surveying the damage when the phone rang—which surprised me, given that the guys had disconnected the electricity at the street to avoid an electrical fire.

"Dylan, it's John."

I knew Caglestock had become comfortable with me when he started calling me by my first name. I also knew that if he was calling me at close to ten thirty, he had something on his mind.

I sat down. "Hey, John."

"Listen, we've got to move one of Bryce's accounts from one trading house to another. We can get a better rate, so it makes good sense. But, as with any transaction of this type, it will produce a commission—of about $45,000." He let that sink in.

I understood. It was the cost of doing business, and Bryce understood this.

"No matter how or where I move them, I'll end up paying a commission to move these funds." He let that sink in too. Then he said what he'd called for. "I want to know if you will let me hire you for a day to make one transaction."

I looked out through the kitchen window overlooking the pasture.

"Dylan," he continued, "Bryce's estate, his LLC, or any of

the partnerships we've formed would pay this commission to anyone regardless of their affiliation with him."

He was right. And in terms of Bryce's account total, which now ran in the hundreds of millions, it wasn't even a drop in the bucket.

"I want to hire you for a day."

I took a deep breath. "John, I made a promise to Bryce that I would never seek to profit from him or the management of his funds."

"Yes, but given the good decisions you've made now over an almost-five-year period"—John paused—"do you know how much money you've made him?"

"John, I gave him my word."

"I don't think this qualifies as—"

"And second, I don't ever want Bryce to think I want any part of his money. I don't. Not one penny."

"That makes you different from most of the people who've befriended Bryce."

"That makes me *me*."

"It might also make you poor."

"John?" I knew he meant well, and his intentions were good, but I also knew that wasn't good enough. "Just because it's legal doesn't necessarily make it right."

He started to say something, but I cut him off. "I was maybe ten, standing with my grandfather in the grocery store check-out line, when the lady at the cash register handed him his change. He counted, paused, recounted, and then handed a twenty back to her and said, 'This one was stuck to the other one. You gave me one too many.' To say the least, she was pretty relieved when she realized he was right. We got in the truck, and I asked him why he didn't just keep it. She'd never know. You know what he said?"

"I'm listening."

"He said, 'I'll know.' He must have seen the confused look on my face, because he said, 'Son, I won't sell my word, my integrity, for twenty dollars. Not today. Not ever.' He stuck his face real close to mine and said, 'Words are what men live by, and once you sell them, not all the tea in China can ever buy 'em back.'"

John chuckled, and I could hear his chair squeak as if he'd just sat back and propped his feet up.

"I would have liked to have met your grandpa."

John was an honest man, and I knew this. Every audit of his firm and, specifically, his firm's work with Bryce's money, had produced nothing but praise from every auditor we'd ever met. Bryce had been good to him, but maybe more important, he'd been good for Bryce.

The problem was not the legality of the action he proposed; of course it was legal. The problem it posed for me was the gray area it presented with respect to my relationship with Bryce and my promise to him.

"I think you two would have gotten along well," I said.

I hung up the phone and leaned against the kitchen sink. I took a deep breath, let it out slowly between my teeth, feeling the pressure in my cheeks, and wondered if my grandfather and I were just plain crazy.

Knowing I needed to quit carrying a loaded shotgun around in the van, I brought it inside, unlocked my writing closet, and slid the gun onto the floor just above our "safe." I locked the doors and walked outside onto the porch. It was close to midnight, but a flicker in the distance caught my eye and told me something about the world was distinctly different.

I stepped off the porch, walked out into the cotton, and ran my fingers along the tops of the white flowers. Beneath the moon, spotlight-bright above me, the cotton field shone with thousands of moon-white flowers, waving ever so slightly in the cooling breeze. They had opened in the last few hours and would remain that way for twenty-four more, in which time a single, microscopic grain of pollen, carried on the breeze, would come to rest inside, pollinate the flower, and start once again the mystery that grows inside.

Maybe it was then that it really hit me. The loss reached up out of the earth, and I felt cold and lonely, like low, dark clouds before rain. I squatted in the cotton, eye-level with the blooms, and the tears came in a flood.

All the world had bloomed, and Maggie had not.

*chapter twenty-three*

I CRACKED MAGGIE'S DOOR AND STUCK MY HEAD IN, and froze. A large, broad-shouldered man stood in the darkness next to her bed. He stood ironing-board straight, towering over her.

But Blue hadn't moved.

The man stood with his hands behind his back, at ease. As I stepped into the room, he turned to face me. He had showered, shaved, cropped his hair higher and tighter, splashed with aftershave—a smell I recognized—and put on clean, starched, and creased BDUs. His boots were polished to a mirror shine. In his right hand he held a black, cylindrical-looking thing about fourteen inches long. The end closest to me reflected light and looked like small circles of glass.

I stepped into the dim glow of the fluorescent light coming

from the bathroom, and the reflection told me that Bryce had been crying. Tears clung to his drawn cheeks and puddled in the bottoms of the wrinkles around the base of his eyes. He blinked and sent the puddles falling off his face. I stepped up alongside him, and we stood overlooking Maggie, who slept peacefully beneath the covers and whatever medication Dr. Frank had prescribed. I glanced at the machine above her bed and saw that her temperature had climbed to 102 degrees.

Standing next to Bryce, I noticed that the baton in his hand was actually a rifle scope. The bluing had worn in spots, and because of the rings and brackets, it looked as though it was rigged with a quick-release mechanism that would allow it to be quickly attached or detached from the top of a rifle.

In months past, as Amos became proficient with more types of weaponry, he had shown me the SWAT team sniper gear. One thing that struck me was the rifle scope. Most were large, came in adjustable powers, and could deliver a projectile with great accuracy up to eight hundred yards, even farther. Many had two protruding adjustment knobs that allowed the shooter to make last-minute adjustments depending on distance, wind, and various other conditions. They were state-of-the-art.

If Amos's gear was fifth- or even tenth-generation, then Bryce's scope looked like a first generation. It was longer, thinner, probably a fixed power, and didn't have the protruding adjustment knobs. He carried it the way a sailor might carry his spyglass.

Bryce didn't say a word. After a few minutes he knelt next to the bed, stretched his neck, and leaned over Maggie. He lowered his head ever so slightly over her tummy, finally pressing his ear against the blanket as if he were listening to a railroad track. He rested there several seconds, close but not pressing into her. After a minute he rose, kissed her forehead, and tiptoed out of the room.

I sat up the rest of the night, eyeing the temperature reading on the machine above her bed. Twice it bounced up to 103.5 degrees, but it spent most of the night at 102. Somewhere in the middle of the night, Blue hopped off the bed and licked my face. I cradled him in my arms, and I guessed we dozed off there.

At daylight, Dr. Frank walked in and nudged my arm. Blue hopped down, and I stood up, balancing myself with a hand on Maggie's bed.

"When was the last time you slept in a bed?"

I scratched my head, smiled, and shook my head. "Can't recall."

"You need to." He stepped closer to the bed and slid his hand under Maggie's wrist, feeling for her distal pulse. He could read it plainly on the machine on the wall, but he seemed to be in thought, and his measurement of her pulse was more subconscious than conscious.

I whispered, "Most of the night it hung around 102. A couple of times it hit 103."

"I expected that. It'll always rise at night. Her body's doing what it should. Fighting."

I nodded, and a few seconds passed. I tucked one long strand of hair behind Maggie's ear. "She is a fighter."

Maggs stirred, and her eyes blinked open. "Hey, guys." She shivered and pulled the covers up over her shoulders. "You two planning on hanging meat in here?"

I grabbed another blanket while Dr. Frank instinctively felt her forehead with his hand. He pulled his rolling seat up to the side of her bed and said, "Well, you want the good news or the bad news?"

"Good news, and let's just skip the bad. We've had enough of that for a while." Maggie's hand appeared from under the covers and grabbed mine.

When I think about my wife, one word comes to mind. *Indomitable.*

"The good news is that my son's team won his game last night and put us in the play-offs. The bad news is that I have no idea what's causing your fever. Your blood work will only tell me so much." He eyed the IV hanging above her. "We're throwing some pretty strong stuff at you, and it should have kicked in by now."

Maggs moved slowly and looked tired, as though the fever was really working her over.

"I have an idea," the doctor said, "but I wanted to check with you first, since it's your body."

Her eyes opened slightly, the sleep almost falling off the edges of her face. "I'm game for most anything that allows me to stay in this bed. I'm afraid I'd fall flat on my face if I had to get out of it."

Frank nodded. "It's just the fever. It'll pass as soon as we get on top of the infection." He patted her foot. "Since your first delivery, have you had any pictures taken of your insides? Uterus, ovaries, etc."

"Other than that really kind lady doctor you sent us to, no." Maggie smiled. "I could've spit nails."

"Yeah, sorry about that. I called her this morning, and she doesn't have what I need." He repositioned himself on his chair. "I want to take some pictures, look around a bit. We'll sedate you."

Maggs nodded. "When do you want to do this?"

Amanda rolled in a cart loaded with medicines and needles. She walked up next to the bed, hooked one arm inside mine, and patted Maggie's leg.

Dr. Frank said, "How about now?"

We heard the seriousness in his voice. Maggie turned toward me, took my hand with both of hers, and looked at me. "You'll be here when I wake up?"

I knelt, my eyes level with hers. "Always."

Dr. Frank nodded, Amanda inserted the needle into Maggie's IV, and in five minutes, Maggs was in that sedated place that fell somewhere between partly awake and mostly asleep. Amanda pushed the cart back out into the hall and clickety-clacked down the terrazzo while Dr. Frank escorted another nurse into the room, pushing an entirely different machine complete with an LCD screen.

I helped him turn Maggie onto her side, and then I stepped back while the nurse prepped her. Frank pulled out a long, cylindrical tube that could flex and bend like a joystick, and while I was thinking, *You're not sticking that thing in my wife,* Amanda walked back in with a hot plate covered with aluminum foil.

"When was the last time you ate?"

I shrugged.

She set it on the countertop behind me, patted me on the shoulder, and checked Maggs's IV. She changed the fluid bags, inserted a catheter, and emptied Maggs's bladder, and then Frank inserted his camera. He turned the screen so that I could watch along with a second doctor I'd never met, who'd appeared just for consultation.

While Frank moved the camera via the joystick, he pointed at the screen with his other finger. "This is Maggie's uterus." He moved the camera. "This is the cervix." He moved it again. "The fallopian tube."

He said something to the other doctor, and while I'm sure he was speaking English, I didn't understand a word. Amanda watched and listened, and the consternation on her face told me that she understood more of that screen than I did.

Maggie's face was pale. When Frank moved the camera, extending it farther into Maggie, she moaned and gripped my hand more tightly. I turned to Amanda and raised an eyebrow. Amanda shook her head and brushed Maggie's forehead with her fingers.

"She's okay. These are pretty good drugs."

Dr. Frank was speaking quietly to the nurse technician who stood alongside him. He nodded at the screen. "That one." He moved the camera slightly. "And that one too."

Twenty minutes later, he pulled the camera out and printed out several pictures from the machine. As the nurse rolled the cart back out into the hall, he called behind her, "Ask the lab to run that to the front of the line."

Then he turned to me and held up the pictures. "Nothing I didn't expect, except maybe this one." He held one up closer to the light. "This is Maggie's fallopian tube, and these are cysts along with some scar tissue from the first delivery." He shrugged. "Many women have them; sometimes they're nothing, sometimes they prevent people from ever getting pregnant, but in this case . . ." He turned the picture sideways to get a different look. "We biopsied these two because most cysts don't look like that."

"What should they look like?"

He rolled his shoulders and shrugged. "Not like that. The lab will send results as quick as they can. We'll know more then."

I pressed him again. "What might they tell us?"

He chose his words carefully. "They'll either tell us it's nothing or tell us it's something."

"Frank, define 'something.'"

He took a deep breath, blinked, and folded his arms. "Best case, just an abnormal cyst that I can remove with little problem."

I grabbed his arm. "And worst case?"

He took another breath. "I don't know, Dylan. I just don't know. Let's wait on the lab."

"Frank, you're hiding something."

"Dylan, Maggie's body is hiding something from me, from all of us. And I think that cyst might be a starting point. Let's wait on the lab."

"So if you remove the cyst, will it lower the fever?" I was grasping at straws.

Frank shook his head. "That's the bad news. Normally, a cyst wouldn't cause a fever like that." He looked at my dinner growing cold. "Why don't you try to eat something? I'll check back in a while."

He walked out and left me alone with Amanda, Maggie, and Blue.

After several minutes, Amanda spoke. "When I get to heaven, I'm going to ask God why it's so easy for some and yet so difficult for others."

"What's that?"

She patted her tummy. "Just doing what He made us to do." She placed her palm flat across Maggie's forehead and whispered, "Why, when some want it so bad, and deserve it so much, is it so difficult to get?"

She leaned over, kissed Maggie's temple, and then eyed the call button. "Holler if you need me."

I sat down, rested my chin on Maggie's bedside, my face just inches from hers, and watched her breathe. I could smell the last remaining whispers of her perfume beneath the waves of antiseptic. An hour later, I looked at the wall of lights. Maggie's temperature had risen to 104 degrees.

TRUE TO HIS WORD, DR. FRANK WALKED IN WITH THE LAB results in his hand, but he wasn't alone. He'd brought most of the hospital with him. Five nurses, dressed in various versions of surgical scrubs, immediately walked to the bed and began prepping Maggie. They worked quietly and efficiently.

Frank pulled me aside. "I'm taking Maggie to the OR."

"Right this second? Why?"

"Because Maggie's body needs help getting rid of the baby."

I was confused. "I thought . . . I thought she'd already done that."

Frank nodded. "She had, in part. Problem is, Maggie was having twins. She had a heterotopic pregnancy. In layman's terms, there's one still in there, and she's being poisoned from the inside out. I'll explain after surgery."

He turned and followed the nurses, who pushed a sleeping Maggie out the door on a rolling bed. I stepped forward to kiss her, but she was gone. I watched them roll her down the hall, then turned to look at Amanda, who was shutting down the monitoring machines. The last one she clicked off was the temperature, reading 105.5 degrees.

I sat down in the hospital room and sank my head in my hands. *Twins?*

Amanda sat down next to me, looped her arm beneath mine, and rested her head on my shoulder. About that time, Amos came running into the room. He was sweating, breathing heavily, and almost slid onto the floor beneath me. "I came as soon as I heard."

I looked up, unable to focus. The world was spinning. "We were having twins."

Amos swore silently. He stood up, wrung his hands together, then finally pulled me up with him and bear-hugged me.

# chapter twenty-four

I SAT NEXT TO THE BED, REACHED BENEATH THE
covers, and touched Maggs's hand. She was hot to the touch,
and her face was flushed. When she opened her eyes, they
were glassed over and heavy. The machine on the wall told me
her fever was now only 102.5. I rubbed her hand gently and
tried to open my mouth, but the words wouldn't come.

She fidgeted, but her ribs were tender, making movement
difficult, and her face was still puffy, slow to heal. She saw me
struggling and touched my lips with her fingers. "I was having
a dream about you."

"Yeah?" I tried to smile.

"You were sitting on the tractor with our daughter, driving
to the river. She was blonde, had your eyes, my toes."

I bit my lip, gritted my teeth, and tried to hold back but

could not. I choked and wiped my face with her sheet. Maggie eyed the wall, her temperature, and then me. Her movements were slow. She looked as if she'd just delivered a child and run a marathon.

I tried again. "Dr. Frank had to . . . you see . . . we were . . . you . . ."

She breathed deeply and turned toward me, pressing her forehead to mine. She placed her palm on my cheek and whispered, "Shhh." She tried to swallow, but her mouth was dry.

I held the glass of water while she sipped through the straw, then she pulled me close. I held her several moments, her eyes studying mine, mine studying hers.

"I want to grow old with you."

"Maggie," I stuttered, "we were having twins."

Her eyes narrowed, and her head tilted like Blue's when he didn't understand. I could see the pieces falling into place.

"The second baby got caught in your tube, and it was just growing and . . ."

Maggie shook her head vehemently, placed a flat palm over her stomach as if it could tell her the truth, and started whispering, "No. No. No!"

I placed my hand on her shoulder. "Honey, Dr. Frank had to remove your . . ."

The words I'd spoken registered somewhere in her foggy mind, and she laid her head on the pillow, unable to hold back the sobs. They came loud and in waves. I tried to hold her, to wrap my arms around her, protect her from the world and take away the pain, but I had no defense strong enough. She rolled into a ball and pounded the bed with her fists.

Amanda came running, pulled a syringe from her pocket, and quickly inserted it into Maggie's IV. The medicine hit her veins, and within thirty seconds her eyelids were heavy and

Maggie

her movements slow and incomplete. They'd given her medicine for the pain in her ribs and the stitches in her uterus. But Maggie was teetering on the edge, and only the oblivion of sleep could give Maggie respite from the pain in her heart.

The last words she screamed before the lights went out were unintelligible. Lost in transmission. But while I couldn't understand the words, I understood the emotion.

*chapter twenty-five*

MAGGIE LEANED AGAINST ME, THE AIR-CONDITIONING cooling our faces as Amos drove us home slowly in his truck. He pulled into our drive and around back, where we climbed out and stood looking at the house. The smell of smoke, burned pine, melted rubber, and soured water met us under the searing heat of the sun.

Maggie couldn't hide her shock. She was too tired to be angry, but that was there, too, just beneath the surface. A blue tarp covered half the roof, the screen door had been torn off, about half the windows were broken, and black smoke scars stained the upper portions of the windows, eaves, and soffits.

She turned and studied the rolling pastures. On one side grew the corn—tall, green, and tasseled out. On the other sat the cotton. She looped her arm inside mine, and we walked toward the rows and finally between them. She chose the cotton, waist-high and gently swathing our legs. Maggie ran her fingers across the tops and then scanned the horizon where the pasture bled into the trees almost a mile away.

In a manner of speaking, cotton is the only flower that blooms twice from the same bud, or "square," as it is technically called. A cotton flower blooms, or opens, only for twenty-four hours, during which time it must be fertilized by a pollen grain to produce the cotton. When the flower opens, it is white; a day later it turns a fleshy pinkish red; and after four or five days, it turns a crispy mauve or purple. At the end of the first week, the petals litter the row in which it grows. Depending on growth conditions, it takes another month or more before the seed capsule, called a boll, develops and opens like popcorn.

Maggie turned, teary and tired. "Did you know that cotton is in the same family as hibiscus?" She pointed without looking toward some shoulder-height bushes planted against the house.

I shook my head.

"When the flower opens, it has exactly twenty-four hours to be fertilized by a single grain of pollen, or there will be no cotton."

I said nothing.

She nodded and picked a fallen flower off the soil. "It's pretty."

I looked at my wife. "Yes."

Maggie walked into the house behind me, followed closely by Amos. She went into the nursery, stood a moment, placed a hand on the crib, and shook her head. Then she walked into our bedroom and stood beneath the tarp where our bed lay. Water dripped off the tarp and splattered about her feet. She took a deep breath, walked back to the doorway, and eased her shoulder under my arm.

"Amos?" She looked around the house, then turned and poked him in the chest. Her voice grew strong and direct. "You catch the people who did this to my house. You hear me?"

Amos nodded. "Yes, ma'am."

He walked out onto the porch, and I laid a watermelon in the back of his truck. "You mind taking this to Vince? I owe him." Amos nodded and pulled out of the drive.

Maggie stood on the porch and looked at me through squinted eyes. "Why do you owe him?"

I retrieved the shotgun and showed her the barrel. She eyed the change, and I didn't need to explain. I held it out. "You remember how?" She palmed the shotgun and slid a shell in the chamber while I placed the smallest of the melons on the grass in the yard.

I eyed the target and then behind it, which was eight hundred yards of corn pasture down to the river.

Maggie shouldered the shotgun, clicked off the safety, and squeezed. The watermelon exploded into a million red and green pieces and sent Blue scurrying under the porch. She ejected the shell, smoke rising from the chamber, handed me the shotgun, and walked toward the barn.

*chapter twenty-six*

ALTHOUGH I'D OFFERED TO MOVE HER TO A HOTEL, Maggie didn't want anything to do with that. The electricity had been restored, and we still had a phone line and plumbing. I agreed to stay with one stipulation. "You point," I said. "I'll clean."

Knowing she was far too weak to dive into a house renovation, she didn't argue. We walked into the smoke-stained kitchen, and she said, "I'll put on some coffee."

While she filtered through the kitchen, I unlocked the closet, knelt beneath my desk, and pried the board loose with the tip of my knife. I lifted the silver box, opened the lid, and breathed more easily knowing my manuscript, wrapped in a dry plastic bag, lay safely inside. Somehow, being below the house, it had survived.

It took me almost two days to haul out all the wet, burned, or otherwise ruined stuff from our house. I carried everything into a pile out back, and on the second night we lit it and roasted marshmallows.

The summer between my junior and senior years in high school, Papa let me turn the hayloft into my bedroom— my first real foray into independence. We cut in a window, added a wall, stuffed insulation between the studs, put up drywall, carpeted the floor, and inserted an air-conditioning unit that blew both hot and cold air. We found some used furniture at garage sales and a four-poster queen-sized bed that looked as though it had come out of some Russian palace. It didn't fit Digger, but at twenty bucks, it fit my budget. When finished, the room looked a lot like an upscale garage apartment and would probably fetch a goodly sum in some place like New York.

Since Maggie and I had married, I'd used the loft to store stuff, but with the house uninhabitable, I got to work. We moved out the stored stuff—old furniture and boxes—and hung a ceiling fan. We bought a new-used mattress and even bought Blue a new bed and laid it alongside ours. I caulked some of the cracks in the floor and walls, rolled on a fresh coat of paint, laid new carpet, and replaced the ladder with steps.

The bathroom was little more than a thin-walled closet in the corner with just enough room for a toilet, a sink, and one person. I repiped the fittings to the water supply, installed a new wax ring at the base, changed out the flushing mechanism so it'd quit running, and put a 40-watt bulb in the fixture above the sink. Within a couple of days, our one-room flat was livable again.

Granted, it was not our house, but because of the height above the ground, the angle at which it faced the rising sun, and the unobstructed view to the river almost a mile away, it had one feature possessed by few homes anywhere. Each morning, when the sun came up over the river, it would light the pasture in that blueberry haze that occurred as the fog was lifting. It then crawled like a wave across the landscape to the barn, where it climbed up the sides, pierced through the window, and took your breath away.

I had swept the floor and adjusted the bed so Maggie wouldn't miss the sunrise. Below the loft, on ground level, I laid a pallet that allowed for better drainage and dragged Maggie's green garden hose through the window and fitted it with a soaking watering head. I hung a piece of cracked glass on the wall, to show half my face when I shaved. While our morning showers were cool to cold, by late afternoon the sun had heated the hose and provided about five minutes of luke-warm water—which I seldom had a chance to experience, thanks to Maggie.

I didn't really care. If Maggie needed hot water, I'd shower in ice cubes.

During all this, Blue chased something he shouldn't have, stuck his nose too close to its back end, and got sprayed. He then went and rolled in the dirt for about an hour trying to rub out the smell. When he finally made it to the house later that night, he was in a bad way. He came walking slowly up to the barn, dirty as he'd ever been and smelling worse. Even Pinky turned away.

Maggie got one whiff of him and gagged. "Oh my," she said. "Your dog needs you."

I grabbed some dish soap from under the sink and every can of tomato soup I could find out of what used to be the pantry. We cleaned him, then scrubbed the soup into his pores, turning our hands and his skin red. When we finished, he smelled like spaghetti sauce—which was better than the alternative. Midway through the scrubbing, I clipped a clothes-pin on my nose. Blue spent the next day licking himself and lying across the porch. He was red from head to toe and looked as though someone had played a bad trick on him.

OUR THIRD MORNING HOME, I STOOD IN THE SHOWER, leaning against the post while the water soaked my back. I reached up, cut off the water, and looked at myself in the tri-angular shape of glass I'd tacked to the wall for a shaving mir-ror. Pinky was looking at me through the slats in her stall like I'd lost my mind. She was probably right. I eyed a few nicks from a dull razor and settled on the wrinkle that had devel-oped between my eyes.

A car engine startled me. I dried, dressed, walked out into the sun, and was met by a man wearing a suit and tie. He explained that he was with my insurance company. After show-ing him around the house, he expressed his condolences and wrote me a check for $5,000.

"This will get you started. We can get the other half to you just as soon as I file my report."

"What do you mean, the other half?"

"Well, your particular policy allows for $10,000 in replace-ment due to theft or fire."

"It does?"

He nodded and continued his explanation. "The police say their investigation is over, that arson is to blame, and that clears us up to get started here."

I thanked him, although I didn't feel very thankful, and

told him I'd be in touch, and he drove off. I was headed back into the loft when a second car turned into the drive. This time a lady, maybe midforties, stepped out, wearing a pantsuit and carrying a clipboard.

She reluctantly shook my hand. "Are you Dr. Dylan Styles?"

"Yes, ma'am."

She pointed at the house. "Is this your home?"

"What's left of it."

She made a note on her clipboard.

Maggie appeared in the barn door, barefooted and wrapped in a blanket and squinting. Pinky was squealing in her stall.

The lady's eyes grew a bit wider. "I'm with the adoption agency."

I cussed under my breath.

"I've come to assess the, for lack of a better word, *living conditions* of your home."

I spat and wished I had a toothpick.

I tried to reassure her. "That fellow driving off there is our insurance adjuster, and he's just cleared us to start work now that the police have finished their investigation."

"Police?"

"Yes, ma'am. See, we had a series of fires the other night, started apparently by some guys who like to play with matches."

She was not amused. Understanding that we were living in the barn, she pointed her pencil. "How long do you think this arrangement will last?"

"Just a couple of weeks while I rebuild."

She perked up a little. "So you've hired a contractor?"

I looked at Maggie, then back at the lady, who had yet to tell me her name. "Well, yes."

She waited, then said, "Who?"

"Me."

She looked at me over the top of her glasses, then through them, and made another note. "I see."

About then Blue walked out of the barn. She looked, then looked again. "What's that?"

"That's our dog."

"Good Lord, he looks like a demon."

"He got too friendly with a skunk. That red is the tomato juice; it neutralizes the smell."

She scribbled some more, and when Blue started trotting toward her, she stepped quickly back into her car without shaking my hand. She lowered her window about two inches. "Dr. Styles, you must know that I have to submit an accurate account to the committee, and that this"—she pointed from the house to the barn to Blue—"is likely not going to help you."

I nodded. "Yes, ma'am. But certainly the committee understands we had a fire that was not our fault, and given some time, we can rebuild." I waved my hands in a large arc. "Maybe run the porch around the whole house."

"Yes, but the committee will also want to look at the company you keep and whether or not those associations provide a suitable environment for children."

I nodded and decided it might be best if I just shut up. She flipped down her visor against the sun and drove off. I rubbed Blue between the ears and decided that this whole adoption thing was just about to hack me off.

Maggie walked out, nuzzled against me, and said, "Who was that?"

I watched the taillights at the end of our driveway. "That was the assessor from the adoption agency who came out unannounced to determine if our home is a suitable environment for children."

"You've got to be kidding."

"I wish I was."

"What'd she say?"

"It wasn't so much what she said as how she said it."

chapter twenty-seven

TWO DAYS LATER I WALKED INTO THE BARN AND found Maggie staring into my shaving mirror. She turned, curled her hair around her index finger, and said, "I think I need a haircut." I wasn't about to argue, so I drove her to town and sat in the waiting area while they cut her hair. The smell of shampoo and the sound of eight blow-dryers was too much sensory overload, so I walked out onto the street and let the heat off the asphalt cook the skin on my face.

An hour later Maggie reappeared, again looking like Audrey Hepburn. I wanted to ask, *What happened to your hair?* but I knew better than to open my mouth. A woman and her hair are a peculiar thing.

We stopped at Home Depot and bought, among other things, some two-by-eight trusses and aluminum sheeting for the roof. An hour later I sat on the porch, missing my own truck and waiting for the lumber delivery. When it arrived, the driver had the audacity to look around and say, "Can't believe you own a farm but don't own a truck."

You ever poured lemon juice on an open wound?

My plan for the house was to repair the roof and ceilings first, pay a painter to spray the entire inside of the house with KILZ and then a color of Maggie's choosing, and then move us out of the barn and back into the house while I concentrated on the finish work.

I walked outside, stepped off the back porch, and meandered through my cotton field, where the midmorning sun was growing high and the bolls were swollen taut with white gold inside. Behind me, Maggie threw open the screen door, tossed Blue out on the porch, and slammed the door, rattling the windowpane. Blue looked at the door, licked the sides of his muzzle, and followed me out into the pasture.

I rubbed his ears and said, "Hey, pal, don't blame her. She's just having a rough time right now. We've just got to give her some space."

Blue looked back at the house and then at me. He wasn't buying it.

I looked across the pasture and road into the blackened piles that remained of Amos and Amanda's house. Amos had hired a bulldozer to push everything into a pile and a dump truck to haul it off. He and Amanda had been staying at Pastor John's house since the fire, and I wasn't the only one who sensed their absence. Blue stuck his nose in the air and, smelling nothing, whined and walked a figure eight between my legs.

A few minutes later Maggie walked out of the house. The sight of her hair was still strange to me. It wasn't that I didn't like it; it was just a surprise, that's all. She stood on the porch, holding her pruning shears and studying the landscape. Then she walked off the porch and began weaving through the flowers.

Everything had bloomed weeks ago. That meant a lot of dead and shriveled flowers now hung limp on drying twigs. Maggie began pruning the garden that surrounded our house. The process looked painful. I grabbed an old plastic trash can and followed her, quietly picking up the pieces. When she got to the roses, she paused, second-guessed herself, and then quietly returned to work. Between her energy level and the number of flowers, the process took her the better part of the day.

Dr. Frank said Maggie had had a heterotopic pregnancy. A 1 in 50,000 oddity. He explained that while we were going to have twins, only one fertilized egg had made its way out of the fallopian tube and into the uterus, where it attached. The second fertilized egg, for reasons we'll never know, became lodged in the tube. As it grew, it burst the tube, destroying itself and beginning a process of rotting inside Maggie, poisoning her blood, killing the other embryo attached to her uterus, and sending her fever to 105.5 degrees. Frank removed the tube, the ovary—which had been destroyed—and our baby. He said another couple of hours and the septic shock would have killed her.

BLUE FETCHED THE MORNING PAPER. I SPREAD IT ACROSS the table, and only then did I realize that we'd missed the Fourth of July. It never even crossed my mind. Which was probably good, because we didn't feel much like fireworks.

While Maggie napped away the morning, Blue and I walked to the river and then north along the edge. Blue kept looking over his shoulder and following close at my heels. Stepping lightly, we walked beneath the oaks and around small bunches of wild iris that had grown up from bulbs Maggie planted three years ago and that had now spread a few hundred yards downriver. The temperature was in the midnineties, and the humidity was just shy of raining.

We came to a small bend in the river that made somewhat of a natural port, if you want to call it that, where Amos and I kept our raft. I hadn't been down here in months, and it looked pretty bad. The raft was covered in leaves and fallen limbs, and had I not known where it was, I'd have missed it. I uncovered it, brushed it off as best I could, and then lay down in the middle. Blue curled up alongside me, and we watched the sun rise above the cypress trees.

I watched the river moving slowly and silently alongside us. Despite the turmoil topside, its rhythm was never-changing. I dipped my feet in, letting the movement and coolness sift through my toes. Blue took a drink and then jumped in, swimming around long enough to cool off. He paddled back over to the raft, and I lifted him up. He showered me in dog-shake, which felt good, and we lay back down. Around noon, I heard footsteps.

Amos stepped onto the raft and sat down. He was dressed in cutoff jeans and a T-shirt, telling me that he'd taken a much-deserved day off. He pulled a soft-sided cooler off his shoulder and unzipped the top. "I've got PB&J, root beer, and Oreos."

I nodded, and he slapped a sandwich in my hand. I pulled back the plastic wrap, took a bite, and chewed without tasting it.

Amos looked at me curiously. "You look like you ain't eaten much lately."

He was right; it was the first thing I'd eaten in two days. I nodded again and stared at the water as if it were a nighttime campfire.

Amos popped the top on a root beer and handed it to me. "Thanks."

We sat on the raft, chewing, soaking in the sunlight and silence while I fed my crusts to Blue.

Amos pulled off his T-shirt and finally spoke. "Need to work on my tan. Been pushing too many pencils lately." He pulled his Kimber and holster out from behind his belt and laid them on the raft. After he finished his sandwich, he lay back and pulled his baseball cap down over his eyes.

We spent an hour in quiet.

AS THE CICADAS AND TREE FROGS TUNED UP THE PSYCHE-delic afternoon, Amos spoke. "We're taking 'Manda to and from work. She doesn't leave the house without one of us going with her. We've rented the house across the street, and some of my guys stare out the windows toward us at night."

I stared at him.

"No, she doesn't know that, but short of leaving town, it's the best we can do." He shook his head. "I've never staked out myself before."

Amos was pretty good at giving me only what I needed when I needed it. He was both friend and brother, but I needed more. I looked across the raft. "Amos, tell me about these guys. I want the *whole* story."

"As Pastor John told you, he got mixed up in some pretty bad stuff. Started out as petty theft in and around Charleston, but given time, and their appetites, it went up and out from there. They had warehouses all over the state stuffed with everything from diamond rings to classic cars. They were smart." He shrugged. "At least they started out that way. Like most criminals who can't keep a secret and love showing off how cool they are, they got greedy and sloppy. Really sloppy.

"They were hitting a jewelry store. Pastor John was the inside man. The other three were parked outside in a car, doping it up and waiting on the signal from John, when an off-duty police officer stumbled onto them. He smelled the dope, knocked on the window, and the driver, a fellow named James Whittaker III, self-proclaimed leader, rolled down the window, stuck a 9mm in the cop's chest, and pulled the trigger. John ran to the window, saw the car leaving pretty fast and a man lying in the street surrounded in streetlight-red. Our guys, having just pulled over a DUI about two blocks up, got there within a few seconds. When they arrived, they found a dead friend, the wiped-down Glock that the bullet had come from, and John Lovett crawling out the jewelry store window carrying a bag worth about a quarter of a million dollars."

I gulped.

"It gets better from there. While John Lovett was trying to explain to investigators how the dead police officer ended up in the street, the other three were feeling their oats. They crossed the state line into Georgia and went out boozing. James, along with two brothers named Antonio and Felix, started buying drinks all around and soon caught the ear of an FBI agent who happened to be in the bar trying to cheat on his wife. An hour or so later, another shooting occurred. This one is a little fuzzy, but according to witnesses, James wrestled the Bureau guy's .40 out of his hand, shot him, then shot the bartender 'cause he wasn't bringing the drinks fast enough. One of the brothers grabbed a bat from behind the bar and started swinging it at people. When the shouting stopped, three more people were dead, and the Three Musketeers drove off into the night.

"They ran out of gas an hour or so later on some forgotten two-lane. Too drunk to walk, they evidently got into a wrestling match, and all three passed out in or near the car. When daylight came, a soccer mom reported the car, along with the three guys sprawled around it, and an hour later they were booked in Georgia.

"It didn't take too long for investigators to put it all together. And while John was very much guilty of grand theft, he was not guilty of murder, nor was he an accessory. During the trial, the prosecution cut a deal, giving him a lesser sentence if he would simply state what happened that night. He did." Amos paused. "He also told them about the warehouses."

Therein lay the problem. Amos had told me several times that criminals don't forget, and they certainly don't forgive.

"When John identified his buddies as the three in the car, along with the locations of their warehouses, he received seven years, serving only four for, oddly enough, good behavior."

Amos dipped his hands in the river, washed his face, and then stood, letting the droplets cascade down his neck and shoulders. "Antonio and Felix got eighteen years, serving eighteen. James got life and served up until last month when his case was brought up for review by an ethics board. They were investigating the activities of the officers, who they thought were too bent on revenge and not justice for the death of their fellow officer, which they say colored the trial proceedings.

"The day you and Maggie saw us leaving the courthouse, we'd been watching video footage of the proceedings. It showed James marking on the table with his fingers, writing 'promises' to John Lovett and family. Seems James isn't too happy about having spent two decades in prison."

Amos pulled out the Oreos and offered them to me. I shook my head. He popped the lid on one, licked off the white center, and then ate the two chocolate sides. He did that for about eight cookies and then fed one to Blue, who was inching across the raft.

"And another thing," Amos said, "prison 'law' dictates that when someone rats on you, what they have becomes yours. That includes people."

After Blue and Amos polished off the Oreos, Amos tore open the wrapper and laid it in front of Blue, who chased it around the raft, wagging his tail and licking the plastic clean.

I looked at my watch and knew I needed to check on Maggie.

Amos put his arm on mine. "'Manda's at the house. Brought some dinner. She'll be okay."

I lay back down and watched the clouds roll overhead.

Amos stared down the river, then at me. "You gonna be okay?"

I shrugged.

"What's the doc say?"

"Says it might take some time."

"How much?"

"Who knows? Technically, we're waiting to see if her other ovary can do the work of two. When he closed her up, he wasn't too sure, so in a sense we're just waiting for her next cycle." I tossed a twig into the river. "If it happens, we'll know it's working. If not, Frank says she'll have to substitute with oral hormones. We'll know in two, maybe three weeks, give or take."

Amos nodded and popped another root beer. "Can you make it that long?"

I thought quietly. A month ago, we were crying at the sight of blood. Now we were hoping for it.

"Don't know."

Amos shook his head and then turned toward me as if he were afraid to ask. "What happened to her hair?"

I shrugged. I held out my hand, palm up. "Right now, life feels like it's just sand sifting through my fingers."

We walked back to the house in the twilight. When we got there, Pinky was grunting at me from inside the barn, so I dropped a bucket of corn in her trough and tried to rub her behind the ears. She rolled in the mud, shook her ears, and rubbed her four hundred–plus pounds against me. It was more of a shove than a love-rub. She wedged me against the stall, ground her muddy haunches against me, and snotted me. She was raising her leg when I hopped out of the stall.

Amos raised an eyebrow. "I thought you two had reached an agreement."

I brushed myself off. "That ended when we sold the piglets. Now she's back to being the devil."

"Can't say that I blame her."

"Feeding pigs ain't cheap."

I crept up the stairs, cracked the door, and peered into our bedroom. Maggie lay in bed, cocooned inside the sheets and sleeping. A pillow covered her head. I leaned my forehead against the doorjamb.

"Maggs, I'm taking Amos home. I'll be right back."

I heard a shuffle beneath the sheets, a creak of the bed, but no verbal response.

Amos loaded into the van for a ride home while I walked across to the house and grabbed the keys off the kitchen counter. The kitchen had been cleaned—Amanda, no doubt—but the nursery door was shut, as it had been since we got home.

Blue met me on the porch, and I pointed to the barn. "Stay." He whined and looked at the van. I knelt down and rubbed his muzzle and neck. "I know, buddy. Me too. But she needs you right now. You hang out here and keep an eye on things." Blue circled, curled into a ball, and kept an eye on the barn.

The ride to Pastor John's house was quiet. Amos said little, and I said nothing at all. I pulled up; he hopped out and leaned against the door.

"Next week, at the station house, we're having a boil. Pastor John wants to thank all the guys. You two are invited."

I nodded. Amos patted the top of the van, shut the door, and walked inside, where Amanda met him at the door with L.D. perched on her hip. Amos lifted him up. L.D.'s face lit up like a floodlight, and I drove off into the night. Alone.

I drove home the long way. Twenty minutes later, I pulled into Digger's outdoor amphitheater and cracked the gate. I walked down the aisle toward a seat in the middle. Clouds covered the moon, and the darkness blanketed me, so I bumped my knee on a few seat backs and tripped over a cup brimming with old rainwater. I tried to see the stage, but only the outline appeared. I sat a long time, listening, but I heard no pipes.

Toward midnight, I climbed back up the hill and cranked the van—a sound I had yet to grow accustomed to. I needed to go home, but I didn't. I drove past the church, but the bulldozer had already been there. Only the foundation remained.

Ten minutes later, I pulled into Bryce's drive and walked up the hill. I smelled the remains of a burnt-out trash fire, but when I prodded the coals, they were cold. I walked to the film house and checked the door. It was unlocked. I read the titles, grabbed a film canister, and loaded it into the machine. I hit the power switch, turned on the reel, and walked to the center of the field in front of the screen, where I leaned against an iron pole, the microphone just above my head.

I have a hard time watching John Wayne movies in which John Wayne dies. As a result, I don't usually watch *The Cowboys*, *The Green Berets*, *The Alamo*, or the one now rolling on the screen, *The Shootist*.

It's a simple story really. It was also the Duke's last. He plays a famed gunfighter named J. B. Books who rides into Carson City in 1901 to visit his old friend Doc E. W. Hostetler (Jimmy Stewart) in the last days of his life. Books is trying to hang up his pistols after he discovers he's dying of cancer, but like Poncho and Lefty, gunfighters aren't allowed to grow old. Only their legends do. Occupational hazard, I suppose.

I lay in the grass, my head resting against the pole, and watched as J. B. checked into the boardinghouse where the proprietor, an attractive widow named Bon Rogers (Lauren Bacall), and her son Gillom (Ron Howard) keep their distance and listen to the rumors surfacing about town. As the cancer eats at his body and the thought of a long, slow death eats at his soul, a few of the next generation of killers seek him out for a final fight. Then and now, what made watching more difficult was knowing that the Duke himself actually had cancer while filming, and it would be that same cancer that killed him soon after.

The movie continued through scenes of doctors' visits in which the Duke refills his prescription for laudanum to the scene at the barbershop in which the barber saves hair clippings to sell and then to conversations in which we learn that the undertaker plans to exhibit his corpse.

I lay on the grass and watched as the Duke walked into the bar. Even then, I wanted to scream like Gillom, "No!" The Duke bellied up to the bar, saw the flash of metal in the window's reflection, turned, and stood heroic one last time.

When my grandfather and I first watched this movie on television in the late seventies, I could not understand why the

Duke turned his back on the bartender. I knew that he knew the shotgun was under the bar. There's always a shotgun under the bar. As a kid, I jumped up off the floor and screamed at the television, "The shotgun under the bar!" But the Duke did not hear me, and he did not hear Gillom.

As I grew older, I understood. It was for that very reason he'd chosen the bar. The gunfighters couldn't get him; he was too good, and he knew it. But he also knew that if he turned his back, there'd be no way the bartender could miss. And he didn't.

Maybe death by shotgun was better than death by cancer. Maybe it still is. When the Duke fell against the bar, I jumped up off the ground and turned my back on the screen, walking down the drive while Gillom finished off the bartender and the end of the reel slapped the machine.

*chapter twenty-eight*

WHEN I GOT HOME IT WAS NEARLY THREE THIRTY IN the morning. All but the barn spotlights were out, and Maggie had left the sprinkler on. I walked around back, turned the spigot off, and in the dim light saw them a second time. Footprints.

I pulled a flashlight from the van, pinched it between my teeth, and crawled on my hands and knees alongside the house. There weren't as many this time, but they were there. And since Maggie had turned on the sprinkler after I'd left, the prints had been made sometime between when I left to take Amos home and just a few minutes ago.

I heard a stick crack in the pasture not forty yards from me and froze. Then I heard it again, followed by a shuffling and another crack.

I slid up onto the porch, unlocked the front door, and crept down the hallway to my writing closet. I unlocked it, slid my shotgun off the floor, and quietly worked the action, sliding a shell into the chamber. I grabbed my larger Maglite, like the kind Amos keeps in his undercover truck, and crept back outside. I belly-crawled off the porch, along the azaleas next to the spigot, and out over the grass next to our house.

When I neared the edge of the pasture, my heart was pounding so hard inside my chest that I thought it would explode out the front. Slowly I stood, holding the flashlight snug against the barrel and pointed in the same direction. I had yet to click it on, but I could with a flick of my thumb. The sound of cracking twigs had moved, maybe another forty yards closer to the river. It was slighter now, not so loud, and when I stepped into the rows of corn, it stopped altogether. With the wind at my back and rustling the leaves of the cornstalks that were two feet above my head, I stood and waited. I heard another shuffling, as if someone were crawling more quickly now, and still the sound was moving away from me toward the river. If he got to the river, he'd be gone. If I could head him off, or get to him first, I had a chance.

I stepped out of the cornfield and circled, the shotgun on my hip and the flashlight and barrel in my hand. The more quickly I moved, the more rapidly the sound out in front of me began moving through the corn. We were mirroring each other. The edge of the corn narrowed like a triangle toward the river, so given our current path, if I took off running right this second, we'd meet at the river. The moon had popped out from behind the clouds and threw my shadow on the dark grass before me. Trying to quiet my heart, I took a deep breath, gripped the shotgun more tightly, and took off running down the side of the corn rows.

Whoever I was chasing did the same, crashing through the corn like a bulldozer, trying desperately to get out the other side. The river was now just a hundred yards off, and based on the sound moving toward me from my left, he'd get there before me. I tried to run faster, but the grass was knee-high, and I'm not a very good sprinter in cowboy boots. He increased his speed, smashing through the corn, and every few seconds I could hear him breathing. Within forty yards of the river, I pulled up, the oaks on my right, corn on my left, and a small field of grass spread out before me and rolling down into the river.

North of me was Old Man McCutcheon's property, south of me a few hundred yards lay my son's grave, beyond that a couple of miles sat the church property, and sitting at a dead stop not ten yards from me in the corn, breathing heavily and sounding winded, sat someone who'd been peeping in my windows. I clicked off the safety, shouldered the shotgun, and placed my finger on the flashlight button. Unable to control either my breathing or my pounding heart, I stood and waited.

The barrel of the shotgun was moving wildly around the sight picture. I stared off into the darkness, trying to see the movement of outlines or images. Then a dark flash caught my eye. Followed by another. I looked straight at it and lost it entirely, so I looked at it out of the corner of my eye and saw the huge form crawling on his hands and knees out of the corn. He crawled out into the grass, trying to hide in the darkness, and when I was certain he had cleared the corn, I fired a shot into the air. The shot rang out and echoed across the river, turning me momentarily deaf, and the smell of burned gunpowder stung my nose and eyes. I quickly and loudly chambered another round, aimed at the shape, shouted, *"Stop!"* and clicked on the light.

Standing broadside, in all her corn-fed porcine glory, stood Pinky, a half-eaten corncob wedged between her teeth. She eyed me, sniffed the air, grunted, and ambled back into the corn, her big ears flopping happily alongside her. I watched her curlicue tail disappear into the corn, sat down on the ground, and breathed for the first time in five minutes.

I clicked on the safety, flipped off the flashlight, and lay down in the grass before I fell over. A couple of minutes later, I sat up, dusted myself off, and laid the shotgun across my shoulder. Then I stood, turned toward home, and ran square into the chest of a rock-solid man.

I dropped the shotgun, the light, and half my bladder before Bryce reached out and grabbed my shoulder. His face was painted in black and green stripes, and into his clothes he had tucked parts of cornstalks. He looked into my eyes, stared over my shoulder, sniffed me, and placed his .45 back into its shoulder holster beneath his left arm.

I picked up the flashlight and clicked it on, waving it wildly around the night and finally centering it on Bryce. The most striking feature was not the clothing, the cornstalks, the face paint, the sidearm, or the old scope dangling from twine around his neck, but rather his feet. His bare feet. I shone down, up, and down again. When I finished involuntarily emptying my bladder, I clicked off the light and said, "Bryce?"

He blinked. His voice was quiet and calm. "Dylan."

I stepped closer. Not smelling the fumes of alcohol I'd come to expect, I said, "You okay?"

Bryce nodded, checked the position of the safety without even looking, and handed it to me. The pungent smell of warm urine reached my nose and, evidently, Bryce's, because he grabbed the light, shone it on the front of my pants, and then clicked it off. He handed it back. "You?"

I took a deep breath, sat down again in the grass, and collapsed onto my back. Just then I heard the barn door slam and saw Maggie walk beneath the fluorescent glow of the light from the telephone pole that lit the yard between the barn and the house. Wrapped in a blanket, she strained her eyes, looking toward us.

I turned on the flashlight, shone it down onto myself, and said, "It's just me and Bryce." I decided it'd be better not to shine the light on Bryce, so I kept it pointing down on me, watching her. She craned her neck, muttered something, and disappeared again into the barn.

I flicked off the light again as Pinky crossed the trail in front of me, waddling her way back to the barn after what was apparently her nighttime feeding.

Bryce stepped closer to the corn and peered at the tops, shining black in the moonlight. He whispered, "They were a little taller than this. It was summer. I was chasing a man, and we came to a field." He raised his hands and touched the tips of the cornstalks.

"He had been assigned to me a month earlier, and I'd been chasing him ever since. That was the thirty-second day. When he cleared the corn and stepped into my row, he was forty-two paces." He pointed at the shotgun on my shoulder. "I'd been working some tunnels earlier in the evening, so I was carrying one of those. I placed the bead on his legs and squeezed." Bryce blinked but didn't flinch.

"He dropped, began spraying the corn around me with AK-47 fire, and one 7.62 round cut through my helmet but missed my head. I fired a second time, and the man stopped firing and clutched his feet. He was screaming. I walked within twenty paces and fired a third time."

Bryce dropped the imaginary gun and pulled the real Colt .45 from his holster. He clicked off the safety and, clasping it with two hands, walked farther down the corn row.

I followed, the shotgun over my shoulder, pointing away, the flashlight aimed on Bryce.

He walked to a spot twenty steps away and stood, feet apart, pointing into the dirt below him. He extended the pistol barrel into the air and stopped some two feet from the ground. He then began speaking in a language I'd never heard. It sounded like a loose cousin to what Maggie and I would hear when we went to eat sushi.

Bryce knelt, the pistol still clutched in both hands, and whispered, "I said, 'Where is she?'" He paused, waited, looked further into the memory, and spoke again. "Where is she?"

Silence followed as Bryce cocked the hammer on his Colt. I backed up one step, and Bryce whispered, pressing his ear hard against the memory of the man's face. He stayed there, listening, shaking his head, and nodding. Then, without another word, he stood up and pulled the trigger eight times. He fired all eight shots into the dirt beneath him, directly through the memory of the man's head. He ejected the clip, inserted a second, and flicked the slide forward, chambering another round. He clicked on the hammer safety, holstered the still-smoking weapon, and breathed in long, measured breaths. Finally he blinked, reached into the cargo pocket on his pants, pulled out a sheet of gum, and popped all twelve pieces into his mouth.

While I tried to make sense of this nonsense, Bryce worked the gum around in his mouth. The mixture of dirt, corn, gunpowder, urine, and spearmint added to the confusion.

"Bryce?"

He blinked and looked at me.

I shone the light on his feet. "Have, umm, . . . have you been, uh . . . do you always walk around barefooted?"

Bryce looked at his feet, the gum filling most of his mouth. "Only when I don't want to be heard."

"You know," I said, trying to sound casual, "if you're ever out this way and want to come in for a cup of coffee or a bite to eat, you can always knock. Or just come on in and have a seat at the table."

Bryce considered that for a moment, then said, "Okay."

I nodded. "Sure. You don't even have to knock."

Without another word, Bryce stepped off into the night. Within ten paces, I could no longer make out his outline. A few more, and both the sight and sound of him had disappeared altogether. Ten seconds later, I heard a covey of quail flush and rise down near the river beyond my son's grave, some two hundred yards away.

I walked back to the barn, stripped, and showered. Cleaner, I walked across the yard to the house and locked the shotgun back in the closet, and only when I'd sat down at the kitchen table, hovering over a glass of orange juice, did I realize how badly my hands were shaking.

When I cracked open our bedroom door, I found Maggie snow-angeled diagonally across the middle of the bed. Her breathing told me she was asleep, so I pulled the door quietly shut and spread out across the front porch with Blue. A few hours later, I woke inside a dew-covered sleeping bag. Pinky was grunting at me from inside the barn, and Blue lay on his bed across the porch looking at me as if I were from Mars.

I sat up and looked at him. "What? What'd I do?"

He flopped his ears forward, laid his muzzle down across his leg, and let out a deep breath. Maybe now he would let himself go to sleep.

THE CALENDAR ON THE REFRIGERATOR SHOWED THAT IT was Tuesday, July 16. Another week had passed. Each day seemed like one long day that rolled seamlessly into another, where daylight and darkness had little meaning other than to suggest something I'd forgotten. According to my count, Maggie had been home eighteen days. Before all this stuff started, her cycles had been pretty regular at twenty-eight days. I wasn't sure, but I guessed we were another two weeks, give or take a few days, from knowing one way or the other. I tried to imagine each scenario. Neither was very good. Whatever the outcome, I wasn't sure how Maggie would react.

I pulled on my jeans, slid on my boots, and combed my hair. I walked around the front of the house and found her sitting in a rocker, wrapped in a blanket, and watching the bulldozer dump burned memories and brick into a Dumpster across the street.

She hadn't eaten much in a couple of days, and I was sure she had lost some weight. Her face was thinner, accentuated by her short hair, and her color was not too good. Her hollow face looked like a reflection of her insides.

I scrambled some eggs, made some cheese grits and toast, and walked out onto the front porch. She smiled, nibbled, but ate little. I kissed her forehead, she brushed my face with her palm, and we sat in the rockers, swaying.

*chapter twenty-nine*

THE PHONE RANG TWICE BEFORE THE HOSPITAL receptionist picked up. "Hello?"

It was late; I cleared my throat. "Hello. I need to speak with Dr. Frank Palmer, please."

"Hold just one minute."

Five minutes passed while the elevator music reminded me that I hadn't been to the dentist in a while.

"This is Dr. Frank."

"Dr. Frank, this is Dylan Styles."

"Hey, Dylan. How's our girl?"

"Well, sir, she's not sleeping much. I was wondering if—"

"No problem. I'll have the nurse call in something. How's everything else?"

I wasn't sure how to answer. Finally I stammered, "I—I just think it'd do her some good to get a good night's sleep."

"I'll tell you what," he said, "why don't you stop by the office. I'll have the nurse pull a few things out of the sample bin. Save you some money."

"You don't mind?"

"I'll have it ready when you get there."

"Thanks, Dr. Frank."

THE BUILDING THAT HOUSED THE DIGGER VOLUNTEER Fire Department No. 1 was little more than a tall concrete-block warehouse with four large front-and-back aluminum garage doors that allowed the trucks to drive through the building rather than just into it and one very tall flagpole that stood adjacent to Mr. Carter's dog kennels. He had donated the land.

Picnic tables and folding chairs spread across the lawn behind the building, and the enormous flag flapped gently in the 98-degree air. Three-foot standing floor fans sat in the middle of the firehouse, circulating the air through the doors and blowing across the red-and-white-checkered tablecloths covering the picnic tables. Newspaper had been spread across the tablecloths, and upright rolls of paper towels sat on top of all that, ensuring that nothing would float away. Mr. Carter's rolling barbecue pit, an old propane tank cut lengthways and set on trailer wheels—and big enough for a man to lie down in—sat smoking, lid open, currently heating three huge twenty-gallon vats.

Draped in a red apron that read "Fire Chief," Mr. Carter tended both the fire and the pots with the same stick. He'd poke the fire, stoke the flames, then dip that same stick into the water and poke the boiling food. He said the mesquite in the charcoal added to the flavor. Badger and Gus, two of Mr. Carter's older and most obedient dogs, had been let out of the kennel and lay at their master's feet.

I parked out of sight because I didn't want to explain the van, and then Maggie and I crossed the street and walked through the firehouse. There's no use denying it; it's pretty much a huge toy room for grown men. All of us signed up in part because of all the cool toys. From chain saws to axes to the infamous Jaws of Life, we are enamored with things that cut, bang, or smash. And what boy doesn't grow up wanting to drive a fire truck?

Mr. Willard, the owner of the corner gas station and grocery, greeted us at the door with a pitcher of iced tea and two glasses. Jim Biggins, evidently taking a break from his land-clearing and firewood business, walked around the side of the building with a hundred-pound sack of charcoal slung over each shoulder. Butch Walker and his boys, free between the morning and evening milking at their dairy, sat at a table laughing with a few guys I didn't know. John Billingsly, Digger's only computer guru, sat hovering over a portable bug zapper that stood like a six-foot chiminea with a purple head. Every three or four seconds it zapped.

The wives of these men all sat at one table, whispering, laughing, and trying to hide whatever they were talking about from their husbands. Which was also exactly what the men were doing, but both groups knew this, so the game continued as it had since Adam met Eve in the garden.

No matter how slowly I walked, Maggie walked a half step behind me, almost hiding behind my shoulder. She hadn't said she didn't want to come, but she hadn't seemed too excited either. I looped my arm inside hers, and we walked to the nearest table, where Amanda saw us and came to our rescue. She grabbed Maggie and led her off to the women's table.

Maggie's eyes told me she didn't want to go, they told me she wanted to run very far away from here, but I silently urged her on, so she put on a smile and acted happy.

I sat with the boys, giving the obligatory laugh when needed, but my eyes, ears, and mind were with Maggie. The women's conversation had turned to children, whose child was in what grade, what sports they were playing, how far each mom drove the car pool each day, how many loads of laundry they washed in a week, and how much their grocery bill had increased because of the rising price of milk. Maggie listened, trying to look interested, but her crossed arms, crossed legs, and stiff neck told me she needed help.

Mr. Carter came to the rescue. Stirring the middle pot, he leaned back out of the smoke and said, "Amos and D.S."

We jumped up from the table and met him at the cooker. He gave us each a hot pad, and we lifted the first vat off the cooker. It was heavy, and I almost stumbled. Amos smiled, eyed my shaking arms, and shook his head. "You need to get busy."

I looked at my deflated biceps and compared them to Amos's. Not much comparison. We drained off the water, then dumped the contents directly onto the newspaper on the center table. Red potatoes, corn on the cob, carrots, shrimp, andouille sausage, Alaskan crab legs, and about four cans of Old Bay Seasoning spilled across the table and sat steaming in the shade of the magnolia tree that towered above us.

Amos and I returned for the other two vats while everyone else grabbed plates and started helping themselves to the mound on the table. We loaded up three tables with dinner and then sat around the tables eating with our hands. A true low-country boil does not involve flatware of any kind. We just bellied up to the tables, rested our elbows on the edges, and dug in.

Everyone, that is, except Maggie and me. We did what we were getting good at. We pretended.

An hour passed. The shrimp tails and crab shells piled up, and people began sitting back and passing around the toothpick cup. Inside the fire station, John Billingsly was tending his ice cream maker, which finished churning about the time someone started telling the story of Amos's and my heroic rescue at the church.

The guys laughed. One of them imitated me with my oxygen tank and rubber boots that were two sizes too big, while another mimicked Amos's attempt to kick in a stubborn door. While they prodded, Maggie, Amanda, and a few other ladies passed out plastic spoons and peach ice cream served in Styrofoam bowls.

While I listened and the fake smile on my face told the guys around me that I was enjoying their fun, my eyes watched Maggie, who had busied herself with cleaning the tables and the ice-cream machine. She tried to look helpful, look interested, look okay, but I knew her, and I knew that she was about ready to jump out of her skin and that when she did, tears wouldn't be far behind. She had held it together about as long as she could.

I threw my bowl away, looped my arm inside hers, and walked her slowly beneath the magnolia and along the grassy lawn that led down to Mr. Carter's duck pond. The shade felt good, the breeze felt better, and the farther we got from the tables, the more her shoulders relaxed and her breathing deepened. By the time we reached the pond, the wrinkle on her forehead had almost disappeared. We stood watching the ducks swim around the turtles and a few well-fed carp feed slowly through the weeds at the bank.

About ten minutes later, Amos and Amanda appeared behind us. Amos held an uncut watermelon on one shoulder. The four of us stood at the water, saying nothing and not feeling as though we had to. Maybe that's the sign of true friendship, when silence is not uncomfortable.

About twenty years ago, Mr. Carter had planted twelve weeping willows along the banks of his pond. Now they were tall, mature, and their branches swooped over and down into the water like Rapunzel's hair. We sat in the shade of one. I leaned against the tree trunk, and Maggie sat between my legs, leaning against me.

Amos drove his Benchmade down the middle of the melon, then cut out large chunks and passed them around. He sank his face into the heart and let the juice drip off his chin. Maggie did likewise, chewed, leaned back, and spit a seed out into the water.

Amos looked out across the pond. "The federal guys have put me in charge of the investigation here. We've got most every agent in the state trying to find them, which shouldn't be too hard to do given what they look like, but we haven't yet, and even when we do, we can't do anything, because technically, they haven't done anything wrong—at least that we can prove. It'd be Maggie's word against theirs, and we can question them but technically can't hold them.

"One more thing." Amos wiped his face, closed his eyes, and spoke as if it hurt. "Antonio and Felix were released from prison about three days before Amanda was kidnapped and tied to a tree in the woods two years ago."

We sat in the quiet a moment while the weight settled down into my stomach. He put his arm around Amanda, who seemed relatively unmoved by the admission. Evidently she'd heard this story before.

"A week later James received a postcard from Charleston. The front showed a picture of a rural country church that looked a lot like one that used to stand not too far from here. And on the back someone had drawn a stick figure wrapped around a tree."

"You think I should move Maggie someplace in town?"

Amos shrugged. "Hard to say. Criminals don't think like we do."

I stood and walked to the edge of the pond, dipping my fingers and then shaking them. I wiped them on my pants, plucked a tall weed from the bank, and began breaking it into smaller pieces.

I nodded. "You think they'll come back? I mean, to the house?"

"The cop in me doubts it." He tried to sound reassuring. "They're probably running now. I've known too many criminals who never make good on their word—even when it comes to revenge." He paused again and looked at Amanda. "But the husband in me does not."

Maggie looked at Amos. "Which one do you believe?"

"I believe . . ." He looked at Amanda, then put his hand on her shoulder, "the one who loves her."

We were quiet a minute.

"I'd keep Papa's 12 handy for a while."


MAGGIE DIDN'T SAY MUCH ON THE WAY HOME. NEITHER did I.

I parked in front of the barn and told her I wanted to check on the house. When I walked up the back steps and into the kitchen, the light on the answering machine was blinking. I pushed *play*, turned down the volume, and lowered my ear next to the machine. Mr. Sawyer from the adoption agency said the committee had reached its decision and would be sending out a letter in the next couple of weeks. When he had finished speaking, I pressed *delete* and walked slowly down the drive to the mailbox. It was empty.

Like me.

*chapter thirty*

BY MIDWEEK, I ADMITTED THAT SEVERAL THINGS were bothering me and I could not shake them. I didn't like having to live like two tramps in the barn; I was worried about Maggie; I couldn't make sense of anything right now; and I knew things were getting worse and not better. But at the top of the heap of things that bothered me most, that woke me up in a cold sweat at night, screaming out of the silence and calling me a liar, sat the story I'd written and given to Maggie. And with Maggie growing more detached by the minute, what troubled me was not what I'd left in but what I'd left out.

I leaned against the shower post and shut my eyes. The water dripped off my shoulders and cooled my skin amid the humid night. I didn't want to live this way. The wrinkle between my eyes told me what was bothering me, but it also said something else: it said I had grown angry and bitter that she had shut me out.

Pinky slammed her stall door, reminding me it was well past her dinnertime. I finally voiced to myself what I had been thinking for days but had not been willing to admit. When I looked at my life, at the torn and frayed quilted patchwork that had enveloped us, I wondered if any part of it could be sewn together again. Because as I studied it in my mind's eye, only tattered remnants remained.

I stood in the doorway, drying myself and studying the house. From the chipped paint to the squeaky screen door to the stick-and-twig ruins of Maggie's landscape design to the smell of Pinky's unkempt stall wafting across the back porch, the place looked and smelled the way I felt.

I leaned over the stall and looked down on Pinky, who was currently digging a hole to China in the corner. She looked at me, grunted through her snout, and flopped her ears forward.

I looked across the overgrown yard to the house and heard Maggie throwing things in the kitchen. I heard a glass break, a pause, then several more crashes for what I assumed was good measure. A door slammed. Blue looked at me, I shrugged, and his face told me what I already knew. We were nearing the end.

Something had been severed. It wasn't Maggie's voice that told me this. It was her eyes. When she looked at me, she was looking at the world beyond me where her dreams once lived. The brilliant light that had once been there was dim and flickering.

"What can heal the human soul?" I whispered.

Blue leaned against me and raised his cold nose to my hand. I stepped into my clothes and admitted that I had grown angry at something I could not see or touch. The irony of my life smacked me in the face: while I could protect Pastor

John from a raging fire, I could not protect my wife from that which threatened to kill her.

I walked out the back of the barn along the edge of the corn and tried counting the stars. I felt little and insignificant—one amid the many.

My sense of helplessness pressed down on my shoulders, grew tighter across my chest, and squeezed out the air. I could not escape the sense of blame. Like a wave of vomit I could not control, the ache cut my knees out from under me, sent me to the dirt, and then exited my heart like a cannon shot. I knelt, clutching the earth, gasping for air, and trying not to let the split in my heart split me.

MIDNIGHT CAME, AND I CRAWLED OUT OF THE FIELD. THE large green leaves of the corn slapped at my arms, and the tasseled tops towered now some two feet above me. I crept toward the barn, slipped through the garden behind the azaleas, and stood next to the barn door staring at the staircase.

Blue looked up at me and even shook his head, but I scratched him between the ears and told him, "I'm just checking on her." I climbed up the stairs into the loft. The room was cold and dark, and I could hear Maggie sleeping in the silence. She lay in the bed, mounded beneath the covers, breathing heavily under the oral sedation she'd grown accustomed to.

I tiptoed to the bedside table, picked up her bottle of sleeping pills, and clicked off the lid. One left. There were five this time last night.

I knelt next to the bed and slid my hand beneath hers. It was limp, frail, and did not respond to mine. I slid my hands beneath the sheets and found her cold feet. I pulled some socks from my drawer, slipped them over her heels, and covered her up. The fan was spinning like a tornado, and the AC was set on "snow." I knew our power bill would shoot through the roof, but I didn't adjust a thing. If that's what she needed, then that's what she needed.

I climbed down, walked across the yard, and found the answering machine light blinking quietly in the dark. The red light reminded me of the hospital and the machines that had monitored Maggie. Maybe we'd escaped the confining walls, but the monitoring continued. I pushed the button and heard Dr. Frank's voice.

"Dylan, it's Frank Palmer. Just checking on Maggie. I'm working the graveyard shift, so call me anytime tonight."

I dialed the number of the delivery ward and asked for Dr. Frank, and the receptionist paged him. A few minutes later he picked up the phone.

"Hey, Dylan, how're things?"

"I'm not too sure."

"Any sign of her cycle starting?"

"I don't think so."

Dr. Frank took a deep breath. "I don't want to give you any false hope. If you don't see something tomorrow, or the next day at the latest, I think, well . . ."

"I understand."

"How are her emotions? Is she on an even keel?"

I scratched my head. "No, not really."

"On a scale of one to ten, ten being really out of whack, where is she?"

"Reaching ten."

He paused as though he was checking his watch. "Today's Wednesday. Why don't you call the office Monday, and I'll tell the nurses to work her in. We probably ought to start her on a hormone replacement therapy. Like we discussed, it's routine for menopausal or sterile women."

The word *sterile* echoed through my head. "I'll call Monday."

He hung up, and I returned the phone to the receiver. When I turned around, Maggie was standing in the doorway, wrapped in a sheet. Her face was as white as a ghost, and she was barefooted. We stood looking at each other.

Finally she spoke. "What'd he say?"

"Who?"

Her eyes were dark and hollow. "Dr. Frank."

"He said he hoped we'd have a good weekend."

Maggie blinked and waited.

I shrugged. "He wants me to bring you in Monday."

"Why?"

"'Cause by the end of the weekend, we ought to know one way or the other."

Maggie's finger slid along the lines of the wall calendar. She reached what would be the end of the weekend, pulled the calendar off the wall, and pitched it into the trash. Then she turned and walked back to the barn.

I walked to the front porch and leaned against the screen door. The streetlight lit the mailbox and reminded me that I had not checked the mail in two days. I walked down the drive and filled my arms with junk mail, then walked back to the house. Sitting at the kitchen table, eyeing the barn door, I filtered through the pile.

The letter from the adoption agency was stuffed somewhere in the middle. I froze, eyed the hallway again, and then slit the top of the envelope.

"*Dr. and Mrs. Styles, We regret to inform you . . .*"

It was signed "*Sincerely,*" which I doubted, and then included a postscript, "*You may appeal this decision in writing,*" and gave detailed instructions on how to do that. The following page was a check in the amount of my deposit.

Over the last few weeks, the facts of my life had festered like a splinter and were now tender to the slightest touch. The letter was like somebody rubbing the tip of the splinter with sandpaper.

I'd had just about enough of this committee. I folded the letter, stuck it in my pocket, and closed my eyes. I needed to work on my appeal, pay off my debt at the bank, and figure out what I was going to tell Maggie.

*chapter thirty-one*

LAST JULY, AS THE HEAT OF SUMMER AND SWARMS of mosquitoes arrived in force, Maggie and I packed enough food for two or three days, whistled for Blue, and hopped on the raft. We shoved off, and I stood at the rear manning the rudder while Maggie lay across the deck tanning, talking with me, and dipping her feet in the river as Blue paced back and forth across the front spotting fish.

The first night we pulled into a small cove, anchored, lit the butane stove, fried fish, scrambled some eggs, and then sipped coffee while Maggie laid her head on my chest and the stars shot by overhead. Two magical days passed before we even blinked. And by the time we thought about returning, we'd been on the raft almost four days. It's a good thing the fish were biting.

Reluctantly we turned around, cranked the Evinrude, and began puttering home. On our trip north, Maggie began spotting flowers that had bloomed, blown off the stem, and landed in the water and now floated carelessly along. They were white and blue, and Maggie said they looked like some sort of iris. She began scooping them off the water, and in an hour or so she had twenty or thirty blooms.

She noticed that the blooms were spilling from the fingers of the Salkehatchie, and her curiosity grew. At the mouth of one narrow stream leading into the river, we saw half a dozen blooms floating single file behind one larger bloom, like ducklings following a drake. We pulled the raft up alongside a tree, marked the tree with a piece of rope, and puttered home.

The next day we borrowed Amos's fishing canoe, an Old Town, and returned to our rope-marked tree. Maggie wanted to find the source of those blooms, but the raft was too big and bulky, and walking was not an option. No one walked in the swamp. Well, not unless you were Jesus. You could be ankle-deep one minute, and in the next you'd be looking up from the bottom of a twenty-foot hole. The Salkehatchie has a way and a mind all its own, and you don't go in there unless you've got a strategy for getting out. Amos and I grew up listening to stories of lost Confederate gold, escaping slaves chained at the ankles, lost Germans manning a submarine, and Indians who lived in the trees.

Rain had overflowed the swamp and, like tidal waters along the shore, spilled over the edges into the larger body, the Salkehatchie River, that ran alongside it. The flooding happened to coincide with the blooming of what Maggie later learned was a rare iris that grew almost exclusively in a unique combination of two types of water that collided in the swamp. The compost created by the tannic acid in the water, the decomposition in the swamp, the water temperature, and the gentle flow of the water from an underground spring combined to make the perfect petri dish for what we soon dubbed Maggie's Iris. I'm pretty sure some botanist had already labeled it, but he wasn't around to correct us, so the name stuck.

The myths surrounding the swamp were many, but what we knew for certain was that the timber had never been cut, ever. Meaning that some trees in the middle were three or four hundred years old, and the canopy in some spots could be a hundred feet high and make the day seem like night. It was the quietest and most peaceful, untouched, virgin, ancient, and prehistoric land I'd ever seen. Few people had ventured far enough in to really get a look, because the first mile or so could be rather creepy. But when you're married to someone like Maggie, who's passionate about plants and where they come from, creepy just adds to the ambience.

We paddled in past our rope, up and into the swamp where the finger lost its boundary and bled into the landscape. Within a few hundred yards we were surrounded by nothing but trees and water. The trees, wide at the bottom and skinny at the top, grew up out of the black water like natural skyscrapers. Once in, everything looked the same, so I took a compass reading and poled slowly past the trees, the smallest of which were bigger at the base than the hood of Pastor John's Cadillac. While the silence engulfed us, Maggie pointed and I poled.

Behind us in the water, the pollen, which had fallen en masse and coated the water in a yellowish haze, was now marked by the wake of the canoe. If we wanted out, the only markers we had were my compass and that oozing trail back through the pollen, which, given a few hours, would bubble, roll, and flow its way along, covering up any track we'd made.

Meaning our trail in the pollen was about as effective as bread crumbs. Couldn't trust it for very long.

Occasionally we'd look into the water and see where an alligator or snake had rolled along the top of the water and made a similar cut in the pollen. The more I looked, the more I noticed that the surface of the swamp was marred with thousands of such scratches and cuts. Dotted amid all of this traffic atop the yellow brick road were the blooms that Maggie was chasing.

And me? I was chasing Maggie, and Oz lay somewhere in the distance.

I poled for hours, dipping under limbs, into the hearts of great canopies, around the bases of trees wrapped with vines and snakes, and over alligator holes and turtle perches. The coolness of the swamp did little to deter the mosquitoes, which had descended straight out of the Jurassic period. The farther in we went and the closer we seemed to get to the source of the blooms, the more Maggie beamed. After four or five miles, she was standing in the front of the canoe, leaning over the bow, pointing me onward like Lewis or Clark.

At dusk, I grew a bit antsy. I did not want to spend the night in the bottom of this canoe floating in this swamp, but I knew absent a miracle that was about to happen. We were almost out of insect spray, and when darkness came I had a feeling that the really big bugs would come out to play. And despite Maggie's Lewis and Clark mentality at the moment, the first really big bug that dropped on her during the night would end her tour of fun and send her across the top of the water like Peter on the Sea of Galilee.

Luckily, we never got that far. Thirty minutes before it grew too dark to see my hand in front of my face, Maggie pointed and started jumping up and down like a puppy in the window at a pet store. I poled another hundred yards and turned into a clearing where the moon, out early, was shining down like a God-sized spotlight. Maggie sat down, dropped her shoulders, and gasped.

A natural spring, flowing up out of nowhere, rose up like a small bubbling fountain and filtered through hundreds of wild irises that were hooked together via their roots and floating free above the spring. They were connected to nothing other than one another and evidently feeding off whatever was shooting up out of the earth. And given their defined perimeter, it was pretty obvious that they would grow only where the black swamp water met the clear springwater. As soon as the water diluted into the swamp, the flowers quit growing.

Maggie sat back on the bow of the canoe, sweeping her fingers through the tips of the irises in the emerald-green water and inhaling the pungency of the swamp through her lungs and into her limbs. She was surrounded by a sea of white and blue that looked almost fluorescent in the growing moonlight. It lit on her hair, which she had pulled back and up, and then cascaded down her shoulders and spilled into the water below. "Promise me that one day we can come back here."

The gates of the Emerald City opened, and I nodded.


I SIGNED MY APPEAL LETTER, DATED IT, AND STUCK ON THE stamp. It was noon, the sun was high, and Maggie had yet to emerge from our room in the hayloft, so I cranked the tractor, ambled across the road to the ruins of Amos's house, and pulled around back, where his shed stood lonely and isolated. I wedged open the door, picked my way through the banana spiders and cobwebs, and unearthed the canoe. I strapped it across the sides of the wheel wells and drove down to the river.

An hour later, draped in sweat and muscle ache, I reached the marked tree and noticed the first of the blooms floating atop the water. I turned into the swamp, took a compass reading, and began making my Osceola-like journey through the limbs and cypress stumps.

Two hours and five miles later, I had paddled my way into what some might have called the heart of darkness. Truth was, I was a long way from nowhere, but if this place had a heart, it was anything but dark. The farther in you paddled, the closer to the light you came—that's the secret of the swamp.

The blooms dotted the surface of the swamp like bread crumbs, just as they had the year before. I followed the trail and finally pulled up beneath the tree limbs, breaking into the cathedral canopy.

The sunlight lit the tops of the irises in a checkerboard of white and blue dotted with golden-yellow tips. The roots waved in the emerald-green water like mermaid fins. Somewhere high above me an owl hooted, and all around me the pungent ripeness of the decomposing yet perpetually reborn swamp filled my nose like menthol.

I worked quickly. The stalks were stiff, some three feet long, and I laid them in the bow of the canoe, blooms up. Within ten minutes I had about two armfuls. I turned the canoe, pulled hard on the paddle, and, thanks to the opposition of the current, landed the canoe on the riverbank below the house about two and a half hours later.

The sun was down, crickets had come up, and a light breeze lifted along the river. It would be a nice night. I grabbed the flowers, hopped on the tractor, and let third gear roll me home. I stopped at the barn, hopped off, and bounded up the steps, hoping I'd find Maggie awake.

She was sitting at the table, dressed in baggy sweats and

hovering over a cup of tea, her fingers nervously tapping the sides of the mug. Her face was thin and pale—like her eyes. She opened her mouth when I walked in, but closed it when she saw the flowers.

I was dripping with both sweat and river water. I didn't know what to say, so I walked to the sink, laid down the entire bundle of stalks, and start filling the basin with water. Her eyes watered, and she shook her head, then walked to the sink, gently feeling the blooms. She shook her head again and loosed a tear that fell like a BASE jumper down toward her once-painted toenails that were now chipped and peeling.

Her voice was hoarse as if she hadn't used it much. "Same place?" she whispered.

I nodded and watched her filter her fingers through the blooms as she would through the hair of a child.

"You follow the trail on the water?"

I nodded again.

She sat down, folded her arms, and looked at the floor as I leaned against the opposite countertop. There were six feet and a thousand miles between us.

When she crossed her legs, her bent knee raised her sweat-pants just above the ankle, revealing a leg that hadn't been shaved in more than a week. Maybe two. I wanted to say something, anything to keep the conversation going. I pointed at the irises. "I wanted you to . . . well." Then I pointed at her stomach. "How's your tummy?" The words slipped out before I had time to take them back.

She reached up, grabbed a single bloom between her index finger and thumb, shook her head slightly, and then snapped off the bloom like a dead twig. She dropped the bloom in the sink, folded her arms again as if a subzero wind had just blown in through the cracks of the floor, and walked out on the porch, where the curtain seemed to be closing on the stage of our lives.

I looked through the kitchen window at the corn standing tall, still, and silent. The cotton was no different. I had only been to one Broadway show, *Riverdance,* with Maggie in New York, and when they finished that magnificent, glorious show, we jumped from our seats—our faces beaming and hearts racing—and clapped for fifteen minutes while the dancers bowed and smiled. Looking through the window, I heard no encore.

*chapter thirty-two*

I SHOWERED, SHAVED HALF MY FACE IN FRONT OF the cracked glass, turned and shaved the other half, and was sitting on the porch when Maggie walked out the door. She hadn't changed, still wore no shoes, and her hair hadn't been brushed out of her face. The only change showed in her eyes—they were red and puffier.

I stood up. I'd have taken her anywhere.

Blue circled behind her and licked her toes, and she pointed toward the river—her eyes lost beyond the horizon. "I'm going for a walk."

I set down my glass. "I'll go with?"

She held up a hand and shook her head. Without looking at me, she said, "I'll go."

I sat back down and watched her disappear into the corn.

Blue looked at me, and I whispered, "You'd better go with her." He slipped off the porch and into the corn just a few rows south of hers.

When dark came, I was about to go find her when Amos drove around the side of the house. His truck was muddy, he was driving fast, and he was half hanging out the window.

He tilted back his black baseball cap. "You coming?"

I had no idea what he was talking about.

"Come on, Ivory. Check the calendar."

I looked toward the house and back at him, but still nothing clicked into place.

He shook his head. "D.S., you need a keeper." He opened the passenger door and sat with the truck running. "Come on, get in."

I looked off into the corn, then back at Amos. "Where we going?"

"Pastor John's house."

"Why?"

He frowned and looked at his watch. "Dummy, it's your birthday." He let the words sink in. "I never met anyone who forgot his own birthday."

I looked toward the river. "My birthday?"

I pointed out into the corn to tell him why I couldn't come, when Maggie walked out. Her knees were dirty, and the hair on the sides of her face was stuck to her temples. She walked to Amos's side window and asked, "Is Amanda at home?"

Surprised, Amos nodded. "Hey, Maggs." He opened the truck door and slid off the seat. "How you doing, honey?"

Maggie walked up the porch steps, opened the front door, and turned around. A pained smile hung on her face. She crossed her arms. "I've got some things I want to bring her."

Amos looked at me, and I shrugged slightly. He nodded. "Well, I'm sure she'll like that."

Maggie walked inside and shut the door quietly behind her.

He spoke to me, but his mouth faced the door. "We thought if we gave you two some time, things might improve." Maggie's footsteps faded off into the back of the house. "Guess not."

I put a finger in the air just as Blue appeared out at the edge of the corn. "Give me just a minute."

I walked inside and down the hall through our construction site. The house was still a wreck. The walls and attic had been gutted, and if you looked up, you could see the underside of the new aluminum sheet roofing. I found Maggie sitting on the dusty floor of what was once our bedroom, looking out the back window toward the river.

"Maggs, Amos invited us to Pastor John's house tonight for dinner. You want to come?"

She turned, shook her head, and said, "No, you go." She paused and looked back out the window toward the oak that towered above our son's grave. "Tell Amanda I'll bring some things by tomorrow."

The thought of Maggie getting out sounded good, so I said, "I'll drive you. Maybe we could go to Ira's or DQ."

She nodded, but there was no conviction in it.

I stepped back out in the hall. "I'll check on you when I get in." I reached to pull the door shut, but she raised a hand.

"You can leave it open."

I stepped off the porch as Amos stepped out of the barn. "You ought to feed that pig every now and then. She might like you a bit more."

I nodded. "I think I'd better hang around here."

Blue hopped up on the porch and up onto the swing. He laid his nose on his front paw and let out a deep breath.

Amos shook his head. "I think that's about the smartest dog I've ever seen."

I nodded.

"And that pig is quite possibly the nastiest animal I've ever seen." He said something else, but I didn't hear him. Then he punched me in the shoulder and said, "Hey, you in there?"

"Huh?"

"I said, 'When did you move back into the house?'"

"Oh, that. Well, we haven't."

He looked toward our bedroom window where Maggie's shadow was moving around. "And?"

I shrugged. "She talks less, cries more."

Amos climbed into his truck. On the seat next to him sat a manila folder, thick with photographs. I leaned into the open passenger-side window and eyed the folder. Amos gathered the folder and set it on the dashboard. "Those will not help you sleep at night."

I looked at him. "Then how do you?"

"I don't."

"Me either."

# chapter thirty-three

MAGGIE AND I SAT AT THE LAUNDROMAT IN Walterboro trying to sift through several loads of clothing. Mostly mine. I'm the dirty one. Our washer and dryer had been out of commission since the fire burst the pipes that ran through the crawl space in the attic. We thought the appliances themselves were relatively untouched, but we wouldn't know until the plumber showed up, and that might not be until next week. So we sat in the incredibly hot dryer room while the television above played some soap opera. When one of the short episodes flashed back to a woman who was trying to get pregnant, I stood up and turned it off.

Trying to lighten the heaviness, I slipped a pair of my boxer shorts over my head and poked my ears out the leg holes. Maggie was not impressed, but she smiled, even laughed a bit, and then threw a pair of jeans at me. I took the underwear off my head before someone walked in and I embarrassed us both. With my luck, Mr. Sawyer from the adoption agency would appear, and our chances of appeal would vanish.

Earlier yesterday I had stamped my appeal letter and asked for a hearing before the committee to plead our case. According to the letter I had received, an appeal was granted at request and they'd inform me via a phone call—which also had me scared—within two days of receiving my letter.

I pulled a white load from the washer and immediately realized my mistake: I had put a red T-shirt in with the whites. The entire load looked like a chemistry experiment gone bad. All of my underwear and T-shirts were red, which was sort of funny, but then Maggie's white cotton gown came out looking pink and splotchy. There was little we could do, so I threw the whole load in the dryer and started it spinning.

Maggie needed a few things, so I sent her on ahead to the drugstore next door and told her I'd finish folding as soon as things were dry. I fluffed, folded, and dropped the three baskets in the van before catching up with her.

The air in the store was filled with what sounded like three kids arguing over a toy. An overloaded mom with one child on her hip, one tugging on her shorts, and two more rolling in the aisle at her feet, fighting over a wooden airplane, was the center of attention and distraction.

I found Maggie two aisles over. Listening. Leaning against the greeting cards. She was trembling, trying not to lose it, and she fell on me when I walked up alongside her. She buried her face in my chest and clutched my shirt. I turned her, and we walked slowly from the store, having forgotten what we came for.

When we got home, Maggie had collected herself enough to walk inside and put on a pot of coffee. The answering machine was blinking at me, and I punched it without thinking.

"Hello, Dr. and Mrs. Styles, this is Kayla Sommers at the Charleston Adoption Agency."

Maggie froze, holding the percolator under the faucet.

"We received your letter of appeal and have set your date with the committee for Monday, August 13."

*Two more weeks.* I wasn't sure we'd last another day. Maggie's eyes were lost out the kitchen window, across the cotton toward the river.

Kayla continued, ". . . is scheduled for 10:00 AM. Please try to be on time." Her voice fell to a whisper. "They prefer you are early."

Maggie set the percolator in the sink and walked quietly outside and onto the porch while the water overflowed the container.

I followed her. "Honey, I was going to tell you. I just . . ."

She touched my arm gently and shook her head. "That's—" She folded her arms and, despite the 94-degree heat, stepped into the cotton and didn't look back.

A LIGHT RAIN WOKE ME BEFORE THE SUN ON SATURDAY morning. I lifted my head and listened to the heavy drops as they pounded the corn and made their way to the house. Seconds later, they hammered the tin roof above. The warmth beneath the sheets told me Maggie lay beside me. I reached across the mattress and found her back turned to me and her body rolled into a ball. I doubted she was asleep.

I stood, scratched my head, and climbed downstairs, leaning against the barn door. The itch and high-pitched sound in my ear broke my gaze on the river. I swatted the mosquito, but he'd already bitten me. My fingers crawled around my neck and found that he hadn't been alone.

I hurried across the yard, sat on the railing, and rested my head on my knee, listening to the deluge. Rainwater gathered in the rows and trickled in tiny creeks down toward the river. With this much rain in such a short amount of time, the ground could not absorb it all. Most of it would run to the river and raise the water level a foot or so.

I grabbed one of Maggie's two remaining watermelons off the porch and slit it down the middle. Cracking it open, I gave half to Blue, who sank his muzzle directly into the meat. I sat my half on my lap and slowly began cutting out the heart. It was sweet, perfect, and only served to impress upon me the gulf that had spread between Maggie and me.

I grabbed a paper plate from the kitchen, cut a large piece of melon, and walked to the barn, where I climbed back up to the loft. I knocked quietly and waited. When she said nothing, I turned the knob and pushed. With the sun just coming over the pasture, I could see her lying in bed, turned on her side, facing away from me. I sat on the edge of the bed and held the plate in my lap, "I brought you some watermelon."

Maggie said nothing.

I placed my hand on her bare shoulder and shook her ever so gently.

She lifted the covers over her shoulder and covered her head with a pillow.

The ceiling fan above us had been set on "tornado," so I clicked it twice to "gentle breeze." I whispered, "Maggs?"

She made no response. Dr. Frank had said that while her emotions and hormones got squared away, I'd do well to give her some space. Well, I'd done that, and the more I gave her, the more she took. I shook her gently again. "Maggs?"

Without warning, she sat up in bed, turned toward me, and looked me square in the eyes. Hers were puffy and covered in red streaks, and they told me she'd been crying. I opened my mouth to say something, but she pointed her crooked, double-jointed finger in my face. Her voice was low and on the verge of cracking. "Don't."

"Maggs, I know you're hurting, but—"

"No!" she screamed. She grabbed the plate of watermelon and hurled it across the room, covering me in red puree. "You *don't know*. You can't possibly!"

"But why won't you talk to me?"

She turned, picked up the lamp from the bedside table, and hurled it across the loft. I ducked, and it, too, exploded on the wall behind me. Maggs lay back down in bed, pulled the covers up and the pillow over her head, and began a muffled sob.

I picked what was left of the watermelon off the floor, placed it back on the plate, and laid it on the bed. I stood there for a minute, watching her shoulders shake. One heel was sticking out from underneath the blankets, so I covered it.

I tried to make sense of it but couldn't. Maybe it was the hurt talking. I pulled a pair of socks from the dresser, set them on the bedside table, and walked out, pulling the door shut behind me.

# chapter thirty-four

I HUNG AROUND THE HOUSE UNTIL LUNCH, BUT Maggs never showed, so I went for a drive. I pulled around the house and almost ran into the front end of Amos's truck.

Amanda was at the wheel. She rolled down the window. "She in?"

I thumbed over my shoulder at the loft. "Yeah, but I don't think she wants to see anyone right now."

Amanda nodded. "Maybe I'll try anyway." She tilted her head and chewed on her lip, sizing me up. "How're you doing?"

I shrugged.

"You sure?" She was getting more like Amos every day.

I turned toward the barn and said, "Make sure she knows it's you. Otherwise, get ready to duck."

I meandered along back roads until I found myself weaving

in a rather straight line to Jake's car lot. The closer I got, the faster I drove. I turned into the lot going a little too fast, hit the brakes, and slid to a dusty stop in front of his office. When I looked at my hands, my knuckles were white.

Jake walked out, holding the last bite of a hot dog. Both mustard and ketchup streaked across his white shirt and blue plaid tie. He shoved in the last bite and wiped his mouth with his tie.

"Well, hey, Dylan. Looks like you've grown to like the family minivan."

I hopped out and looked across the lot. My heart sank. I stuck my hands in my pockets and looked again. "Hey, Jake."

He pointed at the van. "How's she running?" He seemed to ask for both my sake and for his.

"Oh, fine, fine. No problems."

He rubbed his hands together and looked relieved. "Good, good. Well, what can I do for you?"

Jake was one of the unlucky follicle-challenged guys who had started losing his hair in high school. He was now combing one of his sideburns clear over to the other ear.

"I was just in the neighborhood and thought maybe I'd stop by and see if I left some old sunglasses in my truck. They're not worth much, but . . ."

He laughed. "Yeah, I know what you mean. I'll check the drawer in the office, but we searched that thing pretty good before we sold it. I don't think—"

"What?"

Jake stepped backward. "Yeah, we searched under the seats, in the glove box, everywhere. We do that with all the cars before we sell them."

That was the second time he'd said that.

"You sold it?"

Jake looked at me and tilted his head. "Well, yeah. Ummm, see, a fellow I never seen come in here, offered me cash, and drove out five minutes later. It was like he was looking for that exact truck, 'cause when he got in it, he just knew."

I leaned against the van and whispered, "You sold my truck?"

Jake pulled the three-by-five-inch card from his shirt pocket and said, "Well, if you're in the market."

"No." I waved my hand. "No thanks. I just thought . . . since I was driving by . . ."

His wife opened the door and shaded her eyes against the sun, and two kids pressed their noses against the glass.

"Hey, Dylan, you want some lunch? I just made some spaghetti."

The kids' fingers were covered in spaghetti sauce, as was the window.

I stepped forward. "No, ma'am. Thank you. I won't be a minute; thanks anyway."

Jake stepped forward and spoke softly. "Dylan, I'm real sorry. It's just that—" He pointed behind him. "This guy offered me—"

I shook my head and patted him on the shoulder. "No, Jake, it's not . . . I'm sorry. You did right."

"I know how you loved that truck. I was surprised when you wanted to trade it."

"Well, we're trying to adopt, and—"

"I can keep an eye out."

I stepped into the van. "Thanks. That'd be just fine." I cranked the engine and shifted the lever down into drive. "Thanks again."

Jake held an imaginary phone to his ear and called above the sound of crunching gravel. "If I see anything, I'll give you a holler."

I waved out the window and drove slowly toward Digger.

*chapter thirty-five*

A MILE OUT OF JAKE'S DRIVEWAY, SOMETHING thumped the underside of the hood, and then the air conditioner turned from cold to hot. I checked the rearview mirror and saw bits and pieces of my shredded compressor belt strewn across the road. I rolled down the windows, felt the heat blast my face, and missed my truck.

Bryce's place was immaculate and empty. The only signs of life were five crows that had lit atop the center screen and squawked at me when I emerged from the tree line. I walked through the trailer, across the deck, and back into the woods where the obstacle course had been extended. Somebody had brought in some heavy machinery and extended the run section down into the soggy lowlands. The wet, grassy ground ran beneath the oaks and around the bamboo for almost a mile before it encountered the edge of the swamp, which fluctuated with the rain.

By the time I reached the swamp, sweat trickled from every pore in my body, sticking my shirt to me like a vacuum seal. When I reached the edge of the water, I didn't feel like going back, so I sat up on a hickory stump and tried to exhale my anger. That's when I saw the rope.

It was new black nylon, looped around a tree and tied in a hitching knot much like someone would use to tie up a horse. One pull on the free end and it would pull itself loose. The rope led me around the tree and about six feet away to a fourteen-foot johnboat. It floated empty, dry, well used, and complete with one hand-oiled oar. I looked off into the water and saw that as recently as today, someone had paddled through the pollen. The trail had yet to erase itself in the water.

I pulled the rope, pushed off, and dipped the oar in the water, following the cracks in the pollen. They weren't too hard to follow, and neither was the small canal that frequent use had created between the trees. Nighttime would be another story, but between fresh scars on the trees and places that were only wide enough for the boat, the path was hard to miss in the daylight. A mile passed, then another, and finally another.

Three hours later, I tried to find the sun and realized I had made a big mistake. I was about to spend the night in the swamp. If I'd had any sense at all, I'd have looped myself to a tree, lain down in the bottom of that boat, pulled my shirt over my head to protect myself from mosquitoes, and tried to get some sleep. Problem was, I wasn't feeling very sensible.

I poled another hour into the darkness until I could scarcely see twenty feet in front of my face. I set down the oar, coasted across the black water, and checked Papa's watch, which I think told me it was after eight, and only then did I smell the smoke.

Trying not to bang the side of the boat, I poled and paddled closer. Finally I sat down in the back and inched toward a cluster of trees. High above me, maybe thirty feet in the air, I saw a single flame, flickering like a kerosene lantern. It shone through what looked like slats in a tree fort, except this fort was about the size of our bedroom at the house. The timbers supporting it were rough-cut beams that stretched across the cypress trees shooting up out of the swamp.

The light from the lantern shone down through the hole in the floor and illuminated a rope ladder. I tied up the boat, stepped quietly onto the ladder, and pulled myself up. Some thirty-five feet later, I poked my head through the trapdoor and looked around. What I saw amazed me.

The roof above was made of aluminum sheeting, supported with rough-cut trusses, making the inside watertight. The tongue-and-groove cypress floor had been swept clean and looked loosely octagonal in shape. The eight walls also were cypress plank, and each had been fitted with a window.

On two walls there was a kitchen of sorts. A large farmhouse sink had been sunk in the countertop; it was fed by a hand pump connected to a series of pipes that disappeared through the floor and evidently into the tannic black water of the Salkehatchie below. I worked the pump, and crystal-clear water flowed out, meaning someone had either dug a well or tapped into a spring. Maybe both.

Across the room was a built-in bunk, and on the bedside table sat a worn copy of Herodotus. Occupying the rest of the room were two chairs, a shelf with about a hundred Louis L'Amour books, and a large footlocker. Leaning in a rack along the last wall rested three rifles and as many shotguns. One of the rifles was fitted with a large telescopic sight, making it look like some sort of sniper rifle. Four handguns—two revolvers and two automatics—hung from nails driven into the wall. Each was oiled, and despite the fact that most had a matte black finish, each glistened slightly in the pulsating light behind me.

The idea had crossed my mind that Bryce had simply built himself a summer home, which was odd given that he could have owned a slope-sided chalet in Aspen. But my other idea said that someone had built a getaway shack, hidden in the middle of nowhere, that allowed him to keep an eye on his moonshine still, marijuana plants, or meth lab with little fear of intrusion.

My shadow stretched across the room like Peter Pan's, and my heart pounded like a war drum. I looked down into the water at the boat, around the room, and in search of fading shadows. All of that told me one thing: I could not make it out of this swamp tonight, and the best opportunity I had was to sleep right here. Yet I also knew that whoever had built this place and left that light on would be back, and based on the difficulty of finding this place, I wasn't sure he wanted to be found.

I stepped toward the wall and lifted one of the revolvers off the nail. A Smith & Wesson .357. I clicked open the cylinder and found it loaded. I stuffed it inside my pants and stretched out on the bed, where for two hours I kept my eyes pried wide open. Finally sleep set in, and I dozed off. Sometime later, I woke to the sound of someone standing at the sink.

I cracked open my eyes, but the lantern had been dimmed. I could see the form of a person standing some eight feet from me. I slipped the revolver from my belt and lay as still as I possibly could. From the smell in the room and the repetitive motion of the man's arms, I figured he was cleaning a fish.

Only when I sat up did the bunk creak. I slowly aimed the pistol at the broad dark frame in front of me and waited. It was useless to try to aim, because my hand was shaking like a leaf. When the person turned, and the lantern lit his face, I nearly lost my bladder again.

I lay back, shaking my head, and dropped the pistol on the floor. *"Bryce!* What the—!?"

Bryce clicked on a gas stove and threw the fish filets onto the skillet. He poured in a touch of oil, then reached out a window over the ledge and lifted the lid on a propane grill that seemed somehow built into the side of the tree house. He used some tongs to flip over whatever was on there and returned to the fish. He added seasoning and some pepper and popped the tab on a Chek soda. Then he pumped the hand pump in the sink, filling a glass of water, which he swigged down in three gulps.

While the fish sizzled and the grill cooked whatever it was cooking, Bryce set the table with two plates, two forks, and two glasses of water. He pulled plates from above his head, flipped the fish one last time, and then slid two filets each onto the plates. He reached across the ledge and pulled in what appeared to be two ears of corn and two baked potatoes, wrapped in aluminum foil.

While I worked to reinsert my jaw into its rightful place, Bryce sat down and turned his attention to his food. Beneath the light, I could see he was decked out in all black, his feet were bare, and his .45 was tucked in its shoulder holster on the left side of his chest. He looked at me and continued eating as if he were judging the food for its culinary details.

I sat at the table and looked at the breakfast before me while Bryce took small bites and paid me little mind.

"How long have you had this place?"

Bryce chewed, pushed his food around his plate. If he heard me, he didn't appear to care.

I tried again. "What do you do out here?"

Bryce looked around, scraped the last of his fish onto his fork, and filled his glass again. Conversations with Bryce were often one-sided. He'd talk when he felt like it.

I looked at my watch and knew that I'd been gone too long. "Bryce, I don't mean to be unkind, but I need to get going, and I need some help getting out of here."

Bryce finished off another glass of water, then walked to a bare wall and opened a shoulder-width door that led onto a balcony, four feet by four feet square and surrounded by a railing. On the balcony sat a wooden box fitted with a porcelain white toilet seat. With his back to me, Bryce lifted the seat and peed through the hole.

I listened as the stream fell thirty-five feet to the water below. I tried again. "Well, I need to get home to Maggie."

Bryce shut the door and spoke for the first time. "She's fine." He washed his hands in the sink, sat back down, picked up his corn, and started into it like a typewriter.

"Bryce." I set down my fork and wiped my mouth. I noticed that since being up here, I hadn't swatted at a single mosquito. "How long have you been watching my house?"

He shrugged.

"Why?"

He grew very still, and his eyes glazed over as if someone else had entered the room. He cleared his plate and then climbed down the ladder to the boat. Alongside it sat a small black-and-green two-man canoe.

We loaded into his boat, and with the two of us paddling and Bryce's sense of direction, we banked the canoe onto the grassy landing below the obstacle course before daylight. I stepped out and turned to thank him, but he had already backed up and was poling himself back into the swamp. When I tried to open my mouth, he just waved. For the first time since I'd met Bryce, I saw an expression of pain on his face—the kind that had sewn itself into the sinews of his person.

I turned down our drive at daylight and pulled around the house. Blue came trotting out to meet me. Maggie too. She was wrapped in a blanket, and her short hair was sticking up as if she hadn't slept.

She saw that I was okay and looked as though she wanted to say something, but the words didn't make it out of her mouth. She returned to the barn, her blanket dragging on the ground, climbed into the loft, and then shut the door and clicked on the AC unit.

Blue licked my fingers, and his quiet whining told me what Maggie's silence and my heart already had—that I'd been stupid to leave, selfish to go to Jake's, and that spending the night out was a dumb thing to do.

*chapter thirty-six*

FROM THE KITCHEN, I WATCHED MAGGIE WALK OUT of the barn and into her vegetable garden—a small forty-by-forty-foot patch where she experimented with growing vegetables. Ordinarily, it was overgrown with produce; now it sat overrun with weeds. Even the raccoons had quit coming around.

I poured her a cup of coffee and met her midway through what was once the tomato section. She took it and sipped beneath the broad rim of her hat. I tipped her hat back slightly and then leaned on a tomato stake. "You sleep any?"

She shook her head and sipped again. The caffeine did little to raise her eyelids.

I looked at the weeds around us. "You want some help?"

She smiled and let me off the hook. And while that was nice, it reminded me of how much Maggie had withdrawn.

A little later I drove to Walterboro, stopped by Dr. Frank's office, and then found a hat store that I'd heard about in the whispers around church. An elderly lady helped me find what I needed, wrapped it in a box, and sent me on my way with a remembering look in her eye.

Evening brought a blessed cool breeze, a warm shower, and some welcome cloud cover that blocked out the late afternoon sun, dropping the temperature into the upper seventies. Understanding that she was allowed to change her mind at a moment's notice and without reason, I was not surprised when Maggie told me she wanted to get out of the house. We cleaned up, dressed, and drove the four miles to the church property.

A blue circus tent had been erected above the cement foundation, which had been cleared of ash and rubble and new portions poured. Another tent stood alongside, and beneath it sat tables loaded with food.

Cars lined the roadside, and despite the impromptu service, women showed up wearing their favorite and newest hats. Amos had assigned a young deputy to direct traffic, and elsewhere young men in coats and ties were escorting ladies across the dirt parking lot to folding chairs beneath the tent.

Maggie stepped out of the van and looked both ways across the highway before I could get her attention from the rear of the van. "Honey?" She walked around the side, and I handed her the box. "Didn't want you to feel underdressed."

She accepted the box, untied the bow, and lifted the hat from inside. It was a blue sun hat with a broad white band and feathers on one side. Miraculously, it matched both her eyes and her dress.

I held the tail of the ribbon while she settled the brim on her brow, forcing tears out of the corners of her eyes. I pulled my white handkerchief from my pocket and gave it to her, and she dabbed her eyes. She kissed me on the cheek—which told me she was sorry—and hooked her arm inside mine—which told me that she loved me—and we crossed the street.

We took a seat near the back while those around us filled up. Amos looked spry in his coat and tie, which Amanda no doubt had matched because he hadn't displayed that much style in his entire life.

Amanda was busy with the flower arrangement and white tablecloth spread across the folding table up front. Her tummy had grown some more. She was now into the full-on pregnant woman waddle, and she glowed from head to toe. She saw us and hurried down the aisle to hug Maggie.

Maggie smiled, teared up, and placed her palm across Amanda's tummy as though feeling the ripeness of a melon. Amanda gawked at Maggie's hat while I marveled at my wife.

I watched her—the way her shoulders moved with the tilt of her head, the way her smile lit up the six people around her, the way her hair, tucked behind her ears, framed her face like baby's breath. I thought about the way her heartbeat sounded the rhythm for our dance atop the magnolia floor. I wanted to tell her all this but didn't know how. Just because something is broken doesn't mean it's no good. Doesn't mean you throw it away. It just means it's broken, and broken is okay. I wanted to tell her that broken is still beautiful, still works, still wakes me in the morning, and at the end of every day past and those to come, I can love broken.

The choir, a purple mass of matching robes and sweaty faces, appeared and started swaying and humming. The congregation stood, ladies fanned themselves with bulletins, and the choir began clapping and singing a responsive hymn, proving once again that they had more rhythm in five minutes than I'd had in my entire life. We swayed, sang, and clapped until fifteen minutes later when Pastor John stepped up and the choir lowered their voices to underscore his.

He stood several minutes, smiling and looking for an entrance. Finally he raised his hands, the choir dropped their voices even more, and he said, "If you're with the fire department, please raise your hand."

We did.

He laughed. "Well, if you needed a reason not to end up in hell, now you've got it."

The laughter spread like a wave. It felt good.

Pastor John tucked his Bible beneath his arm. When he looked up, his face was soaked, but it wasn't with sweat.

Up front, Li'l Dylan said, "Daddy! Daddy!" Amos picked him up and bounced him on his knee.

Maggie grabbed my hand and squeezed it.

Pastor John raised his chin and began, "I've been asking the Lord to forgive me for the things in my past that brought this upon all of you. I have asked before, and I will ask again, please forgive me."

The choir swayed and hummed a melody, and Pastor John placed his Bible on the altar. He palmed the sweat off his cheeks, dabbed his eyes, and returned his handkerchief to his pocket. Finally he picked up his Bible again, turned toward the back, and read, "And God will wipe away every tear from their eyes; there shall be no more death, nor sorrow, nor crying."

Maggie's fingers wrapped more tightly about mine.

"There shall be no more pain, for the former things have passed away."

Maggie dropped her head and fought back a sob, and I started looking for an exit.

"Behold, I make all things new."

Maggie dropped her head, stood, and hurried between the chairs and out the back of the tent. Pastor John waited while I followed her out. She ran across the parking lot toward the river, hit her knees, and buried her face in her hands. The moss hanging from the oak above looked like arms swaying in the wind, reaching down to sweep the riverbank.

I knelt next to her, and she fell against me. Finally she managed a breath deep enough, and I helped her to her feet. We made our way across the parking lot toward the van.

Midway through the cars, an SUV pulled up to the back of the tent, and the driver got out. He was tall and broad-shouldered, and his skin was dark as night. Although I couldn't see his face, his body posture told me that he wasn't here for church. Maggie, too, picked up on it and stopped walking.

The man walked up to the back of the tent and began striding confidently down the middle aisle toward Pastor John. I led Maggie to the side of the tent where we could see and hear inside.

Pastor John saw the man, stopped midsentence, and said, "Welcome, James."

The man called James stopped and laughed loudly. "Thought I'd stop in and see how the flock was doing, Preacher."

Amos, sitting in the front row and still holding L.D. on his knee, tensed like a dog before a fight.

Pastor John never skipped a beat. He pointed to a seat down front. "There's always room for one more."

James laughed. "No, no, I think I've given you enough of my money for one lifetime."

Amos's deputy slipped out the side and around the back. He stood at the rear of the tent, speaking into a radio clipped to his uniform shirt.

Pastor John addressed the congregation. "Friends, this is

CHARLES MARTIN565

James Whittaker. James and I were once partners, stealing everything we could get our hands on and even some things we couldn't."

Not a foot shuffled; not a person could be heard breathing. If Pastor John was afraid, he didn't show it.

James smiled. "You know, John, after twenty years in prison, I learned something very important." He twirled in the aisle, walked toward the front, and pointed at him. "In the end, we all get what we got coming!"

Pastor John nodded and stepped forward again, now just a few feet from Whittaker. He looked him in the eyes. "Yes, we do."

Whittaker looked down his left arm where Amos sat two feet away—ready to pounce. Had L.D. not been on his lap, I think he would have. Amanda sat next to him, her arm hooked inside his—both holding on to and holding down.

Whittaker looked at L.D., then at Amos. He leaned closer and said, "I don't think he has your eyes." Then he turned and walked sideways across the front of the altar and out the side of the church. He weaved among the ropes that held down the tent.

I don't know the cause—it had something to do with the smug look on his face. The look sparked something I hadn't felt in a long time. Somewhere inside me, deep down, something snapped. I stepped in front of him, started at my toes, and threw everything I had through my fist and into his face. It was the hardest I'd ever hit anyone in my life.

His head jerked sideways and blood trickled off his lip, and faster than a cat, he backhanded me four feet in the air, over a tent rope, and flat on my back, where the stars spun in circles above me.

I looked up, tried to balance on an elbow, thought I might vomit, and saw a black freight train flying sideways through the darkness.

Amos's body-tackle toppled Whittaker like a bowling pin. The collision sounded loud and painful—like two Mack trucks meeting head-on in an intersection. Amos landed on top, fended off a vicious right, and then landed his own squarely on Whittaker's chin. Two seconds later he had Whittaker facedown and hogtied. Little mud bubbles were circling around Whittaker's nose and popped every time he exhaled—which was often as he fought the thick zip ties that bound his hands and feet.

Amos's suit was smeared with mud and soaked with sweat, and the seams behind his shoulders were stretched taut. He squeezed the sides of Whittaker's cheeks so that they'd have a better chance of being cut by his teeth. He pointed Whittaker's face at me and leaned over him, whispering low enough that the folks sitting a few feet away in the folding chairs couldn't hear him. "That is my best friend on the planet. You ever do that again, and I'll finish this fight."

Whittaker outweighed Amos by maybe eighty pounds, but Amos's adrenaline seemed to be making up the difference. He pulled back my eyelid, studied my pupil, slapped me gently on the face, and then picked up Whittaker like a sack of potatoes, dragged him to his deputy's car, and flung him onto the backseat.

Amos and Amanda followed Maggie and me home and helped get me settled in the loft. My eye was turning black and puffy, but my jaw was still connected. And I still had all my teeth. Amanda gave me something for the pain, and while my arms and legs turned to noodles, the three of them stood over me and talked in whispers.

"You be all right?" Amos asked.

I tried to nod, but my words sounded as though I'd just come from a drill-happy dentist. "I've been hit harder."

Amos shook his head. "I doubt it." He pulled the door

behind him and whispered in hushed tones, "We can hold him tonight, until he makes bail, then . . ."

Amanda spoke up, louder. "Amos, this is not going to stop."

He poked his head back through the door and nodded at me. "Keep your guard up."

"You too."

They left, and I climbed right out of bed and watched their truck's taillights disappear. Then I fumbled my way down the steps, hobbled across the yard, and found Blue standing on the front porch, stretching. I walked into the house, using the hallway walls like curbs, unlocked my writing closet, and pulled out the Winchester. I slid a shell into the chamber, clicked the safety on, and walked back into the barn.

ABOUT MIDNIGHT MAGGIE GOT OUT OF BED AND STOOD A long time in the shower. Long after the hot water ran cold, she turned off the stream and stood dripping, eyes closed, leaning against the post that held the showerhead and shaking her head.

I watched from the loft and saw only what one eye and one slit allowed. Maggie's lips were trembling, goose bumps traveled up and down her arms, and her shoulders were tilted at an angle. I climbed down out of the loft and handed her a towel.

She wrapped it around herself, tucking it beneath her arms but not bothering to dry with it.

"You hungry? I could fix some—"

She looked at me as if I'd lost my mind. I turned to cross the yard and find something in the kitchen when she called, "D.S." It'd been a long time since she called me by that name.

Maybe it was time. Maybe I could come clean and tell her the stories I'd been hiding. I stepped closer, into the single bulb above the shower. "Maggie, I know how you—"

She stood straight, her back rigid, and pointed her finger at me. *"Don't* tell me you know how I feel!"

"Honey, I was just saying—"

"You don't know anything! You can't possibly!" She dropped her towel and stood clutching her stomach as if she'd been shot. "You don't know what it's like." She held out her fingers. "Three of your own!"

She clutched her stomach again, and I walked closer.

She held me off. "What kind of a woman am I!? What good is—" She pounded her stomach and chest and squeezed the taut skin. *"Why!?"*

She fell to her knees and beat the pallet that served as the shower floor. I picked up the towel and draped it over her shoulders. Blue hung his eyes over the loft, afraid to come down but troubled by the sound. Her crying quieted Pinky, who had started to complain about her lack of a midnight snack.

I turned around, kicked the stall, and told her to hush.

Maggie collected her towel, climbed naked up to the loft, and shut the door behind her.

I walked to the house and into the kitchen, where I percolated some coffee, threw some ice in a ziplock, and then walked back to the barn and nursed both my eye and my caffeine need at the base of the loft. I looked across the yard at our house, draped in a blue tarp, smelling like smoke, and by most definitions sitting in shambles. I looked up at the closed door, thought about Maggie tossing tearfully inside, and then considered the state of our lives, which was by most definitions much like our house.

I shook my head, spat, poured out the cold coffee, and wiped my eyes—loss is a painful thing.

*chapter thirty-seven*

AROUND 3:00 AM—SOME THREE HOURS AND FOUR cups of coffee later, I sat leaning against the barn door, downwind from Pinky, when Amos's voice crackled over the scanner. It took a second to recognize him because he was out of breath and nearly screaming.

"114 to 110, 114 to 110!"

"110 to 114, go ahead, 114."

"207 in progress. Suspect is 962. I've got a 998 and 999, NOW!"

"114, what's your 20?"

"Parking garage southeast of the hospital."

"10-4, 114. Do you know the name of the person who's been kidnapped?"

There was a pause, then a click from Amos's radio. His whisper was barely audible. "Amanda . . . 'Manda Carter."

I jumped off the steps, climbed the stairs, and burst through the door. The sound woke Maggie, who jumped up angry and cross. I grabbed the shotgun and jumped into my boots.

"Come on," I managed. "It's Amos. They took Amanda."

Maggie moved quickly, and we met at the van about the same time. I placed the shotgun in the backseat and made room for Blue while I dropped the gearshift into drive and dug a trench spinning dirt out to the road.

Ten minutes later I slid to a stop in front of Pastor John's house, which was lit up like a runway. Police cars and flashing lights were everywhere. Standing on the front porch, Li'l Dylan was crying and could not be consoled. Maggie jumped out of the van, ran barefooted across the grass, and picked him up.

She wrapped her arms around him and pulled a pacifier out of her pocket. She smiled at him and put the handle end of the pacifier in her mouth, and he bit. He laid his head on her shoulder, his crying quieted, and they disappeared inside.

Several deputies had gathered around the trunk of one car as a SWAT truck pulled up and several men jumped out. Amos stood in the middle, spouting orders like a man possessed. He ripped the microphone off his shoulder and screamed, "And tell the judge I need that warrant now!"

The dispatcher responded, and Amos swore. "I don't care what his aide says; you get him out of bed now!"

Pastor John stood nearby in a white T-shirt, slacks, and slippers.

I eased up next to him and asked, "What happened?"

He swallowed. "Amanda was on call. Her beeper went off about two o'clock. Amos drove her to the hospital and dropped her off. When she walked in the door, a truck pulled up, blocking Amos, and two men jumped out. They wrestled her into the truck." He crossed his arms and walked back inside the house.

I edged closer to the circle of law enforcement men huddled in the street. I heard them say that the highways and streets leading out of town were covered, but the expression on their faces told me they were looking for a needle in a haystack. I wanted to help but knew I'd do well to stay out of their way.

I walked inside and helped Mrs. Lovett make coffee, then I found Maggie in the den. The lights were off, and L.D. was asleep in her arms. When I walked in, she held a finger to her lips. I offered coffee and she shook her head, pointing outside and waving me off.

I walked back outside just as the men loaded up and squealed off down the street. Jumping into the van, I followed them across town to what looked like a duplex. Three men in black with *POLICE* written across their backs in reflective white letters, carrying shotguns and pistols, ran to the door on the right, while three more ran around back. They waited five seconds, then kicked the door in and stormed inside the house. I sat in the front seat of the van a block down the road.

Within seconds, fifteen more police cars and a dozen undercover cars had parked in front and lit the house with both spotlights and headlights. Amos ran into the house, followed quickly by a team of thick-muscled men.

I stepped out of the van, leaned against a fence, and noticed a small boy looking out the window of a house next door. He waved at me, and I waved back. Five minutes later, he crawled out through a hole in his fence wearing Spider-Man pajamas and carrying a plastic squirt gun. He was a good-looking kid, might have been ten, and his eyes were as big as half-dollars. He started to wave the gun at me, and I quickly said, "Hey, let's not get confused with the bad guys."

He looked at his gun, then at the swarm of law enforcement

a block away, and nodded. He sat down on the curb and said, "They ain't there no more."

"Who's not?" I said, sitting down next to him.

"The fishermen."

"Who?"

He pointed at the house. "Two guys. Lots of tattoos. Said they liked to fish."

"They say what they were fishing for?"

He shook his head. "Nope. But they had a canoe."

I stood and started to walk away when the kid offered, "But I don't think they really liked to fish."

"Why's that?"

"'Cause," he said, "they didn't have no fishing poles."

I asked permission of one of Amos's deputies, and he escorted me inside the house where Amos and his men were huddled around a big table, poring over maps of the Salk and a printout of times—almost like a TV guide but without the stations or programs. Amos saw me, and his eyes returned to the printout. He studied it another minute, turned his attention to the map, then back to the printout. Finally his head tilted back and he sat down in the chair behind him.

I stepped up alongside, and he laid the printout on the table. "It's Amanda's on-call schedule," he whispered.

DAYLIGHT FOUND US AT THE POLICE STATION, WHICH HAD been transformed into a multi-agencied communications center. Law enforcement of all colors, sizes, and uniforms were busily manning phones and radios, hovering over maps, and bumping into one another.

Around 9:00 AM Amos disappeared into an office and shut the door. I followed. The room did not have windows, and the lights were off. Amos was kneeling on the floor, his head in his hands.

I sat next to him and said nothing.

After a minute he looked up, wiped his eyes, and shook his head. "They just released Whittaker. Made bail. Can't hold him." He wiped his eyes. "We've got most every agent in the state out looking for her. If they're in a car, on a road, at a rest area, or within a city limit, we've got a chance of finding them. The first forty-eight hours are the most critical."

About then the lightbulb clicked on. "What if they're not traveling by car?"

Amos looked at me suspiciously.

"I talked to a kid a block down from the house your team stormed. He said two guys with tattoos had a canoe, said they liked to fish but didn't have any fishing rods."

Amos scanned the floor, then jumped onto his feet and walked back out into the command center.

BY EVENING, THINGS HAD COOLED DOWN. ALL THINGS except Amos. I called the Lovetts' house, and Maggie picked up.

"Hey," I said.

"Hey," she whispered, as though someone was sleeping.

"You okay?"

"Yeah, you?"

I shut the door of the office I was in and sat in the chair. "Yeah, just standing around trying to figure out how to help. How's L.D.?"

"He misses his momma."

Just then an undercover officer ran into the room and tapped a superior on the shoulder.

"Hey, something's happening. I'll call you later."

"Be careful."

I walked out into the room where the superior was handing Amos a sheet of paper. He read the dispatch, and his face turned nearly white. He looked down at the ground, steadied himself with both hands, and said, "I'll go." He spoke to a man sitting behind a desk. "You're in charge. I'll be back in a few hours."

Amos walked to a water dispenser, filled a cup, and swigged it down. Half the water dribbled down his chest.

"Wherever you're going, I'm going."

He looked at me, his eyes a road map of red. He nodded, swallowed hard, and managed, "Thank you."

We loaded into his truck, and Amos drove through town and onto I-95 south toward Savannah. He flashed his lights, increased our speed, and drove without saying anything until we reached the outskirts of town. The AC was on high, and he was sweating. He spoke above the noise.

"Amanda has a birthmark about the size of a quarter on her left hip. You wouldn't ever see it unless you were married to her." He tried to laugh. "I kid her sometimes that it looks like a set of Mickey Mouse ears."

He fell silent then as we pulled into town and parked in front of the city morgue. Amos steadied himself on the front of the truck and took a deep breath. We walked through the swinging front doors and were met by a man in a white coat who looked like a doctor but did not smell like one.

"Sergeant Carter?"

Amos nodded.

"Follow me."

Another man in uniform stepped aside as Amos passed and then stepped in front of me and put his hand on my chest.

I looked at him and didn't blink. "I'm with him."

We walked down a long hall and into a sterile room where three black bags lay zipped up across three stainless steel tables. Two lay together on one side of the room; the third lay alone against the far wall. The white-coated man led Amos to the single bag and cleared his throat.

"She was found in an area of woods outside of town. We know that she's twentysomething, was wearing medical scrubs when we found her, in her third trimester, and—was decapitated after death." He looked from Amos to me and back to Amos. "We haven't found her head yet."

Amos steadied himself on the table, gritted his teeth, and placed his hand on the zipper. His hand trembled, he sucked in a deep breath, and one knee buckled. Finally he placed both hands on the table and shook his head.

I put a hand on his shoulder and looked at the bag. "Which hip?" I whispered.

Amos squinted and managed, "Right."

I stepped between Amos and the bag, grabbed the zipper, and pulled it toward the feet of the person. I pulled back on the bag, and at my nod, the doctor slid on a pair of gloves and rolled the body on its side. I studied the hip, turned toward Amos, and shook my head. "It's not her."

Amos turned and walked down the hall and out the front door. He turned into the grass along the front walk, fell to his knees, and vomited. His sobs and groans pierced the quiet Georgia night. It was the most painful sound I'd ever heard in my life, and I did not try to stop him.

We returned to the command center about daylight. I was pretty sure Amos had not eaten in thirty-six hours and was running on fumes. I asked a deputy to bring him some breakfast. An hour later, color-swatch Ira—wearing orange from head to toe—appeared carrying bags of steaming hot food. I helped her clear off the conference table and lay out the spread out for anyone who wanted it.

She saw Amos sitting alone in an office to one side, walked in, kissed him on his bald head, and walked out. I followed her to her car and tried to give her some money. She folded it, stuffed it into my shirt pocket, and drove off.

By the second evening the media had picked up the story, and most of South Carolina and the surrounding states were looking for Amanda Carter. I watched the news reports, the interviews with Pastor John, with Maggie, with other nurses, and the shots of L.D. playing in the front yard, asking, "When is my mommy coming home?" And finally the interview with me.

Deputies had set up cots in two of the offices where men and women could nap for an hour or so. By nighttime I was dead on my feet, so I slept for thirty minutes, then splashed my face and drank three more cups of coffee. My hands were shaking.

I found Amos sitting at a desk, listening to the radio reports. His eyes were heavy. "Hey," I whispered, "why don't you lie down for a few minutes. You're no good to us if you can't keep your head up."

He shook his head and kept listening, waiting.

At daylight, some fifty-five hours after Amanda had been taken, I stepped out of the command center and looked around. The sky was a brilliant blue, not a cloud anywhere. I loaded into the van and drove to the Lovetts' house, where I found Maggie asleep on the couch. L.D. lay on her chest, a pacifier in his mouth. Drool had spilled out the side of his mouth and trickled along her chest. Her eyes opened, and she reached out to grab my hand. I knelt by the sofa and watched L.D. nuzzle his nose against Maggie's bosom.

She kissed my fingers, and I brushed her cheek and said, "You're good at this."

She smiled and pulled the blanket above his shoulders.

"I'm going to take Blue for a while. I'll be back." I walked out the back door, grabbing Amanda's sweater—the one she often wore to work—off a hook and tucking it under my arm as I went.

Blue and I drove down roads with no names and no lines. Some had been paved with asphalt; most had not. I didn't know what I was looking for, but I couldn't sit in that station any longer. I thought about Felix and Antonio and what that kid had said about the canoe.

Blue and I drove to Mr. Carter's house, where he was looking every bit as helpless as I felt. I pointed at Badger and Gus and held Amanda's sweater out the window. I didn't have to say a word.

Mr. Carter, seventy-two years young, jumped off the porch and flipped the gates on the dogs' kennels, and we hopped in his truck. Blue sat up front with us, smelling the sweater and pointing his nose everywhere Mr. Carter turned.

We drove every road that crossed the Salk, and at every bridge or entry into the water, we stopped to let out the dogs. We waited, but the bark never came. Throughout the day, we kept up with reports on the scanner, but we could tell by the tone that the men had disappeared—completely. In midafternoon we heard a report that Whittaker had walked into a movie theater in Walterboro and shaken the tail that had been following him since he walked out of the courthouse. For some time after that, the radio was relatively quiet.

By dark we had scoured the south end of the swamp, but the Salk was huge, and we knew it was useless. Around midnight we drove back to the command center. Seventy hours had passed.

I found Amos leaning over the conference table, eyeing the map of the Salk. He was in a bad way. I knew he hadn't slept or eaten, but I also knew better than to say anything. His dad walked to the map and explained what we'd done.

While Amos thought, a commotion erupted just outside the doors. I heard somebody scream, "He's got a gun," and then a loud crash. I ran to the door and looked through the glass.

Bryce stood in the middle of the room, four agents piled at his feet on the floor. Three other agents knelt behind a desk, pointing their Glocks at him.

I shoved open the door and walked into the room.

One of the deputies screamed at me, "Get down! He's got a gun!"

Bryce's .45 lay untouched in his shoulder holster, but I knew if he so much as twitched a finger, he'd never clear the leather before thirty shots cleared his center mass. He was covered in mud from the waist down. His feet were bare, and he was chewing a wad of gum the size of a boiled egg. The room smelled of pungent swamp decay and spearmint. He was a picture of calm.

Bryce looked at me and at Amos, who stood, hand on his SIG. He spoke slowly, his eyes level and steady. "The girl's not with them."

Amos's eyes narrowed. Two of the agents on the floor moved slowly, both holding their heads.

Bryce looked at me, then at Amos. "You'd better come with me."

Three minutes later, eighteen police or federal vehicles followed Bryce and me to Willard's store, where Mr. Carter and his coon-hunting brigade had assembled en masse. It looked like a bad marriage between a coal miner convention and a SWAT exercise.

Mr. Carter stood in the bed of his truck and conferred with Bryce, who nodded and pointed at the map, lit by Mr. Carter's headlamp. Amos listened and spoke into the microphone on his shoulder, then addressed the sixty-some-odd men around him.

"Two men and a woman were spotted in a canoe making their way downriver. We believe that one of the men is injured. They are armed and dangerous, but nobody does *anything* without my order." Amos's eyes glared like rubies into the night.

As if shot out of a gun, forty vehicles ranging from muddy pickups to shiny Hummers cranked their engines and followed Bryce and me toward his place. We wound up the drive, around the back of his property, and up to the entrance of a logging road I never knew existed. I stopped the van, and Bryce jumped out. Without a word, he began walking into the trees. I shouldered the shotgun and followed.

The moon was high, the temperature was somewhere in the nineties, and there was no breeze to speak of. Two miles into the swamp, I was wheezing, and Bryce was barely breathing hard. We came to the water's edge, and somewhere in the distance an owl hooted. Bryce motioned to Mr. Carter, who walked up alongside.

Mr. Carter took Amanda's sweater and some clothing taken from the duplex, rubbed them in Badger's and Gus's faces, and unhooked their leashes. Badger and Gus disappeared like two ghosts in the darkness while we waited. Five minutes passed as we caught our breath. Badger sloshed off into the darkness, sending out periodic barks, which were occasionally answered by Gus.

Ten minutes passed. The whispers behind us grew. Most of them were directed at Bryce and sounded something like, "Who does this guy think he is?"

Mr. Carter looked off into the swamp, raised his chin, and then raised his hand toward the men behind him. Silence fell across us, and the smile on Mr. Carter's face spread. About the time that his teeth shone through the darkness because of his smile, Badger broke out into a full-blown howl.

Amos didn't hesitate, and neither did anyone else.

Except Bryce. He listened and looked somewhat confused, and when the entire hunting party ran off into the darkness—say toward twelve o'clock on a watch—Bryce ran off the dial toward three o'clock.

I watched the lights scour the darkness ahead of me, then turned and ran as hard as I could after Bryce. I caught up just as he stepped into the water. I stepped down into the cold, swirling blackness, raised the shotgun above my head, and tried to keep up. We partly waded, partly swam through deep water, up onto mushy earth.

Bryce ran through the darkness as if he were following streetlights. The vines and limbs tore at me, and I stumbled and fell, smashing my head against a stump and planting my face in the mud. When I stood, Bryce was waiting on me. We ran what seemed like two more miles, while the sound of Badger's howl faded off into the distance. When I could, I grabbed Bryce by the sleeve and said, "Bryce, are you sure?"

He held a finger to his lips and motioned me to follow. A few hundred yards later, I was neck-deep in muck and paddling. Bryce lifted me onto a log, said, "Wait here," then reached up and grabbed a rope. I looked up and saw his "summer home" directly above.

He disappeared through the trapdoor and reappeared a second later. He slid back down, the sniper rifle strapped over his shoulder, and stepped off into the water. Waist-deep and walking against the current, we waded through the swamp where the mosquitoes sucked a pint of blood out of my neck and flew constantly into and out of my ears.

Thirty minutes later, listening to the sounds of my own breathing and my heart pounding outside my chest, I saw Bryce turn and hold his finger to his lips again. He pointed. Maybe two hundred yards through the trees ahead, a light flickered. I checked the safety on the shotgun. We lay on a mound of fern. The sound of Badger's moaning came out of the distance maybe a mile beyond the house and started a commotion in the structure ahead of us.

"Poacher's cabin," said Bryce softly.

In the distance, I heard one man screaming at another. Then a door slammed, someone splashed into the water, and footsteps started coming at us fast.

Bryce's face was a picture of focus. He turned quickly, jumped up, and swung the butt of his rifle into the running man's face with pinpoint precision. The man's head rocked back, his feet flew out in front of him, and he fell two feet from where I lay. Bryce grabbed him by the belt and started dragging him through the swamp.

The other man was still hollering, frantically trying to load himself into a canoe. The dim lantern light from the shack shone down on him. He wasn't wearing a shirt, and he seemed to be limping. He put his bad leg into the canoe and tried to shove the canoe off the bank.

Bryce dropped the man he was carrying, slid the rifle off his shoulder, aimed, and squeezed. The shot rang out, and the man flew back, clutching his left knee. He lay on the ground, grasping for the paddle with one hand while holding a shotgun in the other and screaming at the top of his lungs.

Bryce picked up the first man again and crept through the stagnant water. We slithered through the mud, and at sixty yards, Bryce stopped. He knelt, breathing slightly, and said, "We met in Saigon. 1970."

"What?"

Bryce watched the man writhe in pain on the far shore. The river, some twenty yards wide at this point, separated us from him.

"She was not American."

The man grabbed the oar and pulled himself up on it like a crutch. Bryce aimed a second time. The man limped toward the canoe, Bryce squeezed, and the shotgun in the man's left hand exploded in the middle. Something must have blown into the man's face, because he fell again, clutching his face and hand.

The man at my feet was bleeding profusely from a huge gash in his face, and his nose was badly twisted out of place. He had yet to move.

Bryce whispered, "There was a chaplain in my unit. Had been an Episcopal priest before we drafted him."

The sound of Badger's moaning grew louder, but not yet closer.

"We got married in a hut, and I kept her a secret until my third tour of duty when they saw me coming out of her village."

We walked to the edge of the water where the man on the other bank lay screaming and clutching his face, his left leg twisted.

Bryce stepped into the water and began swimming across, bringing the first man with him. I stepped into the current, and it pushed me along after Bryce. He kept the man's head above water while I struggled to do the same.

When we reached the other bank, the man on the ground began yelling obscenities. Slowly the first man came to. He, too, clutched his face as Bryce threw the first man down on top of the second. They lay there, tangled, unable to move and cussing both each other and us.

Bryce chambered another round, slid the rifle over his shoulder, and squatted. His eyes were focused out over the swamp. The sounds of Badger and Gus grew closer, as did the sound of sloshing feet and the sight of flashing lights.

Bryce spat in the water. "They burned the village. Lined everyone up and shot them while I watched from the trees. When they shot my son, I . . ." Bryce trailed off. "My unit thought I'd been taken, thought I'd been pinned down. So they came in to get me, but the enemy was good. There were too many. The last one they shot was the bugler."

Bryce shook his head and cracked half a smile. "We used to talk about home, about Scotland—and at night, he'd been trying to teach me to play the pipes."

Badger cleared the trees, took three steps, and pounced on the first man. He opened his jaw, placed it over the man's throat, and stood there waiting. Like a ghost in the darkness, Gus bounded alongside him, clutched the other man's throat, and waited.

Bryce smelled the air and looked southward. "It took me nearly a month to find them all."

The memory of Bryce in my cornfield came flooding back. I pointed in the direction I thought my house sat. "The cornfield?"

Bryce nodded.

AMOS CHARGED OUT OF THE TREES. HIS SIG WAS UP, IN HIS hands, along with his SureFire light, and his eyes were scanning the dilapidated cabin. He saw us and the men at our feet, then jumped up onto the porch and kicked in the door. He shone his light inside, saw nothing, and then walked to the bank. He was breathing hard, but he was hardly out of breath.

He knelt next to the first man. "Antonio, where is she?"

Several of Antonio's teeth were missing, and he couldn't breathe through his nose. He cussed Amos while the remainder of the hunting brigade emerged from the swamp. Their lights lit the area around us like daylight.

Amos holstered his pistol and turned to the other man. "Felix—my wife."

Felix clutched his knee, laughed a sickly laugh, and said, "Yeah, that sweet young thing was so sweet, we just thought we'd come back for more."

Amos cocked his fist and was throwing it forward when Bryce caught it in midair. He shook his head and stooped over Felix. He pulled a knife out of a sheath that ran along the belt at his back, grabbed Felix's right hand, turned it backward in a direction it was not meant to go, placed the blade to the first digit on the man's finger, and pressed.

Felix writhed and screamed, and even the SWAT guys stood back.

Bryce looked at Antonio, but he was of little use because he was fading in and out of consciousness. Bryce leaned closer to Felix's face, raised his eyebrows, and waited.

Felix spat in his face and kicked the ground.

Bryce pressed harder.

Felix pointed his face downriver. "She ran that way!"

Amos leaned in closer and spoke through gritted teeth. "Define 'that way.'"

Felix tried to point with his other hand that had been shot while holding the gun. He began to cry. "She ran that way." He pointed downriver. "Two days ago. Little witch stabbed me in the leg and took off."

Amos looked downriver, then at his dad. Mr. Carter rubbed the sweater against the dogs' faces and pointed them that direction.

Amos looked to one of his men, then pointed at Felix and Antonio. "Handle this." Without hesitation, he ran into the darkness, followed by his team of men and their lights.

Bryce stood up, eyed the river, stepped in, and began swimming—upstream.

I watched Amos disappear, turned toward Bryce's wake in the water, and dove in. We swam against the current a couple of hundred yards until we came to a sandy bank.

Bryce climbed out by the roots of a pine tree that were exposed because of erosion. I extended my hand, and he lifted me up. He smelled the air and spoke without looking at me. "I don't like it when men lie to me."

He walked along the edge of the water. Behind us, Badger's bark faded into the night, and I followed the dark frame in front of me. Bryce studied the waterline, following God only knew what. We weaved for a mile through the brush until we came to a huge canopy of trees that must have been at least two hundred years old. If there was a heart to the Salk, we'd just found it. The ground was soft with moss and smelled of mint.

Bryce turned hard right, away from the water. He smelled the air repeatedly, weaving among the trees. We circled a huge oak tree, the top of which had been twisted off in a tornado, and he paused. He walked again in a circle around the tree, listened, then quietly thumped the side of the tree with the butt of his pistol.

From within the tree, I heard a woman's voice whimper.

I hit my knees and dug with both hands at the soft dirt mounded against the tree. Bryce dug too. We cleared roots, dirt, and sand, and soon I could hear her crying inside. When my hands broke through into the cavity inside the tree, she began kicking at me.

"Amanda! It's me. It's Dylan."

She kicked harder, screaming frantically.

I climbed through the hole while she backed up against the far side of the trunk. She was looking at me, but she had yet to see me. The inside of the tree was hollowed out and as big around as the interior space of our van—maybe five feet across. Moonlight shone directly above and threw a shadow on the ground.

"Amanda, honey." I crawled closer. "It's just me."

Despite the visible rounding of her stomach, she had tucked herself into a ball and shook her head. I sat up alongside her and gently took her hand. "Amanda, it's me, Dylan."

She blinked, looked at me, and could not speak. Her face was swollen from ten thousand mosquito bites, and one eye was shut, but she was breathing. I reached out, and she took my hands.

I carried her through the trees to the river, while Bryce followed. It was dark, the ground was uneven, and she was pregnant, but for some reason none of that really mattered. We reached the bank, and I set her gently down in the water. She drank like a man in the desert.

Bryce unholstered his .45 and pointed it into the air. Just before he squeezed the trigger, I held up a hand, and he waited. I wrapped my arms around Amanda's shoulders, pressed her head to my chest, and covered her other ear with my hand. She clutched me tightly.

I nodded, and Bryce fired three times; his shots were answered immediately by two shots downriver. Bryce fired three more, and I watched as the brass shell casings arced out across the river and disappeared into the water.

Ten minutes later I heard Amos screaming in the distance, "Amanda! Amanda!"

Amanda looked up, her hands shaking. "Take me to my husband, please."

I picked her up, and we walked along the bank through the shallow water. A hundred yards down the river, Badger and Gus emerged from the trees, followed quickly by Amos. He ran into the water, reached me, and looped his arms under mine.

Amanda let go of my neck, wrapped her arms around his, and said, "I want to go home now."

He heard her speak, and the cries of a man in anguish exited his chest. I knew what they sounded like because I'd heard them before. Amos fell to his knees, the water lapping up around his waist, and held Amanda. Finally he placed his hands on her tummy and whispered, "The baby?"

Amanda tried to smile. "Playing soccer right now."

Amos lifted her off the sandy bank and sloshed toward the trees, the sound of feet, and the sight of lights. When I turned around, Bryce was gone.

AT 3:00 AM MAGGIE AND I DROVE HOME. SHE HAD BABYSAT L.D. for the better part of three days. As we drove, a smell that I couldn't place filled the car. I wrinkled my nose and was sniffing the air like Bryce when Maggie noticed. She held her hand to my nose. "It's Desitin."

I nodded. A few minutes passed while I tried to figure out what that was. The look on my face betrayed me.

Maggie placed her heels on the dashboard and leaned back. "It's a cream for diaper rash."

"Oh." The adoption committee can say what they want, but my wife will make a great mom one day.

Emotionally we were about as strung out as two people could get. Physically we weren't much better. The events of the night, and of the last six weeks, had taken their toll. I knew that I was breathing and that sleep was only moments away. All I wanted to do, all we wanted to do, was lay our heads on a pillow, close our eyes, and wake up next week. We'd worry about tomorrow, tomorrow.

I parked, cut the ignition, and opened the door. Blue hopped out and began sniffing around the house. Maggie and I were inside the barn when a light in the kitchen caught my eye. I tried to ignore it, but I heard Papa whispering over my shoulder, *"Money doesn't grow on trees."* I turned to Maggie. "I'll be up in a minute."

I whistled for Blue, but he had disappeared. Probably down by the river or running down a corn row. I climbed up the porch steps, pushed open the door, and walked through the kitchen to the hall to flick off the light. That's when I saw the blood. Three spots of fresh blood led from the kitchen into the den.

"Blue?" I waited, followed the trail, and saw several more spots. Darker red. I called again, "Blue?"

The only noise was the sound of Maggie tossing corn out of a pail and into Pinky's stall. I turned the corner into the den, and there lay Blue. His eyes were half-open, and I couldn't tell if he was breathing. I knelt and reached out, but a huge hand flashed out of the darkness, grabbed me by the throat, and choked off any thought of screaming or breathing. The hand lifted me off my toes, pulled me toward a tormented face, and threw me into the fireplace, where my head hit soundly on the brick hearth.

The room spun. I heard a laugh and the muffled thud of someone kicking Blue's body. The sound told my ears what my heart already knew.

I pulled myself onto my hands and knees, felt a boot in my rib cage, then something hard came down over my head and everything went black. Somewhere between awake and not, I heard heavy footsteps fading down the hall and heard the screen door squeak. I stumbled to my feet, fell, and pulled myself up on the sofa as the blood blurred my vision. A few seconds later I heard the gunshot.

I pulled myself down the hallway, trying to get up but unable to steady my knees. The pressure in my head was growing, my eyes were blurry, and the sides of my vision were narrowing, like a tunnel. The floor felt as if it were moving, like the first step onto an escalator. I reached the kitchen, then the screen door, and finally I rolled down the porch steps, spilling blood all around me. I got to one knee, where the ground felt like a spinning merry-go-round, tried to yell for Maggie but muttered something inaudible instead. I fell again, then elbowed my way past the van.

Maggie stood in the barn doorway, holding Papa's Model 12 and pointing it in the face of Whittaker, who lay unmoving on the ground. She wasn't trembling, but her forehead was wrinkled, her finger was wrapped around the trigger, and her knuckles were white. It struck me that the barrel wasn't smoking. I steadied myself on one knee and saw a flash of gunmetal out of the corner of my left eye. I jerked, the blood spraying off my face, just in time to see Bryce stride out of the cornfield. He was carrying his rifle, and a thin line of smoke was trailing out of the barrel.

Pinky started kicking her stall, snorting and squealing.

Barefooted, Bryce approached slowly, his toes digging into the mud like fingers. He reached across Whittaker's body and gently placed his hand on the Model 12's barrel. He lifted it, and Maggie's eyes followed. When they made eye contact, Bryce hesitated, then shook his head. Maggie looked down, then at me, and finally let go. When she did, the darkness returned.

THE HEADACHE WOKE ME. I OPENED MY EYES, A WAVE OF nausea hit, and I arched over the side of the bed where two hands sat holding a bucket. I must have been doing this awhile, because I opened my mouth and nothing came. The sheets were white, the bed was hard, the air was smoke-blowing cold, and my left eye was completely swollen shut. I studied the room and knew that while it felt familiar, it wasn't mine.

Maggie set down the bucket, touched my arm, and kissed me. She looked three days past tired. Somewhere out of the left side of my bed, Amos came into view. Farther down, I recognized Pastor John. Somebody else I couldn't place, dressed in white, stood at the foot of my bed. I leaned back, braced my hand on the bed, and tried to stop the world from spinning. Somebody spoke, but the words just ricocheted around my head, eventually singing off into nowhere. Maggie said something about not going anywhere, but I felt as if I were breathing the air atop Everest and couldn't respond.

Sometime later I cracked my eyes slightly, looking through the psychedelic crisscross of my eyelashes. Daylight was coming in over my shoulder, my feet were cold, and I smelled Maggie's perfume, Eternity, wafting through the air, mixed with the scent of Pine Sol. My head felt thick, but my left eye was letting in some light, which meant progress.

I felt a hand on my left arm, tracing the lines of my scar. I turned slowly and saw Maggie looking back at me. She waited. All I could muster was a whisper. "I'm hungry."

She smiled, and her face flooded with tears. "What do you feel like?"

"Eggs. Toast. Grits. Some bacon. Biscuits. Maybe a few pancakes. Some—"

She kissed me above my eye, her tears wetting my face, then walked out the door. I heard someone speaking over the intercom outside the door and felt the blood pressure cuff inflate on my right arm.

A few minutes later Maggie returned, her running shoes squeaking on the waxed floor. She slid the rolling table over my lap and set down a tray. The eggs were steaming, had been scrambled with some sort of cheese, and tasted better than anything I'd ever eaten in my life. I tried to sit up, but the pain in my rib cage changed my mind. Maggie held a straw to my mouth, and I sipped orange juice, thick with pulp, which tasted almost as good as the eggs. I ate slowly—eggs, then a piece of bacon, a biscuit with butter and honey, two helpings of grits, more bacon, all the orange juice.

My stomach full, I sat back, breathed, and closed my eyes. "I could get used to this."

Maggie leaned in close, her breath brushing my face. She was smiling and crying at the same time. "Not me. I don't know how you did it. I'm about to lose my mind in this place."

I pulled back the covers, exposing my flowered gown, patted the bed, and lifted my arm. Maggie lay down beside me, gently laying her head on my shoulder.

I was dozing off again when the thought hit me. "How's Amanda?"

Maggie was almost asleep. "She went home two days ago."

The phrase ricocheted around my head and finally took root somewhere in my understanding. "Two days? How long have I been here?"

"Five days."

I thought about her sitting here at my bedside for five days. That meant that between Amanda's being taken and my time here, Maggie couldn't have really slept in almost a week. I replayed the events, those I could remember, in my head.

"Blue?" I asked.

Maggie took a deep breath, one of those that told me she'd not been looking forward to answering that question. She closed her eyes and shook her head.

## chapter thirty-eight

THEY RELEASED ME FROM THE HOSPITAL A WEEK after Whittaker tried to beat my head in with the fire poker. He'd been moved to a hospital that specialized in spinal injuries, but even if he ever made it out of prison, which we doubted, he'd never walk again.

The doctor said my concussion was about as bad as it gets while still being considered a concussion. Given the fact that they couldn't wake me up, they were worried about the swelling causing permanent damage. Maggie said that when Amos heard that, he shook his head and kept telling them I was tough and I'd pull through. But that was little comfort, because every time I woke up, I promptly vomited and my eyes rolled back in my head. They didn't know about my ribs until day four in the hospital, when Maggie noticed the bruise while bathing me.

In the late afternoon, we left the hospital and drove by the vet to pick up Blue's body. I cradled the cardboard box that held my buddy and knew that Blue deserved better. As we drove out of town, I turned to Maggie. "I want to stop at the nursery."

When I told Merle what I was looking for, he nodded and helped me pick three young good ones. We loaded them into the van and headed home.

Near our son's grave I dug another hole, laid Blue's box in the ground, and tried to say something, but the words wouldn't come. Maggie stepped up alongside me and hooked her arm inside mine, and I felt a part of my heart crack off and float away downriver.

She wiped her tears and whispered over the hole in the ground, "Blue, thank you for taking care of Dylan when I couldn't."

I knelt, rubbed his cold muzzle one last time, and clenched my teeth so tightly I thought they'd crack. I closed the top of the box, shoveled the dirt down on top of him, and then stood there leaning on the handle. But something felt wrong. Really wrong.

I dropped to my knees, pawed away the dirt, and opened the lid of the box. "Hey, pal—since you'll get there before me, take care of my kids. All three of them. They'll need a buddy to run with." My tears fell into the hole, landed on his shoulder, and trickled down the side to his heart. I touched his muzzle one final time. "You're the best."

I closed the box again and covered the hole. The pain hurt. It hurt deep down where my soul lives. I walked to the van, pulled out the three weeping willow saplings, and began digging the holes down by the river. They were young, maybe three feet tall, but if I planted them closely enough, they'd sink their roots into the riverbank and in years to come shade both my son and my dog.

Maggie helped me pull back the sandy earth, set the root bolls in, and then cover them back up. We used the plastic pots to pour water over the roots. When I stood back, the sight satisfied me. The three young trees stood some ten feet apart and, when mature, would lean over the river, allowing their long limbs to dip in and drag along the tops like floating fishing lines or maybe a woman's hair when she washed it in the sink.

I think the sight comforted Maggie, too, because she stood alongside me, sweat rolling off her temples, the veins in her biceps throbbing beneath the skin. Her shoulders fell, relaxed, and her face showed signs of having come to terms with what is our life.

We climbed into the loft, turned the AC on "snow," and pulled the curtains across the single window. If there was any type of normalcy to our lives, I lay half-awake thinking we were pretty close to it.

THE NEXT DAY, MAGGIE SLEPT PAST LUNCH. SOMETIME after two o'clock, she appeared out of the barn and started across the lawn to me on the porch, where I'd been sitting and thinking. She shaded her eyes against the sun, walked barefooted across the grass in the 99-degree heat, and sat on the porch while I scrambled some eggs. When I handed her the plate, she set it beside her and rested her head on her arms across her knees. Even under the porch, the heat was oppressive and the humidity stuck like spray paint to my skin.

Maggie tried to whisper, but the emotions that had built over the last six weeks choked off her voice. She disappeared into the kitchen and came back with the calendar from off the wall. When she sat back down on the porch, she crossed off the last few days and whispered, "I'm sorry. It's not . . . It's not coming."

The marks showed that she was somewhere between twelve and seventeen days overdue.

I tried to hold her, to hug away the pain, but some pains must be shared before they can be carried. A hot breeze rattled through the corn and brushed across my face. She pressed her chest to mine; her face was wet, and her tears slid along my cheek. Her sobs shook her entire body.

Finally I just lay down on the porch, holding her. When I did, the dam burst, and I felt her soul crying.

She looked up at me. "How can you love a woman like me?"

There was no answer to the question she had just asked. Love is not a noun; it's a verb. I walked into the house and into my writing closet. Hands trembling, I pried open the floor-board where the truth lay wrapped in a plastic grocery bag.

I walked back out onto the porch. "Maggs, I lied to you. This is the story I could not tell you."

The look of confusion on her face grew when I placed the manuscript in her lap.

"I wrote two stories: one for you, one I thought you could handle. The other—this one, I wrote for me—the one I needed to write."

She registered the pain in my voice.

"This is the story of a man who loves his wife. Of a man who died for a time and then lived again. Of a man who felt pain unknown for what seemed like a thousand lifetimes and then joy untold. Maggs, it's the story of us. It's everything I've wanted to tell you but didn't know how for fear of letting you know how far down I fell."

She held the pages, then sat up and handed them back. Her voice cracked, her fear apparent, as she said, "Read to me."

"Honey, I—"

"Shhh . . . Read."

We took the phone off the hook and spent the day on the front porch. Maggie lay on the swing, swaying, while I sat on the steps or walked back and forth.

My story started with the pink line that announced that she was pregnant and went through my ride in the back of the truck when I held my son's casket between my legs. I took her through the painful weeks that followed, and when I read about my walk through the cornfield where I tried to peel the skin off my arm, Maggie slid off the bench, knelt, and ran her fingers along the scar.

"Why, Dylan?"

"Because I couldn't get clean."

She patted the page, and I continued. I took her to church, communion, the baptism. I brought her back to the bed she slept in, my longing, my tears, the wrinkle on her forehead, the doctors' dire predictions, and the first time she squeezed my hand. Somewhere in there, she realized that walking into her room every day was killing me. She also realized that no matter how many times I died, I'd keep walking in. Forever.

Around dusk my story brought us into Pinky's stall, to her snorting and slamming me into the fence rail. I told Maggie how I jumped into the truck and pegged the accelerator till it leveled out somewhere over a hundred, and then tripped up the stairs where a mass of people were standing outside her hospital room. We reached the part where I walked into her room, covered in pig smear, and I set the book down. I didn't need to read anymore. I knew that story by heart.

"When I walked into your room and saw those beautiful

brown eyes looking at me, I didn't know who to be; I didn't know who we were. I needed you to tell me."

Maggie slid off the swing and lay down beside me on the porch. We lay on the wooden boards, both out of tears, while the manuscript surrounded us like a blanket. Her chest rose and fell, and her breathing told me that the healing had started. She placed a hand across my chest, hooked one leg around mine, and dug her head into my shoulder.

*chapter thirty-nine*

BY SUNDAY AFTERNOON, WE WERE BOTH DREADING Monday morning. We had slept through church, eaten a late lunch, and spoken hardly a word throughout the day. We had a pretty good idea what they were going to tell us. Talking about it wouldn't make it any better.

A vehicle turned into the drive, crunching gravel, so we stepped off the porch and craned our necks around the corner. In front of me was what might have been one of the most beautiful things I'd ever seen—next to my wife's open eyes. A 1972 Chevrolet C-10 pickup, the spitting image of my first truck, except this one had been restored to its original condition.

Bryce sat behind the wheel. The truck's paint matched his hair—classic orange—and it shone like the sun. The engine sounded like a dream, and if you listened closely, you could hear the lope of the cam in the big block. That's engine-talk for "It sounded wonderful."

Bryce stepped out, pulled a rag out of his pocket, and started shining the hood. He was wearing shorts—or cutoff BDUs—a T-shirt, boots, and his shoulder holster. Absent the pistol, he looked rather normal.

The truck bed had been sprayed with a padded black liner, all the metal trim had been dipped and re-chromed, the windows looked like new glass, the tires were oversized Michelins. Bryce popped the hood. Somebody had put his tender loving touch under the hood as well as everywhere else. Most of the engine had been chromed, the tubes were made of a shiny metal material, the spark plug wires matched the truck, and there wasn't a speck of dirt or grease anywhere to be found.

Bryce was really beaming. Because he's not one to start conversations, I walked up alongside him and was about to open my mouth when he walked back to the driver's side, pulled the keys from the ignition, and placed them in my hand. I heard Maggie suck in a breath of air as if it would be her last on earth.

He held the keys there for a minute while his mouth and mind searched to find each other, then connect. He nodded and said, "I always did like this truck."

I looked at the truck again, and my eyes grew as round as half-dollars. "That's my old truck?"

Bryce nodded and wiped his hands with the rag. "What time is it?"

I pulled Papa's watch and said, "Almost seven."

He eyed the sky, tilted his head, and said, "Movie starts in about thirty minutes. We'd better get going."

Maggie looked at me. "What movie?"

Bryce looked at us as if we should know. "*The* movie." His eyes twinkled, and he tried to conceal his smile. He had really pulled out all the stops, and even though I had no idea what movie he was talking about, if it meant I got to drive my truck to his place, I'd have watched just about anything.

Maggie ran inside to grab her bag and a couple of blankets, then threw everything into the back of the truck and slid across the seat. Bryce sat in the passenger seat and clicked the door shut, and both waited on me. I slid onto the driver's seat, pulled the door shut, and turned the key.

When I get to heaven, I hope God lets me drive a truck like that.

I dropped the gearshift into drive, and we idled around the back of the house, down the drive, and out onto the hard road. At sixty miles an hour, I almost started crying.

We pulled into the drive-in, where Bryce hopped out and ran into the projector house. I heard him shuffling pans in what used to be the concession stand, and pretty soon I smelled popcorn. I parked the truck in the middle of the lot in front of the biggest screen, next to one of the hundreds of iron poles topped with microphones. I let down the tailgate and spread Maggie's blanket across the back.

Bryce soon appeared carrying three large bowls of popcorn and a six-pack of Old Milwaukee. Then he returned to the projector house and started flipping switches.

I looked at Maggie and said, "Do you have any idea what movie we're about to watch?"

Maggie put her hands on her hips and looked at me over one shoulder. "Why, Rhett Butler—"

"You've got to be kidding. Please don't tell me." I looked at the screen as the first of the credits began rolling.

Maggie flipped a piece of popcorn at me and said, "Yup."

I scanned the property and saw that Bryce had made a few more changes. To our right, beyond the film house, he had laid out a long-range target with eight rifle targets some eight hundred yards away. Like a golf range, every hundred yards was marked with a large white sign. I pointed and asked, "You doing some shooting?"

Bryce nodded. "When your buddy saw my trophy, he asked me to teach his team some of what I know." He looked at me, and his eyes grew quizzical. "You think that's okay?"

It was the first time Bryce had ever asked me a question that required us to swim below the surface.

I studied the target, then Bryce's face. "Yes, I do."

I thought about what he said. In the years that I'd known him, Bryce had never shown me a trophy of any sort whatsoever. "What trophy was that?"

He pointed to a glass case just above the old concession stand. Inside was a four-foot silver trophy polished to a reflective shine. Evidently it'd been there for years, and I'd walked by it a dozen times, but I'd never seen it. "What's it for?"

"The Wimbledon Cup. 1970."

"You played tennis?"

Bryce shook his head. "It's given to the winner of the Marine sniper competition."

"How many other marines did you beat out?"

Bryce considered that. "All of them, I guess."

"How far away was the target?"

Bryce looked downrange, his eyes coming to rest beyond the farthest target. "Thousand yards."

I started putting the pieces together. I thought about Antonio, Felix, Whittaker. "Bryce?"

"Yes."

"Were you *trying* to hit Antonio in the hand?"

He nodded.

"And were you *trying* to hit Whittaker in the spine?"

Bryce looked at Maggie, then at me. He nodded.

"Why?"

Bryce pulled a pack of gum from his pants, popped all twelve pieces into his mouth, and walked toward the film house.


FOUR HOURS LATER, THE END OF THE TAPE STARTED FLIP-ping in the projector house and woke me. I looked up and saw Bryce crashed out alongside me, sleeping as quietly as a church mouse. On my other side was Maggie, who'd eaten almost all of our popcorn and was now sniffling and drying her eyes.

I stretched and yawned. "Wow, I just love that movie."

She elbowed me and dumped the rest of her popcorn in my lap.

"Come on," I said, hopping out and then helping her down out of the truck. "Big day tomorrow."

Bryce lifted an eyebrow. "What about tomorrow?"

I brushed him off. "We've just got a meeting with the, um, the folks down at the adoption agency."

Bryce's eyes narrowed. He pulled a fresh pack of gum from his leg cargo pocket and started popping all twelve pieces into his mouth. "'Bout what?"

"Well, it's the appeal board."

The smell of wintergreen was overwhelming. Bryce moved the mass to the other side of his mouth. "What're you appealing?"

"Their decision." I looked at Maggie. I didn't want to make it any harder on her.

She looked at Bryce. "They rejected our application."

Bryce looked all of a sudden angry. He chewed harder, and it looked as if his lips and cheeks were pulling his face in two different directions.

I shrugged, thinking more about Maggie than Bryce. "It

doesn't mean we can't go to other agencies, but we'll have to disclose that they refused us."

Bryce scratched his head and looked confused. "Oh." Without so much as a good night, he stood up, disappeared into his trailer, and started banging around inside.

We cleaned up, cut the lights in the projector house, and hollered good night across the parking lot. If he heard us, he made no response.

*chapter forty*

WANTING TO PUT OUR BEST FOOT FORWARD, MAGGIE asked me to wear a coat and tie. I did, but I couldn't hold a candle to my wife. I descended the stairs out of the loft and found her standing in the middle of the barn, where the sunlight had broken through the slits in the walls and lit her from calf to halo. She stood heel to arch, hands in white gloves. I'd missed a belt loop and cut my face shaving, and my tie was crooked and too short. She was the canvas on which God had painted all the wonder and beauty of summer. I stood open-mouthed. She touched my chin, closing my mouth, and smirked. "Well, say something."

I gulped. "Will you marry me?"

She straightened my tie and peeled the toilet paper off my cheek. "That'll do."

It'd been nearly a month and a half since the white flower of the cotton plant had bloomed, turned pink, faded into red, then grew deep purple and fell to the earth below. By rough calculation, time was drawing near, but how near was anybody's guess. While some farmers have attempted to make farming a predictable science, it is not. Never will be. You can beg, cuss, dance, even manipulate conditions, but she will grow, blossom, and produce only when she's ready. Nothing short of the hand of God can change that.

Evidently God thought it was time.

We walked out of the barn and were met by a hallelujah chorus of white. As if sprayed from heaven, the fields had exploded into a seamless sea of fluffy white. Hundreds of thousands of cottony white hands rose up out of the earth and reaching to heaven blanketed the landscape with texture, tenderness, and promise.

We eyed the cotton, Maggie's dress flapping gently in the warm breeze. She stepped into the field, snapped off a fist-sized boll like a rose, and raised it to her nose.

*Indomitable.*

I held out my elbow, she slipped her hand inside, and we drove the back roads to Charleston.


ALTHOUGH WE ARRIVED EARLY, MR. SAWYER AND MS. Tungston were waiting on us. Kayla, the receptionist, led us into the conference room, where Mr. Sawyer pointed us to our seats and then rested his hand on his notebook, which had grown thicker. He tapped the vinyl cover. "We've received several letters in support of you. Many of them quite complimentary."

I nodded. "Yes, sir. Like your letter suggested, we asked a few of our friends."

Maggie sat listening, watching the proceedings, but I could tell she didn't like being under the microscope.

He was opening his mouth to speak again when the door behind us opened, and John Caglestock walked in. He was carrying a tape recorder under one arm and several folders under another.

Mr. Sawyer stood up. "Excuse me, sir, but these proceedings are closed."

John nodded and set his things down on a side table. He straightened his bow tie and extended his hand. "I'm John Caglestock. And that's part of the problem."

Maggie smirked.

John spoke softly to us. "Hi, you two, hope you don't mind." He addressed the committee. "Dylan called me a couple of weeks ago and asked me to write a letter in support of them. I said I would, only to find out that I could not. I'm good with numbers, not letters, and what I have to say, well, I can't make it fit in a letter."

Mr. Sawyer sat back down and waved his hand. "While unprecedented, please continue."

"I manage an investment firm. I met Dr. Styles here when our best client marched him into my office and told me that I was to do whatever he said. Needless to say, I wasn't too happy to have met him." John paced the room and looked at me. "I had a few questions. Like, just what did a farmer from the sticks know about investments and managing money? But when your best client, who's worth"—John looked at the ceiling and calculated in his head—"somewhere north of three hundred million dollars, speaks, you do what he says."

"You mean to tell me that Dr. Styles is a member at your firm helping to manage that amount of money?"

John waved his hand. "Not technically."

"You're not making much sense," said Sawyer.

John nodded. "Think I'm bad? You ought to meet my client. Let me explain: my client trusted Dylan, placed faith in his common sense. He instructed me to run every decision by him. In a sense, he tied my hands, and I could not move a penny without first consulting the man in cowboy boots at the table here."

John continued pacing. "I have an MBA from Harvard Business and a Ph.D. from Stanford, but I quickly learned that Dr. Styles knows a good bit more than his cowboy boots and farmer's tan suggest. I wasn't the only one who studied in school. Nor was I the only one worth listening to." He looked at me. "I've learned a lot from him. And I and my client have made a lot of money as a result. At last count, Dr. Styles has helped make my client somewhere around a hundred million dollars."

Maggie gulped. "You never told me that," she whispered.

Sawyer tapped the notebook beneath his elbow. "Dr. Styles, why did you elect not to include this? Obviously its omission was purposeful on your part."

I shrugged. "Well, sir, I'm not officially an employee for either John or Br—his client."

"Then just how do you get paid?"

"I don't."

"You mean to tell me that you helped a man increase his portfolio by some 30-plus percent over—"

He looked at John, who interjected, "Five years."

"Five years, and you've never been paid?"

I nodded. "Yes, sir."

Sawyer paused and looked at Ms. Tungston, then back at us. "Why?"

"Well, sir, " I said with a shrug, "I never figured it any other way."

Sawyer sipped from the mug in front of him and considered.

John plugged in his tape recorder and said, "I wonder if you'd allow me about two more minutes."

"Please."

"When this process began several months ago, Dylan called me, and this is a recording of our conversation."

Sawyer broke in. "Did you tell Dr. Styles that you were recording him?"

John shook his head. "Not directly, but if you call our 1-800 number, the answering voice tells you that all calls are recorded for quality assurance." John paused. "And to keep us out of trouble with our auditors."

Maggie grabbed my hand as John pushed *play*. We all listened as John offered me a one-day employment opportunity and I declined. When the conversation concluded, Caglestock clicked off the machine and rolled the cord around it.

Sawyer looked at me. "Dr. Styles, I don't understand. Why didn't you accept the offer?"

"I couldn't."

"Why not?"

"Because, sir." I looked at Maggie, at John, and back at Sawyer. "I gave my word."

Sawyer whispered with Ms. Tungston briefly, then said, "Thank you, Mr. Caglestock, for your input. You have confirmed that Dr. Styles is a principled man. But you haven't offered insight into the character of Mrs. Styles."

Maggie twitched uncomfortably.

A Scottish brogue barked behind us, "I can."

I turned and saw Bryce, clothed in all his military-dress glory, standing at ease in the rear of the room. Evidently he'd been there awhile. His chest was gleaming with medals, his saber clanked at his waist, his beret tilted down over his left eye, his boots were glistening, and his white dress shirt was starched and creased. Last of all, his kilt hung to his knees.

He approached the table, clicked his heels together, and quickly placed his beret under his left arm. Tied with twine around his neck, carried almost like a bugle, hung the worn rifle scope. He nodded. "Good morning to you."

Sawyer and Tungston sat back, eyeing the growing spectacle in front of them.

"Sir, my name is Bryce Kai McGregor. I understand the point of this hearing is to determine whether or not these people will make good parents."

Sawyer crossed his arms and said, "Yes, but for their sake, we don't usually make these hearings public." He pointed at us. "For *their* sake."

Bryce pointed at Caglestock, who was leaning against the desk and smiling. "I'm the client. And I'm here for two reasons."

Sawyer's face told me that a lightbulb had just clicked on.

Bryce cut to the chase. "Is money the issue here?"

Ms. Tungston raised a finger, but Sawyer spoke first. "No, not really. Dr. and Mrs. Styles have satisfied this committee in that regard."

"Then what is?"

Ms. Tungston finally got a word in edgewise. "Frankly, Mr. McGregor, the issue concerning this committee is Mrs. Styles and her medical and mental history over the last twenty-four months."

I turned to Maggie and watched her bite her lip as she uncrossed and then recrossed her legs.

Bryce raised an eyebrow and scratched his head. "Are you talking about that lady right there?"

Tungston nodded.

Bryce walked over and put his hand on Maggie's shoulder. "This one?"

Maggie patted his hand and then folded her own in her lap.

Bryce walked behind us. "You two feel that she—Maggie— is not capable of loving someone, like a child?"

Tungston didn't respond. If she intended to speak, Bryce didn't give her much time.

"Ma'am, I am one of the most unlovable people I know. I have more issues than you've ever thought about. I've seen more death, more hatred, more acts of evil than any one hundred people put together, and I've committed most of them. I know issues."

Maggie grasped my hand. She had tucked a tissue in the palm of her right glove.

"I also know love and what it looks like, how it feels, and I know it when it's freely given." Bryce stood behind Maggie. "There was a time in my life when I knew what love looked like and how it felt. Then there was a long period of time when I forgot I ever knew it. When all the evil stuff covered up the good. When even the smell of it escaped me.

"Then I met these two people, and they reminded me. Both in how they love each other and in how they have loved me. I will stake my life, these medals hanging on my chest, and my honor that the finest two people I've ever met in this life are sitting in these two chairs right here.

"I watched my son, my wife, and our unborn daughter die in another country at the hands of very angry people. I held my son in my arms as he took his last breath, so I know loss. Please . . ." Bryce choked. "Please don't give that to these two people here. Give it to me, but not them." A single tear fell off Bryce's face and splattered across the mirror toe of his boot.

Ms. Tungston opened her mouth to speak, but Bryce zeroed in on her and approached the table. "When an angel flies too close to the ground and clips her wings, she needs time to heal. But this one—" Bryce pointed at Maggie. "She'll fly again."

Maggie's bottom lip was quivering, but her eyes were sparkling.

Bryce brushed his stomach against the table, used both hands to place his beret on his head, nodded at the committee, and turned to leave.

Mr. Sawyer sat up and spoke softly. "Mr. McGregor?"

Bryce turned.

"You said there were two reasons?"

Bryce stopped, breathed deeply—his chest round as a barrel and his stomach flat—and looked at me. "As my friend John Wayne once said, 'Words are what men live by.' And he kept his."

Without warning, Bryce clapped his heels to attention and saluted me. Standing wrought-iron straight, his hand shading the eye that had puddled with tears, Bryce blinked, and the corners of both eyes broke loose at once, sending long trickles down the sides of his freckled nose. After a moment he slowly released his salute, straightened his saber, and then lifted the twine around his neck that held the rifle scope. He eyed it several seconds, laid it on the desk in front of me, and strode out the back door.

I watched him leave, amazed at the complexity that was and is Bryce. Maggie patted my leg and kissed my shoulder. She was sniffling, so I reached in my pocket for my handkerchief, but a hand appeared over my right shoulder and beat me to it. I turned and found Amos, Amanda, and Pastor John sitting quietly behind us.

Caglestock collected his things, nodded at me, and then

turned toward Mr. Sawyer. "Thank you again for your time and for allowing me a few minutes."

Tungston leaned in toward Sawyer and attempted to whisper something, but he waved her off.

"Sometimes we fail to get a complete picture. This may be the case here today. The committee—we had decided prior to your coming in here that we would not approve your application."

Maggie let out a deep breath, and her shoulders dropped slightly.

"But I wonder if we don't have an alternative." Sawyer pointed over our shoulders and said, "Sir, are you Pastor John Lovett?"

Pastor John, wearing a black suit and his clerical collar, nodded. "I am."

"In his letter here, Pastor Lovett offers to provide counseling. Mrs. Styles, would you agree to this over the next several months, and upon completion allow us to return here and reconsider this?" Sawyer looked at Tungston, then back at Maggs. "At such time, I think we'd look more favorably upon your application."

Maggie looked at Mr. Sawyer. "Yes, sir, I would."

He set his pen down on top of his notebook. "Let's put a hold on this for six months, at which time I'll confer with Pastor Lovett. Does that suit you?"

We nodded, and I spoke. "Yes, sir."


THE FIVE OF US WALKED OUT INTO THE BRILLIANT SUNSHINE, where Amos slid on his sunglasses and smiled at me.

Amanda looped her arm inside his and said, "He's such a baby. Don't let the biceps fool you." She put her hand on her stomach. "How's everybody feel about some lunch? My baby needs some of Ira's biscuits."

We drove a glorious hour in my new-old truck back to Walterboro. Amos was so impressed that once we hit the city limits, he flashed his lights and gave us an escort. Having noticed the commotion, along with most of the rest of town, Ira met us at the door of her café. Today she was lime green, including her lipstick, eyeliner, and the scarf holding back her bushy, long red hair. If I hadn't known her, she'd have scared me half to death.

She kissed me on the cheek. "Hey, sugar, ya'll come in here, and I'll have the food out in a minute."

About ten minutes later, she delivered plates filled with steaming eggs, biscuits, bacon, grits, and pancakes.

While we talked, I watched Maggie change like a chameleon before my eyes. The wrinkle was mostly gone, some color had returned, and if hope really does spring eternal, then a trickle was coming up through her eyes. Under the table, she hooked her heel around my leg and pulled my foot a little toward her.

We walked out into the sunlight, where Amos's dad waved to us. He was sitting on his tailgate and holding something little. Its feet were too big for its body, its ears were long and floppy, and its wrinkly body seemed to follow its nose like a slinky. It lay half-asleep and looked like a chocolate chip cookie.

We stepped off the curb, and Mr. Carter walked over to me. He extended his hands and placed the puppy in my arms. "Ten weeks old. Badger's son." He sucked through his teeth. "He's certified bluetick hound. I haven't named him. Thought I'd let you do that."

I looked down, held the puppy to my face, and felt his wet tongue lick my cheek. "I'll call him Tick."

Mr. Carter nodded and pulled a red handkerchief from his back pocket. "It's a good name."

*chapter forty-one*

IT WAS WEDNESDAY NIGHT, AND WE'D BEEN PAINTING
the better part of three days. We'd started in the kitchen and
then moved down the back hall and into our bedroom. When
we got to the door of the nursery, holding a paintbrush and a
roller, we looked at each other and scratched our heads. Neither
one of us wanted to tackle the real issue—guest room or nursery. Amplifying our dilemma was today's date—a fact that was
not lost on us.

I looked at Maggie, who was staring blankly into the room,
and said, "I'm tired of painting."

She dropped her brush in the bucket. "Me too."

The sun was disappearing, the tree frogs were tuning up
down at the river, the wood ducks were jetting like F-16s overhead, and daylight was almost gone. Maggie and I watched in

amazement as an enormous moon, as big as Christmas, rose directly in front of us and popped its glowing head over the treetops.

We sat on the porch teaching Tick how to eat the last of Old Man McCutcheon's produce. Maggie sat on the top step, feet spread, watermelon between her knees, and her face, hands, and cutoff jeans covered in red juice. When the wind blew, the frayed edges of her shorts flittered like tiny fingers. She took a bite, chewed, leaned back, funneled her lips, and then blew like Shamu out across the front yard. Messy but effective.

The shiny seed spun like a football some fifteen feet across the yard and into the grass where about fifteen other seeds lay. In the process she'd pretty well covered the porch steps, and me—sitting downwind—in spit spray. I looked at the yard and knew in about three months we could quit stealing from McCutcheon, because we'd have watermelon growing right here at the base of the steps.

Given everything that had happened, Dr. Frank had held off starting Maggs on a low dose of oral hormone therapy. But now that life had returned to mostly normal, he'd scheduled an office visit. Tomorrow. Maggs didn't like the idea, and neither did I, but she'd been moody lately. Knowing this, and seeing its effect on me, she agreed to try it a month and see what happened.

Because eating watermelon makes me have to pee a lot, I walked inside. When I came back out, Maggie was staring out across the cotton, looking at the river, white paint caked on her forehead and red watermelon juice smeared across both corners of her mouth. Resting at her feet were two clean, folded towels. She looked at me, the river, then back at me. "You want to go swimming?"

With all the pregnancy stuff the last few weeks, I hadn't really pressured Maggie to be with me. I just figured that was not what she needed. I looked from the river back to her. "Do you mean swimming or . . . swimming?"

She smirked ever so slightly, waved her head back and forth as if she were weighing the options, and said thoughtfully, "Swimming."

I scooped Tick into my arms, and we raced barefoot through the grass—corn on one side and cotton on the other. Midway down, we spooked two deer that were feeding through the corn, and then Pinky spooked us. She was rooting along the edges of the corn rows and looked up as we passed by. Her massive jowls, caked with mud, shook like jelly rolls as her lower jaw ground the kernels of corn against the top.

We reached the river, and I climbed the gently sloping bluff and Peter Panned off into the moonlight while the Milky Way showered down about me. The black water covered me, and the gentle current pulled against me. Few things in life were sweeter. I surfaced, swam toward the bank, and dug my toes into the sandy river bottom.

Maggie stood on the bank, pulling her tank top over her shoulders. She slipped off her jeans, waded in, and wrapped herself around me, her short hair sticking up and out. Chill bumps ran up and down her arms, but she pressed her warm chest to mine. The river moved around us, carrying away old memories and filling the empty places left behind.

Because that's what rivers do: they do life.

From downriver, the sound approached slowly. It filtered up through the trees, then across and around us like fireflies dancing on the daylight. Moments later, Bryce appeared. Butt-naked but for the boots, he stood, his face beet-red, blowing through the pipes. He stood, his soul spilling out through his fingers and the tips of the pipes. He played for several minutes. If I'd ever worried about Bryce, and I had, my fears disappeared with those fading notes. Moments later, having said what he came to say, he stepped into the water and faded away downriver, carrying his song with him.

When he had disappeared, Maggie nodded toward the bank and tugged on my arm. Fingers locked, we waded through the current and climbed up the bank. While the moon lit the water droplets cascading down her back, I handed her a towel and spread the blanket across the sand. She toweled off, knelt beside me, and ran her fingers through my hair.

She was just about to kiss me when something out of the corner of her eye grabbed her attention. She tilted her head and stared. Leaning closer, she squinted and held the towel up to the moonlight, and that's when the wrinkle reappeared between her eyes.

Seeing the change, my voice cracked. "Are you okay?" Maybe I had pressured her too soon. Maybe something reminded her of something she wanted to forget.

Without a word, she jumped up, grabbed her clothes, and started a fast jog back to the house. By the time I got into my jeans, she was out of sight. I slipped on my shirt, picked up Tick, and walked back to the house, kicking the dirt and wondering where I had just messed up.

I reached the barn and climbed the steps into the loft, where the light in the bathroom was shining through the crack at the floor. I laid Tick on the bed and tapped lightly. "Maggs?"

"Yes."

"You okay?"

She didn't answer, so I took a cold shower, climbed into bed, and counted to a million. Maggie finally stepped out of the bathroom, wearing sweats, and quickly got in bed. Her feet were cold, and she pulled the covers up around her shoulders. She scooted over next to me and placed her arm around my stomach.

I didn't know much, but I did know that if I opened my mouth, I'd only get in trouble, so I started doing my times tables, and when I got tired of that, I started trying to think of the largest prime number I could find.

Finally Maggie whispered, "I don't really want to go see Dr. Frank tomorrow."

He had told me she'd be moody without the hormones and would probably protest right up to our appointment.

"Okay." I figured we could talk about it tomorrow when she had gotten over whatever was bugging her.

A few minutes passed, then she tapped me on the shoulder.

I was getting a bit exasperated. "Honey. What?"

Tick heard my change in tone and dug his muzzle under a fold in the sheet.

She laid her head on my chest and placed her palm flat across my heart as Tick climbed up our legs and plopped himself in a cavity created by the sheets and shapes of our bodies. "I don't want to go because I don't need to."

Dr. Frank had predicted that too. She'd argue that she didn't need any hormones, and it would take me to convince her that she did.

"Well, okay, but Dr. Frank said it might help."

She patted my chest. "No, you don't understand."

I was getting a bit angry, so I sat up straight in bed. "You're right. I don't. Why don't you—"

Maggie shoved me backward onto the pillow. She hooked her right leg over both of mine, wrapped her right arm around and under me, and then tent-pegged it into the bed.

She raised her head, the moonlight shining in her eyes and revealing the tears and the smile painted there. "I don't need them because my body is making its own."

I squinted one eye while trying to translate what she was saying.

She pulled up the covers, closed her eyes, and said, "Don't worry. I'll take you swimming again in about a week."

Tick had rolled over on his back, paws in the air. He was out cold.

LYING ON AN OLD LUMPY MATTRESS IN THE LOFT OF OUR barn, beneath all the star-filled wonder of the Milky Way, God spread his blanket over us, and when I studied it, the frayed edges and seams had been hemmed. Faint stitching meandered across the quilt like country roads on a state map. I shook my head. *What makes the broken whole? How does deep-down pain, interwoven like sinew, come untangled?*

I looked at my wife, her breathing easy, her spiky hair growing out, her fingernails scratching my chest. Then I looked at us—two chipped and cracked cups, and yet despite the fact that we were leaking like a spaghetti colander, we could still pour water. Still laugh. Still hope. Still cry. Still dream. Still take a swan dive into the moonlight where the mystery of the river would meet us, bathe us, and make us whole.

I wrapped my arm around my wife, pulled her toward me, and felt her heart pounding powerfully inside her. My drumbeat. Our rhythm. It resonated, filtered back down within me, and came to rest somewhere alongside my soul where I'm most alive, where I am me and we are us, where I know pleasure and pain, heartbreak and rage, where I hope, dream, and begin again—down where my love lives.

Brimming with relief, maybe some fear but all excitement, I pulled the blanket up around our shoulders and slid my fingers inside hers. She hooked her leg around mine like a wisteria vine spiraling up a fence post, and we slept.

# acknowledgments

SUMMER 2000.

I was sitting in my office, paying bills, shaking my head at the numbers looking back at me. It was over. My pipedream had come to an end.

I had shut my door because I didn't want Christy to see me hanging my head in my hands. *Maybe I should've taken that job.* In my file cabinet next to me, hung the folder where I kept all the rejection letters. Currently, there were 85.

For eight months the letters had been returning. Slowly at first, then almost one a day, now maybe one a week. I had quit going to the mailbox months ago. Broken man.

I looked at the yellow note stuck to my computer screen that read, "126"—my reminder of the number of times that F. Scott Fitzgerald's *This Side of Paradise* had been rejected. It was little consolation.

Early in 1997, Christy and I had returned to Jacksonville. Thinking I'd continue working as a teacher, I applied everywhere from college to high school. When the phone didn't ring, my brother-in-law took mercy on me and gave me a job working at his insurance agency. Fast forward to 1999. After two years of hard work, we had taken his agency from a rather small one to a very successful one. That had everything to do with Tommy's ability to sell and, to a much lesser extent, my ability to help him put legs on his promises.

Because of this, I had caught the eye of the corporate officer of the insurance company we represented. Friday afternoon came and, with Tommy's blessing, I found myself sitting in the President's office. He was offering me a job—asking me, in short, to do on a much larger scale what I'd been doing the last few years for Tommy.

Did you ever see that scene in the movie, *The Firm,* when Tom Cruise was brought in to meet the Memphis attorneys? Remember the feeling in that room? How they laid the envelope on the table? My experience reminds me of that scene. The red carpet, the leather couch, the view out the windows stretched for miles. So did the opportunity—six-figure money, benefits, signing bonus, yearly bonus. Life on a silver platter.

There were just three problems. The first was travel and lots of it. I'd be living on planes and in hotels. The second was the job itself. I just didn't enjoy the insurance business. I needed it, still do—I'd just rather someone else sell it. The third was that little voice inside my head—and he was screaming at the top of his lungs.

Before I left the President's office, he paused and looked me in the eye. Dick Morehead had risen to the top because he worked harder than anyone else, was pretty close to brilliant, and because he was good at reading people. In that instant, he was reading my emotional pulse. He said, "Charles, life's too d—n short to not do what you love."

I nodded, "Yes sir."

He paused again, this time longer, "Charles . . . life's too d—n short to not do what you love."

I knew my decision before I left his office.

He asked for an answer by Monday, so I shook his hand, stepped into the elevator, and asked myself not what new car I was about to buy or what new white-picket-fence-neighborhood we were moving into, but how was I going to explain this to my wife.

Word spread quickly, and before I got home the phone started ringing with congratulations. "Vice President? Wow!" I found it difficult to talk with my stomach in my throat.

After a few hours at home, I'd made little progress with Christy. She was already painting our new house.

I didn't sleep much. Somewhere around three in the morning, Christy tapped me on the shoulder and whispered, "That's a lot of money." I watched the ceiling fan spin and knew it was going to be a long weekend.

My argument was simple. I could survive the travel, could work at the job and maybe even excel, but no matter what I did or how I tried to appease him, I could not quiet that little voice inside my head.

Christy's argument was also simple—take the money. Write in the morning. Late at night. Do both. Do whatever you've got to do, but take the money.

We argued most of the weekend. Not finger-pointing, shouting, or ugly stuff, but gut-wrenching, who-are-you-and-what-do-you-want-to-be-when-you-grow-up stuff. Our son, Charlie, was almost two, John T. would be here in a few months, and we had outgrown our house. The only thing I had working for me was that Christy knew my heart—she had read my novel (what is now *The Dead Don't Dance*), and she believed it was good. Maybe even good enough.

Saturday afternoon, I went for an aimless drive trying to find the words to explain to my wife and family that I really didn't want the job. That I was sorry if I'd failed them. That I was grateful for the opportunity, but I wanted to follow my heart. I knew they'd think I'd lost my mind. Especially the older generation who had lived through the 1930's. To them, this was a once-in-a-lifetime deal. My ship had just come in. All aboard.

Sunday morning came, and I found myself facedown, clinging to the railing after communion. It was the first time all weekend I could hear above the racket in my head. I don't remember what all I said, but I think it sounded something like, *Please help.* When I opened my eyes, Christy was there too.

By Sunday afternoon, we were both cooked. I sat on the couch, dreading Monday morning, nauseous from the knot in my stomach. I couldn't throw up because I hadn't eaten in three days.

I don't know what happened or how, probably never will, but Christy walked in, her big brown eyes puddling with tears. She stood at a distance, took a deep breath, and said, "We're going to do this one time. Nothing held back. If we fail . . ." She shrugged and took another deep breath. She waved her finger like a windshield wiper across the air in front of me, "But, I don't want you to turn forty, look back, and wonder *what if. . .*" She blinked and the tears fell, "I don't want to take that from you."

Those words still echo in my heart.

For the next year I worked briefly for a non-profit, then started my own Mr. Fix-it business—if you can call it that—and begun pressure washing, building docks, decks, cabinets, you name it. Whatever would put money on the table. Hitched to my truck was a trailer full of hoses and machinery—my cell phone number prominently printed across the back in billboard-sized letters. My family was not impressed. We had lasted almost a year.

Christy cracked the door of my office and walked in with a single piece of mail. I couldn't even look at it. *Please, not one more.* She laid it on the desk, kissed me, and shook her head, "You're not a reject to me." I dropped the letter in with the others and cried like a baby.

That was six years ago.

Today, I've published more than a half a million words, and this morning I received a fax showing where *Southern Living* has picked *When Crickets Cry* as their 'Read of the Month.' If you could see me as I sit now, I'm scratching my head.

When people hear this story, they often respond, "That's incredible." Or "Wow, you really stuck with it." While that does wonders for my ego, I know the truth.

Neither my talent nor perseverance got this book in your hands. I'm neither that good nor that strong. The miracle of our story is not me. It's a girl who, with a single kiss and six words, reached down beyond my fear and doubt, down where my love lives, and gave me a gift—she stood beside me and believed.

# READING GROUP GUIDE

*Maggie:* The Sequel to The Dead Don't Dance

1. In *The Dead Don't Dance,* Maggie Styles spent four months in a coma after she and her husband Dylan lost their first son. In *Maggie,* she's awake, and her desire to have a child is as strong as ever. How does motherhood define Maggie in this novel? Do you think she is obsessed with having children, or does the novel simply show the honest feelings of many women? Have you or someone you know ever struggled with fertility? If so, how does that experience relate to Maggie's?

2. Gardening could act as a metaphor for Maggie in the novel. What does her love of plants represent at the beginning of the book? Does this change by the end of the novel?

3. Maggie and Dylan deal with grief and loss in different ways. Describe these differences. In the midst of her emotional struggles and hormonal changes, does Maggie's behavior ever cross the line, or would any woman who has experienced such loss act similarly? How does Maggie's character change over the course of the novel?

4. The deep relationship between Dylan and Maggie is the central force of the novel. When asked if Maggie could hear him while she was in the coma, Dylan says, "Of course she could. Love has its own communication. . . . It is written on our souls, scripted by the finger of God." How is this godly love displayed in the novel? Are you, or have you ever been, in a relationship of this kind?

5. Adoption seems like a good solution for Maggie and Dylan, but the adoption agency sees things differently. Why did the

agency turn them down at first? Why did they change their minds during the appeal? After reading about the couple's experience, what impression do you have about adoption? How does that impression illuminate Maggie and Dylan's situation in particular?

6. Pastor John Lovett's former life of crime involved three other men. Two of them—Anton and Felix—are covered in tattoos, which reminds Pastor John of Queequeg in *Moby Dick*. The last names of these twin brothers are never given. The third convict, James Whittaker III, is a former Hollywood pyrotechnics expert who earned the nickname Ghost in prison. What do these descriptions tell you about the men?

7. John Wayne is mentioned more than once in the novel. As kids, Amos and Dylan play cowboys and act "like John Wayne in *True Grit*." In the present time of the story, Dylan watches *The Shootist* as The Duke, who has terminal cancer in real life, plays a famed gunfighter with terminal cancer. Why is *The Shootist* particularly relevant? How does The Duke's death reflect Dylan's emotions at this point? What values does John Wayne represent, and how do those relate to the story?

8. At one point, Dylan says about Maggie: "Just because something is broken doesn't mean it's no good. Doesn't mean you throw it away. . . . I can love broken." In what ways is Maggie "broken"? When Pastor John reads from the Bible "Behold, I make all things new," why does Maggie leave the church? In what ways does the couple try to make a whole from the broken pieces? Are they successful?

9. Dylan writes two stories about what happened during Maggie's hospitalization and coma. Describe the differences between the two. Why does Dylan decide to give Maggie the "watered-down, G-rated version"? Do you agree with his decision? Why or why not?

10. When Maggie loses the twins, she isolates herself more and

more. At one point, she tells Dylan that he can't know how
she feels and throws a bedside table across the room. Do you
think Dylan is unsupportive of Maggie? Does he grow more or
less supportive over the course of the novel? Is there any way
he could have shared the stress of her experiences more fully,
or can he, as a man, never really understand?

11. *Maggie* is a distinctly southern novel. In what ways does the
southern setting propel this story? How does the small town
of Digger and the mythical Salkehatchie act as characters in
and of themselves? How do food, church, dogs, guns, clothing, and automobiles signify the south in this novel?

12. The river plays an important role in this story, as it did in *The
Dead Don't Dance*. Before Maggie's coma, she and Dylan
floated down the river on the raft and discovered a rare iris
that can only grow in a particular spot—where the tannic
swamp water meets fresh spring water. What was their journey
into the heart of the swamp like? What does this location represent in the story? Why did the author choose an iris rather
than some other flower?

13. What impact does the past have in this novel? Dylan's grandfather said that farmers "cut the soil and get rid of what
remains of the old. . . . The past fertilizes the future." How
does this relate to Maggie and Dylan's present situation? To
what extent do characters in this story seem able—or
unable—to break free of their past?

14. Through Bryce, the novel takes a hard look at the role of
human sacrifice and the loss of life in war. As part of the
Marine's elite Delta Force in the Vietnam War, he was a "one-
man killing machine" who became "a highly-decorated veteran." Bryce tells Dylan about the loss of his Vietnamese wife
and son during the war. What are your thoughts about
Bryce's military experience? Ultimately, how do you view
Bryce—as a killer, a hero, or something else?

15. *Maggie* tackles the nature of loss. In chapter twenty-nine, Dylan notices the utter emptiness in Maggie's eyes: "Something had severed. . . . When she looked at me, she was looking at the world beyond me where her dreams once lived." He then asks, "What can heal the human soul?" Have you ever experienced loss this deep? What do you think can heal the human soul? Do Maggie and Dylan ever heal?

16. Discuss the theme of forgiveness in the novel. Who forgives whom? What does Pastor John say about forgiveness in particular?

17. Children and childhood are themes in *Maggie*. What particular meaning does the novel ascribe to them? Why is it significant that a boy in Spiderman pajamas with a plastic squirt gun tells Dylan that the convicts left with a canoe?

18. Integrity—keeping your word and telling the truth—are important character traits to Dylan. How are these traits exhibited—or not exhibited—in the novel? What significance do the following words from Dylan's grandfather have in the story: "There's just one problem with pulling the wool over someone's eyes. And it surfaces whenever they take it off."

19. The novel mentions the "fight of good versus evil." What does this battle look like in the story, and what meaning does it have?

20. Dylan and Amos discuss the need to protect their wives from the former convicts, and Dylan is troubled that he cannot protect his wife from the emotional pain that "threatened to kill her." Which threat do you think affects Dylan the most, and why? What do these suggest about the differences between men and women, if anything?

21. Just as in *The Dead Don't Dance*, blood is a recurring motif in *Maggie*. Name the references to blood and discuss their relevance. The concluding reference occurs when Maggie begins her cycle. What kind of future do you envision for Maggie and Dylan? For Amos, Amanda, Little Dylan, and their coming baby?

*about the author*

CHARLES MARTIN'S novels, including the ECPA Novel of the Year *When Crickets Cry* and the Christy-award winning novel *Chasing Fireflies*, have been acclaimed by reviewers and readers alike. He lives a stone's throw from the St. John's River with his wife and their three boys.

A *Southern Living* BOOK of the Month Selection

CHARLES MARTIN

WHEN CRICKETS CRY

A NOVEL *of the* HEART

THOMAS NELSON
*Since 1798*